Edelweiss

K.F Goblin

Playlist

Salutations, reader.

If while you are reading you wish to immerse yourself into this story, I strongly encourage you to listen to the official Edelweiss playlist linked below. Simply scan with your phone, and let your senses fully immerse into this final chapter of the Petrokov Flowers series!

Acknowledgements

This book would never have reached you if not for the dedicated work of my amazing friend and editor, Cassandra.
Thank you, girly, I love you so many!

Chapter One

When most creatures imagine Krampus, it's safe to say they imagine a large, black goat-monster with a basket full of children strapped to his back. Save a few nights of the year, however, this was far from true. The demon behind the story of Krampus enjoyed a very humble, simple life of solitude, high in the densely wooded forests of the German mountains. Oalfus Petrokov was a simple creature; he desired very little, aside from being comfortable and the occasional woman he would sneak into the woods when he ventured down to collect supplies. Maintaining the lifestyle he had meant befriending a select few women from the nearby villages, but, more importantly, being clever. Seeing as Oalfus was a demon, he had little need for regular meals; his true feast came from the fear of his victims on Krampusnacht, or the unsuspecting locals he might stumble upon in his roaming.

There were some things, though, that the old demon enjoyed so much that he required the few female contacts he had scattered across the mountains. The first guilty pleasure was obvious: Oalfus adored having a woman to bury himself in. What demon didn't enjoy a good romp after all, and truly, could you blame him? The others were much simpler, comically so, in some cases. Oalfus was terribly fond of chocolate. He had grown a taste for it in his early years as Krampus, when he stumbled upon a little lad stuffing his cheeks full of chocolate bonbons that had been left out for Christmas morning. His curiosity had gotten the better of him and he simply had to see what the fuss was about. Now it was common, on Krampusnacht, for good boys and girls to leave large bars of chocolate out for Krampus, in hopes he would not steal them away. He was rather fond of the tradition, and perhaps a little extra weight around his midsection could be blamed on it as well.

His other pleasures came with drink, two in particular being his absolute favourites. While coffee was his favourite drink because of how hard it was to get his hands on it, he had learned to make tea with the local flora. Oalfus had also grown quite the taste for Schnapps thanks to another tradition, this one made by most adults in the villages he would frequent. It started off as just shots being left out, but over the years, as the liquor became more commonly available, whole bottles would be left out for him. Another vice, but one he tries not to over-indulge in, especially in his older years.

Despite demons being able to live as long as they wish, time catches up with all of us eventually. Oalfus felt himself growing a little slower as decades wore on, but his desire for life never truly dwindled. He enjoyed his time spent here in the mountains. He savored every day and enjoyed playing the role of Krampus, even if it had come to him by accident.

Today was another day of wood cutting. The last breaths of winter were still clinging to the mountain as Oalfus tossed another log into his large basket. Normally, he only wore this on Krampusnacht, but it was far less annoying to haul four or five loads of wood rather than ten or fifteen arm fulls in the few remaining daylight hours. The wood stove in his cabin had been working hard all winter, and hopefully these last few loads would be its last bit of work, as the warmer weather would allow him to use outdoor fires to brew his teas or cook the occasional meal when the mood struck.

With a great heave, the huge demon lifted the load of wood onto his back, his massive, shaggy, black-and-gray frame standing at a near eight-feet including his long curved horns. His pointed ears flicking, the light jingle of his gold earrings carried on the breeze as he turned his one good eye to the north and took a deep sniff of the frigid air. His claws dug into the handle of his axe as he let out a deep sigh. A snow storm was coming; he could smell it on the breeze. Perhaps his stove wasn't quite done for the season yet after all. Stomping on his vast cloven hooves, he hurried back towards his cabin through the thick trees. If he was quick, he could have the wood stacked to dry out and a fire burning before the snow hit.

Just a few kilometers west on the very same mountain, the snow was just beginning to float down around a young backpacker. Freshly turned a century old and very far from home, Deirdre Shea was a bright eyed Cu-Sith in the final stretch of a backpacking trip she had been on for just over three years. The young demoness had been on a mission to find herself. Traveling from country to country, she had been stuffing her backpack full of piles of photographs. It seemed no matter where Deirdre went, her trusty Nikon FA camera was around her neck. Even now, as the snow was beginning to fall, she couldn't help but stop and snap a few more photos.

She had promised to reward herself by flipping through the newly developed envelope of photos once she had found a good spot for camp. One advantage of being a Cu-Sith was how quickly Dierdre was able to cross land, her light chocolate-coloured coarse fur bristling against an icy breeze as she lifted her camera towards a snoozing owl. When her mass of copper coloured curls flopped over her face just as she was about to press the shutter, she took it as a sign. *Alright, no more photos for now*, she thought to herself with a grumble. Tucking her camera under her windbreaker, Deirdre glanced west once more. The sky was darker than before, and now snowflakes were whizzing past her at a much more frantic pace.

"Oh, well done, Deirdre. You've really done it this time," she groaned to herself. Turning back towards the trail, she began jogging up the path. The woods were dense and unyielding. At this rate, she could be stuck setting up her tent right in the middle of the trail, or at least what she assumed was a trail. There was a faint shadow of what looked like a path she had been following for the last few hours. She thought it might have been a proper path, but now with fear rushing into her heart it looked alot more like a deer trail animals would use.

Just as her heart began to pound in her ears, the young demon's eyes caught the sight of a thin plume of smoke rising above the trees. Against the graying sky, it was hard to see at first, but then the scent caught her nose. Oh bless the sky above! The wind almost pushed her forward into a run as a sudden crash of icy snowflakes and even sharper cold enveloped her. Her curls were a mass of wild tentacles slapping around her face. With a frustrated grunt, she stopped, tearing the thick hair tie from her wrist and wrestling her mass of copper coils into a sloppy bun. Tugging her mustard coloured beanie down over the lump of hair, Deirdre could finally turn her eyes back to the sky. *Follow the smoke, Deirdre. Where there is smoke, there is a warm fire to huddle by.* While the young one raced as quickly as her legs would carry her, the much older demon was none the wiser; he would soon have an unwanted visitor at his door.

Blissfully unaware, Oalfus hummed to himself as he set a kettle on the stove. His cabin was a small, circular space. Well, to him it was small; most would find it rather large. It was a single room with a near ten foot tall ceiling that met in the center at a large point. It had been built to resemble a yurt, and Oalfus had spent years adding his own touches to the space. A small table with two stools was in front of one of the only windows in the structure. It was only in the last few years he had been able to fit it with glass, so now he spent much time in front of it.

The one stool was clearly for him to use, but the other had become another space to store items. At the moment, it was home for the new stack of books he had recently acquired from one of his connections in the village due south. Another nicety he rather enjoyed was reading; next to the door was a simple shelf crammed full of books he had collected over his long years here.

Above it hung the few pieces of clothing he kept when he was forced to venture away from home: a heavy wool cloak, a pair of gray wool trousers with leather suspenders, a lighter gray collared shirt and a wool vest that matched the trousers. It was his only outfit, and, thankfully, he rarely ever needed it. Thanks to his shaggy coat of fur, it was easy to maintain modesty, though he did occasionally wrap a wide piece of black cotton around his waist as a sort of loin cloth if he truly felt the need. At the moment, it served as a half hearted curtain around his window. The logs that made up the wall had been insulated with moss wedged between every last crack and gap Oalfus could find over the years.

The wood stove was next to his makeshift counter and a wash basin. There were several streams nearby that served as his water source, so under the small counter were four large containers of different shapes filled with water. The walls were lined with shelves, many containing jars of all sorts of edible plants, berries, and roots Oalfus had foraged. Most he used for making tea, but as he occasionally craved a meal, some contained wild herbs. He was by no means a chef, but his rabbit stew was one of his favorites.

Aside from the jars and books he would add to any space he could fit, there were also little oddities. Glimmering stones he had stumbled across in his wandering, skulls or antlers from different animals, the wings of a bird had been fastened to the wall, and there were several containers with dried flowers in them. The largest occupant of the space was his bed, or rather, his nest to the average onlooker. It was a mass of dried grasses he had bundled, wrapped in layers and layers of different furs, a blanket stitched together from hides, and several pillows he had clearly made himself and stuffed with feathers. It was rustic, simple, and a little wild-looking. It was a time capsule of his years here, his disconnect from the ever-changing and modernizing world.

Fashions had changed, and technology had surpassed anyone's wildest dreams and was going even further every day. The new millenia had brought a whole new meaning to the world, and Oalfus had purposefully stayed blissfully unaware of it all. He was content remaining as close to the past as possible. He relied on the magic of his ancestors to remain connected to his only surviving family, if he so chose to call on them. He lived as if it was still the 1800s, not the early 2000s. But his ignorance was not going to stay much longer, oh no. Just as the swelling storm outside hammered against the door of his cabin, the new world was about to come crashing in on him.

Oalfus jolted, suddenly realizing it was not just the storm banging on his door, but *someone*. Just loud enough to be heard over the howling wind, Deirdra called out to the occupant inside the cabin in total desperation. Her voice broke with a sob as she banged her fist once more and called out in her broken German.

"Please, help!"

Oalfus groaned. He wanted to cover his ears and pretend the woman's voice wasn't there. This was supposed to be a peaceful night in his home, but the fire was lit and candles filled the house with an undeniable glow. With a great sigh, he crossed the space, taking hold of the door As he opened it, it slammed open against him as a snow covered bundle fell onto the floor at his feet.

"Danke, danke!" the girl said as she got up on her knees and quickly slammed the door shut. She was a backpacker; Oalfus had encountered them before but certainly not so close to his home! Her massive pack had an aluminum frame with a bright yellow tent strapped to the top and several bits of cookware hanging off it. Under the thick layer of snow, he could make out that her pack was *that* particular shade of purple he had noticed becoming more popular some decades ago. Her windbreaker was the same irritating shade of purple, but the lower half was teal. She wore a mustard-coloured wool hat and leg warmers, gray skin-tight pants that one would hardly call clothing for this weather, and seemingly a large sweater under her thin flimsy jacket. Shaking the snow off out of instinct, Deirdre sheepishly smiled up at her host, her

jaw going slack and her neck craning back to see his grouchy face glaring down at her.

Chapter Two

"O-Oh! Oh my, er...*Es tut mir Leid!*"

"For fuck sakes girl, your German is wretched," Oalfus grumbled, crossing his arms as he looked down at her with a raised brow. "Most start screaming by now. You're braver than most travelers I come across, I will give you that. Do you plan on staying on my floor all night?" he growled.

"You speak English!" Deirdre said rather dumbly, her ears folding back as she realized how foolish that sounded.

Oalfus rolled his eyes, turning back to the kettle that was now whistling for his attention. Deirdre shouldered her pack onto the floor, sheepishly raising to her feet as she began peeling her wet jacket off and freeing her hair from under her beanie. Oalfus shot her a double look when the voluminous mass of copper curls fell down to her hips, his eyes widening as she looked around the cabin, in awe of it all. It seemed they both had found something to admire; Oalfus unfortunately needed to burn himself to regain composure. His cup flooded with boiled water, spilling over his fingers as he had stupidly watched his new guest. Swearing loudly, he dropped the cup with a slosh onto the counter, grumbling to himself as he reached for the towel draped over the edge of his table. Deirdre had suddenly bolted for the door, which hadn't entirely surprised him, but he raised a brow at her leaving all her possessions behind. What surprised him even more was when she reappeared in the doorway just as he was about to close it behind her. She had a large handful of snow, her brows knit together in a worried expression as she looked up at him.

"Well don't just stand there, give me your hand!" she demanded suddenly.

Oalfus felt foolish now as he stared at her in total bewilderment. She rolled her eyes, grabbing the hand he had just burnt and pressing the snow onto it. He let out a low huff, the cool relief rather welcoming.

"You needn't fuss, I will heal quickly," he said, urging her inside so he could close the door once more.

Deirdre rolled her eyes again, shaking her head with a smile. "Well, obviously; you're a demon, after all. It still hurts, though. This will help."

Oalfus raised his brows at her, his eyes widening as he looked down at the small female running the melting snow over his burn.

"You know what I am?" he asked, his voice hardly a whisper. Deirdre smiled, nodding.

" 'Course I do, I should know one of the old orders when I see them. Been a long time since I last saw one as old as you."

Oalfus pulled his hand back suddenly, a loud growl rattling out of his throat as he narrowed his eyes at the girl. Deirdre raised her hands innocently, her deep green eyes wide with worry. Oalfus smirked. He could taste her fear already growing, but suddenly, he froze. Long curls of vines sprouted from the crown of her head and ran down her shoulders much like the copper-coloured hair outlining her plump frame. Her white selaras shifted to a deep charcoal and those once-emerald eyes turned to a deep ruby, much like his own good eye. Peeking out from the collar of her sweater and the ends of her sleeves, it appeared like moss was growing where her fur once had been. Carefully, Deirdre stepped forward with her hands still raised.

"I am not here to cause troubles for you, old one. I am a demon, too. I just need a place to stay until the storm passes and then I promise I will not bother you any longer."

Oalfus snorted, letting his shoulders relax as he raised a brow at the little demoness.

"What are you, youngling? I have not seen your kind before."

"I am Cu-Sith. In English, we are called Moor hounds. Back in Ireland, there are many clans of us, but I have yet to meet another of my kind during my travels."

Deirdre stiffened when Oalfus suddenly took hold of her chin, turning her head side to side as he inspected her with his only seeing eye. His brow rose higher as he examined her.

"You look similar to the Grim, or Black Dogs as most call them."

"My granddad was a Grim!"

Oalfus released her, grinning as he watched her tail wagging frantically behind her. Her eyes changing back to that gorgeous emerald and those patches of moss in her fur faded away rather quickly, he found it all *fascinating*.

"You young ones look exactly as mortals do, it's becoming harder to tell you apart," he said as he turned back to cleaning up his spilt tea.

"How else would we live alongside mortals without conflict? Not all of us can hide in the mountains away from the world like you, old one. Or perhaps you would prefer Krampus?" she said with a cheeky smile. Oalfus grimaced at her, shaking his head as he poured himself and his rather lippy guest a fresh cup of tea.

"So, you know the stories. You should be wiser to know that is not my true name."

"Well, of course it isn't, that's just what they call you, I am sure. Most of the locals in town said I was a mad woman for coming up into these mountains. They warned me Krampus lived here and would suck the marrow from my bones," she said in a mocking tone, nodding her thanks as he held the cup out to her.

"I have no interest in your bones, nor eating you, I can assure you. I suppose you pose little threat, youngling. You may call me Oalfus."

"You can call me Deirdre. It's nice to meet you, Oalfus. Thank you for letting me hide from the snow here. You're very kind."

"You would be the first to call me kind. It is no trouble so long as you dont *cause* me any trouble. Do you think you could do that for me, *mein Liebchen*," Oalfus purred out the pet name, his gaze growing heavy on her, and it caused Dierdre to shift nervously.

Waste not want not, as they say. Oalfus could not help but notice the supple curves of Deirdre's body, the way her wide hips swayed as she walked to admire the cabin and how perked her breasts were under her damp sweatshirt. He rather liked how plump her figure appeared under her loose shirt; those tight pants certainly left little to his imagination. Deirdre was slowly wrapped in the warm, spiced scent of cloves and cinnamon, with a subtle sweetness of oranges and cranberry. She felt her tail begin to wag, her thighs pressing together as the warmth of the scent felt as though it were fingers wrapping around every inch of her body. Her ears drooped; somehow her body was throbbing with desire and a grogginess was taking over her all at once.

She only realized what was happening when she felt the looming presence of Oalfus right behind her. Shaking her head, she spun around and stuck an accusatory finger in his face.

"What the hell do you think you are doing?! Are you using your charm on me?" she barked at him, her ears tipping back as she let out a growl.

He was stunned. No one had ever accused him of this before. An odd feeling bubbled up in the old demon. A smirk cracked his features and a sudden burst of laughter spilled out of him.

"I suppose I am, though it's a little stupid to attempt it on a clever young demon, isn't it?" he said, more to himself than anything. Deirdre knew better than to truly be angry; demons were all the same, after all, but it still felt rude to her. Crossing her arms, she gave him a grumpy huff, sipping her tea indignantly.

"The least you could do is ask, for goodness sake."

Oalfus laughed once more, leaning against the table and crossing his arms as he looked down at her.

"Believe me, *Liebchen,* there is nothing good left inside me."

"Even demons have goodness. You stopped, didn't you? I suppose I can't blame you; you must get rather lonely up here," she said with a coy little grin.

Oalfus simply shook his head; best not get into the details. He lumbered over to the chair by the window, crossing one leg over his knee as he eyed the storm outside. *Damnation, it was only getting worse outside.* His ears twitched when he heard her shuffling the books off his other stool, glancing over he was a little put off by how "at home" she was making herself.

"What brings you to these remote mountains anyway, *Liebchen?"* he asked, though he really didn't care. Perhaps if he kept her talking she would stop *moving* his things.

She beamed at his question, moving the stool so it was closer to him before turning to her backpack and rummaging through it. She produced several bundles wrapped in colourful twine and, setting them down on the table, he could see they were bundles of printed photographs. They were *coloured* photographs, which made him lean in with a bit more interest.

"When I came of age, my parents took me to every charity shop in Northern Ireland so I could collect as many camping supplies as I could. My parents were travelers before they settled down in a moor outside Belfast. They had seen all of Europe together and wanted me to do the same. So, I have been on the road for the last three years, and have been taking photos of every country I've passed through. I have more than this tucked away in my bag, though I mailed a lot of my early photos back home for my Mammy and Da to see."

As if she was handling the most precious jewels, Deirdre carefully untied the red and blue twine wrapped around photos with a little tag reading 'France'. Smiling to himself, Oalfus could not help but admire the burning desire for all that life had to offer, shining in those lovely emerald eyes. He leaned across the table, his elbow just inches from her hand, as she began flipping through the photos. Many were of landscapes and what Oalfus had to assume were cities. Much had changed in the world; motor cars seemed to be more common from the photos she showed him, and fashions were *very* different from what he could recall. What impressed him the most were the portraits she had taken. They were incredible, the way she made candid positions or activities bare the very essence of who the subjects were. He rather liked the photo of a group of women cradling babies in one arm while smoking cigarettes and chatting on a veranda. Oalfus smirked, tapping the photo with a considerate claw.

"Reminds me of my great-nephew's mother, Tatiana. She was never seen without a cigarette in one hand, even when Rikovic was just a tiny babe. Probably why he smokes like a chimney now."

"France was so interesting. The women were like vipers, but every rude thing they said was delivered with a smile! The men, too. It was hard to take photos without being sneaky," Deirdre giggled, reaching for another pile while Oalfus sifted through the photos still scattered in front of him.

"You have a good eye. These are lovely, I must say."

This made Deirdre's face warm, her head lowering as she shyly twirled the twine in between her fingers. Oalfus grinned, leaning a little closer to the girl. She may have been a demon, but she was some kind of terrier, from the looks of it. He had a fondness for canines, even one as oddly tempered as this one was. His closeness only flustered her further as he plucked the new stack from her hands, offering the collection of photos from France in return.

Clearing her throat loudly, Deirdre turned her attention to carefully tying the bundle back up. "T-those are from—"

"Italy. I recognize some of these places," he said with a grin, glancing in her direction, which only made her squirm more. Swallowing hard, she fumbled with the twine once more as her tail betrayed her with its wild wagging. Oalfus smiled inwardly this time, clearing his throat and asking her about some of the photos. She was incredibly glad for the silence to be over; the distraction of sharing her travel stories was well-appreciated.

As the storm outside raged, the little demoness regaled all her stories with great passion. Oalfus could not help but notice he was growing a little more fond of the girl with the passing hours. The candles were low, and, save the white tornado of snowflakes, the world outside was a deep inky black. High above, hidden behind the clouds, the moon was the only witness to these two demons brought together by fate.

The large demon had his chin resting on his folded arms, listening contently to Deirdre as she spoke of the incredible meals she had while in Spain. His interest peaked at the mention of the hot chocolate with cinnamon and chili flakes, which earned a great peel of laughter from Deirdre. As night faded into early morning hours, Oalfus seemed frustrated as fatigue began to set in. With a sigh, the old demon rose and stretched before bowing his head as he spoke.

"An old demon knows when to admit fault. I misjudged you, youngling. You have proved to be delightful company, though I regret to say I am not as young as I once was. The joys of aging, it seems, as I require much more sleep than I did in my younger years. You may do as you like, but my eyes are heavy, I am afraid."

"Oh goodness, it really has gotten late! Thank you for listening to my rambling, I won't keep you any longer." she mused, flashing him a bashful smile.

"I was glad to listen. Your stories are impressive. For one so young, you have seen and understood much more of this world than I ever have," Oalfus rumbled, a tired smile warming his features.

"Don't be foolish, you talk as if you're dying! The world may not be the same as you remember, but it is still out there for you to enjoy."

Oalfus smiled at her naivety, shaking his head.

"Old demons like me are not welcome in this world. Unlike you, I can not hide my true nature. I can hardly control my charm when in the presence of a charming woman, it seems. I am glad the world has accepted our kind in more ways, as it gives me hope for the younger generations."

Deirdre flushed once more, her tail wagging, as much as she wished it wouldn't. She glanced towards him as she tucked the photos back in her pack and pulled out her sleeping bag and foam roll. "Where would you like me to set up," she asked, " just in case I sleep late? I wouldn't want to get in your way."

Oalfus raised a brow at the flimsy looking mat she intended to lie on. He nodded towards his bed and spoke in a gentler tone than he had with her all night.

"Don't be foolish. Lie here. I give you my word, I won't lay a claw on you. I can lie above the blankets if it makes you more comfortable. I can't allow my guest to sleep on the floor."

Deirdre nervously pushed her hair away from her face, gripping her sleeping bag a little tighter. Her ears tipped back as she timidly stepped towards the bed.

"I won't rob you of your blankets. You've been kind enough already. I can just lie inside this if you don't mind me being beside you."

"If that is what you wish, do as you please," he said, before settling himself down. Laying on his stomach, he nestled into the pillows and, within moments, the steady rhythm of his deep breathing was all Deirdre could hear from him. She covered her mouth to stifle her giggles. He fell asleep as quickly as a babe!

Squirming into her sleeping bag, she tugged the hood up over her head and pulled the drawstring tight so that only her face stuck out. Moving in a rather child-like, inch-worm routine, she wiggled up onto the bed and rolled onto her back. The loud rustling of the nylon had made Oalfus' eyes snap open as soon as she got into sleeping bag. Lifting his head, he let out a loud snort before chuckling darkly.

"You look like a caterpillar in that foolish thing," he muttered, before lowering his head and allowing sleep to take him once more.

Chapter Three

Oalfus shifted, trying his best to ignore the light filling his small cabin. He froze. Something very warm was pressed close to his side. Peeking his one eye open, he was met with the immediate sight of a mass of copper curls. Craning his neck, he got a better look of what was dozing beside him.

Deirdre was half out of her sleeping bag, her arms folded against her chest and she had wiggled herself under his arm some time in the early morning. He tried not to smile in spite of himself, though the little groans she made from his stirring only made his smirk widen. Suddenly, her legs pulled free of the sleeping bag as she curled into a little ball at his side, nuzzling her head under his shoulder so her face was hidden between the furs and his body. He hardly made out her muffled 'Five more minutes, Ma,' as she pressed closer. Oalfus tried not to enjoy the feeling too much. He was certain her cuddling would stop the moment she woke properly. Instead, he thought for a moment, arching a brow as he considered his options. He could be a gentleman and move away from her, make a pot of coffee and pretend it never happened...though what was the fun in that?

A wicked grin spread over his face as he carefully shifted himself so she was cradled against him. His arm wrapped around her back, he slowly edged the blanket up over them both before settling down and feigning sleep. He struggled to relax his face. Once he slowed his breathing, he shifted his snout so it was just above hers and let out a huff of air. Closing his eyes as he felt her shift and stir awake, he truly struggled to keep from laughing when he heard her gasp as her heart began racing. Oalfus let out a rumble, pretending he was still asleep as he wrapped his arm tighter around her. Deirdre let out a little whine, her face flushing so much Oalfus could feel the heat coming from her cheeks against his snout. Blinking his eyes open, he grinned down at her sleepily and let out a yawn.

"Guten Morgen, mein Liebchen."

"G-good morning..." she stammered, her tail tucked between her legs as she looked away from him. Oalfus chuckled, sitting up and raising a brow at her worried expression.

"Relax, nothing happened. You probably just got cold in that flimsy little thing. I told you to take the blanket, stubborn girl."

Deirdre smoothed over her hair nervously, nodding and hurrying over to her backpack as she rolled her sleeping bag back up.

"I always did that when I was small," she mumbled quietly, glancing over at Oalfus. He had gotten up and was getting the fire lit once more, a kettle already set on top. The scent of coffee reached her nose as she watched him intently, all but forgetting she was trying to roll up the sleeping bag.

"Most pups get close for warmth; it makes sense what you did," Oalfus grinned at her, nodding towards the mess she was making. "Perhaps paying attention might get that done properly, *Liebchen.*"

Deirdre flushed even more, turning her attention towards her bag as she quickly rolled it up and tucked it away. She decided before any more of these flustered feelings arose that it was time she left. She pulled out her extra base layers, wiggling on the thicker pants over her leggings and pulling another jumper on over her sweater before her windbreaker. Oalfus only noticed her hasty attempt at an exit when he heard her bulky pack get slung onto her back.

"I should be off then. You have been most kind but I feel I have overstayed my welcome," she said in a hurried tone, rubbing her now mitten-covered paws together nervously.

Oalfus shrugged, gesturing towards the coffee now steeping. "There is no rush, but should you like to go, I will not stop you. Safe travels, little one."

He didn't want to admit that even a small fraction of him was disappointed to see her go, but, then again, this was never going to be more than a single night affair like most of his other encounters. He was more disappointed he never got to enjoy more of her. Perhaps he would go see if any candles were lit tonight. A shiver ran across his body when the cold air from outside hit him.

Deirdre made an odd sound before she suddenly let out a great sigh. "Well, I suppose I will be staying for coffee."

"Don't sound so disappointed. What changed your–"

Oalfus half turned to face her when he saw what she was looking at. A massive snow drift had formed in front of the door and only a tiny sliver of light at the top of it was visible. His expression dropped, just as hers had, as they stared at the wall of snow keeping them trapped inside. The two were equally irritated, but for very different reasons.

Oalfus detested being trapped in any space, even if it was his own. He had been trapped inside a cave for two weeks in his early years as Krampus. A town had come together as a mob after he had carelessly been caught enjoying the company of one of their women just beyond the tree line. Ever since that incident, any confinement that was not of his own accord made him incredibly on edge.

Deirdre was annoyed for another reason entirely. She got a very odd feeling in the pit of her stomach when she watched Oalfus too long. The flutter she felt when he closed his eyes and smiled as she had spoken last night, and the incredibly delicious scent that was now lingering on her from being so close to him all night. She hated how foolish she felt, how badly she wanted to reach out and touch the thick fur that draped over his forearms.

Shaking her head suddenly, she put both hands on her cheeks trying to will the stupid thoughts away. It had to be his charm. Surely she was not actually attracted to this old demon? She *had* to get out of this cabin, come hell or high water.

Oalfus was already pulling down the black cotton hanging around his window and wrapping it securely around his waist. He shifted the bookshelf out of the way until he found a metal shovel he kept for just such occasions.

"Are you really going to try and dig out?" Deirdre asked, going to the window in attempt to see how big the drift was. Unfortunately, it seemed to have covered most of the front of the cottage and she could hardly see a damn thing.

"What else am I going to do? I don't have the patience to wait for it to melt."

"Well, have you got another shovel? I don't want to just sit and watch."

Oalfus smirked at her, raising a brow as he gave the wall of snow a hard jab with the shovel. "That eager to get away, *Liebchen?*"

He pushed hard on the handle until it sunk down to his wrist. When he pulled it free, he stooped and peered into the hole it had left. A deep frown set his features as he glared at it.

"Damn it all...this will take a while. You best get comfortable. It will get damned cold in here, keep your layers on."

She was more than happy to oblige. Even under his casual gaze, she felt he was looking at her just a little too long. Setting her pack down, she sat cross legged on the floor in front of the wood stove and watched as Oalfus got to work.

At first, they chatted idly, Deirdre avoiding any topics that might venture past any sort of small talk. Today, she wanted him to do the majority of the talking. The less she spoke, the less he would look back at her. She asked him about being Krampus, which he laughed at, but obliged. He explained how it had started as an accident, how he enjoyed the few perks that came with it. He also shared how, in his youth, it was his only way to have freedom, not to have to hide away from mortals. Somehow, this topic (she had hoped) would stop her stomach from knotting and fluttering did the opposite.

The sadness in his voice was like a vice on her chest. When he explained how lonely it used to be for him, she caught herself swallowing back tears. She felt like she was losing her mind. What was happening to her?

Quickly, she scanned the room for anything to change the subject. She hoped for anything at all. Her eye fell on a sizable box up on a high shelf. It was stuffed to the brim with chocolates in all shapes and sizes. Even from her spot on the floor, she could see nearly a dozen bars poking out, and that was just what was at the top. He sounded a little sheepish when he explained the tradition, how he had grown quite the fondness for the sweet over the years. His tail even flicked from side to side when she began teasing him over it, his ears tipping back as he glanced back at her between shovels of snow.

Damnit, Deirdre! She swore inwardly when her stomach fluttered at his smile. It was time for another distraction, one she could enjoy alone. Digging through her pack again, she fished out a large white envelope.

"I nearly forgot!" she exclaimed, with a new found giddiness. Oalfus glanced over as he saw her dump out several smaller envelopes onto the table.

Pausing only long enough to discover they contained more photographs, he chuckled and returned to his work. "Are those new photographs?"

"Yes, from my time in Berlin," she said, only giving him half her attention as she inspected each one intently.

His interest was piqued, but the nervousness of leaving this wall of snow was more demanding than his desire to go look at her photographs. With a grunt, he continued gouging away at the never ending wall of snow.

Deirdre wasn't entirely sure how long she had been pouring over her photos, and she couldn't recall when his grunts of exertion had turned into snarls of rage. It was the sudden bang of the door against the wall that made the younger demon jolt upright. Oalfus was smashing the shovel into the wall of snow, his one eye glowing brilliant crimson and his long fangs bared as he sent sprays of snow into the cabin.

"W-whoa, whoa now! Easy!" she called, leaping to her feet and getting between the snow and the furious demon. Oalfus paused mid-swing, his eyes widening when Deirdre wrapped her arms around her head and let out a yelp. The shovel clattered to the floor and he took several steps away from her, looking down at the floor in shame.

"I–" he started, but Deirdre quickly stopped him.

"No harm done. I should have known better. Da always said never get between an angry man and whatever project is making him foul. I think you need a break, but Lordy look at the dent you made! Come on now, don't look so disappointed. Look how far into it I can walk!"

Deirdre was able to take several large strides into the sizable hole Oalfus had made in the snow. Much more light was able to make it through now. In fact, if she just climbed up, she was sure she could poke her head through the gap between the snow and the roof's wide overhang.

Scrambling up the slippery snow, Deirdre wedged herself up as high as she could. Scraping away at the snow, she managed to pop her head past the roof's edge and see how much further there was. To her dismay, the drift looked as though it went all the way to the trees. That, or there was just that much snow covering everything.

"It's bloody April!" she whined, trying to back herself out of the tight space. A new round of dismay washed over her: she was totally stuck.

"Is it that bad?" she heard Oalfus' muffled voice call.

Swallowing her pride, her tail tucked between her legs, she called back to him. "Afraid so, and what's worse...I am stuck"

"You're WHAT?!"

"Oh stop whinin', you great big brute, and help me!"

Oalfus pinched the bridge of his nose, sighing heavily before reaching up and tugging away handfuls of snow around her neck. His long claws kept brushing against her neck, which produced flurries of muffled giggles. Showers of snow fell down on him as he continued trying to free her.

"Would you stop all the squirming? I am trying to get you out, dammit!"

"Well stop ticklin' me!"

Oalfus smirked, shaking his head and pulling a few more large scoops of snow away from her before wrapping his large hands around her waist.

"Hey, what are you–?"

"Oh relax! Turn your head to the side and I will pull you out."

Gingerly, she turned her face to the side, and with a curt tug on her hips, she was pulled free of the snow. She had tumbled back right into his arms. Cradled against his chest, she was now nose to nose with him. Her breath caught in her throat; he was holding her like she weighed nothing. The thick arm wrapped around the back of her thighs flexing against her behind made her press a little closer. Her hands against his chest, she could feel his steady heartbeat under her fingers. The incredible spicy-sweet smell hit her, like clove, oranges and cinnamon sticks. Oalfus had to bite back a grin when he felt her thighs flex and press together under his arms. This time, he had to do nothing at all and she was already heavy with desire.

Her voice was a breathy whisper as she desperately clung to any fragments of clear thought. "Y-you really are layin' that charm on thick..."

"On the contrary, *Liebchen*. I have not used it once since last night," he rumbled, leaning in a little closer.

"T-then why...?" she breathed.

His nose pressed against her throat, his breath hot against her as he spoke in a hushed tone. "Most likely the same reason you smell so damned good to me..."

"I smell good to you?" She sounded surprised. As badly as she wanted to shove his head away, she melted when he pressed his nose a little harder against the neck of her sweater.

"Like a morning after rainfall," he whispered, his eyes locking onto hers as he slowly opened his mouth and hovered just above her throat.

Was he waiting for permission? Deirdre's jaw trembled. Swallowing hard, she let out a little whine and timidly looped her arms around his neck. Her fingers slid into the long charcoal coloured hair that hung well past his shoulders. The white streak at either temple had been rather charming, she had to admit. A moan slipped between her parted lips as he slowly ran his long forked tongue over her throat and up to her jaw.

Oalfus could smell the heat growing between her thighs as they began to wiggle under his arm. Backing into the cottage, Oalfus clamped his mouth down on her throat. The flurry of moans that came from her as he started sucking on the tender little dip between her shoulder and neck only encouraged him. Her hands were tangled in his hair, gripping fistfuls as she held his head firmly to her neck.

His will power snapped like a dry twig. Kicking the door shut, he crossed the space in a few short strides before pinning her down below him. Her head was in a fog. *How was this possible?* She was hardly a virgin; what demon her age would be? But the haze Deirdre was in was nothing like anything she felt before.

Oalfus was a little shocked at how hungrily he desired her. Mortal women had always served him well; they were incredibly easy to break, but, nevertheless, he had always been satisfied. This desire, however, felt more wild. Something inside him was growling deep in his mind.

Their eyes met, and, like a unified moment of clarity, they both stared at each other in perfect silence. Oalfus hesitated, leaning back slightly. Perhaps he had gone too far with this girl. Her hand shot forward and took hold of his shaggy beard. Deep in those emerald eyes was a blazing inferno of desire. She may not understand why she was feeling this way; part of her still wanted to blame it on him using his charm, but an even deeper part of herself wanted to believe he had told her the truth.

Never had she ached in such a way to be with a man, to be touched or caressed. She wanted to know just how strong his hands could be, how hard his claws could scratch. She wanted to know what it felt like to be pinned under him.

"Don't tell me you're gettin' cold feet now?" she breathed, leaning in a little closer to him.

Oalfus was hardly one to hesitate, even he was surprised he had stopped. The way her green eyes bore into his only made him want to ravage her more than ever.

"I might hurt you, Deirdre..." he said with a heavy swallow, his eyes sliding from her face down over her body.

"I was counting on it," she said in an almost alien-level of confidence.

Oalfus snarled loudly, grabbing her wrists and pinning them above her head. His free hand lifted her onto his lap as he growled out his words.

"Careful who you challenge, little one. You know not what you're toying with."

She leaned as far forward as he would allow, her mouth just a breath away from his ear as she whispered out her words, each one dripping with a carnal desire she had never imagined she was capable of.

"I think I would like to learn, old one. Show me what a *real* demon can do."

Chapter Four

Deirdre was shocked at how efficiently the large male was at pulling off the layers she was still bundled in. What she assumed would turn into a shredding frenzy was some of the most considerate and swift movements she had ever seen. He handled her like she weighed nothing; practically a doll in his hands as he slid her final layer free of her legs and slowly began slipping his large hands up and under her sweatshirt. She shuddered, his strong fingers adding enough pressure, his claws gently raking across her sides as he pulled it up and over her head.

It was like a feast for his eyes. She was much plumper under her layers than he had originally imagined. A *glorious* surprise, he must admit. Oalfus was not a picky lover; he was keen to enjoy anyone willing to allow such company. His favorite, however, was when he had something substantial to play with. His bulk and looming stature always made things precarious, especially with a petite partner such as Deirdre. His advantage in this moment was that she was, in fact, a demon, leading him to think she was much more resilient than any mortal partner he had enjoyed in the past.

Her breasts were barely a handful for him; he could cradle them easily with just his thumb and index finger. Her thighs were just as plump as he imagined. Trailing his hand down her side, he relished the breathy gasps she made as he took a rough grasp of her ample behind. It spilled between his splayed fingers, which only made him rumble loudly with satisfaction.

Using his other hand, he slowly raked his claws down over her midsection before taking a rougher grip on her plush stomach. He watched her with heightened interest as her hands suddenly shot up and covered her face. His bushy brow arched as she peeked between her fingers at him, that long forked tongue dragging over her maw as he leaned in a little closer to her.

"Getting shy now, *Liebchen?*"

"N-no! I...It's just..."

Oalfus leaned down and dragged his tongue over her torso, starting just above her belly button. His hot breath and that deliciously firm tongue ran over every little curve and the roll under her breasts, up and over them both before finally trailing over her throat and up her jaw.

Her head was spinning, she could hardly manage anything but breathy moans and little whimpered gasps. His lips brushed against hers as she gasped out her words.

"It isn't fair...I can hardly think..."

"One might be glad for such pleasure," he rumbled out, rubbing his snout against the side of hers as he eyed her hungrily.

"I've never been with someone who has such a strong charm...I feel like I'm going mad."

Oalfus chuckled darkly, hooking an arm under her knee as he pushed her a little further up the bed. His knees settled just under her legs, which forced them as far apart as she could manage.

"I already told you, Deirdre. I have not been using my charm on you."

"B-but then–"

"Even mortals get this worked up when they fuck. It's rather obvious, isn't it? Sexual tension does not have need for charms or tricks, little one."

Deirdre hesitated, watching him lean down and nuzzle against one of her breasts before letting his long forked tongue coil around it. The way his mouth clamped over her nipple sent a jolt of pleasure through her body like an electrical shock. *There was no way he wasn't using his charm, he had to be...he had to be, right?* Her back arched under his touch, his large hands trailing over her sides and fondling any little curve or roll he could blindly grab at. Her gasps and whimpers only spurred him on further as she was spiraling inside. It didn't make sense: how could this perfect stranger do all of this to her? How was this even happening right now, had it not been for him using his charm?

Her mind raced and her moans becoming more frantic as he licked over her other breast and trailed down her stomach. He hooked under both her knees, lifting them up and over his shoulders as he wrapped both arms tightly around her midsection. She hung upside down a moment before it dawned on her what he was about to do. She yelped in surprise when his mouth clamped down over her mound, that devilishly wonderful tongue dragging roughly over her folds before roughly circling her sensitive little clit.

Deirdre cried out, gripping onto anything for support as her hips instinctively rocked forward into his eager mouth. She had to be losing her mind; there was no way this was normal. How could anyone, demon or not, make her boundaries completely crumble in just a single day? She didn't even know him; she had hardly learned anything about him! Sure, he had told her about being

Krampus, how he lived alone in these woods since he was young, but there must have been secrets he kept.

She cried out once more as his tongue delved even deeper inside her, splitting her open and filling her melting core. Oalfus shuddered at the taste, his pleasure completely clouding his mind as her heated scent utterly enveloped his senses. He growled deeply when he felt her hands gripping onto his arms. Her short claws digging into him and her hips rolling into his mouth was almost too much for him. He had been with a multitude of women over his long years roaming this earth, but never had he been so utterly entranced by their desire.

His eyes were partially rolled back, his mouth moving automatically. The more she cried out in pleasure, the faster his tongue worked inside her. Deirdre was hardly able to keep her wits about her. Her head was in a total fog when something began rubbing against the side of her neck.

In a daze she reached for whatever it was, only to find herself grabbing at a very stiff length trapped under the black material Oalfus had wrapped around himself earlier. It wasn't too difficult to get it out of her way. Her curiosity blazed when she realized he was full mast and eager to be attended to. Her eyes went as round as dinner plates when his member finally sprung free. He was incredibly well endowed. Her eyes were unsure where to focus first. Between the glittering gold ring wrapped snugly around the base of his length (which she now realized matched the two gold rings hanging from his nipples) and the three intimidating spikes that came out of the underside of his length just below the tip, she could hardly find a clear thought.

Oalfus was watching her very intently now. His mouth had slowed on her needy slit and he was eager to see what she would do. This was always when he could gauge just how far he could go with his partners. His length was intimidating just in its size, but the soft and very sensitive spikes that went down his length were always a place of hesitation for most women.

Deirdre had impressed him. Her hand immediately began to explore them, her fingers rubbing over each one, which made him gasp and tighten his grip on her. A little moment of clarity came over her; looking up at the strained expression on his face only made her grin as she slowly began rubbing his length. She took special care, letting those very soft spikes pop between her fingers as she rubbed him, his hips rocking forward into her hand.

"Someone is sensitive," she cooed, her legs wrapping a little tighter around his shoulders as he tightened his grip on her.

"You're one to talk," he growled, suddenly lashing his tongue over her perked clit and rubbing his tongue roughly over and around it.

Deirdre gasped before a chorus of uncontrolled moans poured out of her, her grip tightening on his length as she whined and rocked her hips into his mouth once more. He was relentless, lapping at her sopping folds and bucking into her hand still wrapped around his throbbing member. Deirdre needed to level the playing field; he was certainly skilled at taking the upper hand but she had a few tricks up her sleeve. Shifting to the side, she did the best she could to position herself so she could reach his length with her mouth.

The guttural snarl that tore out of him when her mouth wrapped around the head and her tongue flicked over the top spike was exactly the reward she longed for. He nearly dropped her, gripping her even tighter now. Pressing his forehead against her thigh, the big demon began bucking into her mouth with gusto. He had only ever had one other woman take his length into her mouth, and it had been fleeting at best.

He sucked in a sharp breath every time her tongue would circle over his *very* sensitive spines, and his claws only dug into her body further. Deirdre was working much more eagerly than she had thought; the sticky pre-cum that was flooding her mouth was surprisingly pleasant. Her previous partners had been mortal, admittedly, so she was not sure if it was simply a demon trait or if it was an *Oalfus* trait. Just as his scent was a mixture of spices and sweetness, his pre-cum was equally as tantalizing. She was shocked how badly she wanted more, her hand now helping her as she worked her mouth with a little more eagerness. Her ears perked when Oalfus let out a low *whine* and gasped her name. This finally made her stop, looking up at him and freezing when she saw the strained expression knitting his brows tightly together.

"Oalfus?"

"I...I can't take much more..." he breathed, his face rubbing against her thigh and finally his eyes opened, his one blazing red one locking on her face before he quickly shifted her down on the bed.

Admittedly, she had been growing rather light headed; dangling upside down for so long was beginning to get to her. He was very close to her now, looming over her with a much different expression on his face. Settling between her legs once more, he trailed his hands from her knee all the way up to her breast before he clamped his mouth down on it. She let out a moan, running her hand across the top of his head and digging her fingers into the thick fur at the back of his neck. She was impressed with how attentive he was to her; his mouth had always been in some kind of service to her.

He was keen on delivering as much pleasure to her as possible. By now, he would normally have his cock buried as deep inside his partner, but this time, it felt different. He wanted to get every last moan he could from her, every last breathy gasp.

Deirdre let out a little whimper when his tip pressed against her folds. Oh, she wanted him inside her *badly* now. She was struggling to keep her lewd thoughts to herself; the idea of begging for him to fuck her was becoming much too tempting.

Oalfus, however, was eager to hear her ask for it. He didn't realize he was pushing her to the brink of begging already, but he simply wanted to hear her ask him. Lifting his head away from her breast, he glanced up at her. The mixture of desperation and pleasure painted over her features was exactly the reward he had wanted. His finger trailed over her lip as he leaned in a little closer, but when her arms suddenly wrapped around his neck and her mouth pressed roughly to his, he froze on the spot.

No one had ever kissed him before. Sure, there had been moments he had pushed his tongue into open mouths in the throw of passions, but never had someone *chosen* to kiss him. Deirdre pulled back just enough to look at him. Why had he gone so stiff? Her eyes searched his stunned face but her brows drew together suddenly.

"Did I do something wrong?"

Oalfus shook his head cursing internally before he finally found his words. "No, not at all. I am sorry, *Liebchen.* You just caught me off guard, I suppose. Believe me, you have done everything perfectly," he purred, pressing his nose into her neck and letting his tongue trail over it.

This time, he grew a little bolder, running his tongue up her jaw and just the very tips over her lips before he gently pressed his mouth against hers. Deirdre was all too happy to return the gesture, her tongue running over his bottom lip before both of them deepened their passionate embrace. Deirdre could hardly hold back her moans as his tongue invaded her mouth, her nails digging into his long hair and thickly furred neck. She lifted her hips just high enough that his tip was pressing against her. She couldn't wait any longer; his teasing had gone on long enough.

Oalfus' arms caged around her, his claws digging into the furs and blankets under them as he began pressing into her. She spread her legs wider, wordlessly inviting him in as she held him locked in their passion-fueled kiss. Only when he began pushing into her slick entrance did their lips part and a loud gasp tore out of her. She was clutching onto him, her face buried in his neck as he used one arm to lift her into his lap.

"That's it, open up for me," he breathed against one of her short folded ears. His voice was like velvet, and a shudder ran down her entire body as he finally began to slip inside her.

She sucked in a sharp breath as the first spine popped inside her. *Oh lordy, he was big, and he had hardly started pushing inside!* His loud growl of approval was intoxicating. Leaning back, he lifted her up into his lap to let gravity help ease her further down his length. Her arms and legs wrapped around him, inch by *glorious* inch plunging deeper inside her incredibly snug folds. Oalfus adored how tightly she was clamping down on his length, the way she gasped and whimpered as each of those spines finally slipped inside and she began to quickly sink down to his hilt. It was a struggle for her to take all of him initially; her body shuddering as his vast length finally seemed to end. She was sitting in his lap now, her ankles crossed at the small of his back and her face pressed firmly into his chest.

"*Was für ein gutes Mädchen du für mich bist,*" he purred as he pressed his nose against the top of her head and began slowly rocking his hips back and forth. Deirdre's eyes went wide as she hid against him. Her German may have been rough but as he purred out those sweet praises, something deep inside her melted. Her reservations, her last little scraps of self control, washed away the second he called her *his* good girl.

Perhaps it was a routine of his. Perhaps she was being utterly foolish for letting some corny line shake her so deeply. Oalfus felt his breath catch in his throat when those gorgeous emerald eyes finally looked up at him. There was something different about the way she was looking at him. Desire was one thing, but this was *so* much more.

The way she reached up around his neck, lifting herself just enough, he grit his teeth as she began to rise and fall on his length. All of it was incredible, but what made *him* melt was the way she moaned his name. Not Krampus as every other mortal he had been with. No, she moaned out his true name.

"Oalfus, please..." she whispered to him, her chest pressing firmly against him as she worked her hips a little faster now. Desperate moans bubbled up from both of them as he took a firm grip on her wide hips to urge her on.

"Please, what, *mein Liebchen*?"

"Please fuck me! I want all of it!" she whimpered, her ears tipping back as she let her head fall back from a rather rough upwards thrust he had given her.

"Mmm, I rather like the sound of you begging. Ask again; perhaps I shall consider it."

He wanted her to beg? Well, he would get begging. With a desperate determination she lifted her knees so her feet were firmly under her. Leaning back and bracing herself on his knees, she began working her hips with a passion as she gasped and moaned out to him.

"Oalfus, please, please stop teasing me! I need it, I admit it! I can't stand a second more of this teasing, Oalfus, please...!"

His eyes were partially rolled back as he gripped onto her hips, lifting and pushing them to only force himself even deeper inside. He could hardly contain himself; this woman would drive him *mad!* She was unlike anything he had encountered, but the eagerness to please him was becoming addicting. He snarled viciously as he finally pulled her off his length, throwing her firmly down onto the mattress so she was face down. He handled her like a doll, pulling her hips up and pinning her head down before she felt him begin to push back inside her. Her tail was wagging with a fury, so much so her hips were wiggling side to side making his job a little more tedious.

"So eager you can't even stay still long enough to let me back in. Such a desperate little thing you are!" he growled, grabbing her tail and pulling her towards him by its base. She practically screamed as he forced himself back inside, but the delirious smile spread over her face told a very different story.

"That's a good girl. Look at you. You took me without hesitation this time," he hissed, bending over her as he pressed his nose against her neck and cheek.

Deirdre felt completely lost, but it was such a wonderful feeling. He truly had her under his spell, or perhaps she was simply losing her grip on reality. In any case, she couldn't care less; she just wanted to feel good. She wanted to be in the throws of passion with him. She whined in total bliss, her tail wagging against his stomach as his hips began to work roughly against her. The slapping sound of their hips colliding only grew louder and more frequent as he pinned her down with both hands on the back of her shoulders. Loud snarls tore out between his clenched teeth as he truly started his onslaught of aggressive thrusts.

Her moans began with what little control she could muster, but soon they devolved into a mixture of delighted squeals and yelps. Oalfus never wanted the lovely sound to end. As foolish as he felt, he desired nothing more than for her to make that sound as long as he could. He had never felt such a torrent of desire rush through him, his body aching from the amount of edging he was doing. He refused to let it end yet, but he was quickly losing this battle.

Deirdre's hand had slipped between her legs, her fingers making tight circles around her aching clit as she felt her own orgasm build to an almost painful level. Soon, her moans were becoming little shrieks as she looked back at him, her tongue hanging out.

"Oalfus, please! I—I think I am going to—"

"Yes, that's my good girl! You don't stop until that pretty voice is screaming my name, you understand?"

She was already nearing her limit, but his growl in her ear was too much for her to bear. She let out a hysterical shriek, her voice muffled slightly, thanks to his weight pushing her firmly into the bed.

"Oh *fuck!* Oalfus, please, don't stop!"

He relished every shriek and whimper she made; her moans in the shape of his name were unlike any sound he had ever heard. He hated that it had to be done. Oh, how badly he wanted to bury every last inch of himself into her while he released, but the risk was much too high with demons. Tearing away from her was torturous, his hand only just good enough to help him finish but not nearly as delectable as her tight folds.

Stream after stream of his load painted across her back, his teeth grinding together as he snorted out his heavy breaths. Deirdre had made such a disgruntled sound, as if he had robbed her of a reward when he pulled out of her. It took him several minutes to finally open his eyes. Wave after wave of pleasure had shuddered through his body. He finally lifted himself off her, enjoying the afterglow as he let his head fall back and eyes close once more.

It was short lived. A jolt of electric sensitivity tore through his body and his eyes flew open. Deirdre had turned around and was sucking on the head of his length. He gasped, grabbing a fistful of her hair to prevent her from taking any more of him into her mouth. He shuddered visibly, his knees buckled and he groaned loudly.

"You minx! I was rather enjoying myself, fuck sakes..."

Her tail was wagging as she looked up at him, a mischievous grin spread over her face.

"Sensitive?" she teased, reaching out with her tongue and licking off the bead of cum that had formed at the tip of his length.

"Someone is clearly insatiable!" he chuckled, releasing her hair. She hugged him around his waist, nuzzling against his lower stomach and trailing feather soft fingers along the underside of his member. He sucked in a sharp breath, running clawed fingers through her mass of curls.

"You pulled out; I need my revenge," she giggled, kissing up the side of his length. She smiled a little wider at the sound of his low rumble, his long claws scratching gently over her scalp in little circles. She melted against him, nuzzling a little firmer against him and leaning into his hand.

"I pulled out in an attempt to be responsible. You are not mortal. You could actually get pregnant, and I am sure that is the last thing you want."

She hadn't considered that part. *Would that truly be such a bad thing?*

Her eyes went wide as she hid her face against his hip, horrified at her own thoughts. For the love of all that was good, what in the world was coming over her? Had she completely lost her mind? Just as she was about to delve even deeper into her inner spiral, those wicked claws started scratching at her scalp once more and a heavy tail wrapped under her behind.

"Let's get you cleaned up, hm?" Oalfus murmured.

She was glad for the distraction; anything was better than being trapped in her own thoughts right now.

Chapter Five

Oalfus had returned to his work trying to dig through the snow drift, leaving Deirdre dangerously alone in her thoughts. He was completely unaware that inside his cabin, the little demon was sitting on his bed, chewing her claws down until her fingers were bloody stumps. Her mind was a vortex of fear as her emotions spiraled into self destruction.

She was reeling from what she had just done with him; how she had so willingly given herself *entirely* over to him. She had participated in many one night stands in her travels. She had stayed with those casual lovers for extended periods, even. All of those previous interactions were easy, fleeting, in a sweet way, but this was sitting heavy in her stomach.

A vice was clamping down hard and heavy on her heart. *Why in the world was she acting so foolish?* Her mind raced, this strange feeling of dread weighing her down more and more. Oalfus had been an incredibly generous partner. He had pleasured her better than any of her previous encounters could have imagined. She was satisfied beyond words, and he had not forced her or made any move in a harmful way. He had *washed* her after, for fuck sakes, so what on earth was her problem?

A faint waft of his scent rose up from the bed when she shifted to sit cross legged once more. Her eyes fluttered closed before she slowly edged up towards the pillows and wrapped both her arms around one. Pressing her face firmly into it, she felt as if that incredible spiced scent was wrapping up every inch of her. She gasped, dropping the pillow and scrambled back off the bed.

"What the hell am I doing?" she whispered to herself, backing far away from it.

She backed up until she bumped into the wooden wall. Covering her eyes, she let out a loud groan and slid down into a heap on the floor. Why was this happening to her? Why did she wish he would stop shoveling so efficiently? Why was she *dreading* having to leave?

Her heart started racing and tears burned her eyes, the swirling chaos in her mind pushing her to an emotional melting point. Hugging her knees and pressing her face against them, she let out a pathetic little sob as embarrassment, rage, confusion, and desire roared their arguments inside her mind. Her bloodied fingers dug into her knees as she tried to control the emotional outburst, but more tears only fell.

Oalfus had heard the little cry, but when he saw Deirdre in shambles on the floor, he could only stand there, frozen in the doorway. He felt like a stunned idiot, a helpless child, as he gripped the shovel in both his hands and watched her as the gut wrenching sound of her muffled cries filled his small space.

His breath became uneven, his heart began racing and confusion began to gnaw at his mind. Had he hurt her? Perhaps he had done something she didn't like? What if he had been too forceful or said something too crass? When he had left her, she seemed so content. She had been affectionate towards him during the whole affair, but perhaps it was just an act, after all.

Suddenly, memories of when he had been trapped inside the cave came back to him, panic rising inside him, but now he was unsure why. How could this be happening? Surely this was some mistake or simple misunderstanding? He was Krampus, for fuck sakes, a feared monster, the things of nightmares and scary stories. He was not some weak little dolt prone to fuss over the affairs of others, but, in this moment, he felt like all his control was gone.

Taking in a slow, deep breath, Oalfus silently set the shovel down. Edging carefully towards her, Oalfus willed his voice to work. His mouth felt terribly dry as he slowly approached Deirdre. Stopping so there was still space between the two, he gingerly sat himself down onto the floor to avoid looming over her. Finally, after opening and closing his mouth several times, he spoke in a very dry whisper.

"Deirdre...?"

The little canine's head shot up, tears still visible in her eyes. Her grip on her knees tightened and her toes curled in fear as Oalfus was now very aware of her distress. The demon normally enjoyed the scent of another creature's fear, found the energy that came from it very delightful, but this cut into him like a knife.

Almost instantly he dropped his gaze from her, visibly struggling to come up with something to say. His mind was now racing just as frantically as Deirdre's was, his facial expressions clear as if he were holding up a flashing neon sign. Somehow, seeing how much he was struggling with this situation helped ease her, even if just slightly. Oalfus avoided those emerald eyes, her perplexing expression only making him more uncomfortable.

"I...well, I heard you while I was...you seemed upset and I just wanted–" he gritted his teeth, snorting loudly before finally speaking in a frustrated voice. "Have I done something, anything at all, to upset you?"

Deirdre's chest ached further, but this time she knew why. Seeing him so confused and now taking the blame for her own turmoil was more than she could endure. Wiping her eyes quickly she shifted onto her knees and edged a little closer to him, in hopes it might reassure him. She was careful not to touch him, though, for fear of how her body might react again.

"Oh, Oalfus, no! You have done nothing wrong, I promise you. It's just, I...I don't really– I just sometimes get trapped, up here," she gave a timid tap to the side of her head, looking down at the floor as shame began to well up inside her.

Oalfus knew that feeling all too well. Glancing up at her, he carefully moved closer. Even on his knees, he was like a towering wall of fur and muscle. She could tell he was trying so hard to be small; he was being so considerate and delicate with her. *Why was he going to such lengths for a near perfect stranger?*

"I also get trapped in my mind. More so when I was younger, but even now, I find myself locked in a battle with my thoughts," he spoke gently as he held out a hand to her. She hesitated, which made him quickly pull his hand back and avoid her eyes once more.

"I apologize if I have–"

"Why are you apologizing to me? I am the one who barged into your home, a total stranger, and disrupted your life. I– we just had sex and, while it was absolutely mind-blowing and likely the best I will ever fucking have, I am sitting on your floor crying and clearly making you uncomfortable! You owe me *nothing* and, for some damn reason, you are being so incredibly gentle and I– I don't know if I want to run far away from you or throw myself into your arms!"

Deirdre was crying again, gripping the sides of her head as she tried to bite back the growing frustration in her mind. It was so loud. All of her worries spiralled no matter how badly she wanted them to stop. Tears poured down her face. Nothing in this moment made sense. Oalfus knew better than to try and speak; nothing he said was going to be adequate or eloquent enough to help.

He hated this paralysis he was in. His claws dug into his palms as he tried to remain as still as possible. His voice was distorted when he finally spoke, looking at the little trickle of blood running down his fingers as a ground.

"Perhaps it is good timing then, I just finished digging us out. The snow is deep but–"

He winced when she scrambled desperately to her feet, stumbling over herself she grabbed her backpack and, in several very loud chaotic moments, his door flew open and swiftly slammed behind her. In the blink of an eye, he was plunged headfirst back into the heavy loneliness that was his life before a little Cu-Sith fell through his door the day before.

Oalfus had not moved an inch, his mind painfully blank as he stared at the spot Deirdre had been sitting. He sat, and stared in pitiful silence. He had not even noticed the setting sun and darkness that was beginning to fall all around him. Finally, a flicker of an emotion lit in his stomach, a spark of anger. An alien smile spread over his face, he was screaming internally to get up and continue about his business but not muscle moved for him. He just kept staring at the empty space in front of him.

Deirdre had hardly made any real progress, having sunk waist deep into the snow the moment she got past where Oalfus had cleared. The freezing trudge left her breathless and clinging to a tree for support only a few hundred feet away from the cabin. With her forehead pressed against the rough bark of the pine, Deirdre fought back yet another round of tears. Her mind was slowly beginning to quiet down. Instead of several blaring emotions racing inside her mind, only a few thoughts were left swirling. *What on earth was she doing out here? The snow is deep and wet, suicide, even for a demon.* Still, she clung to the tree in desperation. She hoped somehow her mind might finally decide what it wanted, even if it was just for the moment. With tear-blurred eyes, she looked back at the cabin.

She could almost see Oalfus as she looked at the yurt-like structure. He was likely very hurt from her harsh decision; she had not even said goodbye to him. Maybe she was a worse monster than the so-called nightmarish Krampus all the locals had warned her to stay away from. How could a beast so gentle, so considerate, and genuinely kind be the truth behind the scary tale told to keep children behaving throughout the year?

He was nothing like the act he put on on Krampusnacht. There was such a strange sadness in his one red eye, and here she was, likely being another reason for that sadness. What was she gaining from running away, and what was she truly running from? He was kind, and, for once in her life, she had found someone who was fond of her endless prattle about traveling and photographs. Was she afraid of what might come with growing close, *truly close,* to another creature?

Deirdre realized this might be the first creature she might be able to call a friend. She had been alone most of her life, with only her Mammy and Da as company. She had always been an outsider, loud and overly chatty; in school her teachers had scolded her for her outlandish personality. Going through school in the 1910s and 20s was certainly no help to her isolation, either. She had never found comfort in the company of others. Sure, while she traveled she was a social butterfly and would chat to anyone giving her the time of day. Perhaps, though, it was because she knew she never had to see them again. She had been dreading the idea of leaving the cabin where the friendly Krampus had lived. Yet here she stood, soaking wet and shivering as she stared back at it with a mixture of fear and longing.

Oalfus felt his brows knit together as he realized the sun was beginning to set. Even inside the cabin with the dying fire, it was beginning to become very cold. *How on earth would Deirdre survive*

out in waist deep snow once it was dark? What sort of demon was he, if not one with self-pride. If he wanted to live with himself, he could not allow her to die, even if she wanted nothing to do with him.

Oalfus' body finally began to listen. He rose to his feet and made quick work of wrapping himself in his black cloth. He would be no use to her if he was freezing, so he also pulled the black cloak off the hook beside the door. With a great heave he threw the door open and would have bowled Deirdre over, had he not looked down first. He stepped back in surprise. The pair of them stared at each other in disbelief. Deirdre was the first to speak, though it was through chattering teeth.

"O-Oalfus I am so sorry, I-I shouldn't have run from you the way I did. I-it was cruel and I am sure you're very upset with me, you have e-every right to be. I d-don't have any good reason for what I did. Y-you will think I am a total fool but the t-truth is—"

"Stop talking, you foolish girl and get inside!" he growled, scooping her up into his arms and quickly shutting the door."D ammit all, Deirdre. You're soaked through," he grumbled, pulling off her backpack and dropping it beside his table.

He once more quickly peeled her out of her layers. This time there was far less to fuss with, which may have added to his deepening frown. Deirdre was completely stunned. She had expected him to tell her off, to slam the door in her face. Yet once again, he was doting on her.

He had her wrapped tightly in several of his fur blankets, sitting her beside the wood stove as he bustled around the cabin. He lit a much larger fire, and, thanks to the smoldering coals, it took little time for it to begin throwing huge waves of heat through the small space.

Deirdre shuffled even closer, her head resting on the edge of the counter as she watched him hurry about setting a fresh kettle of water on the stove and preparing a pot of tea. He then turned his attention to her soaked clothing. As he began draping it over the edge of his table, it also occurred to him her other clothing in her pack might have gotten wet since half the bag was now soaked. Spring snow was always wet, and, from how sore his back was from shoveling the heavy stuff, he figured it was better to be safe than sorry.

Deirdre was about to protest as he unzipped the back, but the fierce glare on his features quickly made her shut her mouth. Oalfus was in total shock at the priorities of this girl; her clothing was crushed into the bottom of the large pack, under her sopping sleeping bag. Everything was wet, including the little rocket stove and other odds and ends she had. The only thing that had been wrapped inside water proof bags were her collection of photos and camera. Oalfus looked over at her with an unimpressed raised brow. She quickly looked down at her feet peeking out from under the fur blankets. He decided to just dump the contents of her bag to let everything dry out properly. Soon most of the floor and any counter surface not being used had her wet possessions draped or laid out to dry.

Deirdre was too ashamed to speak. Her ears tipped back and tail curled around her side under the blankets. Oalfus finally eased himself down on a stool beside her, holding out a cup of mint tea towards her as he held his own cup and a bottle tucked under his other arm. She whispered her thanks, taking the cup and avoided looking at him as she watched little flecks of crushed mint leaves swirl in her cup. Suddenly a bottle of sharp smelling liquor was stuck under her nose, which she quickly jerked her head back from.

"It smells worse than it tastes. Drink this. It will warm you," he grumbled, taking a mouthful of tea.

"What is it?" she asked as she gingerly took the bottle.

"Schnapps. Just drink it."

Deirdre took a mouthful of the incredibly strong liquor and struggled to swallow it. Her throat and stomach burned at first, but then a gentle sweetness of apple and cinnamon filled her mouth. It was not overly sweet; she had drunk sweeter whiskey than this. It reminded her of a dry cider... if cider was made of 80 proof alcohol.

Handing it back to him, she watched as he took several long gulps of the liquor before capping it and setting it on the floor between them. The silence was heavy between them. Deirdre wished she had the courage to speak again but her tongue felt too big for her mouth.

"Why did you run?" Oalfus finally asked, his eyes seemingly glued to the flames as he watched the fire burning intently. It took a few gulps of tea before Deirdre managed to find her voice once more.

"I suppose because I was afraid..."

"Of me?" he asked. His words cut her like a knife.

"No, gods no...Oh Oalfus, I am so sorry..."

"What are you afraid of then, if not me?"

She sat in silence, a sad chuckle slipping out as she finally spoke.

"I suppose my feelings..."

"So you decided to run into waist deep snow, possibly getting yourself killed, because you were afraid of your *feelings?*"

"I don't expect you to understand—"

"No, I don't, but I am trying to understand. Enlighten me!" he snapped, closing his eyes suddenly and pressing his hand over his face. He took a slow breath, exhaling through his nose before he spoke once more in a much more controlled voice.

"When I left you earlier, you seemed happy. I came back in to find you in tears and your fingers practically mutilated. I...what did I do wrong?"

"I already told you, Oalfus. You have done nothing wrong! You have done everything *too* right. I...I feel comfortable with you. I feel like I can be myself and tell you my ridiculous stories. Apparently, I can tell you my inner thoughts rather easily, and I am afraid of what that might mean. You and I hardly know one another and...I was *dreading* the idea of...of leaving here once the snow cleared."

"Have you not felt comfortable with others before me?" he asked in a careful tone, his eyes glancing towards her more frequently now.

"Not the way I do with you...I suppose we have one thing in common. I know it doesn't seem like it with all my traveling and stories, but aside from my Mammy and Da, I have never really had friends. I have been an outsider almost my entire life..." she squeaked out in a small strained voice.

Oalfus' long tail began to sway slowly, eventually wrapping around the back of her stool and tugging her a little closer.

"I suppose I understand a little of what you might be feeling. I have never enjoyed the company of another creature as I have with you. It may have also crossed my mind that I would be unhappy to see you leave..."

"Do you mean that?" she asked, looking up at him with a little more hope in her voice than she liked.

He turned to look at her, his one red eye looking deep into her lovely emeralds. Nodding as he leaned a little closer to her, his tail now able to curl around her legs as he spoke gently.

"I do, and I can not lie to say I was not incredibly glad to see you had come back to me safely, even if a bit frozen."

Deirdre shuffled her stool so it bumped up against his, her ears still tipped back as she looked up at him shyly.

"I was really glad you didn't shut the door when you saw me. I didn't want to truly say goodbye to the first friend I have ever made...i-if I am allowed to call you that."

"I am honored you think of me as such, *mein Liebchen,*" he rumbled, his voice gentle and a small smile tugging at the corners of his mouth.

"I don't think normal friends call each other such old fashioned pet names," she said with a little smile, her ears lifting and tail thumping against the blanket.

"I don't think normal friends have...oh, how did you put it, 'absolutely mind blowing' sex?" he said with a wide smirk.

"Well, then, I am glad you are not a normal friend."

"As am I."

Chapter Six

It took several days before the snow melted down to a manageable amount. Deirdre was still in shock by how much it had snowed and so late into spring. She had worried Oalfus may have come to regret having her, but it was quite the opposite. He had never had company this long before, and the more time the two spent together, the more fond he grew of having someone to tend to.

He did not fuss or fawn over her, that was below him, but he did enjoy being able to share a cup of tea with her or have someone to talk with while he cut wood to replenish his dwindling stores. What he truly loved was having someone to read with, or, rather, someone to read to.

Deirdre was not nearly as fond of poetry and philosophy as Oalfus was, but she always entertained his chatter on the subjects. In the last few days, she had gone from listening to his occasional outbursts while reading, to *asking* for him to read to her. She was much more fond of the poetry than the philosophical books; they were too boring and stiff for her taste. She found a few books on folklore among his modest collection, and this was when Oalfus discovered something he enjoyed even more than discussing poems with her.

She would read the tales to him, and the emotion she would put into her reading was breathtaking. She had caught him with his eyes closed and a wide smile across his face several times while she would read to him. It was rather endearing, so between endless pots of different herbal teas or their morning coffee, the pair would read and chat away as they waited for the snow to melt.

Now that she was not to her waist in snow banks, Deirdre was able to offer her help when Oalfus went to cut wood. She practically leapt for joy when, one morning, he mentioned it would be safe to go foraging soon. When the morning came when Deirdre's cabin fever could no longer be contained, Oalfus busied himself with buckling on the deep red leather harness he hooked his basket onto while Deirdre dressed herself and got her camera loaded with a new roll of film.

Deirdre tried not to stare, but something about the thick leather strapping across his chest and midsection was incredibly enticing. She *so* badly wanted to ask if she could take his photo; he was truly very handsome considering he was an old order demon. His dark red eye shone so brightly against his charcoal coloured fur, and even the eye which was heavily scarred and clouded over had a strange beauty to it.

The milky silver colour of it was so mysterious, her mind wandered as she imagined what two profiles of his face framed and hung on the wall might look like. They would be such a lovely contrast. Deirdre had not realized she had been staring right at him as she was off in her daydream. It was only when Oalfus finally walked up to her and rapped his knuckle on her forehead that she realized she had been off in her head again.

"Are you in there, *mein Liebchen?*"

"Sorry," she mumbled at first, her eyes still unfocused. Once her mind registered him, with a swift shake of her head she smiled up at him and spoke in a shy tone.

"Just off in space again. Are we ready to go?"

Oalfus ran the backs of his fingers over her forehead. He had been making a habit of this gentle gesture. Any time Deirdre had been off in her imagination, he would reach over and trail the backs of his fingers over her forehead and down her snout, sometimes even tickling the scruffy fur on her muzzle to regain her attention.

He never said anything. When he noticed that dazed expression or emotionless stare, he would gently attempt to bring her back. Sometimes, he would not even lift his eyes from the page of his book, simply reach over and return to his reading once she came back. She nuzzled into his palm, looking up at him with those beautiful emerald-coloured eyes. Oalfus only smiled, reaching behind her and lifting her windbreaker off the table's edge.

"Put this on, the wind is still sharp," he rumbled before turning towards the door and stepping out into the clear blue day. Deirdre followed behind, tugging her windbreaker over her head. She looked delighted to finally be able to stretch her legs properly, skipping out ahead of him and spreading her arms as she spun around.

"Oh, bless the morning air! I have never been so glad to be outside!" she said in a sing-song voice, her tail wagging wildly behind her.

Oalfus warmed at the sight of her, smiling as he finished hooking the large basket onto his harness. Deirdre eyed him, grinning coyly as she pulled her camera out from under her windbreaker.

"Is that the famous basket Krampus stuffs the children he steals into?" she teased. Oalfus rolled his eyes, smirking at her and nodding.

"It is, though I must admit I have never stuffed a single child in here. The supplies I collect from my connections in town and the offerings left for me on Krampusnacht are the only things I've ever put in here. I still don't know how that rumor started," he said with a snort.

Deirdre circled around him to look closer at it. It was more of a barrel than a basket really. It was narrower at the bottom than the top, finished with the same red leather that his harness was made from. She grinned, tapping her finger on her chin as her mind began to wander. Oalfus raised a brow at her.

"What is going through that devilish mind of yours?" he rumbled, leaning down as he eyed her accusingly. Deirdre giggled, pushing his snout away from her as she looked a little embarrassed.

"You will make fun of me!" she said with a mock pout.

"Try me," he huffed.

"Well...I was wondering what it might be like..."

"To be thrown in my basket and stolen off with?" he chuckled.

"See?! I told you! You laughed at me!"

Oalfus flashed her a dangerous smile before she was suddenly hauled up off her feet and tossed quite literally over his shoulder and into the large basket. She couldn't contain her wild giggling, snorting between bouts of laughter. Oalfus had to readjust his harness, mockingly huffing and giving a little hop to jostle her. She couldn't help but squeal with laughter as she was shaken around, and soon Oalfus was letting out a gruff laugh with her.

It took Deirdre a moment to get herself upright in the basket, her head popping out over his shoulder and her arms reaching around his neck so she could prop herself a little higher to see. The old demon grinned broadly, one of his hands resting over hers as he continued walking towards the thicker trees. Deirdre felt her face warming; he had never held her hand before. Finding a shred more courage than usual, Deirdre gently wiggled her fingers between his and gave his hand the gentlest squeeze.

Oalfus rumbled loudly, which surprised both of them it seemed. He cleared his throat, turning his head away from her to hide his embarrassed expression. He could feel Deirdre craning to look at him, but, instead, gave her a firm nudge with the side of his head. She giggled, running her free hand over the top of his head.

"Aw, the big bad Krampus is bashful now!" she teased, which earned her an annoyed glance.

"Quiet back there. I might take up a new habit of eating my captives," he grumbled, but, to his surprise, Deirdre simply leaned in closer to him and whispered against his ear.

"You mean the same way you ate me up the other day? If that's the case, I certainly welcome it."

Oalfus grinned wider, his long canines exposed as he glanced back at her, that gloriously long forked tongue running over his maw as his one clear eye bore into hers behind a heavy lid.

"You tease and tempt me now, little one... Be careful, I might just have you right here."

Deirdre's face grew much warmer, her tail wagging wildly and her thighs pressing tightly together. No matter how much she tried to hide it, Oalfus could smell her excitement, and it only made him growl louder.

"You are full of surprises aren't you, *mein Liebchen?* Do you enjoy the idea that much?"

Deirdre gave his head a shove and looked away from him with her ears tipping back.

"No fair, you're cheating!"

"You know I won't use my charm on you, so it's hardly cheating if my teasing works on you just as yours works on me."

Deirdre ventured a downward glance and was shocked to see the tip of Oalfus' length peeking out behind the thick fur that ran down his stomach and between his legs. Her face only warmed further, her tail wagging a little faster as she squirmed.

"You really should wear your pants more often if I am around you. Clearly, someone doesn't have much self control," she said with a sly grin.

"You try wearing clothing with this much fur and tell me how comfortable it is. I used to have to clip my fur short twice a week back when I still lived in Moscow. I refuse to do it unless absolutely necessary now. Besides, I have never had an issue with it until a certain little moor hound fell through my door," he said with a grin.

Deirdre had to admit, he was very heavily furred. He looked more wild than other demons. Aside from the ancient ones her kind guarded, the creators, she had never really met an old order demon like him before. They were incredibly rare back home; the world wars had been devastating for demons in her regions as they had all been forced to join the fighting. She was shocked Oalfus was even here the longer she considered it. Demons from all over had been forced to participate in the wars. Then again, he lived in such a remote place and was very good at hiding; perhaps they walked right past him in their search.

Deirdre was busy admiring his more feral features; his gait was more animalistic than hers was. She wondered if he ever ran on all fours. *What a sight it would be*, she thought. His long tail swayed side to side behind him, another trait long since bred out of demons. Demons had been clever in their cross breeding in the early years with the mortals, making themselves less and less like Oalfus and his kin, and more like the mortals they walked among.

There were little traits that lingered, the eye colour being a big one. Longer canines as well, and claws were all dominant give-aways that someone might be a demon. Demons tended to have brightly coloured eyes, canines that hung over their bottom lip and long claws. Many like Deirdre could change their shape when they felt certain emotions or simply by their own will. There was a trade off though: much of the ancient magic that ran through their veins had to be sacrificed in order for the new order of demons to be born. In the early days, demons had to use blood magic to breed with mortals, and it took an incredible toll on them. These days, it was rare that mortals would become pregnant from a demon, and if it did happen, it was from relentless attempts at breeding. Demons conceived much easier with other demons, but many stayed within their own species.

Deirdre felt a flicker of a thought tease her mind. *What would her and Oalfus' child look like?* She shook her head. *Let's not entertain such things,* she reminded herself. Quietly, she reached out and ran her fingers along the long curve of Oalfus' long horns. They both came to a wicked point, and as her blunt claws trailed along the bone, she could feel something like a purr rattling through his body. She grinned widely at him; he looked terribly embarrassed.

"You can purr?" she gawked, almost laughing as she ran her fingers over his horns again. The vibrating sound only grew louder, which deepened his grimace.

"I didn't even know I could. No one has ever touched my horns before," he huffed, rubbing his neck in embarrassment. Oalfus had enough of her poking and prodding; kneeling down, he reached back and pulled her out of the basket.

"That's enough from you, we have work to do," he grumbled.

Turning towards the woods, Oalfus reached for the ax he had slid into the loop on his hip. He seemed to be considering which tree he was going to cut, pulling the basket off his back and setting it down before finally making a decision Deirdre grew bored waiting for him to need her help, so she wandered off to take pictures. She never strayed farther than a few hundred feet, or, at the very furthest, still being able to hear his ax hammering into the trunk of a tree.

She was disappointed she didn't see any birds, but there were still things to take photos of. She found a lichen-covered tree and took several close ups, some kind of deer skull half-buried in the mud and overgrown with moss, and, just as she was lifting her viewfinder to her eye, there was a rustle in the trees beside her. Through the trees, only a hundred or so feet away, was a massive red deer, completely unaware of Deirdre. She bit back her gasp and turned her camera quickly, snapping several photos. She grinned and carefully backed away as quietly as possible. Scurrying back to Oalfus, Deirdre looked positively giddy.

"Oalfus! Oalfus, you won't believe what I just saw! It was so close!"

"Spit it out then," he said over his shoulder.

"I have never seen one so big! It was gorgeous!" she continued her excited prattle.

"What was so big, what was gorgeous?"

"Oh, right," she said with a sheepish grin. "It was a red deer"

Oalfus perked up, looking in the direction she had just come from. "Did you scare it off?"

"No, why?"

Oalfus tossed the ax into his basket and quickly unfastened his harness. He smirked, shrugging it off and tossing it over with the basket before he took several long strides, leapt up and hauled himself up a nearby tree. Deirdre watched in stunned silence. The way he perched on the branch and loomed over her made a chill run down her spine. In the shadow of the thick pine branches, his long teeth gleamed and his red eye looked like it was glowing.

"You have nearly run out of the bits of food in your bag; I know you younger ones prefer to eat more regularly. I suspect some fresh meat would be appealing."

"Y-you're going to kill it?!" she gasped.

"How else am I going to feed you?" he said with a smirk before he began leaping from tree to tree. Deirdre hurried after him, her eyes wide with shock and jaw slack. For such a huge creature, he moved with an eerie silence. The wind blowing through the trees hid most of the noise he was making, and what impressed her more was how a creature with hooved hind feet was able to climb trees so damn well. Oalfus' secret weapon was his incredibly strong tail; he used it to help him balance and steady himself in the trees.

He had learned at a young age that his bulk made his footfall much too loud, and, after a lot of practice over these long years, he had mastered the practice of climbing above any prey he was after to drop down on it. Deirdre had somehow lost sight of him. He was surprisingly quick. The only reason she had found him was the horrible sound the deer made when Oalfus had inevitably found it. When Deirdre finally came upon them, Oalfus' muzzle was covered in blood and a limp deer was under him. Deirdre shivered; the feral nature of his shape crouched over the deer's broken body made her heart catch in her throat.

As he stood and lifted the deer over his shoulders, Deirdre couldn't stop herself from blurting out. "Could I please take your photo?"

Oalfus arched a brow at her, suddenly dispelling the more animalistic appearance he had just had on. It was like he was two different creatures wrapped into one. One moment, he was the charming demon who would read poetry to her, and the next, he was a wild beast tearing the life out of a deer with his bare hands and teeth.

He grinned when he caught the scent of her excitement and noticed her thighs pressing a little closer together. His tongue ran over his mouth as he licked the deer's blood from his face.

She suddenly shook her head and whined a little. "Oh no, don't! You'll ruin my shot! Please, could I take a picture of you?"

"You want to take a picture of me with blood all over my face?" he asked, raising his brow a little higher.

"I mean, right now I do. But I also want to take a photo of you without the blood, and one of you with the basket on, and maybe one of you cutting wood, too..." Her voice had grown a little smaller and more shy with each scenario she confessed to wanting. Oalfus was a little surprised; this was a new feeling for the old demon. Perhaps a little vanity flickering into his mind, his grin widened and he gave a shrug.

"Fine, why not? If it is what you truly want–"

"Yes please!" she gasped, holding her camera up.

Oalfus chuckled at her sudden excitement, her tail wagging once more. He dropped the deer down to the ground and put his hands on his hips.

"Alright then, little photographer. What do you want me to do?"

Chapter Seven

Deirdre held onto her camera like it was solid gold, a permanent smile on her face since the moment she pointed the camera towards Oalfus. The old demon couldn't help but feel a little bashful; he had never been the subject of such attention before. It was not a bad feeling per se, but he also was a little nervous of what she had captured. He had only had his portrait painted once in his life, when he was a young man and not the sole subject of the photo. It was of him, his brother, and his father. His mother had been too ill to sit for the painting at the time.

Oalfus felt his chest ache at the memory, quickly shaking the thoughts from his mind. He was glad for the distraction of handling the deer. While he had allowed the animal to bleed out properly, he had continued to cut more wood to replenish his dwindling stores. He still had plenty of wood to burn, though he never allowed his pile to go below a certain point as fresh wood was a pain to burn. He would have to return again for more, though. Even with the deer gutted, he was still weighed down with both it and his wood-filled basket.

Deirdre suddenly looked over at him, her eyes widening as an even toothier grin spread over her features. Her camera once more rose and pointed at him. He rolled his eyes and smirked, looking away from the lens as she had insisted so many times that day. She practically squealed with delight as the little mechanical shutter went off.

"Oh bless you! I can't wait to have this roll developed. I think it might be my best one yet!"

Oalfus smiled; it was becoming a little less embarrassing with every photo she took of him now, but still he felt a small pang of fear. What if someone else saw these photos? He could be discovered so quickly...

"Tell me, *mein Liebchen*, how exactly do you get the photos out of the camera?"

"Oh that's easy!" Deirdre chimed, holding the camera up and pointing at a small door on the camera. "Inside here is a little roll of film, so when I take it to the print shop, they have a special machine that shines light through each photo onto special paper. Then it goes into a few chemical baths that do...uh...well, they make the picture nice and then pictures come out how you saw them!"

Oalfus raised a brow at her, smirking slightly. "You haven't a clue how it's actually done, do you?"

"No...I'm too clumsy for that sort of work. Why do you think I pay folks to do it for me?" she giggled, cradling her camera to her chest. "I don't know if I'm patient enough to finish this roll! Oh, I want to know how they turned out! I might hike to the village in the morning and–"

Oalfus suddenly tore the camera from Deirdre's grasp, panic painted across his face as he looked at her.

"You can *not* have these photos printed anywhere near here. I would prefer it not even done in the country! I...If anyone were to find out what I am–" His words caught in his throat when he saw the hurt expression on Deirdre's face. Her ears had dropped and she was looking down at her feet.

"I...I suppose I will just have to wait until I leave, then..." she said in a small voice, her tail tucking between her legs. Oalfus swallowed hard, his brows drawn together as a heavy ball of regret made his throat feel tight.

"Deirdre, I just—"

"I know, I promise I won't have them developed until I am far from here."

He had no words, the hurt had been done. He gingerly returned her camera, and the rest of the walk was done in an agonizing silence.

Oalfus had remained outside, skinning the buck and butchering the meat. He was doing several things at once, hanging thin strips to dry on a small rack he had made with thinner branches. He had started a fire to smoke a few larger pieces, but this would take some time to complete. The last step he was doing was salt curing in a large container.

All these different tasks were giving him time to think of how he would apologize to Deirdre. What on earth would he say to her? He had basically told her to leave if she wanted to see the photos she was so excited about. *Damnation, why on earth had I gone and said that?* He clenched his fists, the knife handle in his hand letting out a little crack as if pleading for mercy. Oalfus sighed, but jolted when a small voice spoke suddenly from behind him.

"Can I help with anything?"

Oalfus was surprised to see Deirdre; she had seemed so hurt when she had gone inside upon their arrival. He swallowed once more, his tail curling around his ankles. He had not yet figured out what to say to her.

Clearing his throat, he nodded and attempted to untie his tongue. "O-Of course, yes. Would you mind adding more wood to the fire? The dried logs, though, not the wood I cut today. It needs to season over the summer"

Deirdre was also trying to find her courage to speak. She had been thinking long and hard on what had happened. After filling her arms with split logs, she set them down near the fire, took a seat, and finally spoke up. "I have been thinking about what you said–"

"Deirdre, I need to–"

"Please let me finish," she pleaded, her face very serious. Oalfus sighed and nodded, turning back to the meat he was slicing to hang dry.

"Apologies, please go on..."

"I thought about what you said, and I agree. I can't have these photos printed near here, as people still think you are some spirit. They have never really seen demons, not like the people in the cities have. I don't know why you hide here, but you know that things have changed out in the world. Demons are not hunted down anymore, not like when you were younger..."

His knife stopped, his ears tipped back and his shoulders raised. She had struck a nerve. *Shit.*

Gingerly, she stood, moving to his side and placed a gentle hand on his arm. "I know it's not my place to ask about your past, and you have every right to deny me, but would you at least tell me why you have hidden away all these years?"

His eyes closed tightly, taking a deep breath before opening them once more and looking at her. "When I was young, the world was different. Demons were feared by mortals; they did not blend in as you do. Most looked like me, and most slaughtered relentlessly for power and status amongst our kind. Mortals had every right to hate us, to hunt us down.

"My parents were no exception to such behavior, and it's why they were hunted and slaughtered, just as they had done to countless mortals. It is how I lost my eye; a demon hunter who wore iron claws tried to gouge my eyes out as trophies. I watched my parents get torn to pieces by a mob of demon hunters. If it had not been for my brother, I would have been dead long ago. I lost my trust in the world; I hid myself as far away as my legs would take me.

"At first, I simply roamed the wild and fed off animals; even the fear from a buck is better than nothing. I roamed as far as France before eventually settling here. I had survived off animals so long, I had nearly forgotten the taste of mortal fear. I stumbled on a village late one night in December. A lone boy was out in the woods, likely to defy his parents. He saw me, and the scent of fear was just *indescribable*. I couldn't help but give chase. I would have killed the child had he not ran back to his village. I suppose that's how it all started. I just...stayed.

"These people did not try to hunt me, not in the beginning, anyway. They thought of me as some ghost, so I had a banquet of fear to feed on. After that...well, you know the rest."

Deirdre lowered her head, her ears drooping and sorrow flooding her voice as she spoke in a low tone. "You have no reason to trust mortals, or anyone else, for that matter. The fact you are so kind is a wonder to me, but I promise you, things have changed so much since then. I can not promise that everyone will be kind, nor can I promise it will be easy, but...what I am trying to say is, would you..." Deirdre gripped her hands together over her chest, sucking in a sharp breath with a nervous tight wag of her tail. "Would you ever consider coming along with me?"

Oalfus gawked at her, his jaw slack and a perplexed expression spreading over his features. He stammered the start of several sentences, but no words could truly form.

Deirdre winced, looking down at her feet once more as she took a half step back from him. "Y-you don't have to say yes, I just–"

Oalfus never had the chance to reply. The dry snap of a branch only a few yards away in the tree line made his head snap up and scan their surroundings. He suddenly shoved Deirdre behind him, his teeth bared and a loud snarl rattled out of his clenched teeth. A flash of black and, was that pink he saw blur through the trees? Oalfus felt slightly less worried, no mortal could be such an odd colour. He could not smell a mortal either, but the scent that did hit his nose made his hackles stand on end.

"W-what is t-that?" Deirdre whispered, her eyes wide with terror as both hers and Oalfus' gaze fell on four glowing yellow eyes peering out at them from the cover of shadows. Oalfus let out a loud growl, his stance widening as his protective grip tightened on Deirdre's arm.

"Come out where I can see you. Only cowards hide in the shadows and taunt like little wretches!"

Deirdre gripped onto Oalfus' fur tighter, a choked gasp coming from her as one of the two creatures gingerly stepped forward. It looked something like a sheep, its thick wooly coat covering most of its body. It walked in a hunched fashion, with oddly coloured pinkish flesh covering its face and limbs, and two small wings flapping nervously on its back. The creature had two tall horns that curved back dramatically from its forehead just above two very large yellow, goat-like eyes. Its long black ears lopped down beside its cheeks, and sharp, pearly teeth were revealed as it gave a timid smile. From the sounds of its wispy voice, Oalfus had to assume it was a female.

"P-please, we come as friends. W-we mean you n-no harm," the little demon whimpered, her hands folded against its chest as it stayed low to the ground. A long tail with a tufted end swept nervously behind it.

"It's corrupted!" Deirdre wheezed, trying to scramble back but Oalfus held her tightly.

"If it was corrupted, it could not speak. This is...this is something else," Oalfus said, narrowing his eyes.

"N-no, no! We are not corrupted, please don't fear us! No please, I promise you we are no threat," she whimpered pitifully, covering her head and trembling as she folded against the ground.

There was a rustle in the trees before a second creature, much like this one, hurried forward and hunched over the smaller female defensively. It was larger, with long spines sticking from its back. Its fur was less like sheep's wool and more similar in texture to Oalfus'. This one had two sets of horns, a smaller set over its eyes and a second, much larger and curved set further back. Only his face and forearms were the same pink-coloured flesh. Its long tail, which came to a pointed end, was flesh as well, unlike its smaller counterpart. What caught Oalfus' attention was the heavy metal shackle around its neck, the faint but clear scent of iron coming from it.

"She speaks true, we do not come to harm you!" it growled in a much deeper voice as it hissed out to them. Clearly male, his large yellow eyes narrowed as he bared his sharp teeth and his hackles rose. The little female suddenly crawled out and faced him, holding her arms spread wide as if she were protecting Oalfus and Deirdre.

"Cert no! You must not growl at friends, you must be calm!"

"But Blednica–!"

Oalfus raised a brow, clearing his throat loudly before speaking to the pair in his very rusty mother tongue. It had been many years since he had to speak Russian, but he could understand the pair of demons rather easily.

"You two hail from Russia?"

The little one called Blednica turned, smiling widely and nodding frantically.

"Yes, yes! We come from Moscow, sent here especially for you, Mr. Petrokov."

"You know me, little one?" Oalfus asked, bewildered at the use of his last name.

"Yes, er...well, not really. We have been sent here to bring you a message, from your nephew!"

Oalfus was stunned, but a sharp tug on his fur reminded him Deirdre was completely lost to what was happening.

"What the hell are they saying?" she hissed at him.

"It seems these two are here to speak with me. Apparently my nephew sent them." He turned to face them once more.

"Speak in English. My...er, companion is not able to understand you. What you say to me can be said in front of her."

"Y-yes, of course, apologies. M-my name is Blednica, this is my 'brother' Cert," the little demon said, giving a bird-like bob of her head, seemingly some kind of bow.

"What do you mean 'brother'?" Deirdre suddenly said, raising a brow over her narrowed eyes. Clearly she did not trust whatever these creatures were.

"Oh, yes, well...how do I explain," Blednica tapped a spindly finger on her chin before seemingly finding an answer. "We are children of chaos, you see, demons born from the secret breeding program that happened during the war. All of us who survived call each other brother or sister. We are some of the few who still live. We are a family, of sorts."

Oalfus and Deirdre looked confused. Cert gave a snort and spoke in a sullen tone as he sat dog-like on the ground.

"You know nothing, it seems. During the wars, corrupted demons were common. Starvation in battle drove soldiers and civilians to devour their enemies and each other. With so many corrupted demons available, both sides began experimenting on how to weaponize their wild and unruly nature. Some twisted bastard came up with the idea to forcibly breed them. Those subjected to the breeding program were our parents. Countless demons died to create us..." Cert seemed to spit out his last few words, his eyes flickering red as his anger grew.

Blednica frantically patted his hand, trying to sooth his growing rage.

"It is thanks to Cert I am alive; it is why I call him brother. I was a runt, you see. I am much smaller than the others were. We were meant to be weapons to tip the scales of the war. The chaos demons born in the program were thrown into battle like lambs to slaughter. Demon hunter techniques became common upon the battlefield. We saw so many of our brothers and sisters torn to pieces.

"Cert and I only survived because we met Rikovic. I believe if the great slaughter had not happened at the end of the first World War, more chaos demons would have been made for the second. The compound where we were being made outside Moscow was burned to the ground after many of our siblings were rounded up and locked inside with the scientists who were leading the program. We had been assigned to work with Rikovic and his company as trackers and to sniff out the deadly gas the mortals used to kill each other. He helped hide us when our kind were being betrayed by those we served. Demons are very untrusting of us...but Rikovic trusted us."

Oalfus could not help but feel a bit of pride for his great nephew; he had always known Rikovic to have a good head on his shoulders. Deirdre looked horrified, coming out from behind Oalfus and stepping closer to the pair. Blednica flinched by her closeness, her eyes widening with fear when Deirdre knelt in front of her.

"I am so sorry for all you have endured, and I am sorry for hiding from you both..."

Blednica smiled sheepishly, her eyes softening as she edged a little closer. "It is alright, you only did what is natural"

Oalfus stepped forward, kneeling behind Deirdre as to not loom over them. "So you say my nephew sent you. What is it he needs?"

"It seems your gate would not open for him. He has been trying to reach you with his happy news! He is to be married and wishes for your attendance. The wedding is soon, so it might be best you return to the Petrokov estate sooner than later."

Oalfus rubbed both his hands over his face with a great sigh; he sounded a little annoyed, to Deirdre's surprise. She thought a wedding sounded like good news, what on earth could he be so sour for?

"You're unhappy?" Cert asked, tilting his head.

Oalfus let his shoulders droop and he gave a half smile. "No, I am glad to hear of my nephew's joy. I just...it has been a long time since I have been anywhere near my family," he said with a sigh, looking a bit apprehensive.

While tending the fire throughout the night, Deirdre had decided to get to know the strange visitors a little better. It seemed they were planning to return to Moscow with Oalfus regardless, so until he was ready to leave, they refused to leave. Deirdre was happy for the company; these two did not make her feel uncomfortable as most other demons did. They were almost child-like in their awkwardness. They were fascinated with her when she showed them her full form. Blednica seemed very fond of plants, and when Deirdre made little white flowers bloom in the vines that grew in her hair, the little demon squealed with delight.

Deirdre plucked a few of the flowers and wove them into a little crown for the smaller demon. Even as the sun sunk behind the mountain and the cool night air surrounded them, the three were rather content around the fire.

Oalfus had eventually disappeared inside the cabin, and, based on his expression, Deirdre thought it best to leave him alone for the time being. Only when it became too cold for her to manage without a fur wrapped around her shoulders did she dare venture inside. She had certainly not expected the spectacle she walked in on.

Oalfus was sitting on a stool, clipping away thick tufts of his long shaggy fur with a pair of silver scissors. He seemed very skilled at it; his coat was clipped rather evenly considering the mountain of fur piled around his feet. He looked very frustrated, as the thick fur around his neck was almost entirely gone and his torso was the same. Deirdre's face warmed when her eyes ventured lower and saw his now very exposed private parts. Oalfus had turned just in time to catch her staring, which softened his expression slightly.

"You are no better than a peeping tom," he teased, pulling his long hair forward and attempting to clip the thick strip of long fur that remained on the back of his neck. Deirdre smiled, walking over and taking the scissors from him.

"Let me help, though I don't know why you're making all the fuss. I thought you hated clothes," she said, as she began clipping his fur down to match the rest. He had set up a small hand mirror on the counter, and, tilting it slightly, he was able to look at her through the reflection. A warm smile teased the corners of his mouth as he watched her cut his fur with such care.

"This makes wearing clothing much more comfortable, though it is a pain in the ass. Now I will be stuck wearing clothing until my coat grows back in," he said with a chuckle.

Deirdre hated to admit, but he looked much more regal without the shaggy fur. Her fingers trailed up into his long, charcoal hair streaked with two stripes of silver. Holding the scissors between her teeth, she slowly began to braid his hair. Oalfus let out the same purring sound as she used her fingers like a comb to get rid of his tangles. Thick and slick, his hair reminded her of a horse's mane more than hair. As she worked the strands into a braid, his heavy scent filled her nose. Her eyes fluttered closed a moment as she took in the sweet citrus-and-spiced scent. She wished so badly to shove her face into his hair and hide there forever, but his chuckle made her eyes flutter open.

"What are you doing back there?" he said, blindly feeling over the braid.

"I thought it might make it more manageable for you. Your fur normally held your hair back, didn't it?"

He nodded, and when she told him to hold the end while she dug through her bag for an elastic hair tie, Oalfus had a hard time not watching her. He was beginning to become very attached to the little moor hound, her gentle hands and the sound of her voice so soothing to him. As she returned, he turned away to allow her to tie his hair finally. Closing his eyes, he took a breath and spoke in a low voice.

"I suppose you are getting what you wanted..."

"What do you mean?" she asked, tilting her head.

Oalfus turned, pulling her up into his lap and wrapped a possessive arm around her back and hips. "To travel with me, if you still desire to do so. I would be lying if I said I was not scared to go see my family after all these years. It would bring me great comfort if you were by my side..."

Deirdre grinned, her tail wagging as she looped her arms around his neck and pressed her cheek against the top of his head. "I get to be your plus one?"

"I would like that very much. Have you ever been to Moscow?"

"No, but it was on my list. Oh, I am so excited! I have heard so much about Moscow! St.Basil's Cathedral and Red Square. Oh, and of course the–" Deirdre stopped speaking suddenly, her eyes going wide when something very obvious occurred to her.

"I'm going to meet your family..." she whispered.

Oalfus' brows drew together as he forced a smile. He was not sure what would come of this whole situation himself. It had been over two centuries since he last saw his remaining family. A funeral had been held for his brother after he and his wife had been killed during one of the many riots that broke out in Russia. He had attempted to make himself available to his nephew and great-nephew when Rikovic had been a young boy, venturing to the estate to spend time with them. He wanted to be closer with his family, but back in those days, travel had been very hard for him. Being seen, especially considering his age and appearance, made him a target. The riots that seemed to plague his homeland only made him more uneasy and, unlike the younger members of his family, he was unable to blend in easily. As Rikovic grew older and more independent, he would come to find Oalfus when his visits became less frequent.Oalfus grew more and more unsettled by the growth of Moscow, it was left to his nephew to maintain their connection before it ultimately was severed by the old hermit.

Anxiety was bubbling up in the old demon; his chest grew uncomfortably tight as he gripped a little tighter to Deirdre. The young demoness quickly took notice, her sides aching from how Oalfus was gripping onto her. His hands were trembling! She strained against his might to lean back and see his face, his brows pressed tightly together as he looked deep in uncomfortable thought. Her gentle hand ran over his head as she leaned down to kiss the spot between his eyebrows.

"Oalfus, it's okay to be scared..." she said softly, her hand running over his cheek.

"And yet I feel like a pathetic child," he mumbled, avoiding her eyes now.

"You won't be alone. I promise I will stay by your side. I don't know your family but I'm sure they can't be so scary. They are related to you, after all, and you are so wonderful."

He wrapped her in his arms, resting his cheek against her chest and taking in a deep breath of her delicate scent. Like the forest after rain, she was so calming to him. His eyes slowly closed and he loosened his tight grip on her sides.

"They are not what I fear seeing. I have not left these woods in many long years. I worry I have been so set in my ways, I won't recognize the world around me any more"

"But isn't that the fun of it all? I never know what I am supposed to expect or what will happen when I travel to a new place. I certainly had no idea I would get caught in a snowstorm and find you! The joy of exploring is discovering all the new things you never knew before. I promise the world is not as cruel as it once was. However, if we meet cruel people, I will scare them away from you. All it takes is one bark!" she said with a broad grin, wrapping her arms tightly around his head as she cradled him close.

"One bark?" he said with a chuckle.

"Of course! Moor hounds are known as terror dogs by the English folk. We guard the sacred land of the ancients, the creators of all of us. The moors are ancient gateways for them to come and go from our land to theirs, so when they made the hounds to guard it, they gave us a special bark. One bark is a warning; it makes a grown mortal's blood run ice cold and fear grip his heart. Two barks means death hangs over their heads; their heart will beat so fast it might burst. And three barks, not even the angels could save them; their hearts will freeze with fear and they will drop dead where they stand."

Oalfus raised a brow, a smirk spreading over his face. "So you create fear in those who trespass on the moor lands?"

"Yes, we are the protectors of the ancient gateways. Since my Mammy and Da are still alive and live in a pretty isolated moor, they let me travel while I still can, just as their parents did. Once they decide it is my time to take up their mantle, I will have to return to our moor. But for now, I am free as a bird to see the world."

"Perhaps I have been hidden away too long. You amaze me with how someone as young as you are is so full of wisdom and confidence. I wish I had half your strength when I was your age."

"You give me too much credit, Oalfus. You are a wonder all on your own, a living legend known all over Europe!"

Oalfus scoffed, shaking his head. "Be quiet, what nonsense. I am known only here because I remained here."

"Do you seriously not know?! Oalfus, they hold Krampusnacht parades in most cities throughout Europe during Christmastime. They have been making greeting cards and writing stories about you!"

Oalfus looked at her in total disbelief, rubbing his neck bashfully. "I-I knew that perhaps in wider areas of Germany I was known, I did not think..."

"You are a living, breathing legend, I promise you! Every country I have traveled to knows who you are, and your stories have spread far and wide. You have done so much more with your life than you give yourself credit for. I suppose I am truly blessed by fate for having found you." she said, looking up at him with such adoration.

Chapter Eight

Blednica and Cert were curled up outside the door of the cabin when Deirdre had woken up. The young demoness could not help but think how very animalistic the two seemed as she peered out the window at them.

Oalfus had hardly slept. He had spent most of the night tending the fire for the meat he was smoking. His nerves were hardly being kind when it came to sleep either, as he was incredibly on edge about going to see his family. Deirdre had nagged him to allow her to finish clipping his fur on his back; he had truly hacked at it, and it looked dreadfully uneven in the morning light. With another jab to his side, she grumbled at him to keep still.

"Sorry, *Liebchen*. It's—"

"Yes, yes, I know you're nervous, but if you keep shuffling around I am going to nick your skin! You really hacked it short in areas. I have to try and make it look even. You should have asked for help, you stubborn old goat."

Oalfus snorted, raising a brow and crossing his arms "Old goat? Snotty little know-it-all..." he grumbled to himself, which earned him another jab with the points of the scissors.

Deirdre grinned to herself when he pursed his lips at her, huffing loudly through his nose. The pair's heads lifted when Blednica poked her head in.

"Are you two ready to–" she had got an eyeful of a very exposed Oalfus and quickly squealed and shut the door. Deirdre snorted loudly, trying to hold in her giggles as Oalfus covered his eyes with his hand.

"This is why I don't have company..."

Oalfus hated wearing clothing; he felt foolish from how incredibly dated he looked. Snarling loudly, his large fingers fumbled with the button strap on his trousers that was supposed to go over his tail. Deirdre took pity, buttoning his shirt for him as he stood there complaining loudly about how useless clothing was. He really did look out of place in his clothing; it was very early 20th century styles. Deirdre remembered boys wearing trousers like this when she was in primary school, and the suspenders certainly didn't help him from looking much older than he really was. It was something her grandfather would have stubbornly insisted to wear, had he been alive, but Deirdre kept her thoughts to herself. She smoothed her hands over his chest, smiling up at him and reaching up towards his face on her tiptoes. Tugging a shorter strand of hair out of his braid so it hung along the side of his face rather suited him. Her gentle caress over his cheek made him lean into her hand.

"You make this bearable, *Liebchen.*"

"You will be fine, and, if you want, I am sure we could find you something else to wear. Moscow is a big city, I am certain we could find the time to slip away."

"Is it that bad?" he asked, looking down at himself and letting out a long sigh as he covered his face in his hands. "It's bad..." he groaned. He knew it would be dated, but he certainly had not expected fashions to change so much so quickly.

Deirdre laughed, patting his hands and pulling down the thick black cotton wrap he had used around his waist. "We can try this, maybe like a scarf. It could help distract from it a bit. Who knows, you might look wonderful!"

He shrugged. Anything was better than nothing. With a little fussing, Deirdre wrapped the 'scarf' in a more modern fashion around his neck. Then she unbuttoned the cuffs of his shirt and rolled them up to just below his elbow. Stepping back, she tapped her chin and gave a smile.

"It's certainly better than before!"

The old demon's nerves were beginning to fray. He ran both his hands over his head and turned away from her. This was foolish, this whole thing was a farce. He had not been around anyone so long. Deirdre made him comfortable but the idea of seeing his family was like jumping into a viper's pit. Two very delicate hands ran across his back and looped around his front, causing a low rumble to shake through his chest.

"Your family wants to see you. They *miss* you. They would not have gone to such lengths to send tracking demons to find you if they weren't anxious for you to visit."

He turned and knelt down in front of her, his arms wrapping around her before she was lifted up off her feet into the air. She was perched on his forearm and his head pressed firmly against her chest. She squeaked and used a hand to brace herself against the ceiling that was suddenly very close to her head.

"How do you manage it? You make my worries seem so small..." he murmured against her.

"I know how you feel. I just say the things I had always wanted someone to tell me when I was having a panic attack," she said bluntly, running an affectionate hand over his head.

"Is that what this is?" His ears tipped back as he held her a little closer. His chest felt very tight, his tail lashing nervously behind him.

"It looks like it to me, but this feeling will pass. It feels impossible right now, it feels painful and lonely but I promise I won't leave your side. You won't be alone in this."

"Do you mean that?" He felt like a child when the words left his lips, his ears now pinned flat against his head.

Deirdre stroked one of his velvety ears and smiled warmly at him. "I give you my word. I won't stray from your side once while we are there. I am with you as long as you need me."

The look she gave him made his chest throb with a desire he had not felt in many years. His arm slid up her back and cradled the back of her head as he slid her down his front. Her legs were forced to wrap around him to keep herself steady in his arms, but there was safety in his strong embrace. Deirdre's heart was pounding in her ears; her face felt like it was burning as she held onto him tightly.

"I don't deserve your kindness, but I am eternally grateful for you," he said in a hushed tone before letting his lips brush against hers.

Rikovic was standing with his hands on his hips, a raised brow on his face as he watched the demon gate begin to open. Cert had arrived not long ago to let them all know of his great-uncle's arrival. Viktor smirked at his son, running a hand through his much shorter hair. With all the changes that had happened over the last year, the older demon decided a refresh in his appearance was needed.

He was still adjusting to such a modern haircut. The short sides and back with longer hair on top felt drafty. Still, he figured he looked much better than his son, who stubbornly kept his long locks. Viktor was pleased with the positive progress he had made with his only child; their relationship had been very fractured only a year beforehand, when Ricky, as he preferred to be called, showed up unannounced with a mortal woman. He could hardly believe that in just a few short days he would be watching his son marry her. Thankfully, she was no longer bound to the mortal clutches of death. Viktor's eyes drifted down to the leather strap around Ricky's wrist. The piece of his soul stone embedded into the leather stared back at him like a fiery eye.

Viktor cleared his throat, gesturing to the bracelet. *"Are you sure you want your uncle to see that immediately? I thought we were keeping Carmen's 'status' subtle for now,"* he rumbled in his gruff baritone.

Ricky perked, muttering a few curse words before struggling to get the thing off and stuffed it inside the pockets of his tattered jeans. *"Remember, not a word of Carmen to him until they meet. I don't want to deal with the headache,"* Ricky hissed as the gate began to glow brighter and grow twice in size. They were moments away.

"I bet it doesn't change a thing. He will still throw a fit when he finds out," Viktor said, smirking wider and straightening himself out a bit.

"You're on, old man. I have faith in Uncle Oalfus. He isn't as stuck up as you think."

"1000 rubles says you're wrong," Viktor chimed in a sing-songy way.

"Oh you're so on," Ricky sneered.

A blinding flash of red flooded both their visions as the gate finally opened. Oalfus' head appeared, followed by the rest of his daunting stature. Even though both Rikovic and his father were well over six feet tall, including their horns, Oalfus towered over them. The old demon gave his head a shake, clearing his vision. He had hardly noticed Rikovic and Viktor standing in front of him. Blednica quickly popped out of the gate before it closed and she scurried off to find Cert.

Ricky and Viktor stood slack jawed as Oalfus stood in front of them. In his arms was a petite female, clearly reeling from using the gate. It reminded Ricky of his first time taking Carmen through the gate. This little female was not mortal though. Her form kept shifting as she visibly struggled to gain her orientation. Strange moss-like fur spread over her face and neck before melting away several times. Strange vines sprouted in her hair before wilting and falling out. Ricky was bewildered, looking to his father who was equally clueless.

"Don't look at me, I don't know!" Viktor hissed. His bewildered expression gained him a very unimpressed raised brow from Oalfus as he finally took notice of them both.

"Or perhaps you could simply ask, though I would prefer a greeting before being interrogated," Oalfus grumbled. His attention was suddenly taken from his two winging nephews as Deirdre gripped his arm and groaned.

"Oalfus put me down, I-I think I might be sick..."

"Easy now, *mein Liebchen.* The sickness will pass quickly, take a breath," he practically purred as he gave the side of her cheek a gentle nuzzle.

Deirdre gripped onto his shoulders and let out a whine. "How on earth do people travel like that?"

"Did he call her 'Liebchen'?" Ricky whispered to his father, raising a brow at his uncle.

"I think he did, and I think we have quite the tale in store," Viktor chuckled.

Oalfus walked past them both and subsequently smacked the pair with his heavy tail. They were knocked flat on their backs from the incredibly strong blow.

Ricky laid there, groaning loudly as he pressed his hands over his face. *"He is going to completely freak out...he is already in a shit mood."*

"What happened to 'having faith in your uncle'?" Viktor snickered between groans, getting up and dusting himself off. He straightened the collar of his long-sleeved gray button-up, brushing the seat of his dark-wash jeans before offering a hand to his son. *"One hit from the old man has you knocked down already, boy?"* Viktor said with a grin.

Ricky scoffed and grabbed his dad's hand, throwing him down onto the ground once again before getting up and dusting off.. Viktor growled, glaring at his son before the pair hurried after Oalfus.

The old demon was incredibly uncomfortable already. The estate looked nothing like he remembered on the outside. There was still scaffolding around the house; it was clearly being renovated. Oalfus' grip tightened on his little demoness as he began to climb the short set of stairs up to the main door.

The massive wooden doors flew open and Tatiana appeared. She was dressed in a perfectly tailored, red pencil skirt and a flouncy leopard-print blouse as she stepped out onto the top landing. When she threw her arms wide and began to hurry towards Oalfus, he could very clearly see the black bra she wore through the rather sheer blouse.

"Uncle Oalfus! It is so good to—"

Tatiana looked absolutely horrified, looking him up and down before putting both hands on her hips and scoffing at Oalfus.

"Are those the same clothes I bought you the last time you were here?!"

Oalfus swallowed, gripping Deirdre, who was completely oblivious to what was being said due to her lacking knowledge of Russian, but got the idea rather quickly based on how fashionable this woman looked. Oalfus nodded sheepishly. Tatiana threw her arms in the air and bellowed for Safiya to come to her. Deirdre looked up at Oalfus and wished she could do something to help, but all she managed was giving him an empathetic glance.

"Who is that?" Tatiana asked as Safiya appeared holding a clipboard and a pack of cigarettes for her. The sharp-looking blonde goat snapped up her cigarettes and lit one immediately. The feline beside her wore a flattering pantsuit with wide leg trousers and glossy, pointed kitten heels.

"This is Deirdre. She does not speak Russian, and I would prefer to speak in English when she present," Oalfus grumbled, finally setting Deirdre down.

Tatiana eyed the scruffy-looking female with a raised manicured brow. Her red lipstick was pristine, which made her curled lip even more intimidating.

Quickly sticking her hand out, Deirdre forced her best smile and added a little tail wag to it. "It is a pleasure to meet you. My name is Deirdre Shae."

Tatiana smirked at Oalfus, rolling her eyes before reaching out and returning the handshake rather delicately. "A pleasure. Any friend of Uncle Oalfus is welcome in our home. My name is Tatiana Petrokov, Oalfus' niece by marriage."

"I assume the two following us are your husband and son then?" Deirdre asked.

Ricky, his hands in his jeans pockets and a wide smirk on his face, was the first to climb the stairs and rested his elbow on his mother's shoulder. Tatiana quickly smacked him off and gave a great huff, her eyes flashing red and her canine growing longer.

"Easy, Mama, just teasing! So you are from Ireland then?" Ricky asked, holding out one hand and allowing a little of his charm to slip in as he grinned at the little demon. Deirdre's eyes softened for a moment as she nodded, the scent of smoke and cloves surrounding her before she suddenly shook her head and narrowed her eyes at Ricky.

"Does everyone in this family try to use their charm on strangers?" she huffed, crossing her arms and looking accusingly at Oalfus as well.

"Damn, she can tell?" Ricky said, genuinely shocked and quickly retracting his hand.

Oalfus rubbed his neck, shrugging and giving a little smile. "It seems so. She even sniffed mine out."

"Well, ain't that a neat trick. Might have to get some pointers," came a southern drawl from behind Tatiana and Ricky. Viktor had reached the group just in time for the show, grinning wickedly at Ricky as he hung back on the lower steps, watching Carmen step out from the doorway.

"You weren't gonna tell me your uncle was here, or did you expect me to wait all day upstairs?" the Afghan mix said with a raised brow.

Deirdre's eyes immediately fell on the stunning choker she had on. The black leather and gold finishings hugged her neck snuggly, but the real eye-catcher was the red and yellow stone. It looked like liquid fire trapped inside glass, a long black line running down the center of it, almost resembling a demon's eye.

"Sorry, Carmen. Uh..." Ricky rubbed the back of his neck, a move nearly identically to his uncle's, glancing up at the older demon sheepishly before he gestured towards him.

"Carmen, this is my Great Uncle Oalfus. Uncle, this is Carmen. My fiancee."

"Don't sound so down about it," Carmen chuckled, stepping towards Oalfus and holding out a hand to him. The old demon was about to take hers when the unmistakable scent of mortal hit him. His eyes widening before quickly narrowing as he glared holes into Ricky.

"This has to be a joke," Oalfus suddenly snarled.

Ricky's instincts moved him before he could stop himself; he grabbed Carmen and hauled her back behind him. His horns were already doubling in length and his eyes blazed red as he let out a loud snarl at his Uncle. Oalfus was shocked. Tatiana immediately took Carmen inside, and Viktor hurried to get between Ricky and Oalfus.

"Let's just calm down, Rikovic. No harm was done. Breathe, boy!" Viktor hissed to his son. He could see his horns already starting to split; this was hardly the time to drop another bombshell on Oalfus.

Ricky took a deep breath and closed his eyes, pinching the bridge of his nose. Viktor went on, *"Uncle, this is very much not a joke. Rikovic is attached to Carmen, you must understand. The pair have been through much together. You will find out sooner or later but–"*

"I am blind in one eye, not both! I saw the stone. I can't believe you have allowed him to do this, Viktor!" Oalfus snapped, his eyes narrowing as he glared down at the pair of young demons.

"No one was going to stop me, so stuff it, old man!" Ricky snapped, his temper flaring again. Suddenly a small voice piped up, one Oalfus had certainly not expected to get involved.

"Are you arguing over the soul bond?" Deirdre asked, her arms crossed over her chest.

"I hardly think this is any of your–" Oalfus started, but Ricky suddenly grinned in a rage-filled way before cutting him off.

"No, let the girl speak! She seems to have some fucking sense. Yes, in fact, we are!" Ricky snapped, his hands on his hips as he shook his head.

"I had fucking hoped *you* of all people would be more understanding, Uncle. I wanted you here because you were always open to hear my side of things. I always trusted you, but now you are kicking up a fuss over me finding a partner? One I actually love? For fuck sakes, Oalfus, you encouraged me to cut off my engagement with Katrina because I hated her!"

Oalfus growled, clenching his fists as he loomed over Ricky. "That is hardly the same as throwing your life away on some little mortal girl!" he hissed.

"Oalfus!" Deirdre suddenly snapped, stepping between him and Ricky, and gave him a great shove. She hated to admit, but it took all her strength to get the great oaf to back away from his nephew. "I am shocked! You are not a fool. You might be cut off from the world, but you are not a fool! Demons and mortals have *always* bonded. Who are you to judge your own kin for doing something that is, quite frankly, very common these days?"

"Yeah!" Ricky grinned, stepping forward to look at Deirdre. "What was your name again? I like this girl! How the hell did a grouchy old fuck like you get such a reasonable girl?" Ricky sneered, crossing his arms to mirror Deirdre's now very unimpressed expression.

Oalfus felt his last shred of self-control snap, his fangs doubling in size as his horns curled viciously at the end. His eye blazed with rage as he stepped forward and snarled out his words in a throaty rattle.

"Fine! You want to throw you life away on some little mortal, be my fucking guest. I had to bury my parents and my own brother, what's a great-nephew? You want to throw your life away, do as you fucking please, but don't drag me into your suicide!"

Oalfus turned on his hoof and stormed off towards the gardens, the only shred of familiarity in the damned place. His tail lashed violently behind him as he spun, knocking Deirdre into Ricky's arms. She cried out, gripping her shoulder where his tail had collided. Oalfus immediately turned, but before he could get a word in, he got a sobering taste of his own medicine.

"No, Oalfus! Not a word! Go have your baby tantrum and piss off!" Deirdre barked, her eyes burning red, her hair nearly doubling in length. Oalfus could hardly see any of the original coppertone through the heavily thorned vines that seemed to take the place of her hair. A loud throaty growl came from her as she stood there gripping her arm, tears blurring her eyes as she could no longer contain the rage-filled bark she let out. It echoed through the house and across the property in a deafening clap of sound.

Ricky and Viktor covered their ears from the pain it caused being so close to her, fear flooding their senses as their blood ran cold from the haunting sound of it. Oalfus would never admit the bone-chilling fear that washed through him when he heard that sound, his ears tipping back against his head as he slowly backed down the steps away from her. He turned wordlessly and disappeared around the corner of the house.

Chapter Nine

Ricky couldn't stop grinning as he eyed Deirdre with great interest, tugging on his beard while he lounged on the sofa beside Carmen. Deirdre had finally calmed down enough that her hair length had returned to normal, but her body refused to relax for her moss and vines to recede. Carmen tried not to stare, but the strange demon was so beautiful, and she was brimming with curiosity.

"I-I feel like I should apologize for how Oalfus was behaving," Deirdre said weakly, her flopped ears drooping further.

Ricky snorted loudly, shaking his head. "Couldn't be further from your fault. Unfortunately, all of us have a similar temperament; uncle has just been cooped up too long. He always has a fit over something eventually," he said with a smirk, busy playing with a strand of Carmen's hair now that she had settled against his side.

"How long have you two been together?" Carmen asked, trying to keep her voice gentle as she spoke.

Deirdre visibly stiffened, her hands waving frantically as she awkwardly stumbled over her words. "Oh my, n-no I wouldn't– I mean, I just don't– W-we have only known each other a short w-while! I would never assume–"

Carmen and Ricky both exchanged glances before Carmen smiled knowingly at Deirdre.

"Understood. It was only a year ago I was saying nearly the exact same thing as you are right now. It's complicated; it seems the men in this family make it hard for us girls, don't they?"

Ricky and Viktor rolled their eyes. Tatiana and her husband had been perched on a nearby arm chair. Viktor sat on the seat while his wife was half in his lap and half on the arm of the chair. Deirdre could feel very strong charms radiating off both the males in the room. A familiar smokey, spiced scent filled the room to a near suffocating extent as they both idly traced fingers along their respective partners or twirled their hair around clawed fingers. Deirdre balled her hands into fists on her knees, the sexual energy now becoming incredibly obvious.

"A-are all the men in this family obsessed with using their charm all the time?"

"Yes," Carmen and Tatiana said in unison, though the strange smiles on their faces made it seem like they were completely fine with the situation.

"Doesn't it make you feel manipulated though?" Deirdre asked shyly, feeling more and more like an outsider as she shrunk into her seat.

Carmen gave her a comforting smile, patting Ricky's arm before he finally let her up. She sat on the couch beside the very shy demoness; Deirdre never felt tongue-tied like this. She hadn't felt this alienated and small since she was a child, but the oppressive energy filling the room felt like a set of hands closing in around her throat. Ricky's eyes never left Carmen, even for a moment. Deirdre thought he was watching something he was about to pounce and eat, rather than his soon-to-be wife. Carmen's gentle pat on her hand pulled her attention back.

"Do you know what kind of demons they are?" Carmen asked in a whisper. Deirdre shook her head. She was too nervous to try and ask. Carmen nodded, leaning in to whisper in her ear, covering her mouth with her hand so Ricky couldn't read her lips.

"They are lust demons. It's very normal for them to always be 'in the mood', if you catch my meaning. Don't let them scare you, Ricky is about as soft as they come. His dad over there, Viktor, is so infatuated with his wife he could hardly give a care about anyone else in the room. You're safe, girl. I won't let them pick on ya."

Carmen grinned and gave Deirdre a broad wink. Somehow, this mortal girl was her only lifeline right now. Funny how things turned out...she was supposed to be here as a lifeline for Oalfus, and now she was all on her own with a group of strangers.

Deirdre hugged herself. Her ears suddenly perked when she felt her camera hanging around her neck under her windbreaker. Quickly unzipping it and pulling the camera out, she cradled the comforting item in her hands and took a few deep breaths.

Carmen's eyes lit up, pointing at the camera with a big smile. "You take photos too?"

"Oh yes, I have been traveling all over Europe for a few years now so I take photos of everything!" Deirdre said, her tail wagging behind her.

Ricky raised a brow, finally looking away from Carmen. "Odd for one of your kind to be away from their moor, isn't it?"

"You know my kind?" Deirdre said, rather shocked.

"Of course. You moor hounds were some of the best fighters we had in the war. The way your bark could bring down dozens of mortals and tip the fights in our advantage was incredible!" Ricky said, sounding rather impressed.

Deirdre, however, looked rather somber, her finger running nervously over the edge of her camera lens. "I suppose it would be impressive, but I guess we look at it very differently. My granddad, brother, and many other family members never came home from the war. We were forced to leave our moors and fight. My Da was one of the few lucky enough to come back home to my Mammy and I…"

Ricky hummed thoughtfully, leaning forward and resting his elbows on his knees. He seemed genuinely sorry for the girl, giving a shrug as he spoke more carefully. "Apologies, I suppose it is not an easy topic for many."

"It's alright. So I take it you were a soldier?"

"Yes, but after the first World War, I had my fill. I have been a soldier most of my life, so I didn't want to see any more death. Your father and I were some of the lucky ones, it seemed, we got out with our lives," Ricky said somberly.

"He much prefers his role on the moor with my Ma," Deirdre responded. "It's why they both encouraged me to travel and see the world while I'm not tied to our moor. They are who I send my photographs back to," she explained, smiling warmly as she looked down at her precious camera.

"Have you taken any photos of Uncle?" Ricky sniggered, which earned him a nasty glare from Carmen.

"A-actually, yes I have…I need this role of film to be developed to see how they turned out. Oalfus was very adamant about not having them developed near his home, though, so I will have to wait…"

Tatiana grinned, her morbid curiosity getting the better of her. The blonde goat picked up a nearby little bell, ringing it and, moments later, one of the many house staff appeared.

"I could have one of my girls run it into town, and it'd be back here by the afternoon," Tatiana purred, eyeing the camera with a little more interest than Deirdre liked. The canine swallowed hard, gripping her camera closer.

"I-I suppose I would like to see—"

"It's settled then!" Tatiana declared rather happily.

After much fussing and explicit instructions that Deirdre had to repeat many times, she finally handed over the small film spool. Her heart was racing as she watched her precious roll of film walking away from her.

"Well, this is just silly! How long have we all been sitting around while your uncle sulks over the fact we are getting married?" Carmen said, crossing her arms back on the couch beside Ricky.

"Give him time, he needs to sort himself out before he rejoins us. It seems it might take longer, seeing as he..." Viktor glanced towards Deirdre. She was more worried about her film than about Oalfus, it seemed.

"Nope. If this man has such a big thorn in his side over me, I'm just going to go out there and settle this," Carmen said abruptly, standing up.

Ricky was like lightning, blocking the door and growling out his words. "Not a chance in hell. Beezel is back home with Gibel guarding the property. You are not leaving my sight."

"Oh get your knickers out of a twist, do you seriously think your uncle is a threat?" Carmen huffed.

"He is an old order demon, Carmen! He is unpredictable and—"

"He is probably sulking and feeling sorry for himself," Deirdre muttered, more to herself than to the group. All eyes fell on her, which made her squirm.

"T-that is I mean–"

"Haha! The girl knows Oalfus through and through!" Viktor laughed, almost doubling over in his chair.

"See, I think this will be just fine. Move it, goat man. I wanna get things settled," Carmen insisted.

"I am coming–"

"No way, you sit your skinny ass back on that couch and mind your mouth. He has a problem with me, not you. I wanna get this all sorted and you won't help nothin.'"

Ricky wanted to argue, but it was very hard to deny Carmen anything when she set her mind to it. With a great sigh, he relented, went back to the couch, and flopped down in a heap. He draped an arm over his face and waved her away.

"You get 20 minutes before I come out there," he groaned.

"45 minutes," Carmen snapped back.

"30 minutes, final offer," Ricky huffed, lifting his head to raise a brow at her.

"Deal." And with that, she was scurrying out the door.

Viktor smirked, tapping a finger on his chin. *"100 rubles says she makes this way worse"*

"Oh you're so on, old man" Ricky growled, his defensive side was showing.

Viktor chuckled darkly, wagging a finger at him. *"Ah-ah, you lost the last bet. You still owe me"*

Carmen had been searching all over the garden for any sign of the big demon. How could something so massive be so hard to find? She was about to give up when she decided to double back to the tree surrounded by the stone carvings of all the demon gates that belonged to the Petrokov family.

The only part of Oalfus that Carmen could see was his long charcoal-coloured tail hanging *down* from the tree. She approached carefully, leaning to peek up. Oalfus was lounging on a branch as if it was utterly normal for a massive demon to be *up in a tree.*

"Uh...sorry to bother you," Carmen started, trying to be as delicate as possible.

Oalfus was surprised to see the mortal girl had come to find him, his brows drawing together before he looked away from her. "I am shocked they sent you," he muttered, crossing his arms over his chest.

"No one sent me, I came to invite you inside. It seems rather silly you'd stay out here when we're all waiting for you inside. Besides, I feel like this whole thing is sorta my fault."

Oalfus winced at her words; she was *very* wrong. This was *his* fault. Yet again, he lost control over his emotions. He glanced down at the gentle features of the mortal girl; aside from the scar on her lip and around her throat, she was a pretty little thing.

Swallowing his pride, Oalfus had to admit he perhaps had been rash. The soul bond pendant around her throat was a clear sign Rikovic was very serious about this girl. Carefully, the large male slid down off the branch and landed in front of Carmen. She had to crane her neck to see his face. Oalfus quickly lowered himself to a knee to reduce her strain. Carmen smiled warmly. *What a softy*. He was just like Ricky, which made her immediately lower her guard.

"I know you probably have a lot of worries about me, I know I am a big risk for Ricky–"

"Ricky?" Oalfus said, struggling to make the name sound good with his heavy German-Russian accent. Carmen giggled, which was a surprisingly pleasant sound to Oalfus.

"Rikovic, he lets me call him Ricky. If it wasn't obvious by my very *delicate* and *subtle* accent," she said, being incredibly sarcastic. "I'm from Texas, and most folks just call him Ricky to save from butchering his name."

"I am shocked you are being so kind towards me, Carmen," Oalfus admitted, avoiding her eyes with his only good one. "I have behaved rather poorly thus far."

"I think it runs in the family. You and Ricky are two peas in a pod, ya know. I gotta fight with him to leave the house most days. I understand not enjoying leaving where you feel safe."

"You do?" Oalfus asked, glancing back at the girl.

Carmen beamed at him, her eyes closing as she nodded. "'Course I do! I know we just met and all, but I don't exactly have a warm and fuzzy story myself. Ricky and I enjoy being far from folks, but even I get a little cabin fever and need to get out sometimes. I think if I let him, he would never leave the farm. I don't blame ya one bit for bein' a little prickly. You made it pretty clear you're just worried for him, which I expect his family to be. I pose a big risk, but I wanted to let you know that I understand, and believe me, I'm makin' sure I don't put him in harm's way."

Oalfus smiled to himself, nodding before glancing back at Carmen. "You care deeply for him."

"More than anyone in the world. He saved me, as much as he hates when I say that," she replied.

"He saved you?" Oalfus asked, raising a brow and his ears perking slightly.

Carmen smiled, much more sadly this time, and nodded for him to follow. "I'm sure you're sick of kneeling. Wanna walk and talk?"

Oalfus followed quietly. Carmen was shocked how someone so huge could move so silently.

"You see, when I met Ricky, I was in a failing marriage. My ex-husband liked to drink and snort his feelings away, and when he couldn't get drunk or high, he would take it out on me. Fists, glass bottles, rope, it didn't matter. He just wanted me to hurt as bad as he was hurtin'. Sad part was, I let him do it for six years. I lied when people asked about my cuts and bruises. If I hadn't met Ricky, I'd probably be dead already. Billy was only getting worse as time went on."

Oalfus snarled in response, his eye glowing red as he felt rage fill him at the idea. Only cowards beat on women, especially women they were charged with caring for.

"You look just like Ricky when he realized how bad it was," Carmen said with a sad smile, rubbing her arm absently. "Shortly after I met him, Billy found out and went crazy. He beat me senseless. I got lucky and woke up when he passed out drunk. I didn't hesitate; I just took my truck keys and drove as fast as I could to Ricky's place. He was horrified. Poor thing had to deal with a broken and bloody mess showing up unannounced. He hardly knew me then; I showed up and threw his whole life upside down."

Oalfus felt a pang of guilt when Deirdre came to mind. His nervous glance told Carmen everything she needed to know.

"Sound familiar?" she asked, partially knowing the answer.

"Deirdre appeared at my door in a snow storm a little over a week ago..."

"Oh my, y'all really are fresh in it," Carmen gasped, and then laughed to herself. "No wonder she looked horrified when I asked how long you two have been together!"

"She did?" Oalfus asked, his expression filled with dread.

"I think she was more afraid to say the wrong thing without you, not because I implied you were a couple. She was kinda flustered, to be honest," Carmen said, giving his arm a friendly pat.

"Is she alright? I didn't mean to hit her when I left..."

"Oh darlin' she is just fine. I think it was more of a surprise than anything. You're both demons for cryin' out loud, ain't like it would really hurt her," Carmen tried to sooth, but the worry on his face didn't budge. "I'm sure she would be happy to tell you if you came back to the house..."

"I don't know.." Oalfus murmured. .

"Oh c'mon now, don't be a big chicken! From where I'm standin', the only person makin' a fuss now is you! I think things are much easier, though I might be bold in sayin' so," she smirked, a big toothy grin on her face and hands on her hips.

Oalfus was beginning to see the appeal of this girl; she was quite charismatic. He smiled sheepishly at her, rubbing the back of his neck, just like Ricky would. "Thank you...for giving me a second chance. I apologize for being...well, a giant asshole earlier."

"Apology accepted. Now, are you ready to get back in there, sport?" Carmen teased, giving his arm a playful tap with her knuckles. Oalfus smirked, nodding as the pair made their way back towards the house.

Chapter Ten

After a little more convincing, Oalfus finally made it inside, and was shocked to see how different the house looked. The last time he had visited, it had still looked the same as it had when it was built. Now, it was white-washed, the wallpapers he had enjoyed were gone, and off-white patterns on stark white were in their place. The furniture was modern, and vaguely familiar pieces had been re-finished or their upholstery had been changed.

Oalfus felt like anything he touched would become filthy under his claw. He held his hands tightly behind his back, attempting to not touch anything. The only thing that remained, he was grateful to see, was the dark floors.. The house had once been a masterpiece but now felt alien to the old demon.

Oalfus was hesitant to speak to Deirdre at first, the shame of hitting her was eating him alive. The little demoness also felt bad for her words; perhaps she had been too hard on him. The look of discomfort on his face every time she caught him glancing at her made it clear he was beating himself up over the whole affair. Deirdre had slowly been shifting closer to Oalfus as the day continued, the family idly chatting about Ricky and Carmen's upcoming wedding. Oalfus was made to chat far more often than he had wanted to, but he forced a small smile and put up with the small talk.

Tatiana had one of her house keepers, Safiya, take his measurements which was incredibly frustrating. Like a persistent fly hovering around him, she mumbled for him to stand or sit, lift his arms or drop them. He was infuriated by the whole thing, but incredibly glad to see her leave once she seemed to have everything she needed. Tatiana had muttered instructions to the girl before they both eyed him in a way that made him wish he could leave, and then, Safiya was gone.

Oalfus swallowed hard, his ears tipping back as he avoided looking towards Tatiana draped across Viktor's lap. Even Carmen was lounging across Ricky. Oalfus couldn't help but notice how Deirdre looked as if she was uncomfortable. Oalfus attempted to settle himself, leaning against the arm of the sofa he was on and listening as Ricky carried on with a story about his earlier years in America. It seemed the colonies had changed much since he had first heard of mortals sailing across the ocean to the new world.

The looming spiced scent was only becoming heavier, now that Oalfus was present. It seemed the only one discomforted by it was Deirdre. Tatiana was idly curling a strand of Viktor's hair around her finger as she chimed into the idle chatter. Everyone seemed more relaxed and growing more comfortable. Carmen nuzzled gently into Ricky's neck and her tail wagged slowly against the back of the couch.

Deirdre could feel her head beginning to swim; the heavy spiced scent in the air was like a vice on her mind. Suddenly, the incredible scent of oranges licked at her nose. Her eyes darted up to Oalfus, who was now chatting with Carmen. His legs were spread slightly as if inviting her to crawl over to him, his face resting in his hand as he asked more about Carmen's family.

Oalfus could feel Deirdre's eyes on him, but the older demon couldn't help but take advantage of the heavy flow of charm in the room. Glancing towards her, he moved his hand from resting on his knee to draped across the back of the couch. A stronger scent of orange and cinnamon washed over Deirdre as Oalfus tried his best to pay attention to whatever it was Carmen was saying. He caught her edging even closer to him now, a small grin teasing the corners of his mouth. Deirdre was helpless; there was so much charm in the air she could hardly take it any more. She just wanted to stuff her nose under Oalfus' scarf to try and drown it out. A little whine slipped out, low enough only Oalfus could hear it. Finally, he took pity on her, gesturing for her to come to him.

"Komm her, mein Liebchen" Oalfus mumbled in a low voice.

Deirdre was rather enthusiastic as she quickly curled into his lap and shoved her nose under his scarf immediately.

Ricky raised a brow at his uncle, a wicked grin spreading over his face. *"It seems she finally cracked. That took much longer than I thought it would,"* Ricky chuckled in Russian, trailing a hand along Carmen's spine. He stood, Carmen cradled in his arms.

"I can't take much more small talk, you all are much more boring than I remember," Ricky teased, giving his uncle a broad wink. "Besides I want to go fuck my wife," he declared rather matter-of-factly as Carmen gasped and smacked his shoulder.

"For fuck sakes Ricky, could you not embarrass me!" she groaned, though she was smiling at the idea. Viktor groaned and put his head in his hand, which earned a loud giggle from Tatiana.

"Great, now I get to listen to that all night," Viktor whined, looking rather unimpressed.

Tatiana leaned down and kissed his cheek. "We could make it a contest, who can make their wife scream louder?" she purred in his ear, her finger still twirling a piece of his hair.

Viktor moved like lightning, slinging his wife over his shoulder and rushing up the stairs, all the while Tatiana was squealing with laughter.

Deirdre looked horrified. How could people act like that and not be embarrassed? Oalfus' rumbling laughter caught her by surprise; she thought he would have had the same feelings as her.

"Don't be too shocked. My nephews are both Lust demons. It is their nature, they can't help but act a bit territorial and show off when there are other demons present. Though it is refreshing to see them getting along, I think I preferred it when Rikovic and his father squabbled. It's unsettling seeing them *smile* at each other," Oalfus said, giving a mock shudder.

"They really didn't get along before? It seems hard to believe seeing how they act now..." Deirdre said, hearing the jeering upstairs before two doors shut suddenly. Her fur stood on end when muffled, but very obvious, moaning could be heard within a few moments of the doors closing. Deirdre shrunk, her ears tipping back and her paws covering her eyes.

"I think I will die of embarrassment in this house..." she whispered.

Oalfus was sliding his clawed hand up under her sweater so he could trace small circles over her lower back with the tips of his claws. Deirdre squealed, covering her mouth and looking at him with wide eyes.

"O-Oalfus! W-we are in their living room!" she hissed behind her hands, but the old demon only grinned at her. The room suddenly spun as the large male flipped her onto her back, his arms caging around her head as he gave a deep growl.

"Forgive me, *mein Liebchen.* I don't think I will be able to control myself around you while we are here. My nephews are bad influences..."

His incredibly long tongue lolled out and dragged along her throat, slipping under the collar of both her windbreaker and sweater. Deirdre covered her mouth to hold in her moans. *Fuck she loved the way his tongue felt!* She was kicking herself internally; she was supposed to have more self control than this. Something deep inside her was starting to burn, a new flame of desire she had never felt before. It was like a carnal hunger, that incredible scent of orange and cinnamon driving her to insanity.

He was using his charm, but she much preferred this scent to his nephews'. Their smells were sharp and hard to handle, but Oalfus was like a breath of comfort. His sweet and spicy scent wrapped around every inch of her as he grazed his teeth over her throat. Deirdre let out a needy whine, her hand grabbing one of his horns and pushing his mouth harder against her throat.

Oalfus tried to keep a level head, but she was making it impossible. His hands tore away her jacket, his mouth clamped down on her throat as he began snarling loudly. He wanted to rip every last scrap of their clothing off. He *hated* clothing, it always got in his way.

He pulled his mouth away from her throat only for a moment to pull her sweater up over her head. She gasped when he bit down much harder onto the crook of her neck between her shoulder and throat. His teeth pushing harder against her fur and skin, he wanted to *mark her*, to make his claim on her. His claws dug into her hips as he struggled to hold back his burning desire to possess all of her.

It was an old custom, but one Deirdre knew of, and she could feel his hesitation. The way his jaw trembled over her shoulder, the sharp edge of his claws against her skin as he pressed himself firmly against her. She was trapped under his incredible strength. If he wanted to, there was no stopping him, and yet, he was stopping *himself*. A choked whine came from the massive demon as he finally pulled his head away and sat back, his face a mixture of emotions he was struggling to identify.

Deirdre swallowed and slowly sat up so her hands could run over his chest. "Are you alright, Oalfus?" she asked gently, her fingers running up to his cheek. He gripped her wrist, pressing his face against her hand as his eyes closed. Deirdre gently ran her thumb against his cheek, and his brows drew together tightly. She was surprised to see sadness in his eyes when he finally looked at her. It almost looked like he wanted to cry.

"I am so sorry for how I acted earlier..." he croaked, his arm looping under her waist and lifting her up against him.

She loved how his massive bulk could swallow her up, the way his arms wrapped so tightly around her. "It's alright. I know you were just worried about your family. You didn't mean to hit me. I shouldn't have barked at you either..." her voice growing small at her final words.

Oalfus held her tighter, nuzzling against her neck and leaning back so she was on top of him. He just wanted to be close, to keep her in his arms and drown in the very presence of her. The way her copper curls fell around them like a curtain almost made it feel like it was only the two of them alone in the world.

"If I am honest, your bark truly impressed me. I wouldn't want to be on the receiving end of it again, though...you have quite a bit of power in you," he purred, trailing his hand down her bare back.

He adored the little sounds she made under his touch, her brows drawing together as she let out a hitched breath.

"Well, you better behave then," she teased.

He could feel the heat radiating from her cheeks as he raked his claws gently over her back. "I could never behave with you around. I have...I have never felt like this in the presence of anyone before. You make me forget myself. I feel young and foolish when you smile at me, and yet, it is incredibly comforting," he admitted.

Deirdre flushed further from his confession, her chest tightening and her throat squeezing closed. She struggled to find her words. What on earth could she say in return? Her hands came up and cradled his face, her nose pressed against his before her lips brushed against his.

"You are a wonder, Oalfus. I never imagined in my wildest dreams to meet someone like you. I am glad for that snowstorm, I am glad to have found you," she finally whispered, her fingers sliding along his jaw and stroking his thick sideburns.

Oalfus let out a low purr, letting his eyes close. This was bliss, just the two of them here, pure joy. A muffled crash above them, however, reminded them they were far from alone. Oalfus opened one eye, smirking as he heard Carmen shriek Rikovic's name. He chuckled, glancing down at Deirdre's very naked torso pressed against him.

"It certainly isn't fair if *they* get to enjoy themselves so much and we don't," he said, the heavy perfume of his charm wrapping around them both.

This time, Deirdre didn't find it offensive, but rather enjoyed the sweet, spiced scent. Her hips lifted when Oalfus ran a clawed hand over her ample behind. Her eyes fluttered closed and she bit her bottom lip. He growled loudly as she breathed his name. Deep inside her, something new was coming to life, desperately clawing to the surface as she melted into his touch. A tiny whisper kept tugging at her brain. *Yours, all yours* it whispered incessantly. It was the first time in her life such a feeling was blooming in her chest. She had no idea what to make of it, but it felt as if the most wild pieces of her soul were trying to leap out and dig into Oalfus.

The little moor hound was clueless to the fact the same sensations were boiling Oalfus' blood as he began to explore her. His inner voice was roaring in his ears. The ancient demon had lived closely with his inner beast his entire life that perhaps it was why his temperament was so volatile. Younger demons could control and subdue their truest selves, the very thing which made demons, demons. The bestial shape they could hide was simply a constant for Oalfus.

His more primal instincts fighting to take over as he suddenly hauled both himself and Deirdre off the couch. He remembered a smaller drawing room with a lockable door just down the hall, the perfect place to take what belonged to *him*. Oalfus shuddered when Deirdre gripped onto him tighter. He made every stride count for several.

In the blink of an eye, Oalfus had Deirdre pinned down on the floor just inside the drawing room. His foot kicked out and slammed the door shut before his hands desperately tore away at the clothing on his body. He sucked in a sharp breath when Deirdre began pulling at his clothing as well, throwing it aside and kissing his chest and stomach. There was *hunger* in those green eyes. His body trembled as he quickly took a fistful of her hair and pulled her very eager mouth from his body.

"Easy, *my pet*, you will unleash a beast if you continue like this," Oalfus growled, his pupil becoming a thin slit as his long, forked tongue ran over his maw.

Deirdre wanted that tongue on her, or in her, she didn't care. She reached up for him in desperation, her body already beginning to shift, long vines draping around her shoulders like a curtain.

She had not shifted when they had been intimate before. Oalfus was in awe of how gorgeous her true shape was. Her fur was shifting to a shade of green than its usual tawny red, her hair much longer now and those mesmerizing emerald eyes changing to two burning rubies pleading out to him wordlessly. Deirdre was crumbling in front of him, her submission only fueling his desire to claim her. He clenched his jaw tightly.

"Please, Oalfus...*please,*" she whined, completely shattering his last fragment of self control.

He spun her around and pinned her face down into the plush carpet, his claws leaving scratches behind every touch. She melted against the floor; feeling his claws rake her body was like a pulsing delight as the sting faded into delicious ripples of pleasure. Her tail wagged against his stomach as he finally pulled himself free of his damned trousers. Deirdre practically squealed with delight feeling the head of his incredible length press against her needy folds.

Oalfus shuddered, grabbing her hair once more and pulling, so her back was pressed firmly to his chest. His breath was hot against her ear as he growled, "Press your legs together."

She obeyed without question, looking up at him in a haze as he licked his maw and grabbed at her petite chest. He let out a hiss when his length slid between her supple thighs and the head poked out just under her weeping cunt. Her desire acted as the perfect lubricant as he began to use her thighs for his pleasure. Deirdre watched, totally transfixed as his length thrust between her legs, those incredible spikes tickling her inner thighs as he trailed eager hands over her stomach and ribs.

He gripped at anything he could put his hands on, her soft curves and rolls acting as hand holds. The way she covered her mouth with trembling fingers and whimpered little moans when he took a rough hold on her body only drove him further into his madness. He was going to use every last inch of this incredible body. Every little fold and supple surface would carry his scent, if it was the last thing he did.

Oalfus groaned louder as he began imagining Deirdre littered with his mating mark, bite marks peppered across her thighs and stomach only making his thrusts rougher and more erratic. Very quickly, he could take it no longer; he needed her heat hugging his aching cock. He snorted loudly; the way she hardly needed encouragement to bend over for him, drove him over the edge.

"That's my good girl, look how eager you are already," he purred, running a rough thumb over her slick folds and pulling her open. He licked his maw, *what a feast she would be*, but for now, his throbbing length demanded attention. He could feed on that precious little cunt once his cock was finished, but who knew when that would happen. Oalfus clenched his jaw when his head slid into her without resistance, the sound she made like a song.

"Oalfus!"

The way she moaned his name made his eyes roll back. This little demon would drive him to madness, and he was all too eager for it. Her hips suddenly bucked back into his, forcing all three of his spikes inside her before he could catch her and pin her down.

"Such a greedy little pet. You will get your prize, *mein Liebchen,* but you must be patient," he growled, pushing his bulk down on her, forcing her flush to the floor.

She writhed and let out little growls of protest; she didn't want to wait for him! "Stop teasing me, it's cruel! Please, Oalfus, I am going to lose my mind," she whimpered, but this only encouraged his desire to tease her. He was enjoying the shudder and tightening of her folds around his length, the way she clamped down on him as he pushed forward slowly.

"Mmm...but you grip me so tightly when I take my time with you," he rumbled, pressing his nose against her ear before giving one last thrust and hilting himself inside her. Deirdre shrieked with delight, her body trembling as his incredible length filled her so entirely.

He needed to ravage her now. There was no self-restraint left in the old demon. His arms wrapped around her midsection as he kept her pinned under his weight. His hand gripping her jaw as he forced her to look back at him while he began thrusting viciously inside her. Her expressions were like works of art as his thrusts seemingly melted her reservations away. The way her brows drew together, her eyes rolling back, and the very tip of her tongue hanging over her bottom lip was exactly what he craved.

Her mind was blank, save for the constant waves of pleasure. The little whisper was now growing, chanting one word in time with each wave of pleasure. *Mine, mine, mine.* Oalfus watched with adoring fascination as Deirdre's eyes unfocused and refocused on him with a burning intent.

She managed to break free of his iron grip, twisting under him so she was on her hip, allowing him to hit a whole new delightful angle. She had to pause and squeal out a weak little moan, her lip trembling as those delicious spikes scraped roughly on her insides. Her body trembled, but that constant voice inside her very soul reminded her of her real desire. The kiss she gave him was one thing, possessive and deep as she unabashedly forced her tongue into his maw.

The handful of his hair and claws digging into his shoulders was incredible. He snarled into their mashing kiss, his hand gripping her throat as he reluctantly pushed her back against the floor, eyeing her with a blazing look. He could see the glow of his eye reflecting back in hers, but there was no holding back his words. His inner beast was thrashing in his mind as he hissed out his gruff words.

"Be careful, my pet. If you keep this up I won't have a choice but to claim you as mine."

The way his sharp teeth grazed over her throat sent thrills down her body; her climax was close with such rough handling. Her claws raked down his chest, causing a bellow of a moan to tear from his clenched teeth.

Grabbing her leg, he pulled it tight against his chest to take advantage of such a position. His hips were a relentless onslaught of rough thrusts. Deirdre had to brace herself against the carpet to stop from being shoved away from him. She was unable to form words, her moans becoming an embarrassing devolved drone of whimpers and noise. She couldn't even manage his name from how roughly his vast length hammered away at her insides.

Her first flood of pleasure soaked his length; he had only grazed over her clit with his thumb before she began shrieking out her moans. The rougher those tight circles were, the louder her shrieks became. Soon she was a pathetic mess. Had she been of clear mind, she might have died of humiliation. Her hips lifted and she practically screamed through her orgasm. Her head fell back as she arched into his rough teasing, her leg hooking around his waist before another flood of pleasure soaked his length.

The way her tongue hung out and her eyes rolled back as the waves sent violent trembling through her...Oalfus could no longer hold back. He had been edging for a while and, with her shrieking, he gave in entirely. Slamming into her one last time, he buried himself to the hilt and swore loudly before his own flood filled her. He thrust into Deirdre a few more times before his thick seed finally finished filling every last bit of her. His head fell forward, his hands clutching her hips as if it was the only thing keeping him in one piece.

He wished he had been able to pull out. *She will be furious with me*, he worried. His ears drooped, hating how incredible it felt to fill her. How gloriously her folds held him in, she was absolutely *perfect*. Hesitantly, he glanced up at her, and, to his shock, she had a huge smile painted across her face. Oalfus' eyes widened, his tail began to sway happily as he looked up at that blissful smile.

"Oh gods above, never pull out," Deirdre murmured, grinning down at him as she slowly began to rock her hips.

He sucked in a sharp breath; he was very sensitive now. "You wicked little thing, you keep it up and I might take you up on that," he rumbled, wrapping her tightly in his arms before slowly rolling them both over. She snuggled in close to his chest, her hips wiggled as she tried to grind his length a little deeper inside.

Oalfus frowned a little, making Deirdre perk up. "I am sorry...I left quite the mess inside you..." Oalfus muttered, his face feeling a little warm.

Deirdre was in such bliss, she hardly considered such a thing. Her arms were just desperate to be around him. The way she reached out to him in a dazed state made his chest ache; he could not deny his little demoness. He cradled the back of her head as he hooked his chin around the back of her shoulder. A loud purr rattled out of him as he squeezed her to him.

Deirdre slowly came back to her wits, a broad smile spread over her features at his tenderness. He was so calm and gentle with her, even though he had just ravaged her so entirely. She jolted when he slowly rose to his feet, her legs wrapping around him for support as he gingerly opened the door and peered out. A wicked grin spread over his face as he glanced down at the floor. *Of course she did*, Oalfus thought as he reached down and hooked the handles of several department store bags with one hand. Deirdre peeked out, embarrassment washing over her as she spotted the bags.

"Someone was near the door?!" she shrieked, but Oalfus seemed amused by her bashfulness.

"Oh, don't fuss over something as foolish as them hearing us. I am certain whoever left this for us has heard *much* worse in these halls."

Oalfus gave one more glance before he slipped out of the room. His cock was still firmly planted in Deirdre, which made her shriek and bury her face in his shoulder.

"What in the name of all the ancients are you doing?!" she complained, but Oalfus ignored her.

He knew there was a sizable bathroom on this floor. He snickered at her embarrassment, the heat in her face radiating on his shoulder as he quickly navigated them both to the bathroom. It was incredibly different than he recalled; then again this whole damned house was.

Once Deirdre was on her own two feet and looking *very* unhappy with him, she took in the space. The room was floor-to-ceiling, glittering white tile, likely marble, to match the counters. There was an enormous shower stall with what looked like a rainfall shower head, mounted into the ceiling. The number of knobs and nozzles all over the walls intimidated both of them as they stood inside the glass walls. Oalfus didn't dare touch anything; all these changes were very daunting to him. *What was wrong with the bathtub?*

His ears pinned back and he glanced at Deirdre. Relief washed over him when he saw her same level of confusion, her hand hovering over which dial to touch. Finally, she made a choice, and a heavy jet of water shot out and hit Oalfus in the back. He jolted and made a sound similar to a yelp from the shock of the cold water. Deirdre quickly shut it off, her brows knitting together further.

"Uhm..."

"Well, we might as well try them all, go on. I won't die from cold water," he muttered, glaring at the nozzles in the wall.

After two more failed attempts resulting in a very soggy pair of demons, the overhead water finally began to rain down. Once it was warm, Oalfus rumbled with pleasure as he tilted his head back. The space was big enough to accommodate him without much thought. It was a refreshing change from the rest of the house, which he felt too big or unkempt for. He moaned when Deirdre ran her hands over his back, a cool sensation coming with it.

"Sit down for me, let me wash your hair," she said in a small voice.

He obeyed, though he didn't see the need. He was soon eating his words; the way her fingers massaged over his scalp was good enough to make him stiff once more. He leaned back on his hands, his cock standing fully erect but in too much bliss to even bother touching it. Deirdre giggled at the way he groaned and let his eyes roll back, her fingers working from his long hair down to his thick neck. Soon, he was cross-legged and leaning on his knees as she scrubbed his clipped fur. She was shocked how caked with dirt he was. It took several washes before she was content and the water ran clear. She was beginning to think this big demon never used soap, but the mumbled praise kept her eager as she worked down his arms.

"*Liebchen* you are a gift from the Elders. *Fuck* this feels incredible," he groaned loudly, his eyes fluttering closed once more. His tail had been rubbing the back of her thighs while she scrubbed away at him.

Straddling his lap, she took full advantage of his size. He was a much more comfortable seat than the tile. Even if it meant a throbbing length was poking at her, it was more an affectionate feeling than a lustful one. His body drank in her touch; every ounce of her sent waves of pleasure over him. When he noticed her begin to wash over herself, his eyes became much more focused.

"Ah ah ah, *nein. Das tust du nicht.* I won't sit here lazing while you've just washed me. Give me that." His large hand wrapped around hers as he scooped up the palm full of soap she had just poured.

She was not one to object. The way he eased her against his shoulder while his strong hands ran over her back practically made her melt with ecstasy. Her tail wagged furiously as his heavy hands massaged over her back and ample backside. She let out pleasure-filled whimpers as he gently scrubbed at her thighs and stomach.

Flipping her around, he forced her legs apart as his proud length stood firm just in front of her eager cunt. With the way he was washing her, she didn't take long to realize he was after a second round with her. This time was much less primal, though the sounds he made as he massaged the soap into her breasts said otherwise. He was just as attentive to her, his fingers moving from her breasts to her throat and soon they were tangled into her curls as he washed her hair with incredible care. She whimpered and delighted under every stroke of his fingers, his claws scraping her scalp in just the right way as she leaned against his chest.

"My good girl, you make such tantalizing sounds for me," he rumbled, his hips moving just enough that his cock was now gliding over her folds.

Her body was still a little tender from only a short while ago, and yet, her head fell back to his shoulder and a little whimper spurred him on. Oalfus flashed a wicked grin as he finally allowed the hot water to wash away the remainder of the soap. His strong hands gripped her hips and lifted her with ease as he positioned her above his length. Deirdre was leaning against the tiled wall, her head turned so she could peek over her shoulder at him. His one eye glowed in the low light of the bathroom, his long canines hanging several inches below his jaw as he gripped the base of her tail.

"Take what is yours, *mein Liebchen,*" he purred, his eyes locked on hers.

What is mine? Deirdre thought. Her body responded before her mind, one hand slipping down between her legs as she gripped his length and helped tilt it against her eager cunt. She slid onto him with ease, their combined mess still inside her needy folds acting as a perfect lubricant. Oalfus gasped as she easily took him, sliding down to his hilt before her hips slowly began to work.

"Such a delightful sight...look at that eager cunt swallow me whole," he growled, watching her hips work and his cock disappear deep inside her melting core. He ached to fill her once more, to *breed* his little demoness. How he craved to sink his teeth into her tender neck and leave his mark on her. He needed to claim her, his entire body trembling with selfish desires as his grip tightened on her hip and tail.

He was pushing and pulling her hips now, practically using her as a toy for his own pleasure. She couldn't have cared less, the way his spikes rubbed so firmly deep inside her unlike anything she had ever felt. Her mind was going blank; he had just filled her and yet her body was demanding more. She didn't care about the ache in her stretched core, squealing in delight as his hand suddenly swatted her ass.

Oalfus was fighting his urge to bite her, to claim her, but he could mark her in other ways. Pinning her up against the tile, the old demon snarled with a possessiveness Deirdre's soul adored, his hot breath against her ear as he licked over his teeth.

"You are *mine*, little one. *Mine* to fuck and fill. *Mine* to pamper and pleasure. *Mine* to punish and tease as I desire."

"Yes, yes I am yours!" she whimpered, her words falling out like little sobs as his cock throbbed harder inside her. Oalfus had to clamp his jaws shut and press his forehead to icy cold tile to keep some control. The way she pleaded for him, the feeling of her hand wrapping around his muzzle and pulling him closer, was intoxicating. He groaned internally, but the look in her eyes was pushing him past his limits. She looked as if she was begging to be taken, to be claimed and stolen away by him. He snapped his eyes closed as he forced himself even deeper into her, causing a sobbed moan to tear out of her.

"You have no idea what I want to do to you, what I crave from you," he growled, his body trembling as he squeezed her in his arms. Deirdre let her head fall back against his shoulder, her hand stroking his muzzle before she pressed her lips to the side of his snout.

"Do whatever you desire, I never want this pleasure to end," she whimpered, her eyes unfocused.

As badly as the beast inside him roared to claim her, he refused to ensnare such a creature as young as Deirdre. She was a spring bud, full of a desire to experience life, but he was like a dark cloud blocking out the sun. Clamping his jaws shut, Oalfus turned his head away from her and decided to simply enjoy her while he was able. He wanted to please her, to give her all the pleasure he could while he had her, so that was what he focused on.

Groaning, he bucked a little faster now as his fingers found her needy and swollen clit. She took a little coaxing, her body still sensitive, but soon, she was crying out his name as he edged his way up to his own climax. This time, however, he pulled out of her roughly and allowed his seed to be washed away by the water still raining down on them.

Deirdre may have been delirious in her pleasure as she clung to the wall, attempting to catch her breath and refocus her mind, but she caught the pain-filled look in Oalfus' eyes when she glanced back at him. Worry filled her, but he became silent as they did a final rinse off. He toweled her down before he did himself, then dressed in silence. Dread filled the little demon. *What had happened?*

Chapter Eleven

Oalfus had mumbled something about wanting to lay down, and soon, Deirdre found herself sitting in silence, watching him asleep on the large sofa in the main living room. Her hands fidgeted with a dress she was now wearing; Tatiana had sent one of her staff to collect clothing for them. Deirdre simply chose the easiest dressing option: a pale yellow sundress with tiny blue birds embroidered all over it. Oalfus had only bothered to pull on a pair of dark blue jeans before laying down with his back to her.

Sleep had taken him quickly, which Deirdre hoped would solve his odd behavior. Her eyes caught the corner of a large envelope inside one of the bags. Pulling it out, she was delighted to see it was her developed photographs! Deirdre eyed the sleeping Oalfus before quietly slipping out of the room, not wanting to wake him. Wandering down the hallways, she peered around for somewhere to spread out and admire her pictures. Just as she ambled into what appeared to be a dining room, she caught the enticing scent of baking. Closing her eyes, Deirdre followed the sweet scent through a few more doors before she entered a huge kitchen.

Everything was stainless steel: the counters, the appliances, the copious amount of pots and pans that hung from a rack over a center island. Deirdre was surprised to see Carmen working in the

kitchen, her eyes widening as she cleared her throat. Carmen jolted, looking up from her work before smiling at the young demon.

"Hey Deirdre," she said in her southern drawl.

"Hello..." Deirdre replied nervously. The mortal had been very
kind to her, but something about her made Deirdre feel like she was
a little girl trying to befriend one of the big kids at school.

"Whatcha got there?" Carmen asked, pointing at the envelope
with a batter covered spoon.

"My photos...Tatiania had them developed. I was looking for
somewhere away from Oalfus to look them over. He fell asleep..."
her speech drifted off. "What are you doing all by yourself in here?"

"Ricky passed out himself," Carmen laughed. "He has been
staying up all night with his Dad getting things ready for our big
day, so he's been pretty fried. I just thought I would bake something sweet. I always bake when I am anxious," she explained,
pointing. In the corner of the massive kitchen was a small wooden
table with four chairs around it, and a spread of cookies, bars, and
scones covering it. Deirdre marveled at them, her eyes wide and
tail wagging.

"Well, go on, love. Dig in," Carmen said with a grin.

Deirdre was weak for sweets. Eagerly, she sat down and plucked
one of the bars off the plate. It was something with oatmeal and
pecans, cinnamon and cranberries as well! Deirdre's face dropped
a little; it reminded her of Oalfus. Carmen raised a brow, noticing
her drop in expression.

"No good?" she asked.

Deirdre made an alarmed sound in the back of her throat, shaking her head suddenly and swallowing frantically. "No, no not at
all! It's just...earlier, Oalfus seemed to get upset out of nowhere.
We were...er... in the shower together and it all seemed fine one

moment. The next, he looked like he was in pain and just hurried off to have a nap without much of a word."

"If there is anything I have learned about the men in this family, it's that they are fickle and you gotta be direct with 'em. They won't tell you nothin' unless you drag it out or call them out right away," Carmen said knowingly.

Deirdre hummed, rubbing her arm before another voice came from the doorway.

"She is absolutely right," Tatiana said, smiling sleepily at the pair in the kitchen. She was dressed in a wine red velvet tracksuit. Carmen smiled at her. She loved how Tatiana made everything she wore so glamorous. Even in her house clothes, she was perfect. Tatiana's pale gold hair was pulled up in two large curlers with a matching silk scarf holding them in place. She had no makeup on, but still, she was stunning.

Her golden eyes fell on Deirdre. With a kind smile, she plunked down on the chair across from the young demoness. "What is the problem, dear girl? Has that old codger been rude to you?" Tatiana asked, plucking up a cookie and taking a birdlike bite. She let out a little moan before scoffing the rest of it.

It was a sight Carmen had grown used to; Tatiana *loved* baked sweets more than anyone she had ever met. Deirdre was shocked how the elegant woman suddenly looked like a naughty child scoffing back as many cookies as she could before she might get caught.

"Oh Carmen, these are amazing! Will you make those...oh, what are they again, the lemon things?"

"Lemon bars?" Carmen laughed, rolling her eyes.

"Yes! With the powdered sugar on top?"

"Already working on them, I ain't never seen anyone eat them as fast as you Tati," Carmen teased.

"So," Tatiana said around a mouth full of the oat bar, "what has that old fool done now?"

Deirdre explained the sudden change in his mood, her ears tipping back as Tatiana looked very unimpressed.

"He's bottling again, that old fool of a man. Did you notice anything else tonight?" she asked, tapping a half eaten cookie on her lip.

Deirdre was wondering how the fierce-looking demon kept such a slim figure with how quickly she packed away the sweets. Finally, she gave a shrug.

"I suppose earlier on the couch, it almost felt like he wanted to bite me, but then he stopped. I had never seen him tremble so much before, and then in the shower, he...well, he kept saying how I was *his*. I just thought it was in the heat of the moment. I enjoyed the way he was talking, if I am honest..." Deirdre left out the part where the voice in her thoughts was screaming out for him. She shifted uncomfortably in her seat. Tatiana was suddenly eyeing her with much more scrutiny.

"Do you know of the old bonding traditions?" she finally said.

Carmen had finished with her baking and brought cups of tea for everyone. Sitting beside Tatiana she raised a brow when Deirdre shook her head.

"You're a demon and don't know about them?" Carmen asked, a little surprised.

"Be fair to the girl, not everyone studies demon texts like they are solid gold," Tatiana teased, giving a sympathetic glance towards Deirdre who had shrunk in her chair. "In the old days, before your time, demons would not marry as they do now. We had our own traditions and beliefs, but mortal influence has changed that.

Viktor and I still observe many old traditions, which is why we've been in such control of this whole wedding business–"

"Bless 'em both, honestly. I was dreading the idea of plannin' it all!" Carmen chuckled.

"As I was saying," Tatiana continued, raising an annoyed brow. Carmen grinned sheepishly; she forgot how much Tatiana hated to be interrupted. Her annoyance flickered through, the way her pupils slit as she continued to speak. "In the old days, demons would use marks of claim, not wedding rings, to show they were mated. They would sometimes experience a mating bond, or even a frenzy, when they found their fated partners. Rikovic is still recovering from his recent frenzy. After he soul bonded with Carmen, it seems the poor girl was trapped in their home for over a week."

"It's true, he was insatiable. I have a litter of scars on my back and ass thanks to those damned claws," Carmen laughed. Her face warmed at the memory. She ran her fingers over the large soul-stone on her choker, her eyes softening.

"I think it might be possible Oalfus is feeling a bond for you, but I know that stubborn old goat is too much of a chicken to say a thing," Tatiana huffed, rolling her eyes as she sipped her heavily spiced orange tea.

Deirdre held the cup close to her nose, taking in a deep breath and shuddering. "It smells just like him..." she breathed out the words, taking a deep drink. Carmen grinned, glancing at Tatiana and both of them looked rather pleased.

"You are pretty smitten with him, ain't cha?" Carmen asked, grinning into her cup.

"I–" Deirdre felt her cheeks burn, looking down into her cup and letting out a low whine. "I...I had this– voice? It has been calling out to me since the day I tried to leave Oalfus. Originally, I was just trying to find shelter in a snowstorm, I had never planned on staying at his side. My feelings are a mess still. I don't know why I feel so drawn to him, but since we have been here, something inside me is clawing at my mind...it's clawing for him."

Tatiana gave a sympathetic smile, reaching out and gently rubbing the back of Deirdre's hand. "You sweet youngling, I envy your innocence. Has no one told you of fated bonds either?"

The young demon bristled, her brow furrowing as she snapped back much harsher than she had intended.

"I know what they are. That's how my Mammy and Da found each other–!" Deirdre's eyes went wide and her face burned with embarrassment. She suddenly became very small once more, looking away in shame. "Y-you don't think...?"

"If you could not bring yourself to leave his side after fate forced you together, it only seems logical that you two are, indeed, bonded in such a way," Tatiana said, in a much kinder voice than Carmen had anticipated. Normally, if anyone raised their voice at the wrath demon, she would turn into a viper and tear into them. It seemed Uncle Oalfus was a tender spot for this family.

Carmen sipped her tea, raising a brow. "Sounds like a fairy tale," she hummed.

"Well, I would certainly call you and my son fated. I am surprised you don't also think so!" Tatiana snapped.

There it was. Carmen smiled bashfully and shrugged. "It just, I dunno, sounds so sappy," she teased.

The conversation had shifted back to Carmen, and Deirdre was glad for it. Her mind raced. Fated bond? Her and Oalfus? It felt insane...

"Deirdre?" Carmen called, for the third time now.

"Huh? Oh sorry..." Deirdre was snapped back to the conversation.

"How's about showin' those photos, girl?" Carmen nodded towards the large envelope.

Deirdre was suddenly bright again, eagerly opening it and spilling out the contents. Photos spread across the space between the women in an array of colour. Dozens of landscapes, cityscapes, and stunning portraits of the people of Berlin. Deirdre had started this film roll when she first came to Germany. She explained all the locations, recalling each portrait with enthusiasm as she shared her tales of meeting the different creatures in each one.

Tatiana, however, was much more interested in the near-dozen shots of Oalfus that had landed nearer to her. She plucked them off the table and eyed them with a wicked grin. Carmen caught sight and her eyes went wide as well. Deirdre suddenly noticed what Tatiana was holding, embarrassment driving her voice several octaves higher.

"W-wait those aren't–!"

"These are incredible!" Carmen said, holding one of Oalfus and his axe, mid-swing, his body elongated to its full height. His muscles were on full display, his long shaggy fur giving him a much more primal appearance than what Carmen had been introduced to. The leather strapping across his chest strained as his arms held the axe high over his head.

"Oh my God..." Carmen breathed, Tatiana equally impressed.

They passed several back and forth, but both women gasped when they saw the one of Oalfus crouched over the dead deer, his tongue curled over his maw as he looked directly at the camera. His body appeared more feral as he looked ready to pounce at the viewer for even looking at his kill. Carmen thought he looked like a lion over its prey, her heart fluttering in her chest.

"He's gorgeous," she breathed.

Jealousy flared in Deirdre's chest as she suddenly scrambled for the other photos, much to Tatiana's dismay.

"Did he pose for you?" Tatiana asked, holding the two photos in her hands closer to her chest when Deirdre tried to take them back.

"I—well...sort of? I told him I would take photos, and I said what I wanted. Most are candid, except t-the ones you're holding."

Carmen couldn't take her eyes away from the feral-looking demon with the bloody face. Only when Tatiana held the other photos in front of her did she see it: two portraits, one taken specifically to capture his blind eye, while shadows cast over the other side of his face, and the second was the opposite. His red eye seemed to glow in the portrait showcasing his seeing eye.

"You're damn talented, girl!" Carmen exclaimed, admiring the photos. She stood, walked to a wall, and held up together.

"Can you imagine–?" Carmen started.

"In two frames, side-by-side," Deirdre finished, her voice shy.

"I want copies of them," Tatiana demanded, a wide smile on her face. "Would you take pictures for me as well? I have no photographs of our family at all, only old paintings. I want current ones, and ones of Carmen, too," she said, though it was more of a demand.

Deirdre nodded shyly; no one had ever asked for her to take photos for them before.

"Excellent. Tomorrow, we can go out to the garden for a little photo shoot!" Tatiana exclaimed, her excitement was contagious. The women poured over the photos once more, Deirdre a little less shy to share her thoughts behind the shots of Oalfus.

It had grown dark outside by the time the men had stirred and found the women in the kitchen. Ricky and Viktor both appeared, clearly groggy from their respective naps, and both rather disheveled. Ricky yawned loudly as he entered, his hands in his pockets as he peered in on the women.

"Oh great, you're all gossiping," Ricky chuckled, plucking a cup from one of the cupboards and pouring himself some tea. His brows shot up when he saw the photos spread across the table.

"Is that *Uncle*?!" he said, hurrying over and plucking one up. He let out a low whistle, which made Viktor set the newspaper he had been skimming down and join his son.

"Damn! You took this?" Viktor asked, looking up at Deirdre.

"Y-yes..."

Ricky and Viktor grinned at each other, sifting through the other shots and snickering at the ones with Oalfus hauling the dead deer over his shoulders.

"The wild Krampus in his natural habitat," Ricky said in a mocking tone, which made Deirdre wrinkle her nose at him before snapping the photo away.

"Bugger off," she grumbled.

"I was just teasing, no need to be so touchy," Ricky huffed, rolling his eyes. Carmen gave him a slap against his stomach, glaring at him.

"Stop bein' a jackass," Carmen growled at him. "She takes her photos seriously like I do." Ricky gave an apologetic smile, shrugging before stealing one of the lemon bars off the counter where they were cooling.

"Ah ah ah, no sweets for the brat," Tatiana said as she plucked the bar from his hand and popped it into her mouth. She moaned at the taste, which had everyone laughing. No one had heard Oalfus enter, grumbling as he gave a loud yawn and scratched his neck.

"What smells so good?" he said sleepily, glancing towards the large tea kettle. As usual, the old demon was more interested in the tea than the sweets all over the kitchen. That was, until he caught sight of some kind of chocolate dipped cookie on the counter. His ears perked up as he glanced towards them.

"Of course, we can't keep chocolate near the old man," Ricky laughed, which got him an icy glare from Oalfus.

"You like chocolate, Oalfus?" Carmen asked, swatting Ricky once more and forcing a smile to hide her annoyance.

"*Ja*, it is one of the few things I truly enjoy eating. Could I have one?" he asked, smiling sheepishly.

"By all means! I went a little crazy with the baking tonight."

"Stress baking?" Oalfus asked, plucking one of the buttery cookies and popping it in his mouth. His tail curled and ears splayed when the chocolate hit his tongue. Swiss milk chocolate, the best choice.

"Yeah, how did you know?" Carmen chuckled. Seeing his reaction was adorable.

"You're about to get married, it's only normal. I cut wood when I am feeling uneasy. I think I could cut three cords of wood right now," Oalfus mumbled around another cookie, rummaging through cupboards until he found a mug. He was glad for the tea; as decadent as the chocolate was, the shortbread left him parched.

Oalfus' ears twitched when he heard his name being muttered. Looking over, he saw glimpses of photographs strewn across the table between the gathered members of his family. Taking a long drink of tea, he slowly ambled over, pushing his long hair back before he finally caught sight over Viktor's shoulders. Viktor glanced back, holding up a photo of the older demon with admiration on his face. It was the shot of Oalfus carrying the deer.

"These are pretty incredible, don't you think, Uncle?"

Oalfus' eyes went wide as he suddenly pushed forward, snapping the photo from his nephew's hand and frantically looking over the many shots of him spread out. His face burned with embarrassment. How could Deirdre have shared these?

He felt her looking at him, his eyes lifting to see her face twisted with worry at his reaction. He needed to get away, to calm down and breathe. They were just photographs, but why did he feel so humiliated? His eyes fell on the photo of him crouched over the deer and his eyes widened with horror. He looked like some kind of wild animal, a mindless monster snarling at the camera. He slammed his cup on the counter as he rushed from the room, his clawed hands raking through his hair and gripping the base of his horns. Was that how she really saw him?

The distraught look of pain on Deirdra's face was the final straw for Tatiana. Her pupils became tight slits and her horns grew and curved inward at dangerous angles. Viktor nearly spit out his tea when he saw his wife's rage-filled face. Frantically, he tried to sooth her, saying anything to get her to sit down. Tatiana shoved Viktor away, sending him slamming into the wall as smoke huffed out of her nostrils. Ricky quickly put himself between Carmen and his mother, an anxious expression on his face as they watched her, in stunned silence, storm out of the room after Oalfus. Viktor groaned, rubbing his head and whining out his words.

"Of course, we just finished renovating and now she is getting into a fit of rage..."

Deirdre was shocked. She had known Tatiana was an intimidating force, but now she was downright terrifying. The group all scrambled to see what was happening when the first bellow tore out of Tatiana.

"Do you have any idea how childish you are acting?!" she roared out in Russian. Oalfus spun and ducked as a flying vase came hurtling at his head. It shattered and sprayed across the living room, pelting him with broken ceramic. Damnit, now he had to deal with a pissed off wrath demon.

"What are you talking about, Tatiana?" he snarled back, his tail thrashing as he braced for another flying object. Tatiana eyed the table; it certainly would hurt but she just bought it. She opted for one of the fire pokers beside the mantle instead, wielding it like a sword as she pointed it at Oalfus. He held up defensive hands and backed away as she moved closer.

"You ignorant, stupid, selfish old man! Can you not see that that girl is head over heels for you?! My son is about to marry, this is a time of joy and celebration, of love and happiness! Yet you bring that girl into this house and torment her in front of all of us?! You are a beast!"

"How dare you act as if you know anything about my situation! I do not torment her! You pompous little girl, know your—" Tatiana swung viciously at Oalfus, catching his arm and leaving a deep gash along his forearm.

"Don't you dare speak down to me in my own home, old man! You may be my elder, but you are not my father, nor my superior! It is not my

fault you hid yourself away and became bitter and foolish! You are only blind in one eye, so how are you so stupid to not see that girl is your fated one?!"

Oalfus froze, swallowing hard at Tatiana's words. He shook his head and tried to grab the fire poker from her, but he only earned another expert blow. Tatiana jabbed him in the chest and shoved him up against the wall.

"That is impossible!" he bellowed in frustration.

"Why, because she is clever, brave enough to tell you off and absolutely enthralled with you?" Tatiana sneered.

"Yes! Yes that is exactly why, you wicked bitch! I..."

Oalfus' shoulders dropped, looking down at the floor in shame. His eyes closed tightly and he spoke in a weak tone.

"She is so full of life, so eager to see the world. What would such a little thing like that want with an old beast like me? I know nothing of this world anymore. I am a fucking relic of a time long forgotten."

"Do not look for sympathy from me, your stubborn old goat. Have you once said these things to her? Have you asked her what she desired?" Tatiana gave him a sharp smack on the top of his head with the poker. *"Or have you been bottling up your thoughts as usual, waiting for a disaster like this to happen so you can run away AGAIN?"*

Oalfus snarled, seizing the poker and tearing it from Tatiana's grasp.

"You saw those photographs! She sees me as nothing more than some beast, I am nothing more than what she captured. You might dress me in your modern clothing and pretend I am capable of returning to this world, but I cannot! I am reduced to a fairy tale meant to scare children. Perhaps that is for the best. Why must you all torment me and drag me back here?!"

"You ignorant old fool, you only choose to remain a fairy tale because you are afraid. That girl is a blessing to you. She could free you of the prison you made for yourself, and you will only let her run out of your life. You are hurting her to push her away, and you're a fucking coward for it," Tatiana spat out.

Oalfus glared down at Tatiana, her fury blazing as she suddenly slapped him hard across the face. He was stunned; the pain blazed through his face and a familiar stickiness formed where her claws left gashes in his cheeks.

"You want to squander a blessing? Fine! Go rot in your misery out of my home. You are no longer welcome here if this is how you'll act." Tatiana turned on her pointed hooves and narrowed her eyes as she caught sight of the group who had been looking in. They all ran back to the kitchen. She stormed out towards the front door instead, grabbing her jacket to get some fresh air.

Deirdre was the only one who had not run, her back pressed firmly against the wall as she listened if Oalfus had moved. Her ears perked when she heard a shuddered sigh come from him, his back falling against the wall as he dropped the fire poker with a loud clatter.

Oalfus sank down onto the floor and pressed his hands over his face. *What if Tatiana was right?* What if these feelings, this longing to claim Deirdre, were truly her being his fate? He felt tears threaten his eyes. It had been many years since Oalfus had cried and he certainly didn't want to start now.

He froze when Deirdre's scent hit his nose, shame boiling his blood as he could not bear the idea of looking up to see her. She fidgeted with the buttons at the top of her dress, a pained whine slipping out of her as she tried to find the courage to speak.

"I—" she started, taking in a broken breath. He could hear her fighting back tears. "I don't think you are a beast..."

His eyes widened in horror, his head lifting as he looked at her. His stomach knotted. *She was crying*! Tears flowed down her cheeks as she chewed her bottom lip.

"H-how did you—?"

"R-Ricky was t-translating while you t-two were yelling," she sobbed, rubbing her eyes with the backs of her hands. "I d-don't think you're a beast, I...I think you are beautiful and wonderful!" she wailed, fists forming at her side as she bit her lip and tried to look at him as sternly as she could in her state. "B-But I hate how you're acting! I...I don't want to be with you i-if this is how you'll treat me and your family!"

Oalfus rose to his feet, frantically trying to find words as he grabbed a handful of his own hair. Panic spread over his face, but she had to be strong. Backing away from him, she shook her head.

"Dierdre, I—!"

"No! You don't get to just make this go away, you need to make a choice! I need time to think as well." Her voice cracked as she spoke, her eyes downcast and shoulders trembling. Oalfus was helpless, his ears tipping back. *How did everything go so terribly wrong?*

"Alright..." was all he could manage before she rushed out of the room. Once more, the old demon was left utterly alone.

Chapter Twelve

Ricky felt an immense amount of pity for his Uncle, though part of him was enjoying watching the old man flounder. This was certainly a shit show, from one thing to another. His cousins and extended family had not even arrived yet and there was this level of drama. Elders help him when his mother's siblings arrived. Ricky smirked to himself. He would even have to face his snot-nosed little cousin after their 'reunion' in San Antonio.

After everyone else had dispersed, Carmen had taken Deirdre up to one of the guest rooms to try and calm her down. Viktor was off looking for his wife, so the only one left was Ricky. Shoving a bottle of vodka under one arm and pulling two mugs out of the cupboard, he began searching the house for where his uncle had gone off to hide.

It didn't take long. He found the old man exactly where he had expected: the library. Oalfus was pretty easy to guess, as he always sought comfort in books. When he found him, however, Oalfus was holding a book against his forehead with a pained expression on his face.

Ricky sighed and tapped the doorframe with his knuckle. *"Can I join you?"* he asked, holding up the vodka as a peace offering.

Oalfus opened one eye to look at him, shrugging. *"I suppose, though I doubt I am in anyone's favor right now"*

"Oh Uncle," Ricky sighed as he plunked down in the chair across the Oalfus. *"You are a stubborn old fuck, no one is surprised by this. Perhaps a little surprised on the bringing a girl part, but not that you have brought the dramatics,"* Ricky said with a sad smirk, holding out a cup of the strong liquor. Oalfus glared at his great-nephew and shot back the liquor before holding his cup out for more.

"Always the voice of honesty, Rikovic," he grumbled, half-heartedly nodding his thanks for the top up.

"What set you off about those damned photos? You don't seriously believe she thinks you're some kind of monster."

"I don't know, I suppose...? I don't know why I was so angry, I was upset she shared them with all of you before she did with me."

"Ah, jealousy. That makes much more sense," Ricky nodded sagely. Oalfus hated when his nephew acted like such a know-it-all, especially when he was right. *"You didn't really give her much choice, though. She told us you gave her the cold shoulder after fucking her. No self-respecting Petrokov shoves off their mate like that,"* Ricky said, topping off his uncle's cup again.

Oalfus gawked at him, looking away in total embarrassment. *"She isn't my—"*

"Don't give me that shit, I see how you look at her. Hell, she even looks at you that way. As a professional avoider of 'making it official' I can say with one hundred percent certainty that you two got it bad."

"You and your damn mother acting like you know my life—" Oalfus snarled.

"You are pretty easy to sort out. You haven't changed one bit since I was a boy! Look at you, about ready to burst because you hide from everyone and can't stand to be called out for your bullshit. Mama already

ripped you a new asshole, so let's just stop pretending and accept facts. What would you do if she left?"

Oalfus felt sick to his stomach at the idea. The expression on his face was enough of an answer. Ricky pulled out a pack of cigarettes and lit one, pointing at his uncle accusingly.

"Exactly, you would fall to pieces. Stop denying you care. I avoided it with Carmen, too. I feel like all of us are idiots with women in this family, until they get bigger balls than us and call us out. It sucks, believe me."

"Give me one of those, you little brat," Oalfus snapped, holding out a very desperate hand for a cigarette. Ricky smirked, lighting one and holding it out to him. Oalfus trembled as he took a long drag, his free hand pressed firmly against his blind eye.

"Relax, you will be okay. I understand wanting to avoid the world, to hide from it, and stay in your ways. I did it for a while, but not nearly as long as you. Hell, even Viktor and Mama did it. When's the last time they hosted a damned ball or a dinner? Mama is scared shitless to see all the family after a century of silence. We all know what you're doing, that's why we are all pushing you so hard. This girl, she is a fucking blessing to you. She might be the exact thing you need to free yourself, Carmen was that for me. I was starving myself nearly to death until I met her. I haven't felt this strong in years, I finally understand what Mama and Viktor have, and I wouldn't trade it for the world. You are allowed to find happiness, and you should have it Uncle," Ricky tried to find warmth in his voice, but it was forced. While he meant every word of his lecture, there was a bitterness climbing in his stomach. He ignored it, pushing it aside and eyeing his uncle as he listened. Oalfus only shook his head, rubbing his forehead as he hauled once more on the cigarette.

"If I haven't already blown it..." he groaned, rubbing his hands down his face.

Ricky leaned over and gave his knee a half-hearted pat. *"I doubt it. She seemed upset because she cared, not because she hates you."*

"You think so?"

"I know so. You just need to do the hardest thing ever to fix it."

"What's that?" Oalfus moaned.

"Admit you were wrong and apologize," Ricky said with a wry smirk.

It was early morning, but Oalfus had been awake most of the night. He had been mulling over what he would say to Deirdre. Dozens of crumpled pieces of paper scattered around where he was sitting in the library. The bottle of vodka had been polished off between him and Ricky, and at some point, his nephew had dozed off, sprawled out on the couch across from him. Oalfus could no longer think of what else to write. Scanning over the scrawled writing on the page one last time, he folded it and clutched it tightly in his hand as he silently moved out of the room.

His hooves fell lightly on the stairs as the old demon climbed the steps and, once at the top, took a deep breath. The faint smell of the forest after a rain reached his nose; Deirdre's scent. He followed it until he stood in front of a door he knew she would be behind. Part of him wondered if it would be locked. His large hand took hold of the knob and he gingerly turned it, relieved to feel it allowing him entrance. Careful to not make a sound, Oalfus peeked with his one good eye. The lamp in the room was on, and Deirdre was curled up on top of the bed with several photos laid out in front of her.

She had the skirt of a night dress pulled over her knees, and had clearly been crying as she trailed fingers over one photo in particular. Oalfus ached to take her in his arms; this was his doing, why did he have to have such a temper? Seeing her so distraught made this whole affair seem like a pointless upset. Struggling to find his courage, he winced as he tapped a knuckle gently against the door frame.

Deirdre jolted with shock, turning to see Oalfus looking defeated in the doorway. She scrambled to collect the photos and pressed them to her chest.

"O-Oalfus! What are you doing here?"

The large demon bit his bottom lip, nervous to meet her gaze before he finally spoke in a quiet tone.

"I...I wondered if I might be allowed to speak with you?"

She paused for a long moment before nodding. Her nod was enough of an invitation for him to step into the room. Carefully, he closed the door before taking one step closer. He gripped the piece of paper a little tighter in his hand before taking a shaky breath.

"I feel at a loss for words. I wrote something in an attempt to organize my thoughts, but seeing how you are so upset with me, it hardly feels adequate enough."

Deirdre felt her chest tighten, a ball formed in her throat as she looked up at him. "You wrote me a letter?"

"I suppose you could call it that. I doubt it means— it is hardly enough to—"

"Please read it to me," she breathed, her hands gripping the photos to her chest a little tighter now.

Oalfus wished his mouth didn't feel so damn dry. His tongue felt glued to the roof of his mouth as he nodded meekly and looked down at the crushed paper in his hands. Feebly smoothing it over his leg, he let out a nervous huff of a laugh before clearing his throat.

'*My dearest Liebchen,*

'*I do not know where to start asking for you to consider my apology. I do not think I am deserving of it. My actions have been nothing if not beastly, and I am sure you are regretting our encounter by now. I have been wretched, to say the least. In just one day, I have managed to upset this whole house during a time meant to be one of happiness. My nephew is to be married, to continue our family lineage, and I am spoiling it and likely pushing you away. Words are not my strong area. I am an old fool with a stubborn mind and very short temper, so it seems.*

'*I have lived too long hidden away from the world. I have grown bitter and ignorant, and it is no one's fault but my own. Family is not something I ever thought of as precious; my bonds to them were simply obligations. However, the longer I spend with you, the more I realize how wrong I was.*

'*You fell into my life by fate's design, and, in being with you for the short time we have had, I realize how very lonely I am. You are like a light in the darkness and my actions have been attempting to snuff that light out. Perhaps the reason I became so upset when I saw your beautiful photographs was because I was afraid to accept how others see me.*

'*If you can find it in your heart to give me one last chance, I would be honored if you would allow me at your side again. I would love to look at your photographs with you, to drink tea with you, and to make you smile once more. I am deeply sorry for my actions, and I promise, no matter what you decide, I will treat you with only the utmost respect and kindness until you choose to part ways with me.*

Yours, Oalfus'

He quietly folded the paper, avoiding her eyes as he stood there. Never had he bore his soul so much to anyone. Writing it had eased his nerves, but now that it was out of his mouth, he felt like a spring wound to its limit. His body was rigid as he waited, the silence gnawing at his very soul as he stood there.

Deirdre was in shock. No one had ever written or said anything so kind to her before. She could hardly believe this old demon was practically begging her, a nobody little Cu Sith, to forgive him. Her heart soared, as much as she wished it wouldn't. She felt that rush of mad panic fill her from the joy his words brought her. *By fate's design*. Those words felt sweet in her mind as her eyes closed and allowed the rumble of his voice to echo those words over and over. When he began to shift uncomfortably, she realized she had not spoken a word to him in several minutes, embarrassment washing over her face.

"Could I have the letter?" she finally asked. Oalfus hadn't meant for his ears to tip back, but he nodded and stepped forward to hand it to her. She held it with as much care as she did her pictures, which warmed the old demon to see. Her fingers trailed over his scrawled handwriting with incredible consideration before she finally looked up at him.

"You really wrote all this for me?"

"And likely two dozen other versions I threw away," Oalfus mumbled, avoiding her eyes in his embarrassment.

Deirdre perked up, looking at him in disbelief. "You're truly upset over what happened?"

Oalfus had the urge to reach out and grab her shoulders, to shake sense into the girl. Did she not have eyes? Could she not see how much this pained him? His brows drew together tightly, clenching his fists at his sides, setting his jaw before finally speaking.

"Of course I am upset over this. I caused you such upset because of my stupidity. I...I never want to be the one to cause you pain, I only want–" He snapped his mouth shut, looking down at his feet as more embarrassment filled his chest.

"You only want...?" she urged him on, now half off the bed and running her finger tips down his forearm.

Oalfus quickly sized her hand in his, the other cradling her face before he closed the space between them. His eyes closed tightly in fear of her expression as the words finally spilled out of him. He could not restrain these all-consuming and gnawing feelings a moment longer.

"Tatiana was right. She may have had to bash me over the head to get me to listen, but that witch was right! I want you to stay by my side, Deirdre. You are *mine.*" He spoke with a deep seeded desire, not that of an order or demand. He was spilling his heart out to her.

"You are my fate, and I denied it to be true. I denied myself because I did not want to risk my claim, thus becoming your death sentence. You are brimming with life, and have a desire to live every moment to its very fullest. You have passion I have never encountered before, and I fear if I ask you to be mine you will be stuck with an old monster slowly rotting away in a prison he made for himself."

Deirdre felt tears burn her eyes, but this time, she let them flow freely. No sound came from her, not a sob or sniffle. When she pulled her hand from Oalfus', the sound he made almost made her heart shatter into a thousand pieces. His eyes opened and widened in horror at her tears, but before he could turn and run, she took hold of his face in her hands. She forced him to look at her, using as much force as she could muster to keep him where he was. Her soul cried out in a joyous triumph, the inner voice calling out *mine, mine, mine!* The little demon lifted up onto her tiptoes and ran her thumbs over his cheeks.

"I was afraid it was only me who felt this way," she whispered, her ears tilting back and tail tucking as she spoke in a weak voice. "I ran from the cabin because I was scared of why I felt so attached to you. I was afraid of those feelings because no one has ever made me *want to stay*. I am not afraid of you, and I promise you are not a beast in my eyes. I meant it when I said I thought you were beautiful."

Oalfus made a weak noise in his throat, and soon, she was cradled in his arms with his face buried against her neck. Deirdre froze when she felt a very familiar wetness of tears run down her shoulder. Oalfus curled himself around her, hiding his emotions as much as he could. He simply needed her in his embrace. He whimpered and desperately clung onto his little demoness until he calmed himself enough to face her. He pressed his lips against hers, and he was thrilled when her fingers dug into his hair as she deepened their kiss. Her legs wrapped around his midsection and only parted their lips to suck in little breaths.

Oalfus would have been content to stay like this all day, but Deirdre eventually pulled away enough to speak.

"Do you remember what I asked you before we left?"

Oalfus nodded, his mind drifting back to the pair of them outside the cabin, dealing with the deer meat. He swallowed hard. "You asked me if I would travel with you..."

"Have you thought about it?" she asked, her nerves flaring.

Oalfus felt a weak smile touch his lips as he gently ran his thumb over her cheek. The swirling scent of spices, oranges, and cranberries filled the room as he pressed his forehead to hers.

"Relax, *Liebchen*. Do not be afraid to ask me anything. Yes, I have considered it. I am...I am willing to try, if I have you by my side. Perhaps I could manage it, but I only ask you give me a little time to prepare."

"Oh! O-of course! I mean, I–"

"Hush, let us discuss this another time if it is alright?"

"Okay," she said, smiling in spite of herself as she took in a deep breath of his intoxicating scent.

"Does this mean you forgive me then?" Oalfus teased, smiling at her with that mischievous grin Deirdre had come to adore.

"I will forgive you, but you need to promise me one thing," Deirdre said, cradling his head against her chest as she stroked her fingers through his hair.

"Anything you ask and it is yours, *mein Liebchen.*"

"I want you to apologize to your family as well."

Oalfus bit back his groan; his eyes, however, still rolled.

Great.

Chapter Thirteen

Oalfus hated this. His ears were splayed to the sides and a scowl rested on his face as he stood awkwardly in the doorway of the dining room. His family was looking at him with confused expressions after Deirdre had announced he had something to tell them before sitting at her place for breakfast.

"Er...yes, well, I suppose..." Oalfus sighed and pinched the bridge of his snout. *"Listen,"* he began in Russian, the irritation in his voice evident. *"I have been an ass, and I need to apologize for it. Especially to you, Rikovic. This is a time of celebration and I have been a thorn in everyone's side."*

Ricky raised his brows. His uncle was many things, but never before had he been apologetic for his attitude. The younger demon smirked at Deirdre, nodding and holding his mug up in a mock toast.

"I don't know what you did, but I am impressed," Ricky teased.

"Don't make me regret this!" Oalfus snapped, his eyes narrowing at his nephew. "I...I just am not used to all of this. So much has changed, I don't even know where to begin, " he admitted openly, rubbing the back of his neck.

Viktor was the most surprised, standing and putting an understanding hand on his uncle's shoulder. "It wasn't until very recently that Rikovic gave my head a shake. I was stuck in my old ways, too. It is a strange thing to come into this modern world. We are old creatures of habit. It was hard for me, so I can't imagine how it must be for you. Perhaps this girl is a good thing; she can make this adjustment a little easier," Viktor offered, his expressions softened as he spoke.

"She is more than a good thing," Oalfus sighed, smiling at Deirdre. She was so proud of him for opening up, her tail wagging wildly behind her as she rested her head in her hands.

Carmen leaned across the table to whisper in her ear. "Ain't it cute when they all get on?"

"It really is. They're all so similar," Deirdre giggled, smiling warmly.

Even Tatiana had warmed up, a sympathetic smile on her face as she walked over to the side table and poured a cup of coffee for Oalfus. "Here Uncle, you look exhausted. Did you sleep at all?" she asked, holding the cup out to him.

Oalfus took it gratefully, shaking his head. "Not a wink. Thank you, Tatiana," he rumbled, taking a greedy mouthful.

"I am glad the pants fit, but where is your shirt, Oalfus?" Tatiana said, her nose wrinkling at his disheveled appearance.

Oalfus snorted, smirking at Viktor. "Is she always like this?"

"Yes, and I suggest you just do as she says or you'll never hear the end of it," Viktor mumbled around the edge of his cup.

"Well, come now! Look at how cute Deirdre is in the clothes I got for her! You can't possibly look so slovenly when she is so put together."

Oalfus grinned at his companion. She was in a white turtleneck with ruffles around the shoulders, sleeve cuffs, and neckline. The dark blue overalls she wore made her copper-coloured fur and hair shine; she really did look wonderful. Oalfus rolled his eyes and moved to sit beside her, lifting and placing her rather possessively in his lap. Deirdre did not protest; rather, she was glad to be so close to him.

"After breakfast and more coffee. Right now, I just need food," the old demon rumbled, nuzzling into her neck.

The meal moved with ease. Eating was something that never changed and made interacting simple. Oalfus couldn't help himself; now that Deirdre knew his intentions, he was feeling very possessive of her. He kept feeding her mouthfuls and soon, she had resigned herself that he wouldn't let her use her own fork. The fussing was welcome, as it was the first time someone had doted on her like this. Even if it was embarrassing, since everyone kept eyeing them and smirking, she felt very at ease in his arms.

"Seems his apology went over well," Rikovic mumbled to Viktor.

"Apology?"

"Mmhmm. Was up with him half the night listening to different versions he was writing," Ricky snorted around a spoonful of eggs.

"Hah! You were drunk and fell asleep an hour in, no help at all!" Oalfus sneered.

"Oh, whatever, old man, it doesn't matter anyway. Look at your little lap dog perched like a prize. You're falling hard, Uncle," Rikovic teased, which earned an icy glare from his uncle, followed by a piece of bacon being thrown at him.

"Quiet, you lippy brat. You're spoiling my breakfast," Oalfus huffed, turning his attention back to Deirdre, who was cradling a cup of tea close to her chest. "Did you get much sleep?" he mumbled, rubbing his nose against her cheek.

"No, not much...I am feeling a bit tired."

Oalfus grinned. An excuse to slip away. The coy grin on his face was obvious.

Ricky smirked at Carmen before he reached under the table with his foot and gave his uncle a little kick. "You just got here, don't even think about it," Ricky warned. "You need to get fitted for a suit and she has to go with Carmen to get a dress."

"What?!" both Deirdre and Oalfus exclaimed.

"I hope you don't mind, I don't really have many girlfriends and I didn't want it to just be me and my sister up there. Do you wanna be my bridesmaid, Deirdre?" Carmen asked.

"I don't mind. I suppose I am just a bit surprised is all," Deirdre replied, her face warming while her tail began to wag.

"And you are my best man," Ricky said matter-of-factly.

Oalfus spit his coffee, his eyes wide and jaw slack. *"What?"*

"What do you mean, what? You think I would go to all the trouble of getting two demons to track you down just to have you *watch* me get married? You are the only one I want standing beside me," Ricky scoffed. He seemed a little insulted.

"Rikovic...I just never thought—"

"No, you don't think much. What matters is you are going to come suffer with me while we get fitted for some damned suits."

Oalfus was a little flattered, his ears tipping back bashfully as he nodded. "Alright, if this is what you want, Rikovic, I am honored."

"See, was that so hard?" Ricky sneered.

Oalfus was shocked at how much of a sprawl Moscow had become. He hated being cramped into the long black vehicle, and the twenty-five minute drive just to reach the fashion district was beginning to wear down his patience. Every jostle and scrape of his horns on the roof pushed him a little further to snapping. The old demon mentally noted to never set hoof into another cramped 'luxury' vehicle again.

The women were dropped off first, which made Oalfus even more antsy. Deirdre gave him a tight hug before she left, kissing his forehead and whispering to him gently.

"Be brave, my wicked Krampus," she teased, her voice only audible to him. "It will only be for a little while and you have your family with you. I will see you at the restaurant for lunch."

"Be good, *mein Liebchen,*" Oalfus cooed after her, to which she responded with a broad wink before she closed the door.

Oalfus tried not to groan when the vehicle continued its winding journey over the seemingly endless paved roads. Not only was he being forced out into this dizzying sprawl to get fitted for a suit (his own idea of torture), he was about to be forced to go into a restaurant after an already irritating affair.

Oalfus grumbled as he tugged at the high, tight neckline of his black sweater. He was already frustrated with having to wear clothing, but now he had to wear *tight* clothing.

Ricky was lounging across from his uncle, dressed similarly in a tightly fitted black turtleneck with a pair of black denim pants. The difference was that while Oalfus wore a deep charcoal sport jacket, Rikovic was wearing the vintage leather bomber jacket Carmen had picked out for him before his first visit back to Russia.

Rikovic grinned. His uncle was truly a fish out of water, the way he had to hunch over to fit into the limousine amusing enough as it was. The fact that his scowl deepened every time his horns bumped against the roof of the car only made Rikovic's desire to tease him grow. He knew he had to be careful, as his uncle was high-strung enough as it was, but he figured it was a dose of well-deserved medicine.

Oalfus had been such an important part of his younger years. He had confided in his uncle over any upset he had in his life, but then, one day, he just vanished. His gate stopped working and Rikovic had been cut off from him, his only true friend gone in the blink of an eye.

The younger demon was delighted his two chaotic friends had been able to track his uncle down, but there was a resentment in his heart that was beginning to nag at him. Ricky glanced over to his father. A similar resentment had festered and grown into hatred at one point, and it was only until very recently that the two had made amends and were beginning to enjoy each other's company. Rikovic was the picture of his father, as the two bore striking similarities, not just physically, but also in demeanor.

They were both ravenous lust demons and were hopelessly in love with their chosen partners. Ricky had grown up hardly able to finish a meal without his parents getting fresh with each other and shooing him out of the room. It was only in his early adulthood that his parents' marriage had suffered because of the deterioration of his relationship with Viktor.

Tatiana adored her husband, but she truly loved her son most. Seeing them at each other's throats constantly while Ricky was in the height of his military career had driven a wedge between her and her husband. In hindsight, she had realized it was unfair to choose sides, but Tatiana was a wrath demon and she gave into her more primitive habits when upset.

Oalfus had always been an escape. Ricky would constantly run off to his uncle's for a few nights to cool off when he and his father fought. Often, Viktor would have to come through the gate himself to collect a young Rikovic while he was asleep.

Oalfus truly did adore his nephews, but he always had a soft spot for Rikovic. Seeing him now, the old demon realized just how much he had missed out on. He had only just learned of Rikovic running away, of his abandoning his place in the military, and now living in America.

His great-nephew looked older than he should. He was only a few hundred years younger than Viktor, and yet the pair looked more like brothers than father and son. His long charcoal hair had streaks of gray through it, and two long, white stripes sprouting from his temples, much like Oalfus had. It seemed that Rikovic had followed in his uncle's footsteps and grew his hair out, loosely braided and hanging down past his shoulders. Oalfus frowned when he began to really notice the deep-set laugh lines on his nephew's face, the fine lines around his eyes, and the creases in his brow line.

He had missed *too many* years.

Pain filled his chest. His heart ached thinking of all the times Rikovic may have come to him had he left his gate open. If he had been available to his nephew, would things be different? Perhaps he would not be in such a shock over the world and all that had changed. Perhaps Rikovic might not look so aged. Perhaps he would not feel a crushing awkwardness between him and his only close family. Oalfus pressed his palms over his face; he had done all of this to himself. He deserved to feel this guilt, this shame was his self inflicted burden.

"We are almost there. Are you feeling alright, Oalfus?" Viktor asked as he glanced up from his newspaper, his brows drawn together in concern.

"Yes, just feeling a little sick to my stomach."

It wasn't a total lie, though he knew they would assume it was motion sickness and not guilt wracking him that was the cause. He wasn't ready to confront these feelings yet. He needed time to consider. Unbeknownst to him, Rikovic was already planning his method of confrontation. Rikovic had been a commanding officer for many years, strategies were his strong suit, after all.

The shop was rather impressive on the outside. As the vehicle slowed to a stop, Oalfus was eager to be free of the cramped space and stretch to his full height with an animalistic shake of his head. Immediately, he felt eyes on him, his ears flicking and his several gold earrings jingling as he glanced around. The streets were filled with all kinds of creatures roaming about as they window-shopped and chatted.

Rikovic stepped out onto the road next to his uncle, patting his arm as he glanced up at the large two-storey men's clothing store. *"Relax, and remember you have us here. I booked the whole upper studio for the next two hours so no one will bother us."*

Oalfus immediately felt relief, his brows drawing together as he looked down at his nephew. *"Thank you."*

"Don't forget that I take after you. I hate being around people, too. Come on, I want this shit over with," Ricky said with a wink, walking up the few steps before pulling one of the massive glass doors open.

Oalfus ventured one last glance at the busy road, many eyes upon him, before he felt a gentle push on his back. Viktor nodded towards the building and the pair hurried after Ricky. Oalfus was grateful the inside was as big as the outside. The massive store was filled wall-to-ceiling with all sorts of men's clothing. Suits in every colour, casual wear, knit items, high-quality luxury items, and, at the front of the store, an enormous display filled with millions of dollars' worth of glimmering gold and silver men's jewelry.

Oalfus blinked dumbly as he stared wide-eyed at the huge space. This was nothing like the cramped tailor shops he had been forced to visit on his last trip to Moscow.

"Holy shit," was all he could manage.

Viktor smirked and gave the big demon an elbow to the ribs. *"Careful, you look impressed. Someone might think you like this kind of thing, Uncle."*

"Welcome, gentlemen," came a bright voice.

The three were greeted by a curvaceous canine in a very form-fitting dress. She was a doberman, her black and tan fur glossy under the lights and her black hair cut into a dramatic asymmetrical bob with blunt bangs. Viktor and Rikovic let out a pleased rumble in unison, glancing at each other before nodding to her.

"My name is Liliya. Do you three have an appointment?"

"Hello Liliya," Viktor started, his eyes darkening as he glanced over the woman. Her pointed ears tipping back only for a moment as his eyes lingered over her.

Clearing her throat, she pushed her smile a little wider and looked towards Rikovic as he spoke.

"We do have an appointment, it should be under Petrokov. I certainly hope you are our consultant," he purred, flashing a grin at her as his eyes trailed down her figure once more.

Oalfus caught a faint scent of both his nephews' charm, similar notes of smoke and spices. The old demon rolled his eyes. They were both so predictable.

Liliya's eyes glazed slightly, which was a common reaction to their charm. Her thighs pressing together and a perfume of desire flitted past them. Viktor and Rikovic were like vultures, edging closer to her and purring out compliments and small talk.

The little scene was put to a halt when a much taller, and much more vicious-looking female demon approached. Oalfus wouldn't have known she was a demon had it not been for her metallic pink eyes; otherwise, she looked like a regular greyhound. Her sharp features and icy glare made Viktor and Ricky immediately back away from Liliya as she placed protective hands on the little mortal girl's shoulders.

"Yes, well, Liliya is only our receptionist. Come, gentlemen, I will be handling your appointment today. My name is Anya."

Viktor and Rikovic were both very displeased, their ears tipping back before they forced matching polite smiles.

"I didn't know other demons worked here," Viktor said in a strained voice.

"Yes, well, having a mostly demon clientele, we do what makes our customers more comfortable. Please, come this way and we shall get you settled upstairs," she said with an equally strained smile. It seemed their flirting had offended this demoness.

Oalfus smirked, clapping the pair on the back before moving past them. *"Serves you right, you couple of vultures."*

The upper studio had several consulting areas. Booth-style set ups of three large mirrors with a pedestal in the center and a rack set to the side for whatever clothing was being altered. Lush black curtains closed off each space for privacy. Oalfus knew this place meant money; it practically dripped with the charm from the many greed demons who worked here. He couldn't imagine how much this would have cost. It was partially why he did not concern himself with how money was made or spent.

Alongside Anya were two other smaller females, one who appeared to be a lynx, and the other some kind of long-eared spaniel. Their eyes were what tipped Oalfus off. Again, they had a strange metallic sheen to their rose- and plum-coloured eyes.

Rikovic was growing a little more antsy, his irritation evident by his splayed ears and fluffed-out tail. While Viktor took it upon himself to explain the wedding colours, Oalfus leaned down and spoke quietly to his great-nephew.

"What is on your mind, my boy?"

Ricky stiffened hearing his uncle refer to him this way; he had not called him 'my boy' since he was young. Glancing over at the old demon, Ricky swallowed hard and gave a shrug. *"They are all succubi. I had a...er, bad run in with one and I suppose I am not over it..."*

Oalfus stepped closer to his nephew, placing himself between the group chatting with Viktor and Ricky. He tried his best to keep a casual stance as they spoke, but his fur bristled and shoulders rose slightly.

Ricky cracked a small grin. *Just like old times.* His uncle always put himself between whatever caused him strife, like a final wall of defense against the world. A warmth returned to his heart as he eyed the hulking demon before him. Always the protective type, even if he was an aloof old hermit.

"I don't expect you to talk with me about it. I haven't exactly been a good uncle to you. However, if you change your mind–"

"I will, but not here. It's a bit touchy for me...I would prefer privacy when we speak."

When we speak, we are going to talk. Oalfus smiled at his nephew and nodded, his long tail swaying as he took another step forward. His expression dropped, and a nervous hand rubbed the back of his neck.

"I am sorry, Rikovic."

"You already apologized this morning, why repeat yourself?"

"I am sorry for not being here...I have missed so much in these last two centuries."

Ricky nodded. Damn, he wanted a cigarette right now. He was glad when two of the girls came to usher them over to fitting areas. He wasn't entirely sure what to say just yet. He needed them to be alone. *Patience*, he reminded himself, *all that needs to be said will be in time.*

"Oh dear..." one of the girls mumbled as they looked at the rack of suit options they had pulled for Oalfus. Ricky and Viktor smirked at each other; clearly these girls were out of their depth.

The three men were stripping down to begin trying on the options, and, as Oalfus pulled the sweater up and over his head, Anya made a very disgruntled sound. Without hesitation, the succubus ran her fingers through the unevenly chopped fur on Oalfus' arm. He went rigid, his horns still trapped inside the damned sweater, which left him slightly compromised.

"Who hacked at you with dull shears?" Anya sneered, her lip curled in displeasure as she turned to one of the other girls.

"Call the stylist in immediately."

Viktor and Ricky blinked dumbly before positively wicked grins spread over their faces. He was going to have to suffer through the full nine yards, and they hadn't even planned it! This would certainly be entertaining. Between the pair of shocked young demons and the incredibly critical head consultant, Oalfus knew he was in for a torturous morning.

"We haven't had an old order demon come through in quite some time. Forgive my girls. This will be their first time handling someone of your size." As Anya spoke, little plumes of barely visible pink smoke slipped out of the corners of her mouth. Succubi were not a new order, like Deirdre. Oalfus had encountered them before. This one, however, was very forward.

Oalfus swallowed nervously, shaking his head and forcing a strained smile. *"I suppose it is harder to meet my kind, as there are very few of us left."*

"It is truly a shame. Your kind has such lovely features and stature. It is difficult to meet men taller than myself these days," the greyhound lamented, a bit more sway to her steps as she circled Oalfus, holding different off-coloured white shirts against his chest.

Though she seemed to be testing which shade of shirt would be best, her eyes lingered mostly on his face and then down to his groin. He wished to be anywhere but here. Looking over to Viktor was no use, either. It seemed he was all too happy to play into the young succubus' attempts to mimic her superior. Oalfus glanced over at Ricky, who was simply a stone wall, his face twitching with irritation and his eyes darkening with anger. It seemed there would be no chatting with either of them to avoid this very pushy woman.

A thought came to him, and Oalfus rejoiced as an out presented itself. He could mention Deirdre any time she flirted with him!

"Well, I suppose I am used to towering over most. My companion, Deirdre, hardly reaches my chest with the tips of her ears."

Another rack was brought up to the area Anya was fitting him. Several suits in white bags were quickly brought out and the three succubi compared the colours to what matched Viktor's requests.

While they were distracted, Oalfus turned to Rikovic and hissed a whisper. *"I have never met such a pushy woman before!"*

"Just ignore them, that seemed to shut mine up," Ricky grumbled, chewing on one of his claws with clear irritation.

"What's wrong with you two, they are delightful," Viktor said with a smirk, and gave his consultant, who was clearly under the influence of his charm, a little wave while she was supposed to be conferring with her co-workers.

"You called, Anya?" a voice called from the staircase. A flamboyantly-dressed and well-groomed male poodle was standing with a stylists kit in his hand. His black fur was perfectly fluffed and coiffed into a large pompom on the top of his head and ends of his shorn ears.

His metallic purple eyes gave away what he was: incubus. Oalfus groaned internally. Why was this happening to him? The stylist's perfectly pressed lavender suit and bright green pocket square were pristine, the pants cuffed just enough to show off the very boldly patterned socks and matching green leather dress shoes he wore.

"Oh my word, never mind! I see where I am needed!" he gasped when he saw Oalfus, rushing over to him and cringing as he inspected the hack job done to his fur.

"Hello Jacob. Yes, this is Mr.Oalfus Petrokov. I thought you could give him a little finesse. He is going to be the best man for Mr.Rikovic Petrokov in five days. Do your magic, darling," Anya cooed as she had her assistant jot down measurements she was actively taking from Oalfus. His tail lashed and he let out a snarl when her hand ran up his thigh as she took his inseam measurement.

"Careful, Jacob. It seems he is testy today," Anya teased. Oalfus was truly starting to loathe that woman.

"It is a pleasure, Oalfus, was it? I do hope you don't mind, but with my experience, it might be best we get you over to the end booth for some privacy."

"Excuse me?" Oalfus grumbled.

"Well you are old order, and, from what I recall, your kind tends to grow longer fur similarly to my breed. It would be easier if we had you stripped down. That will result in the most even cut so you don't have any discomfort."

Rikovic and Viktor were snickering like children. The large demon gave a loud snarl in their direction before finally moving where the incubus was directing. Once the curtain was drawn, the petit male spoke in a much quieter tone.

"I do hope I am not causing you any trouble, and I can call my female assistant if that would—"

"Ignore my nephews and their childish behavior. I have no problem with you, I have a problem with this whole outing. It is not your fault."

The poodle smiled, nodding and setting his kit down as he began pulling out clippers and several pairs of scissors. His tail wagged happily as he began considering where he wanted to start.

Oalfus had little issue being naked in front of others; he was used to not wearing clothing to begin with. As he dropped his pants and underwear, Jacob let out a little gasp before regaining composure. He was positively huge in every aspect, it seemed. Oalfus smirked to himself as the poodle shifted nervously. It was flattering, even from a male. His ear flicked when the clippers started, glancing curiously at them as Jacob approached and gestured for him to sit on the pedestal.

"*What is that?*" Oalfus asked, his curiosity getting the best of him.

"*The clippers? Are you serious?*"

"*Er...well I haven't exactly been living among most creatures for many years. I...live in the mountains in Germany, actually.*"

The poodle giggled. It was a pleasant sound which helped Oalfus to relax. "*An eccentric hermit are we? I knew your accent sounded familiar. My father is German, he met my mother during the war.*"

"*I suppose I am. Frankly, I haven't been in the city in two hundred years,*" Oalfus said, watching the clippers curiously as the incubus worked on his chest and arms first.

"*Goodness, no wonder you had such a hack job. Did you do it with scissors then?*"

"*Yes, my companion helped, but she is not as well-versed as you seem to be,*" Oalfus said with a smile. He didn't fully realize he was using his charm until Jacob made a small sound in his throat.

"*You are certainly full of surprises,*" he said, trying to clear his head with a little shake. His eyes were glazed only a moment before he tried to focus back on his work. Jacob may have been an incubus, but the heavily spiced scent of this older demon was intoxicating. He had heard rumors about the old order demons being something else but he certainly had not expected this.

They chatted idly, Jacob struggling to keep his head clear and mostly keeping quiet as he tried to even out Oalfus' fur. As he began working on Oalfus' back, he was surprised at the visibly worn down patches on his shoulders. His brow cocked as he ran his fingers over the tattered fur.

"What happened here?" he asked, curious how nearly identical patches of tattered fur formed on his shoulders. Oalfus glanced down at his shoulder, running his own hand over the spot and giving a shrug.

"Ah, it must be from my harness"

"Harness? Do I even want to know?" Jacob teased, continuing on with his work.

"The basket gets heavy, and with how often I wear it, I suppose I am not surprised" Oalfus chuckled.

"Basket...?" Jacob thought for a moment what he might mean, perhaps something to do with his remote home in Germany? Suddenly the poodle's eyes widened and his ears perked.

"Wait a minute, you said you lived in the German mountains? Does that mean..."

Oalfus couldn't help but let a wicked grin spread over his face, his smug expression only solidifying what Jacob was beginning to piece together. As the older demon looked over his shoulder at the incubus, Jacob suddenly blurted out.

"You're Krampus! The real thing, has it been you this whole time?!"

"Hush boy, I don't need the whole world knowing!" Oalfus laughed, gesturing for him to lower his voice. Jacob's face burned with embarrassment as he whispered.

"Are you seriously Krampus? Evil child stealing monster my dad used to threaten me with if I misbehaved around Christmas? That Krampus?"

"So you have heard of me. Well, I can assure you, I have never actually stolen children, and I don't particularly think I am evil. Do I scare the ever-living piss out of children and their families to feed off their fear from time to time? Well, that part is true."

"Oh my stars, I knew Krampus had to be a demon! There was no way the stories were about some ghost. Do you have any idea how famous you would be if you went public with this?!" Jacob gushed, his tail wagging wildly behind him.

Oalfus groaned at the idea, shaking his head and covering his eyes with one hand. *"That sounds like my own personal hell. Believe me, I don't want anyone to know. I am surprised you even know who I am."*

"Are you kidding?! The whole world knows who Krampus is! There are parades dedicated to you all over the world! People dress up like you on Krampus Nacht, they send greeting cards with drawings of you on them. You didn't know?!"

Oalfus felt his face growing warm, shaking his head in total disbelief. Deirdre had mentioned knowing who he was, but he had only assumed it was because of the local towns she had been to. Krampus Nacht was celebrated all over the world? How on earth could word of his antics have traveled so far?

Oalfus was reeling. His ears tilted back and he suddenly slumped down on the small platform he had been standing on. *"How on earth will I travel with Deirdre now?"* he groaned to himself, covering his face with his hands.

Jacob squirmed with guilt, he hadn't meant to upset the poor fellow. *"Is Deirdre your companion?"* he asked gingerly, rubbing his arm nervously.

"Yes. I was supposed to travel with her but if everyone knows who the hell Krampus is..."

"Oh, don't fret over that! You know they don't even portray you correctly. You are far more handsome than any of the greeting cards ever made you out to be. Had I not spoken with you, I never would have figured it out, you know."

Oalfus smiled despite himself. He looked up at the young demon and sighed. *"You certainly are charming. It is a shame I didn't meet you sooner."*

"I didn't think Krampus was interested in men," Jacob said with a smirk, popping one hip to the side and crossing his arms. *"From what I recall, only women would light a red candle to call on you,"* he teased, grinning as his perfectly groomed tail wagged behind him.

Oalfus leaned back and cocked a brow at the boy, clearly he knew more than he originally let on. *"I never ignore a red candle, no matter who lights it. If it should happen to be a man who lit, it I certainly made it memorable for him,"* Oalfus mused, a devilish smirk on his face. Jacob's face burned with embarrassment; perhaps teasing an old order demon was a step too far for the younger demon.

Oalfus took pity on the flustered boy and returned to his previous position, pulling his hair over his shoulder and turning his back to the incubus. Jacob gratefully returned to his work, the chatting easier when Oalfus' eyes weren't on him. The conversation turned into a question and answer session, which made Oalfus a little more smug. He was letting the new knowledge of his fame bolster his ego just a smidge. The incubus had a million questions, all of which got an answer, and some getting rather explicit answers that made Jacob even more flustered.

The old demon was beginning to enjoy the flamboyant incubus; he was very talented with his clippers and scissors. Though the old demon was reluctant, he did allow the boy to style his hair. He was strict on not taking too much off the length, but, with a little of his own flirtatious charm and much reassurance, he got Oalfus to agree to some feathered layers. Soon, he was calling for hair lightening products to be brought and a few pieces of clothing from the store front.

The hair lightener made Oalfus' nose burn, but, according to the fashionable incubus, if he lightened his streaks of gray and added a few highlights to his hair, it would easily throw off any suspicion. Krampus was always depicted with jet black fur and hair, a whip-like tail and a more goat-like appearance.

Jacob finally seemed satisfied with the tight clip job done on almost every inch of Oalfus' body and the highlights in his hair. After an arduously long blow dry and fussing with different sized dress shirts and pants, Oalfus was finally allowed to rejoin his nephews. Just before Jacob was about to pull back the curtain, he paused and pulled out a small digital camera from his stylist bag.

"Could I grab a photo of you for my portfolio? I don't think I have ever done such a good job on anyone in my entire life," he gushed, eyeing Oalfus with total admiration in place of the earlier desire. With a shrug, Oalfus agreed.

Jacob was delighted with the shots he got, Oalfus posed so naturally for him. He tucked the camera away with glee. Oh how wonderfully those shots would do in his portfolio!

Finally, the curtain was drawn back and Oalfus walked over to where Rikovic and Viktor had been sitting waiting for him. It seems the suits had been dealt with long ago and he had been holding them up. Viktor saw him first, his eyes widening. He reached over and feebly slapped his son's arm for attention. Ricky winced when his father finally smacked him. Grumbling as he looked up from the magazine, he went to snarl at his father before seeing his uncle and dropping his jaw.

"Holy shit!" he gasped before a wide grin spread over his face and he began laughing. *"You look like you belong on a fucking magazine cover!"*

Oalfus shifted uncomfortably, glancing down at the shirt with its sleeves rolled up to his elbows and the navy coloured dress pants that were tight on his thighs but a little looser under the knee. He swallowed, running a nervous hand through his hair and realizing just how much shorter it was now.

"It's not too much is it?" he asked nervously.

"You're going to look better than me at my own wedding, you jack-ass!" Ricky teased, shocked at how different his uncle looked. The pair got up and circled him, stunned looks of disbelief on their faces as they nodded approvingly.

"Tatiana will certainly be pleased," Viktor noted.

"Do you think Deirdre will like it?" Oalfus muttered to Ricky, which earned him a loud bark of a laugh.

"I think every woman you walk past will like it! If she has eyes, she will enjoy this!"

Chapter Fourteen

Deirdre stared in total disbelief. How on earth was that Oalfus? He didn't even look the same! The wild, scruffy demon she had come here with was gone! Now he was a sharply-dressed, clipped-fur and highlighted-haired supermodel. Oalfus looked like all the older demons on the cover of fashion magazines. Had Carmen not pushed her mouth closed, Deirdre may have gawked at him all day.

Oalfus was dressed in a light gray dress shirt, fitted navy dress pants, and a long felt jacket. Where was the turtle neck she had helped him into this morning? Her mind raced as the group of men approached the table where the girls were sitting. On top of being put in a dizzying number of dresses that cost more than Deirdre thought possible, she was now sitting in one of the most gorgeous restaurants she had ever seen and felt like a fish out of water.

Carmen gave Deirdre a reassuring pat on the hand. "Easy girl, I know this is probably a lot. When Tatiana took me here after Ricky proposed, I felt the same as you do now. Just let her do this, it makes her happy," Carmen assured, but that was small potatoes now.

Deirdre's brows drew together as Oalfus finally caught sight of her and smiled at her. "He doesn't look the same..." she whimpered.

"He looks fabulous. Oh, Oalfus, they really worked their magic!" Tatiana exclaimed as she hurried over and threw her arms around the old demon.

Carmen leaned in closer to Deirdre and squeezed her arm. "You okay, doll? He looks great, don't you think?"

"I think– I mean I am. I just...he looks *too* good. What if he doesn't want to be seen with me?" Deirdre whispered, her thoughts spilling out a little faster than she could stop them.

Carmen rubbed her arm, giving her a tight side hug before scooting over a seat to make room for Oalfus. "With the way he's lookin' at you like you're the only gal in the room, I'm sure that won't be true," Carmen reassured her with a broad wink just before Oalfus took his seat.

"How was your morning with the girls, *mein Leibchen?*" he asked, shrugging off his jacket before giving her forehead a kiss.

Deirdre felt her cheeks warm, her hand holding his where it was cupping her cheek. "It was fine. You clearly had quite the morning yourself."

"Ah...yes. I may have been strong armed into all of..." he gestured at himself, his ears tipping to the sides bashfully, "this."

"You look..." Deirdre was at a loss for words, her hand reaching up to run through the white streaks of hair over his temple.

"Is it too much?" Oalfus whispered, his brows knitting together.

"No! Oh no, no, no. It is just so different that's all. You look incredible," Deirdre reassured him, pushing her smile a little wider.

"I was worried you might not like it. I don't really know if I do, myself. It is..." Oalfus didn't want to admit it. Swallowing hard he gave a shrug and mumbled, "I look just like my brother. He certainly cared more about dressing well than I ever did."

"I like you dressed up like this, but I will miss running my fingers into that thick fur while we..."

The pair grinned at each other. Oalfus pulled Deirdre up into his lap, despite the displeased look Tatiana shot his way. He nuzzled against the top of her head and mumbled against her flopped ear. "I will be sure to grow it back. I wouldn't want you to lose your hand holds while I am having my way with you."

His clawed hand ran up along her thigh, a low rumbling in his throat as he pressed his nose against her mass of curls.

Tatiana cleared her throat loudly, her eyes narrowing on the pair. *"I am sure Deirdre will manage just fine feeding herself while we are here,"* she snapped in Russian.

With a great sigh, Oalfus let go of Deirdre and nudged her back to her own chair. His hand, however, was immediately on her thigh and gripping it in a rather possessive way. Deirdre squeaked when his hand slid up higher, which only made him grin at her.

Ricky was now beside Carmen, his arm around her shoulder, and the pair were whispering to each other, drawing Tatiana's attention. She began lecturing her son about whispering at the table, wagging a finger at him as her eyes darkened. It seemed Tatiana's temper was beginning to fray.

"Was the dress fitting alright?" Oalfus mumbled to Deirdre.

"Oh, it was fantastic!" she replied enthusiastically. "I don't think I've ever been in such a fancy store. I think Tatiana is still upset about them not having the right lace in stock, but it worked out for Carmen, in my opinion. She doesn't seem the type to wear such a fancy dress. She was really happy with the one she picked out instead. But, because she had to change her dress, mine changed, too, and—what?" Deirdre stopped mid-sentence, squirming a little under Oalfus' intent gaze. A relaxed smile had spread over his features listening to her speak so freely to him.

The older demon just shook his head and chuckled to himself. "Don't mind me, I am just glad you had a good time. I was thinking of you while I was being forcibly groomed," Oalfus said with an eye roll. Deirdre reached up and ran gentle fingers along his shorn neck. Now that he was clipped so much shorter, he almost didn't look the same.

"Will it take long to grow back?" she hadn't meant to say it aloud; the flicker of worry across his features made her chest tighten up.

"I have never cut this much off, but I imagine by winter it will nearly be back to its usual length." He tried to sound unphased, but the twinge of worry in his voice made her ears tip back.

"I shouldn't have said that, you really do look wonderful! I guess I just need to get used to you looking like a supermodel. I'll have to keep the girls off with a bat," she teased, giving his arm a gentle bump with her shoulder.

"My eyes will only ever look for you, Deirdre. You are all I could ever want." Oalfus spoke gently as he cupped Deirdre's face in his large hand.

Ricky made a snorting sound, raising his brow at the pair. "What about the red candles?" he sneered, almost spitting his drink from laughter at the nasty glare Oalfus gave him. He snorted, quickly covering his mouth to try and stifle his laughter, but this only seemed to curl his lip further.

Viktor rolled his eyes at Ricky, cuffing him hard across the back of the head. His eyes narrowed and he hissed at him in Russian.

"Watch your mouth boy. This might be a time to celebrate your union, but it doesn't mean you forget your common manners. Show your uncle some respect. Bringing up something so crass is below you."

Ricky rubbed his head, huffing and glancing over at Oalfus. He looked mortified, looking down at the table and avoiding Deirdre's gaze entirely. Deirdre knew of the red candle tradition; most people who knew about Krampus did, but it didn't bother her. She imagined he must have grown lonely at times. Perhaps it was the only way he felt he was safe to connect in such a way.

Deirdre straightened up a little, giving Ricky a stern look as she spoke very pointedly. "I don't *care* about it, if that's what you are getting at. If this is some kind of cheap shot because Oalfus has been prickly since he got here, it seems a wasted effort. Red candles or no, that doesn't matter to me, I only care about his actions moving forward, not his past."

Carmen smiled at Deirdre, stomping on Ricky's ankle under the table. "See? A girl with a head on her shoulders. It is a shame some people here—" she stomped his ankle again, making him double over and puff his cheeks out as he held in a yell of pain, "don't seem to have their head on straight."

The sore ankle and icy smile Carmen gave Ricky was enough for him to know he had to behave. Wheezing out a weak apology to his uncle, Ricky rubbed his throbbing ankle under the table in silence. Oalfus was really starting to like this mortal girl, but his eyes landed on Deirdre once more. He placed a hand on her leg and simply smiled at her. Nothing else needed to be said, he was just glad to have her.

"I don't know about anyone else here, but I am starving," Viktor said, waving over a waitress. "Let's get something to eat, yes?" he asked, raising a brow at the group. Everyone seemed to agree as they opened the menus on the table. Deirdre smiled as she kept catching all of Oalfus' little glances from the corner of her eye. *Yes,* she thought, *I think I know exactly what I want...*and luckily he was sitting right beside her.

Chapter Fifteen

The subsequent days went by with little issue. Aside from the odd snide remark thrown at each other over the remaining days leading to the ceremony, Deirdre was very impressed at how warm Oalfus was towards everyone. She had even overheard Viktor and him seemingly having a heart-to-heart while she had been looking for Carmen. She couldn't say for sure what was said between them as it was all in Russian, but from the gentle tone they were using and the hug she had spotted before she crept away, it had been a good moment for the pair.

Oalfus was making a real effort to mend the bonds lost over time. After realizing how deeply he could truly care for another being, he saw the damage his absence had caused. Viktor had been very receptive to him. Even though Oalfus knew the relationship between his brother and nephew had been less than warm, Viktor made it clear he found comfort in his uncle's presence. He was a much kinder version of what his father had been, and having Oalfus present reminded him how far he had come with his own son, and still how much more there was to do.

Viktor had fallen victim to the weaker habits of demons, allowing the bonds that knit a family together to fall to the wayside in the pursuit of his own ambitions. It had damaged his relationship with Rikovic, and he was determined to repair the damage he had done. Viktor could see it in Oalfus as well; the lost look in his eyes when he was alone with his nephews spoke volumes. Viktor had been the one to invite his uncle for a chat, but Oalfus had certainly leapt at the opportunity, partly to begin rebuilding his relationship with Viktor, but also to ask his advice.

Oalfus had become increasingly aware of an odd tension grow-ing between him and Rikovic; it had slowly been getting worse as the days passed. He would catch him glaring, or sneering when they spoke, what little they did. He had even caught a snippet of a whispered argument between Carmen and Rikovic when he had been walking past their room. Carmen had been trying to find out why he was acting so out of character; it seemed, normally, Rikovic was not so stand-offish and was much warmer.

Oalfus had not lingered, as he feared it might worsen things if he had been caught. The chance to possibly ask Viktor his opinion had been greatly appreciated.

"I am sorry for my absence, truly. I never should have taken down my gate, but after what happened, I became paranoid, I suppose," Oalfus confided in Viktor. The pair had been talking for quite some time now. The evening was growing long in the tooth, but Oalfus rather enjoyed the comfort of Viktor's office. It was the only space he recognized in the house.

"What happened to upset you so much?" Viktor asked as he poured them both a glass of brandy.

"It was in the early morning after Krampus Nacht. I was careless with a woman and didn't get far enough away from the village. Her husband awoke, found the red candle lit, and put two and two together. Before I knew it, a mob was coming after me." Oalfus' brows drew together,

his face hardening as he recalled being hunted by the mob of angry mortals.

Viktor handed Oalfus the glass, placing a hand on his uncle's shoulder. "That would be hard on anyone Uncle, especially after how you lost *Dedushka* and *Baba*."

"*Hah...you know, it's not even the mob that got to me. Pitchforks, torches and all. It still did not bother me. What bothered me was being trapped...caged like an animal.*" His voice became a dark whisper, staring down at the brandy in his glass with a stony glare.

"*They trapped you?*" Viktor breathed.

"*In a cave. I was there for days. I probably never would have gotten out if that woman hadn't taken pity on me. She pulled away enough of the smaller rocks I could see the light again. That was all I needed. I became very untrusting and paranoid, always looking over my shoulder, and never going to the same village twice in a row. I never imagined my antics as 'Krampus' would become fables across the world,*" Oalfus chuckled dryly.

"*Perhaps it is a blessing in disguise. Yes, you have been hidden away for all these years, but I see a new light in you, Uncle. That youngling of yours is truly something. She has made an impact on you. Just be careful with one of her kind,*" Viktor teased, smirking over the rim of his glass.

"*Careful?*"

"*She is a demon of the new order. Where she's from, they call themselves Fae. They're more in tune with magic than our kind. Think of them like...cousins, to our kind of demons. They have strange magic. It's wild and from an ancient place, perhaps even more ancient than you.*"

"*I will keep that in mind. I am curious of her kind, and hope she will show me more of her soon. I was hoping to ask you something though,*" Oalfus said, glancing up from his glass.

"Anything, Uncle."

"Have you noticed...Rikovic, he is acting very–"

"Cold. I am used to his chilly behavior, but I am shocked he is being so nasty to you. He was so desperate to find you before the wedding that he sent two chaos demons hunting for you, and now he is being a prickly little bastard."

Oalfus' ears drooped as he sighed, looking down at his feet. *"How do I fix this? It seems it is only getting worse as time passes. I know he must be frustrated with me. I don't blame any of you for being frustrated, but I don't know how to even start the conversation..."*

Viktor smiled at his uncle, standing and sitting on the sofa beside him. *"It has only been a year since Rikovic and I began speaking again. It isn't perfect, but when I–"* Viktor paused. He was not sure if telling Oalfus about Ricky's current...state was appropriate. It was not his place to explain that, and he certainly did not want to damage the relationship he had been re-building with his son. Smiling in a sad way, he shrugged and looked up at Oalfus.

"I went to him, and when we spoke– er, he tore a strip off me. Then time began to mend things. I think you will just have to go and speak with him plainly, and though I fear you might get the same harsh treatment, it will get easier."

"I trust your judgment, Viktor. Thank you for speaking with me. I feel a little foolish for coming to my nephew for advice on such things. You would think by my age I would have some sense..." Oalfus trailed off, smiling in a sad sort of way.

Viktor wrapped an arm around his uncle's bulky frame and gave a great sigh. *"Frankly, Uncle, I still struggle to figure out where I stand with my own son. I just appreciate the positive moments, and do my best to avoid getting upset. Perhaps discussion will help most of all, though I must warn you: he has his mother's sharp tongue."*

Oalfus laughed, shaking his head and returning the hug to his nephew. He even kissed the top of his head, which the older demon had not done since Viktor had been a very young man.

"I suppose I will deserve some of his ire, though I appreciate the warning. Perhaps now is the best time to attempt this venture. I have had some liquid courage, and your words have given me a new-found energy. If you will excuse me then."

Oalfus climbed the stairs slowly, following the slow drone of Rikovic's violin. It seemed while the women were occupied this evening, Rikovic was eager to practice a song he was preparing for his wedding. The closer the older demon came to the sound, the tighter the knots in his stomach became. His worries nagged at his mind but his pride pushed him onwards down the hallway.

Oalfus placed a wary hand on the door, edging it open slightly. His eyes widened and his jaw went slack when his gaze fell on his nephew. Ricky, it seemed, had gorged on Carmen after supper like he was starving to death. She had hardly been able to stand when she scurried off to meet with his mother, and his body was practically vibrating with her sexual energy. He still had immense levels of lust pumping through his veins His four eyes were closed, his wings flexing slowly along with the melody of his violin, and his long tail flicking side to side. His ear flicked, *someone was watching him.* Slowly, his red eyes opened. Setting the violin down on the bed in front of him, he kept his back turned to the door.

"Are you going to hide behind the door or come in here?" Ricky hissed, glancing over his shoulder. He had been waiting for Oalfus to find him out; he was hardly surprised to see his uncle step into the room.

"You can save the theatrics. I have been corrupted for a long time now. I won't harm you, if that is what you are worried about," Ricky sighed.

Oalfus shook his head, closing the door behind him as he stepped closer to his nephew. He was more bewildered at the change in his appearance than worried about coming to harm from his own kin. Oalfus eyed him like a curious animal rather than a terror-struck child as his father had. Ricky turned fully, folding his wings tightly to his back and crossing his arms.

"How long have you been like this?" Oalfus asked, reaching out a hand to trace his claws along the taller pair of Ricky's horns.

Ricky cocked a brow at his Uncle's awestruck curiosity. *"Since I snapped during the war. After Viktor and I had our falling out, I tried to find you. I always came to you when Father and I would fight, but your gate was closed. I went on a bender. I was an idiot and consumed a succubus..."*

Oalfus' chest tightened with guilt, his ears tipping back as he looked down at his nephew. He had truly failed his family; the consequences stood before him as plain as day.

"Rikovic... I–"

"Don't bother trying to apologize now. You never bothered before you saw the truth. Why start now?"

"Rikovic, I am here now because I–"

"What, because you care? You haven't cared for two hundred years. If I hadn't sent those two to find you, you would have continued on with your reclusive life and never have known. You would never have had to face what abandoning your family looks like. You only feel bad because you've seen the ugly truth," Ricky spat, his eyes glossed with emotion he wished would go away.

"I know I failed at being here for you; I have failed all of you. It was one thing to punish myself by hiding as I have for so many years, but I never should have punished you. I know I can not make up for lost time, and I can not fix the rage you feel towards me. I can only ask for your

patience with me, Rikovic. I am trying, I truly am. I want to be a part of all your lives again. Things have changed..." Oalfus was choking out his words by the end, emotions flooding his vision as he quickly looked down at his hooves.

Ricky wanted to hurl as much ire as he could, but seeing his uncle become so openly emotional shocked him. Memories of crying on his uncle's shoulder came back, from when he would run away and find his uncle somewhere in the woods of Germany. When there was too much pressure from his father or his superior officers, he would always turn to Oalfus for advice or even a mere distraction.

"I never imagined one little girl would change you so much," Ricky muttered, his wings curling around his shoulders. He avoided his uncle's intense gaze, his wings acting as a line of defense against these invading emotions threatening to pierce his heart.

A year ago, he would have easily held the grudge against his father; against Oalfus would have been child's play. It seemed Carmen was melting the ice around his heart as well, as much as he hated to admit it. Seeing his uncle visibly distraught, struggling to open up to him, and reach out to him was harder than he anticipated.

"I could say the same to you, Rikovic. Carmen truly is wonderful. I know I was apprehensive when we first met, but I can see now how good she is for you."

Ricky tightened his wings around his shoulders, turning away from his uncle and sucking in a sharp breath. *"She and I have been through much, but it does not change how hurt I am with you, even if you have finally accepted my bride."*

"I do not expect your forgiveness immediately. I know I must earn your trust. I only hope, with more time, we might return to a place we

once were. I never should have closed my gate. I would give anything to go back in time–"

"Well you can't!" Ricky blurted, a growl ready in his throat, but he look on his uncle's face made it die quickly. Looking down and carefully unwrapping his wings, he splayed them once before folding them at his back. *"Of all the creatures in this world...I needed you the most,"* Ricky croaked out, his voice threatening emotion as he kept his eyes glued on his hooves.

Oalfus' heart was in a vice, his ears tilting back as he cautiously approached his nephew. Never being one to shy away from physical embrace, Oalfus placed a gentle hand on Ricky's shoulder before pulling his nephew against him. He moved slowly, considerately, as he placed a large hand on the back of Ricky's head, hugging him. He hugged him just as he did when he was a small boy.

"I know, and I've failed you, my boy. I've failed you, and I wish more than anything I could repair the harm I have done. I only wish to find a place where perhaps we can move forward. But if you only wish for me to be here and leave, I–"

"Shut up, old man... You keep running your mouth and you will ruin this moment. I did not have you hunted down to simply allow you to disappear from my life once more." Ricky allowed himself this moment of weakness, his voice wobbling with emotion as he leaned against his uncle's shoulder.

He could no longer dwell so darkly on the past. His broken family was somehow piecing itself back together for the first time in so many years, and, instead of resisting this, Rikovic knew he had to embrace it, all the complicated, uncomfortable emotions included. He knew there would be moments he would not want to face, emotions that would make him want to tear out his hair, but if it meant he would finally regain the uncle who had always been a pillar of support in his life, it might all be worth it.

Ricky's wings began to retreat back into his body, his long horns receding and his second set of eyes melted away. Sucking in a shaky breath, he allowed the younger version of himself a silent moment of healing. His arms wrapped around Oalfus' vast chest, his head tucked against his shoulder and his ears tipped back as he gripped onto his uncle. Oalfus was silent, leaning down and resting his chin on Ricky's head as he returned the hug.

Neither of them needed to speak, there was nothing left to say. They both simply needed time.

Chapter Sixteen

Deirdre fell asleep waiting for Oalfus. He and Ricky had stayed up half the night talking about everything, once their emotions had settled. Sharing stories of whatever came to mind, Oalfus was eager to learn more of his nephew's relationship with Carmen. Hearing their harrowing tale made him proud of how strong they both were.

Carmen had returned some time around one in the morning, exhausted and pleading for Ricky to carry her to a shower. Oalfus smiled at their banter, excusing himself to go find his own companion. Deirdre's scent was magnetic, so bright and welcoming as he slipped in quietly to the guest room she was dozing in.

Her eyes fluttered open when Oalfus eased down beside her, wrapping her up in his arms and curling around her warm body. Rolling over, she buried her face in his neck. Oalfus rumbled happily, feeling her pepper his neck with sleepy kisses and wrap one leg around his waist.

"I missed you," he whispered softly to her through the darkness, kissing the crown of her head. Deirdre's eyes opened slowly, looking up at his shadow and blindly reaching out for his face. Her fingers trailed along his neck up his cheek and brushed back stray hair from his eyes.

"You never need to miss me, I am always here…" she breathed, her words wrapping around his heart and filling him with warmth.

"You have no idea how much that means to me," Oalfus murmured, his nose bumping against hers. Deirdre smiled, kissing him softly and sliding her fingers into his hair.

"I have thought about what you asked me. Perhaps when the wedding is over, we can travel to St.Petersburg together," He murmured against her wild curls.

Deirdre's eyes went wide and she shot up, reaching past him to flick on the lamp at the bedside table. Oalfus grimaced at the sudden brightness, but the look of pure joy on Deirdre's face was well worth the discomfort.

"Do you mean it?" she asked, her eyes wide with disbelief.

"Yes, of course I do, *mein Leibchen,*" Oalfus chuckled, urging her back down onto the bed beside him before reaching over and turning off the lamp. "Hush now, get your rest. We have been roped into some dreadful dance routine, according to Carmen."

"But the wedding is in two days!" Deirdre gasped.

"That's why we're practicing first thing in the morning," Oalfus groaned.

Tatiana was grinning wickedly as she watched Oalfus amble into the large ballroom at the back of the manor. *At least this room was still the same,* he thought as he looked up at the familiarly painted ceiling. Carmen was rubbing her legs, stretching on the floor, and looked about as exhausted as Oalfus felt. Tatiana was a drill sergeant when it came to dance; she was the real driving force behind Rikovic being a dancer in his youth. She wore a sleek,black, long-sleeved leotard, black tights, and satin hoof caps. Deirdre was shocked at how perfect the older demoness' physique was.

"Still the prima ballerina we all know and love," Oalfus teased.

"You know what they say, once a prima, always a prima," Tatiana mused, pulling her hair back into a tight bun.

She had studied dance all over Europe through her youth. Though Tatiana had been born in Moscow, she had spent very little time in the city. She was shipped from dance school to dance school, mastering every form under the harsh scrutiny of her mother. Oalfus empathized with Tatiana; she, too, had lost her parents during the riots just before Rikovic had been born, but her six siblings had managed to survive.

Oalfus' great-nephew was named after Tatiana's father, and though his mother never pushed him as hard as his father had, Rikovic carried the burden of his namesake with just as much weight. Rikovic Molochev had been a well-respected nobleman. He had backed many of Russia's tsars and had been involved in government since his youth. The Molochev family was as well-known and respected as anyone could imagine, so it served to reason they were the first family targeted during the raids.

The only reason young Tatiana had survived was that she had been in Paris studying ballet when the riots broke out. Viktor had been her betrothed since birth, so when the dust had settled, his family sent for her and their marriage was rushed.

Just as Tatiana had been sent abroad, so had her many siblings. Several were in the military, one studied music, and another followed in her footsteps as a dancer. Tatiana was the only girl among seven children. Her brothers were well-respected among the demon community, though, in the last century, they had grown distant due to Tati's own struggles in her marriage.

Oalfus guessed it would be a tense reunion at the wedding, ye another thing to dread.

Tatiana was doing everything in her power to ensure her one and only son had absolutely everything she had missed out on for his wedding, including a surprise dance performed by his new bride.

"Sorry to spring this all on you so suddenly. Tatiana thought it would be a fun addition to this already painful experience," Carmen groaned, which earned her an icy glare from Tatiana.

"Rikovic is trained in this style of dance. He will be able to match your movement perfectly once the music begins. You are the one who has to worry, not them. I expect perfection, Carmen," Tatiana sniffed, but her teasing smile quickly broke her stony façade.

"So what do you need from us? I am not the best dancer, I'm afraid," Deirdre said, her tail tucking nervously.

"Your steps will be simple. Traditionally, a single couple is the highlight while other couples form a line behind them. This was a very popular dance at any special event. It still is today, though many forgo the traditional dances now," Tatiana explained, then, as graceful as a butterfly on the breeze, she moved to the center of the room to demonstrate.

It was a simple enough combination of steps: four to the left and four to the right, a spin and a clap. Deirdre was surprised at the angle she was expected to bend her knees and feet, but, after a little reassurance from Tatiana and some pointers to keep herself steady, it was becoming easier. Oalfus seemed to know this dance;

he confessed he had helped Rikovic with rehearsals when he had been more present in the boy's early years.

"This is a dance they teach little children when they start traditional style. I can't tell you how many recitals the poor boy had to do of this routine," Oalfus chuckled, crossing his arms and crouching a little lower to accommodate Deirdre's stature. He moved considerately with her, helping her balance and adjusting her footing when Tatiana became wrapped up with Carmen. After only an hour, it seemed Deirdre's confidence had grown exponentially. She smiled widely when Oalfus praised her as the music stopped once more.

"Oh *damn*, look at the time," Tatianna suddenly blurted when she saw the digital clock on the stereo. "Alright, go freshen up. The Elder representatives shall be here soon to run through ceremony–"

"What do you mean the Elder?" Carmen gasped, her eyes widening with terror.

"Well darling, who else would officiate the wedding of a high-order demon? Our family has deep ties to the Elders. They insist on all high-order family unions be officiated by the Elders themselves. There are so few of us left after all," Tatiana explained as it was common knowledge, but the dread in Carmen's eyes spoke volumes. She rushed from the room, her voice rang out like alarm bells as she called out for Ricky.

Oalfus swallowed hard. He didn't need to ask why the poor girl was so terrified of the idea of the Elders. Many demons avoided direct contact with them for good reason; they were terrifying beasts. Ancient beyond words.

Deirdre looked up at Oalfus for an answer, but he simply shook his head and frowned. "Stay close to me when they arrive. I had hoped we would forgo this tradition."

"Are they really so bad?" Deirdre asked, her tail tucking once more.

"The Elders are the oldest of demons among our kind. They created all of the original branches of our tree. I am only a third generation from the original creation of the Elders. My great-grandfather was one of the first made in their image. To say we are afraid of them wouldn't be a stretch. We must show them the utmost respect out of habit, but only the wise fear them."

"Back home, our ancients are loved by all. I could never imagine fearing those who gave us life," Deirdre whispered, but Oalfus' fear of the Elders sent a shiver over her whole body.

"You will understand when you see," Oalfus warned.

The garden was being set up for the ceremony. White folding chairs lined up in perfect rows filled the massive green space at the center of the impressive garden. Deirdre swallowed hard. This was going to be quite the affair. Ricky was standing with a very anxious looking Carmen when Oalfus and Deirdre found them up where the ceremony would be held.

"Why did you not tell me a damn *Elder* was officiating!" Carmen hissed, her fur standing on end as she glared at Ricky.

"This was not my idea, Carmen. I hoped my parents would have avoided this whole situation after everything that happened, but a letter showed up two weeks ago. They informed us it was already decided. No one knows how they found out," Ricky explained, again, to his frantic bride.

"It will be over before you know it," Oalfus tried to assure them both, forcing a calm smile onto his face. "Elders have never been known to linger longer than needed."

"Back home, it would be a great honor for an Ancient One to insist on being a part of a wedding. Perhaps looking at it that way will soften the blow?" Deirdre suggested, trying to be helpful, but the stony expression on both their faces made it clear it was all in vain.

Chapter Seventeen

Oalfus had not been sure what to expect, but it certainly was not the looming creature whose eyes fell on him so viciously he nearly turned and ran. It had been centuries since he had been near an Elder, but the fear that filled his veins like ice was just as aggressive now as it had been so many years ago. Deirdre half-hid behind Oalfus as the horrific creature's bone-chilling gaze slid from Rikovic and Carmen, to them. The beast was *enormous*, possibly the biggest demon Deirdre had ever seen. Its horns nearly touched the highest branches of the tree where all the demon gates were kept on the estate. Its body was covered in snow white fur from ear tip to hoof. Its limbs were abnormally long and spindly. It almost reminded Deirdre of a walking skeleton, with how lean it was. She wondered if it was hungry; something so thin must be, she told herself.

Blond-coloured cloven hooves matched the impressive pair of horns on its head. Two pairs, one that went straight up, and the second tightly curled ram horns that hugged the three pairs of long pointed ears, appeared to be growing out of each other. Its canine head was narrow with a long snout, and the six piercing blue eyes felt as if they stared right into Deirdre's soul. This horrific creature was nothing like the Ancients of her homeland.

The few demons that seemed to be its escort scoffed when they caught sight of her. In her state of fear, her body had shifted and long vines were now hanging down to her ankles. Oalfus placed a protective arm around her, pushing her further behind his hulking frame that was now dwarfed by the approaching horror. The smile that spread across its narrow face, revealing long sharp rows of teeth and blood red gums, made Deirdre whimper.

"Do my eyes deceive me? Could it really be you, my beloved Oalfus?" The Elder growled out. Had the thing not been so utterly terrifying, Deirdre may have mistaken the sound it made for joy. She did not understand what it said, aside from Oalfus' name, but the way his whole body froze told her all she needed.

"I won't leave your side," Deirdre whispered as quietly as her voice would allow, to which Oalfus gave her arm a tight squeeze.

"What is that little thing you hide behind you, my ancient child?" The Elder cooed as it stepped in front of Oalfus.

Its long, boney fingers trailed over his cheek and hooked under his jaw, forcing him to lift his gaze and meet the six piercing-blue eyes boring into him. Deirdre pressed her forehead against his back, knowing full well it could see her, but hoping it wasn't staring.

"She is my companion, my Elder. I–"

"Tut, tut. I do not care who she is to you. I asked *what* she is," the Elder purred in a sing-songy way. Somehow, it was even more discomforting when it attempted a sweet voice.

Oalfus was about to answer when Deirdre finally found her courage. She had caught sight of Ricky and Carmen looking on in fear from the corner of her eye. They were just as worried about this Elder as she was. Perhaps it could be a welcomed distraction if she faced it. She was still a stranger to them, but in their short time together, Deirdre had grown fond of Carmen and Ricky. Swallowing hard, she stepped away from Oalfus and timidly looked up at the towering beast.

"I-I am a Cu-Sith, I hail from Ireland...E-Elder."

Deirdre felt her mossy fur stand on end when the cold boney fingers wrapped around her jaw and jerked her head back. She tried to hold back her trembling, to remain still and allow this invasion, but her body betrayed her and she felt her knees buckle.

"A *new* child, yet you are wrapped in ancient magic. Funny how our cousins to the west waited so very long to begin creating your lot. What was their funny name for you now..." The Elder leaned in, its razor sharp teeth mere inches from Deirdre's face as it smiled wickedly at her. "That's right, they call you little ones *Fae*. What a pretty name for such strange creatures. We do not see many of your kind in Russia, yet here you are, with one of my oldest children. My, my, Oalfus. You are quite the charmer to have caught this one."

Oalfus had his eyes glued to the ground, his ears splayed back and fear evident in his expression. Deirdre was shocked to see how poorly he was doing in the presence of this Elder. Viktor and Tatiana were keeping a safe distance, though it was evident the younger generations were less fearful of this terrifying creature. Ricky simply stood defensively in front of Carmen, watching his uncle intently as his gaze flicked between him and the Elder.

Deirdre was relieved when those horrible fingers finally released her. The tall skeletal creature straightened and looked her over with great interest. His lingering eyes felt as though they were boring right into her very soul as she stood trembling. She wanted nothing more than for Oalfus to hold her hand, to keep her hidden as Ricky was doing for Carmen, but he was paralyzed with fear and avoided looking directly at the Elder at all costs.

"How fascinating indeed...*Oalfus.*" The Elder snapped his name, his face pinching into a vicious looking glare as his gaze landed on the old demon.

"Y-yes?" Oalfus muttered, his gaze flicking up to meet the Elder's only once before going back down to the ground.

"You and I have much to discuss later. You have hidden away from us. Until this point, I believed you dead, my child. For now, though, I have my eyes set on our happy couple." The Elder's gaze fell on Ricky and Carmen, leering at the pair as he pushed past Oalfus to get to them.

Instantly Deirdre was in Oalfus' arms, his hands cupping her face as he whispered, "Did he harm you?"

"No, I am fine. You look terrified. What is that...*thing?*"

"Hush! He might hear you." Oalfus' fearful gaze looked to make sure the Elder was not listening, but the old demon knew better than to have hope for such things. "I thought I might avoid seeing the Elders...it's complicated, I will try to explain later..." he mumbled, but now his eyes were on Rikovic. The Elder looked unimpressed, waving a hand which Oalfus winced at when Rikovic was forced to his knees and his body began shifting into its corrupted state.

"What have I told you, Rikovic? I grow tired of you hiding your true shape from me. You know how fascinated I am with you, after all," the Elder practically giggled his words.

Deirdre gasped, covering her mouth as she stared in wide-eyed horror. She recoiled against Oalfus, who immediately pulled her against his chest and hid her face.

"Deirdre, please don't panic now. I know what you are thinking. This is a very delicate situation and I *need* you to trust that I would never let you near Rikovic if I thought he was a danger. Just please,

please trust me and stay calm," Oalfus pleaded in a whisper against her ear.

Everything in the young Fae said this was wrong. Rikovic was clearly corrupted. She had been told her whole life how dangerous the corrupted demons were. Oalfus was begging her to ignore everything she knew, but somehow, she trusted him. Timidly, she looked over her shoulder.

Ricky was on his knees and visibly in pain as Carmen held him protectively. She was so brave to embrace him without hesitation; his corrupted shape was horrifying. Leathery bat-like wings, two sets of lethal looking horns and four red eyes glared at the ground as he panted. Double canines hung low under his chin as he tried to breathe through the agony of a forced shift. It was just as bad as the first time the Elder had done it.

"Goodness, your little mortal is rather bold, Rikovic. I dare say she looks–" the Elder paused, looming over the pair and lowering his vicious looking head so close to Carmen they nearly touched noses. An eerie grin spread over his features that made Deirdre's skin crawl. Carmen wanted to slap that grin off his face; she knew how much pain Ricky was in, and it was all because of this monster. She kept her arms wrapped around Ricky's shoulders, supporting him as he finally lifted his head.

"Something has changed," the Elder giggled, standing up and clasping his hands together. His tail swayed – no, wagged – behind him as he eyed Carmen with absolute delight. "*You* have changed," he declared, pointing a bony finger in Carmen's face. "Oh, this is better than I ever could have imagined!" he cackled, throwing his head back in wicked laughter.

"Ricky, what's he talkin' about?" Carmen growled, glaring up at the Elder.

"I have no idea..." Ricky ground out, swallowing hard.

"You can't tell, Rikovic? You can't even sense the change in your little mate?" the Elder giggled once more, his head tilting side-to-side in an owlish manner. "Your corruption has spread!" he practically squealed with excitement.

"Start talkin' some damn sense!" Carmen barked. The Elder narrowed its eyes at her sudden rage, as if examining her more carefully. She stood suddenly, jabbing a finger against the Elder's chest as she stepped forward and growled her words. "You show up here, throw a damn wrench in all my plans, and set everyone on edge. You grab at Deirdre like she is some kinda toy for you to poke at, and then you hurt Ricky! Now you're talkin' some damn nonsense and makin' out like the rest of us ought to know what you're goin' on about!"

Everyone gasped. As Carmen progressively got more and more angry, accosting the Elder, her eyes had begun to change from their pale green to a deep red. This only made the Elder even more delighted, a wicked grin painted across his face as a bright glow began to fill her vision.

"*This* has never happened before!" the Elder giggled, grabbing Carmen's jaw and studied her closer. She snarled against the Elders grip, but it was of little use. Its grip was iron tight.

"What's happened to her?" Viktor gasped, finally breaking the terrible silence. Tatiana, Oalfus, Deirdre, and even Ricky were all gawking at her in dumbfounded silence.

"What is going on?! Can someone just speak normally?!" Carmen shrieked, finally slapping the Elder's hands away. When she whipped around to scowl at Ricky, he shakily rose to his feet and seemed in total disbelief as he looked at her. His face twisted in a worried expression as he cupped her face in his clawed hands.

"Carmen...what–" he looked up at the Elder, shaking his head. "What have you done to her?"

"I have done nothing. I *warned you* something might come of this, and this is even better than I imagined!"

"What are y'all goin' on about?!" Carmen roared, looking around herself at all the shocked faces.

"That is the most wonderful part, dear girl," the Elder said, leaning down to examine her a little closer. Its bony finger tapped the stone around her neck as he spoke.

"I don't exactly know how this happened, or if you truly are one, but it would seem being soul-bonded to Rikovic has turned you into a demon."

The Elder cackled. It was a vicious and humorless sound. No one saw the humor in this situation, it was unheard of. Never in the history of demon-kind has a mortal been *turned* into a demon. Cross-breeding was one thing, but to turn a living mortal into a demon? No one thought such things were possible.

"Oh, glory of this earth," the Elder giggled. "Here I thought I had seen it all, and then you come along, Rikovic. My blessed child, my little *experiment*. You certainly have piqued my interest now. I will be keeping a *much* closer eye on the pair of you."

The ceremony rehearsal was done with a horrible tension hanging over everyone. Oalfus felt as though he was going through the motions, though nothing was really sticking. Carmen and Ricky could hardly look at the Elder, who was clearly enjoying every tense moment. Viktor and Tatianna were chain smoking, and, for the first time in a long time, Oalfus *needed* a cigarette as well. Deirdre stood off to the side, her eyes often downcast, but Oalfus could see her listening intently. Her ears flicked every time a different aspect of the ceremony carried on.

Traditional demonic weddings were tediously long affairs, irritating, and full of minor rituals on top of the ongoing task. Oalfus would have preferred to not have participated. His blood would be required during the official event, but for now, they simply mimed through the steps. He detested the idea of all those eyes, but he knew his nephew hated it just as much.

Carmen was a trembling mess. It seemed the poor girl was in shock from the news. Who could blame her? To have such a massive realization dropped on her at the whim of a narcissistic demi-god would be shocking for the strongest of creatures. The Elders contained power beyond anyone's understanding. It was terrifying and vicious magic.

Oalfus hated the prolonged proximity to the creature, his sharp eyes and wicked grin made the old demon's skin crawl. Finally, he was able to get away, as it was done for now. He would have to bear this fuss one last time, and then *finally* he could leave Moscow with Deirdre.

She reached out to him with open arms when he approached. Oalfus needed her as badly as it seemed she needed him. Wrapping her in his arms and lifting her up off her feet, Oalfus buried his face against her neck.

"You looked as though you were being tortured," Deirdre tried to laugh, but there was a worried edge to her voice.

"I was. That Elder is dangerous. He makes me anxious. I can't wait for all this garbage to be over with. We can return to Germany and rest, and then we can begin planning our adventures without all these *fucking* prying eyes." He rattled off his words in a flurry of anxiety. His chest felt tight, but the longer he held his little demoness, the lighter he felt.

"You really want to plan our trip?" Deirdre asked in disbelief.

"I promised you, but have pity on me. Small crowds to start. I do not want to attract attention," he mumbled.

Deirdre squeezed him tightly around the neck, nodding and wrapping her legs shamelessly around him. She was giddy, her heart soaring with excitement.

"Oalfus," a slimy voice called.

There went their happiness.

Oalfus slowly turned his head. His family was already heading inside and it appeared that the Elder was staying. *Lovely*. Oalfus set Deirdre down, whispering for her to hurry inside as he made his way towards the Elder beckoning him with a skeletal finger.

"Ah ah, bring your little...*pet* with you."

His fur stood on end. Instinctually, his hand clasped Deirdre's arm and pushed her behind him.

"It's alright, I am not afraid," she whispered.

The Elder loomed over them both, his vile grin making both of them uneasy. "Such a pretty little thing. Come, sweetling," the Elder cooed. It was singsongy and unnatural.

"Y-yes..." Deirdre whimpered, stepping forward.

Oalfus wanted to snap the fingers off the Elder's hand when he traced them along her jaw and neck. The Elder's eyes never left Oalfus' face.

"My my, so very *possessive*. Look how angry he is," the Elder whispered to Deirdre. Its fingers trailed lower, over her shoulder and down her arm. Then it moved to her hip and, just as the Elder reached her midsection, its hand jerked back and its piercing eyes focused on Deirdre once more.

"What?!" The Elder said in shock, its voice an astonished whisper as its fingers edged closer to her stomach. When it touched her, the smile returned. "Well, today is just *full* of surprises. Well done, Oalfus," the Elder mused, pulling its hand back and tapping its chin thoughtfully.

"What does he mean?" Deirdre asked, looking up at the old demon.

Neither of them could speak, but the answer was plainly obvious. Oalfus stepped cautiously forward, his hand hovering over Deirdre's stomach a moment before she placed a fearful hand on her stomach.

"Am I...?" she whispered, looking up at the Elder who was beaming at them. This smile was not sinister as it was before. Oalfus wondered if it was *genuine joy* on its face.

"It would seem one of my oldest has managed to plant his seed in a new generation. I am eager to see what comes of you two. We have very few cases of the Fae mixing with our order. I wonder what shape it might take."

Oalfus dropped to his knees, his hands hovering over Deirdre's stomach as he looked between it and her face.

The Elder snickered, turning towards the house where Oalfus' family had long since disappeared into. "I shall allow you time to collect your thoughts. *Congratulations*. I do hope you'll make an honest woman of the poor girl, Oalfus."

They stared at each other wordlessly, Oalfus still on his knees and Deirdre in total shock. Her ears were ringing. After the Elder had said she was pregnant, the world had gone silent, save the low ringing. She could hardly grasp such news. How in the world had something like this happened? It shouldn't have been possible; she was a new order demon, Oalfus was old order. She never even considered the risks. She had never told him to pull out or even entertained the idea of protection. Were there even condoms that size?

Finally, two huge hands shakily covered hers. Deirdre looked up at the old demon, staring at her with pure fear in his eyes. He looked even more petrified than she felt at that moment. He was talking to her, but not a single word was audible. He brought a hand up to her cheek but she hardly felt it. She blinked, and blinked again. Then she rubbed her eyes and face, sucking in steady breaths; it was like the sound of the world was slowly being turned up. She could almost feel the little ridged dial of her Walkman under her thumb as the sound of birds singing, grass swaying in the breeze, and Oalfus saying her name finally came back to her.

"...Deirdre? Sweetling, can you hear me?"

"Uh-huh..."

Oalfus wrung his hands nervously, looking away from her, down at the ground or over at the garden to his left. "I...oh Deirdre, I am *so* terribly sorry..." he choked out, running frustrated hands through his hair as he slumped further down onto the ground.

Deirdre was taken aback by how upset Oalfus was. It was terribly soon for all this, she knew that, but was it really so devastating? He held the base of his horns and hung his head, shame and guilt swirling inside him like a torrent as he croaked out his words.

"I will support any decision you might make. I can't believe I have done this to you. Deirdre, if I knew then what I do now, I never would have laid a hand on you. This is the last thing I could ever imagine you would want and–"

"Oalfus, stop talking," she said, not cruel, but in a simple, blunt way. He was rambling out what he *thought* she wanted to hear. It was quite the opposite; in fact, he was on the verge of insulting her.

"I...forgive me, *Liebchen*."

"What is there to forgive? We were careless, foolish, perhaps a little over-zealous. Ignorant, I suppose," Deirdre seemed to be considering the correct adjectives more carefully than the truth in front of them. He almost wanted to shake the girl at her nonchalant attitude.

"I suppose neither of us expected this," she said plainly.

"Of course not! Do you hear yourself? You discuss this as if it is the weather! Do you not understand what we have done? What *I* have done to *you?!*" He sounded exasperated.

Deirdre shrugged slightly, running her hand over her stomach for the first time. "I suppose you have given me a baby, though I didn't quite imagine it happening so soon."

Oalfus was dumbfounded. This girl was not distressed or upset as he imagined she would be. He sat back on his hooves, threw his hands in the air, and smiled, despite how very, *very* serious this entire situation was.

"You are taking this much better than I am," he scoffed, running a hand over his hair once more.

"Did you want me to take it poorly?" she asked genuinely, confusion written all over her face.

"I suppose I expected anger, disappointment maybe? I don't know...this is not regular news one would expect less than a month into...into a relationship."

"Well...didn't you say I was your fate? Perhaps this is simply *fate's* design for us. Fate is a fickle thing, but I know I don't feel sorrow or anger. I don't know what I feel...surprised, I suppose, but it is not a bad feeling, I know that much," she said, kneeling down in front of him and shuffling forward. Their knees were touching now, her head lowered and her wild mass of copper curls curtained around her face. She gave a shrug, smiling to herself as she spoke.

"My Mammy and Da didn't know each other long before they had me. Both of my parents might be younger than you, now that I think about it."

Oalfus groaned, his head falling forward into his hands,

"But I think that is a good thing. If my parents have been together for so long and with such unbridled love, that must be a good thing. We are not mortals who live short lives and throw connections away like they mean nothing. You would think demons are more inclined for such things–"

"They are, don't be fooled," Oalfus interrupted.

"Well, I am certainly no such demon. I will fight for us. You told me you want me at your side, and I told you the same. This child, if it should come, will be *ours*. Something we created together. I know this is all...very sudden. I am aware this is my choice, but it is also your choice. I would never force you into something like this, just as much as I am sure you were about to tell me the same. However, I would like to keep it."

The old demon swallowed hard. He had never considered himself a family man, but when Deirdre said that it was their shared creation, a warmth flooded over his heart. He pulled her close to him, cradling her against his chest and placing a protective hand over her stomach.

"You are certain?"

"It is still early, clearly. I am sure even a pregnancy test wouldn't even pick it up yet. That Elder is a being of magic. I trust he knows better than some mortal science. Demon pregnancies vary, too; some are the same as mortals and some are much longer. My mother carried me for nearly fourteen months. This could be a long wait for us both. Are *you* sure this is what you want?"

Oalfus cupped her face, studying her carefully before looking down at her stomach. It was the same as it had been since they met. He knew it was only a matter of days into the pregnancy, but something inside him growled at the idea of this being taken from him.

"I never imagined myself to be a father; I hated mine fiercely. My brother was a bastard, but his children came out alright. Perhaps our little one will benefit from me having had to wait so long to finally bring them into the world. I will stand by you and protect you both. I give you my word."

Chapter Eighteen

Deirdre and Oalfus had decided to keep their news to themselves until after the wedding. Oalfus had plenty of work to do to rebuild the relationship between him and his family. Overshadowing Viktor's only son's wedding with the news of a baby was simply out of the question. He was glad to have this time to process it all. He and Deirdre shared quiet conversations where possible, but today, everyone was preoccupied. Caterers, event staff, house keepers, even Ricky and Carmen were rushing to and fro with things to be done.

None of it, however, was as stressful as the arrival of the extended family members. Viktor had been charged with that headache. Between the extended Petrokov family Viktor hardly recalled the names of and the vast brood the Molochev brothers were bringing in, Viktor was up to his eyeballs in fake smiles and excited reunions. Tatiana's brothers had certainly been busy producing children. A dizzying number of little demons were scampering about, and grandchildren and great-grandchildren were being corralled by older siblings and cousins. It made Viktor strain internally, the jealousy of such a vast brood nagging him. Perhaps he would discuss the possibility of growing the family with Tatiana, but that would have to wait.

The ceremony was nearly ready to begin. Tatianna was at the point of tearing her hair out after Carmen's third time scurrying away from her hair and makeup to take a phone call. It seemed her only remaining family, her sister, was very apprehensive of strangers appearing in front of her home, claiming to be whisking her off to a wedding in Moscow. Carmen had to make several attempts at reassuring her sister and brother-in-law that the plucky little chaos demons were not there to maim them. It did not help that it was ungodly hours of the night back in the United States. Oalfus kept thanking his lucky stars he had grown up in this life. He was used to portals and demons of all kinds, though he did see how a mortal would be terrified of a chaos demon.

It was shaping up to be a gorgeous day, and an even more gorgeous wedding ceremony. Viktor was adjusting his hair for the umpteenth time as he came into the house again, glancing over at Oalfus, who was pacing along the back of the sofa in the living room.

"Uncle? You look more nervous than Rikovic," Viktor called.

"Hm? Oh, I suppose I am in a way. It has been a long time since I have seen...well, anyone, let alone as many guests as you have invited," Oalfus half lied; he was truly busy worrying about Deirdre. She had just been whisked off to have her own hair and makeup done.

"You will be fine. I know this has all been very exciting for you but I am confident this will only open more opportunities for us all," Viktor said, moving over to where Oalfus was with an offering of scotch.

"You are a good lad," Oalfus muttered, taking the glass and shooting back the strong liquor.

"Hell's sake, Oalfus. You really are nervous!" Viktor laughed, taking the glass to pour him another. Perhaps it was best he kept just how many *older* relatives were waiting outside to himself for now.

"You have no idea..." Oalfus groaned.

"Kennedy I swear on my life, this is the private travel I promised you," Carmen huffed, leaning closer to the open cellphone on the vanity in front of her. Tatianna, Carmen, Deirdre, and the hair and makeup team were all together in Tatianna's powder room. Deirdre felt sorry for poor Tatianna; she looked ready to blow her top.

"You made it sound like a private jet! Not a weird...sheep? Goat? Thing! A weird *thing* with a glowing pentagram on my front lawn!" Kennedy shrieked back over the speaker phone.

"Just please trust me. Blednica is very sweet and quite harmless!" Carmen pleaded.

"Listen," Tatianna finally growled, snatching up the phone and taking it off speaker. "Kennedy is it? This is Tatianna, the one paying for this whole thing. If you don't get your ass through that portal, I promise that I will come through it myself and drag you here by your hair. If you delay this wedding–"

Carmen was on her feet and pulling the phone out of Tatianna's hands. "Kennedy *please*, get Jason to hold the kids and just *trust me!* You will literally be in *Moscow* in less than ten minutes!"

Deirdre exchanged glances with her hair stylist, both of whom were on the same page. *Thank goodness that wasn't me.* The young demon smiled to herself, her hand absentmindedly covering her stomach as she turned for the stylist. She was excited to see how her hair would turn out, as she was getting about a zillion braids put in at the moment.

Tatianna was about to light another cigarette when she looked over at Deirdre. She studied her for a moment before her jaw went slack, the cigarette tumbling to the floor. Deirdre's heart raced. She didn't know how, but Tatianna *knew*. She looked down and quickly yanked her hand away, Carmen was too preoccupied, pleading with her sister to take notice.

"You–" Tatiana started.

"Tatianna, please *don't!*" Deirdre hissed.

Too late. The blonde demoness was flying out of the room, her voice shrieking wildly as she bellowed out across the house.

"Oalfus Petrokov, get your miserable carcass up here NOW!"

Down below, Oalfus felt the blood drain from his face, his eyes wide as saucers as he snatched a bottle out of Viktor's hand and downed half of it.

"What the fuck have you done now?" Viktor laughed, turning to see Oalfus looking horrified.

"I'll explain later..."

Tatianna was already at the base of the stairs, brandishing a vase she was prepared to hurl at Oalfus.

"Tatianna, please–!" Oalfus pleaded, holding his hands up helplessly. She lifted it over her head, her eyes blazing red as she charged at him.

"Tati, don't ruin his suit!" Viktor called out as she was mid-swing.

She froze. Grinding her teeth so hard Oalfus could hear them, Tatiana spoke in an eerily calm tone. *"You tell me right now,"* she demanded.

"I had no idea until the Elder told me yesterday! I didn't plan this, I swear. I would never do anything to ruin this day. Why do you think

I have kept this private?" Oalfus hissed, desperate to keep his voice down. Rikovic was outside, speaking with the florist. Carmen was still fussing on the phone with her sister. They had time, but very little, to get this dealt with subtly.

"Tatiana what is going on?" Viktor asked, walking over to his wife and gently taking the vase from her. Tatiana released it without argument, her arms crossed and eyes narrowed.

"Tell him, Oalfus!" she snapped.

Something inside the old demon snapped. Tatianna was always a woman he admired, a woman he revered with respect and admiration. She was a wrath demon, viciousness and wickedness wrapped in a gorgeous package. Oalfus had told Viktor many times how he admired his brave choice in wife, but this time, she had gone too far.

Oalfus had no idea how Tatiana had found out. Perhaps she was eavesdropping while he and Deirdre had been whispering, perhaps she had asked the Elder after supper the night before, or perhaps that wicked bitch was simply too perceptive for her own good. No matter what it was, Oalfus was fed up. He was pushed to his limits with all these damn people swarming, pushed to his limits of family time after centuries of solitude, pushed to his limits with his life being upturned, and now, he finally had his fill of Tatiana and her foul temperament.

His eyes blazed with anger; it seethed out of every pore in his body. Viktor immediately backed away, yanking Tatianna in an attempt to move her, but her pride refused. She stood firm with her nose upturned.

Insolent little bitch, Oalfus thought.

He hardly spoke above a whisper, but it dripped with venom. He was *desperate* to repair the damage he had done between him and his nephews, but even Viktor knew Tatianna had gone too far. He pinched the bridge of his nose and looked the other way as Tatianna glared up at Oalfus.

"Come at me again, little demoness, and find out what comes of it. You are the wife of my nephew so I have given you your shots at me, but no more. This is your own son's wedding day, and you act like an insolent little brat? Are you trying to ruin this for your own child? I don't care what you think you know, what you want me to admit, but I will not draw an ounce of attention away from my great-nephew's wedding day to placate the demands of a loud-mouthed little bitch like you. Shut your mouth, and keep it shut!" Oalfus snapped. He then turned his blazing red eye on Viktor, who visibly shrank back. There was an order to these things. Oalfus was an ancient one. He was Old Order, and that demanded respect, no matter who it was. Tatiana had gone against him twice now, and this time, it struck a nerve. No one knew how scared the old demon was, how his whole world was spinning, and how he was struggling to wrap his mind around what was to come. He was taking this news with much more grace than anyone would likely give him credit for, but he didn't want credit. He wanted to process, he wanted to be left alone, he wanted to *leave.*

Viktor swallowed, straightening himself as his Uncle's ire was directed at him.

"I am tired of her antics, and I have hardly been here a week. Know your place, woman. Stay away from Deirdre, and stay away from me. Muzzle your bitch, Nephew."

Oalfus turned on his hoof and stormed out of the house, throwing the twin oak doors open with such force Viktor swore he heard the timbers crack. He winced when they slammed shut behind his uncle. Rubbing his forehead and sighing loudly, he turned to his wife.

"Hell have mercy, Tatiana..."

"Are you seriously going to allow him to speak to me that way?!" she shrieked.

Viktor turned to her and glowered, crossing his arms and shaking his head. She was so damn stubborn at times, it was truly a wonder the woman hadn't gotten this sort of lecture sooner.

"I do love you dearly, Tatiana, I truly do. But you have gone against my uncle far too brashly. You know your place, and I know mine. Oalfus is Old Order, he is our elder, and we must show him respect. Whatever this nonsense is about – ah, ah, not a word on it until Uncle tells me– it can wait until after the wedding. Today is about our son, not whatever gossip you are chewing on. Uncle Oalfus is trying desperately to reconnect with us. He is my only remaining immediate family, and I will not have you upsetting him anymore. Keep your mouth shut as he asked, or must I remind you of your station?"

Tatiana's perfectly manicured brow arched, her lip pursed and the anger slowly left her features. *"Exactly how might you remind me of 'my station'?"*

She knew exactly what she was doing: provoking her husband was her specialty. Viktor took the obvious bait, but not in the way she had anticipated. In a blink of an eye, she was pinned against the wall, her arms above her head and Viktor gripped her jaw to force their eyes to meet.

"Wouldn't you just love to know, my pet? Keep on running your mouth, and you might not like how I remind you. Though, if you decide to be a good little thing and scurry on back upstairs to finish preparing our soon-to-be daughter-in-law, I might consider making it a pleasant experience for you."

Tatiana's chest heaved as she looked into Viktor's eyes, his intoxicating charm encircling her whole body. It almost felt as if hands were everywhere on her at once, her legs pressing together and face burning.

She forced a smirk, though it faltered when Viktor leaned in a little closer to her. *"Using your charm is hardly fair, dear one,"* Tatiana breathed, struggling not to take another deep breath of her husband's addictive scent.

"I think it's entirely fair when dealing with as fiery of a wrath demon as you are, beloved. Now, will you be a good girl for me?" Viktor purred, his lips brushing against hers. Tatiana swallowed, nodding, and was guided away from the wall and towards the stairs, as if utterly hypnotized. She floated up the steps while Viktor smiled after her.

"That's it, such a lovely girl you are."

Tatiana normally would have thrown a vase at her husband for such a patronizing tone, but the tantalizing prospects of what would come later that night (not to mention the charm fogging her head) only left her scurrying off faster to please her husband.

"If that whole scene hadn't been so disgusting, I might be impressed with how you tamed her," Rikovic called from where he was leaning on the door frame.

Viktor turned to his son, arching a brow. *"I thought you were dealing with flowers."*

"I was until I saw my uncle storm past in such a rage I could have sworn fire was coming out his nostrils," Rikovic chuckled humorlessly.

"It probably was, your mother provoked him. Don't worry about it, he was more angry this whole thing might spoil today than whatever it is she is holding over his head. I think he just needs some air. He will be fine. He knows how much today means to you," Viktor assured his son, giving his shoulder a squeeze.

"*Remember, we must all behave,*" Rikovic said sternly to his father. "*Carmen has not seen her sister in a long time. This is just as much a family reunion as it is our wedding day. Don't make this harder than it needs to. I believe there will be...ugh, mortal children attending as well.*"

"*So...no orgy on the front lawn?*" Viktor teased, patting his son's back as he walked out onto the front steps.

"*Hell's sake, I wouldn't want that even if there were no children coming. Do you know what Mamma was up to that caused this upset?*" Ricky asked as he stepped beside his father.

They were both watching Oalfus pace angrily along the edge of the garden. He was swearing and growling in a mixture of German and Russian. Viktor was impressed he hadn't noticed the swath of *their own* family mingling in the gardens.

The gates were opening and closing non-stop now, and Viktor was pleased to see they could at least entertain themselves with greetings and idle chatting. Rikovic couldn't help but glance from his uncle to the growing crowd of extended family. As much as he viewed his family as small in number, it was far from true. Ricky had hardly maintained bonds with his extensive list of cousins, second cousins, and distant aunts and uncles. He only cared to put energy into those inside the house right now, or, in this case, fuming on the lawn. As a child, he had been subjected to socializing with the growing crowd of demons, but now, he had little interest. They were here only because they *had to be*, not because Ricky was keen to reconnect.

"*I might have an idea, but, as I told your mother, I will wait until your uncle tells us to hold any judgment. Focus on your wedding, Rikovic, not what thorn is up your uncle's arse. He will be on his best behavior for the ceremony, mark my words.*"

Ricky sighed, watching his uncle as his brows pinched together.

"I hope you're right"

Chapter Nineteen

Ricky was already outside, dressed in his fitted suit and his hair slicked back into a tight ponytail. He stood eagerly, waiting for his bride. The lawn was packed with filled folding chairs. Many faces he hardly remembered or didn't know at all; high-ranking demon weddings always drew a crowd. The aristocracy might be dead in the eyes of mortals, but demons never forget.

Broad garden hats, folding fans, over-the-top garden party dresses, and enough pearls to choke a horse were what made up most of these demonesses in the crowd. Stiff-faced and glowering male demons of all kinds had them hanging off their arms as they sat waiting for the whole ordeal to start. It was obvious who were truly connected to the family and who were simply showing up for another event. Several cousins made Ricky's brows raise, as even the Petrokovs from Serbia had attended. He was shocked to see one of his second cousins, Katya, beaming at him from the third row. He had spent several summers in Serbia with Katya and her family. Viktor and Katya's father, Konstantin, were whispering to each other like old friends. Konstantin Petrokov was more closely related to Oalfus than Viktor, and Oalfus had been more shocked than anyone to see him. It seemed two Old Order demons were still alive and well in the Petrokov family.

At the very front, huddled together and trembling, was Carmen's only remaining family. Her brother-in-law, Jason, and their two wide-eyed children were looking very much out of place among these demons. Kennedy had reminded Ricky of Carmen greatly during their very quick meeting, as she had the same face, only on a rail thin and much taller body. Jason was a labrador of some kind. His creamy brown fur was pleasant enough, but he was horribly plain and drastically underdressed. Kennedy had a very simple ankle-length sundress on, her chocolate brown hair pulled up in a bun, and her jewelry was all department store specials. Ricky hated that he could tell, but it hardly offended him; these were humble people. He would rather look their way than at all the stuffy demons glowering at him and gossiping.

Ricky was pleasantly surprised with how mildly behaved the children were. It seemed Kennedy was the quieter of the two sisters, subdued and meek. Their children took after her, and they only dared look towards Ricky, as they were clearly terrified of the other demons.

The sisters' reunion had been short, due to their arrival time. Carmen had to talk them through going into the portal, making it with only thirty minutes to spare. There was a mountain of things the sisters needed to discuss, but that would have to wait.

All eyes turned towards the big oak doors when the music started playing. There, the wedding party (or lack thereof as Oalfus and Deirdre were the only ones in said wedding party) came walking down the aisle. Thankfully, the old demon had calmed down considerably since his run in with Tatianna. His eyes seemed glued to Deirdre. He adored how beautiful she was in her dress. It made it very hard to let her go when the time came. Tatianna carried forward the ceremonial blades and gold bowl, and then came Ricky's bride.

Carmen's gown was perfect for her, simple and free as her spirit. It was entirely made of champagne-coloured lace with a simple slip underneath. It had short-capped sleeves and a babydoll neckline. The skirt started under her bust and ended just at the top of her feet. She wore pearlescent white Birkenstocks, which almost made Ricky burst into laughter when he saw them. He could not be any more in love with her than he was at that moment. Her hair was curled in a simple way, and holding her long veil was a huge crown of summer flowers. Ricky wanted to tell everyone they could leave; as far as he was concerned they were married, and he was ready to consummate.

Viktor, alongside Kennedy, walked her down the aisle holding the only photo Carmen had left of her father, placed in an incredibly gaudy and ornate Victorian frame Tatianna had insisted on. It was set on a small table beside the archway as Viktor went to take his seat.

The Elder stepped forward, which caused a small gasp to burst from Kennedy as she stood trembling beside Deirdre. The Elder was dressed in white robes, and embroidered with gold thread were all sorts of different demonic sigils, representing the binding and reforming of the married couple's lives. Carmen did her best to keep her composure when the Elder's long fingers stroked her cheek and bit her lip when he did the same eerie gesture to Ricky.

"Due to the language barrier of the bride and her family, today's ceremony will be recited in English, to the best of my abilities. Do forgive me, though, if I return to Russian at times. Some things simply can not be translated."

There was audible grumbling, and then the Elder began. The ceremony was long, but, having agreed to do this for his parents, Ricky grit his teeth and tried to keep the boredom from his face. He couldn't keep his eyes off Carmen, and neither could she keep her eyes off Ricky. They were madly in love, it was plain to anyone present.

Even Oalfus found himself smiling, in spite of the discomfort the Elder caused him. His mind began to wonder if he and Deirdre might go through such lengths. Perhaps he would indulge his bride and follow her traditions. It sounded far more interesting than all this nonsense. Perhaps it might involve less blood as well.

Oalfus grimaced when the Elder slid the blade across his palm for the binding. Oalfus had to offer his blood as a sign of protection and blessing to the couple, as did Viktor and Tatianna. Deirdre was exempt from such things, as her Fae blood might 'disrupt' the spell, so Kennedy was called in at the last minute to replace her. She was visibly horrified, but, on shaky legs, she came forward and yelped when her hand was cut. Snickers passed over the crowd. Oalfus could not hide his distaste and glared out towards the audience. Silence quickly returned.

Finally, after what felt like an eternity, the ceremony was finished, and the Elder held his hands above his head as a swirling red orb formed between them.

"With this final act of binding, the blood of our Bride and Bridegroom, and that of their families, shall come together to form a new sigil. One that connects to both their souls, one that shall act as the final element of their union."

The red orb expanded slowly, patterns flowing through it, and a new portal sigil was created. Ricky held up Carmen's cut palm beside his as the Elder lowered the sigil and pressed it over their open hands.

"Just as a sigil binds to the demon it belongs to, this sigil will bind to both of you and in turn bind you to each other. It is with great pleasure that I might introduce to you all for the first time, the newest branch of the Petrokov tree, Rikovic and Carmen Petrokov."

It was done, and Ricky could no longer contain himself. He wrapped Carmen in his arms and spun her around as he kissed her. It was a ghastly display of emotion to many in the crowd, but to Ricky, it was exactly how he felt. He cradled Carmen tightly to him, their mouths melting together and Carmen's arms wrapped snugly around Ricky's neck. Music began to play and everyone waited only a moment before turning towards the cocktail hour that was beginning in the large tent set up in the larger garden.

"C-congratulations," Kennedy said meekly from a safe distance.

Ricky and Carmen finally pulled themselves apart, turning towards their family gathering around them.

"Thank you, Kennedy," Carmen giggled, straightening her dress and flower crown.

"It's nice to see you so happy. I just hope—"

"Kennedy!" Jason said sharply, pushing a stiff smile and shaking his head.

"What? Am I not allowed to ever talk about it?"

"Honey, now ain't the best time."

Carmen tensed. Maybe inviting her sister had been a mistake. Ricky reached for her hand, giving her a gentle squeeze before he spoke in a little icier of a tone than he had intended.

"Well, seeing as I helped Carmen...*deal* with her last husband, I can assure you that I have no intention of slapping her around or breaking glass over her head. I have had my fill of patching up my wife, thank you."

Oalfus and Viktor exchanged smirks. The absolutely horrified looks on the mortal's faces was priceless.

Carmen sucked in a breath and forced a smile, looking at her sister. "Glad nothing has changed. Come on, Ricky. I'm pretty sure we have photographs to take, and this fucker charges by the hour."

As they turned to leave, Carmen heard Kennedy give her signature little scoff, and she froze. Ricky arched a brow as he glanced back at the woman, wondering if he had misjudged her.

"By the looks of this place, that is the least of their concerns," Kennedy half-ass whispered to Jason, who looked about as impressed with her as Carmen was.

"You haven't changed a fuckin' bit. You always have to get the last word in, don't you, Kenny? Well guess what? Not all of us can be the perfect little stepford wife and have the picket fence and two kids. You seriously–"

"*Milaya*, as much as I love seeing you this fired up, it is our wedding day. Let's just go take our photos now, hm? No fighting, not today."

He cupped her face, kissing her forehead and nodded for them to walk away. Carmen took a slow breath and nodded back, following Ricky over to where the photographer was waiting. Oalfus made sure the mortals were aware that they were not welcome, glowering at them when they lingered. They scurried off quickly when he snorted at them, Deirdre hiding her giggle.

"I am so glad I don't have a sister to fight with like that. Poor Carmen..." Deirdre said as she and Oalfus turned to stand and wait to take their photos with the couple.

"I fought like that with my brother. I regret never mending things with him. I imagine Kennedy will as well, when she starts to notice Carmen isn't aging anymore," Oalfus said darkly.

"Are all your people's weddings that long, by the way?" Deirdre said, trying to change the subject to something lighter.

"Unfortunately, most of our class are forced into them, yes. Elders catch wind of weddings quickly. The only way they could have avoided this whole affair was by doing it in America, but Tatianna, I am sure, would have thrown a fit," Oalfus said dryly, but a smirk toyed the corner of his mouth as he looked down at Deirdre. He reached around her shoulders and pulled her close to his side, stroking his hand over the back of her head.

"Why do you ask, *Liebchien*?"

"I might fall asleep if ours is so long," Deirdre said nonchalantly, but the squeak at the end of her words gave her true feelings away. She was testing the waters, and Oalfus was rather fond of it. His chuckle was a low rumble, leaning down and nuzzling her cheek slowly.

"I suppose I ought to make an honest woman of you sooner rather than later, but perhaps your mind might change. Let's not rush such things, hm?"

"I won't change my mind, but I agree about taking our time." This time, her voice left no room for interpretation: she was serious.

"Whatever pleases you, *mein Liebchen.*"

The photographs went by easily. Carmen was radiant, and Rikovic beamed in each one, which was a far cry from the stern expressions and frowns he usually wore in photographs. Even Oalfus found himself smiling with genuine happiness, and laughing heartily at the series of foolish photos he took with his family.

Having stood well over a foot taller than both his nephews, the photographer suggested photos of Rikovic cradled bridal-style in Oalfus' arms. They both outright refused initially, but when both Deirdre and Carmen howled with laughter and insisted they do it, both men broke down. At first, they were rigid, unsmiling, and stubborn, but soon, the foolishness of it all came over them and they were laughing and making the photos what they were intended to be: pure joy.

Cocktail hour came and went. Carmen avoided Kennedy for the rest of the evening and dinner was served. Oalfus could not recall the last time he felt so at ease with his family. He hardly noticed the crowd of demons in the tent with them. It certainly helped having a gorgeous little demoness at his side with her delicate hand resting on his leg. He kept his arm around her shoulders through the whole night, his fingers in her hair or her head on his shoulder.

Oalfus had even tolerated conversation with the only family member he recognized. Konstantin Petrokov was just as formidable a sight as Oalfus, nearly identical in height and build, though his fur was a pale silvery colour and his horns shorter and sharper. Dierdre couldn't help but admire the demoness on his arm. She looked like a sheep of some kind. Her curvaceous figure and perfectly groomed hair and wool made her look unfairly beautiful.

"I am shocked to see you, Oalfus," Konstantin mused, smirking in a charming way as he glanced at Deirdre. "Such a young beauty you have found as well. Where have you been hiding all this time, cousin? We thought you dead."

Oalfus looked down at Deirdre with pride, rubbing her shoulder before looking back to his cousin. "Germany, mostly. Honestly, Konstantin, I am shocked you're still alive. Time certainly has been kind to you and Milica."

"My wife and the cold of Serbia keep me young. My daughters, as well. Have you met our youngest? Katya was born not long before you disappeared like smoke on the wind." Konstantin could not keep the sneer from his voice; it seemed many took Oalfus' reclusive nature personally.

"I recall little Katya, though she does not seem so little now," Oalfus noted, looking over to where she was chatting away with Ricky and Carmen. Deirdre followed his gaze, her brows shooting up and her eyes widening. The girl looked to be about her age, if not younger. She had bright yellow eyes and a baby face, her white curly fur clipped short and two long pale blonde braids hung well past her shoulders.

"She is beautiful," Deirdre spoke without thinking.

"She looks just like her mother," Konstantin mused, grinning down at his wife.

"She has her good nature as well," Olafus teased, smirking at Konstantin.

Though the man was grinning, his eyes were cold no matter what mood he was in. Deirdre thought him far more intimidating that Oalfus ever had been. They mingled a little longer, though Oalfus was glad when they finally let them be. The dance was next, and his nerves were growing frayed. While it was pleasant enough to be with his family, he was eager for this night to end.

The dance went off without a hitch. Rikovic had truly been touched by the effort his new bride had put in. Pride radiated off him as he danced by her side and twirled her all around the dance floor in the choreographed number. Then came the time for their first dance as bride and groom. Carmen snorted and threw her head back in laughter as the song 'Ballroom Blitz' came over the loudspeakers.

"You didn't!" she howled, laughing away as the pair danced wildly to the upbeat song. Oalfus later learned that had been the first song the pair had ever danced to together, though it didn't change his lackluster opinion of the tune.

Deirdre was all Oalfus could think of as the night wore on, her quiet way of watching the events around her enraptured him. Her brilliant green eyes shone with joy, the way the shaggier fur on her upper lip turned upwards as she laughed and sang along to songs. He adored her. He was absolutely and undoubtedly in love with her, and every inch of him longed to make her his.

As the night wore on and the songs became slower, Oalfus guided Deirdre on the dance floor willingly for the first time that night. An instrumental of some modern love song came on, he couldn't name it, but it was slow and sweet to his ears. He wanted to dance with her, to hold her, and feel alone with her, even in this tent full of other beings. Deirdre lay her head against his chest, listening to the steady rhythm of his heart beat. They swayed in a simple box step, Oalfus cradling her head against his chest. Finally, he hooked a finger under her chin, tilting her head up towards him as he lay a brief kiss on her lips.

"What was that for?" Deirdre giggled, brushing her fingers over her lips.

"Must I have a reason to kiss you?" he purred back.

"No, I suppose not," she smiled softly, squeezing his hand.

"In all of Europe, where have you not been to yet?" Oalfus asked suddenly.

"Switzerland was supposed to be after Germany, though I haven't finished with Germany yet. I wanted to go further into the mountains. I also still want to explore Russia. I have hardly seen anything of Moscow or been to St.Petersburg," she replied with giddiness in her voice.

"I used to be of the opinion that St.Petersburg was a shit hole, but it has been nearly five centuries since I was there. Perhaps it is better now," Oalfus ruminated.

"We will just have to find out for ourselves, won't we?" Deirdre mused, wiggling a brow at him.

"I suppose we shall. However, if we are to continue traveling as you have been, I will need some supplies for our journey. Perhaps I can convince Tatianna to take us on one last shopping trip, though I suspect this one will bore her to tears. If it isn't high fashion, Tati tends to throw a fit."

"She can stay home. I never needed anyone to find things for me before. You can speak Russian, at least. That will make things go quickly," Deirdre spoke with contagious confidence.

"You would go into places blindly? No previous plan?" Oalfus looked surprised.

Deirdre only laughed. "Of course! That's half the fun."

"I fear what would have become of you if you had come to Russia alone," Oalfus grumbled.

"Bah, that's what they said about Germany, and look how well I have done!" Deirdre beamed up at him.

"Didn't the townspeople tell you to run for the hills?" he asked, arching a brow.

"They did, and I did as they told me. I found you, didn't I?" She arched her own brow in return. Oalfus laughed, sighing contentedly as the song ended. He led Deirdre off the dance floor towards the tent opening.

"Come, walk with me," he said gently. She was more than happy to oblige. In fact, she was prepared to follow him all over Europe and back.

Chapter Twenty

Deirdre and Oalfus walked together in silence. The music was still blaring out of the tent as the pair walked deeper into the gardens. Deirdre huddled closer to Oalfus' side, her shawl pulled tightly around her arms. Oalfus smirked, shrugging off his suit jacket and setting it over her shoulders. Even though she drowned in it, he did enjoy how she looked wearing something he knew belonged to him.

The old demon sighed, tugging loose the tie around his neck, opening the top three buttons on his shirt, and pulling out the cufflinks as he pushed up his sleeves to his elbows.

Deirdre watched him with her heart pounding in her ears. Something about this side of him was so gorgeous and so modelesque she could hardly believe he was hers. He looked stunning. Her fingers ached for the camera she had crammed into the small purse at her hip. The product in his hair had lost its bond throughout the night, stray stands of his silvery charcoal fell over his eyes as he pulled a glossy metal case from his pocket.

Deirdre almost let her jaw fall when she saw Oalfus pull out a cigarette and lighter from the sleek cigarette case. Oalfus had never smoked in front of her. However, it suited him, much like it suited Viktor and Rikovic. She felt her cheeks warm, watching him intently as he placed the cigarette between his lips and flick the zippo to life. The warm glow cast over his face made for the most perfect photograph, and Deirdre could not stand to miss her chance.

"Wait!" she gasped, scrambling to grab her purse. She had been forced to take the lens off the camera to fit it inside her purse.

"What?" Oalfus asked, a little baffled by her sudden urgency. He smirked when he saw her pull her camera free of the little silk bag.

"You looked–" she paused, her tail wagging and ears tipping back as she slid the lens into place and twisted it to lock on. "You looked so handsome just now...c-could you hold the lighter again?" Deirdre muttered, hiding the lower half of her face behind her camera.

"Like this?" Oalfus purred, smirking as he lit the zippo once more. He could see her lift the camera towards him, lifting onto her toes and letting out a little huff. Without a word, he lowered down to his knee and glanced upwards directly into the camera lens. Deirdre gasped, her eyes wide for a moment before she leaned in and clicked the shutter. Oalfus smiled to himself, tucking the lighter away and rising to his feet once more. Her camera clicked several more times as he breathed out a cloud of smoke.

"You're so handsome..." Deirdre whispered, slowly lowering her camera as she looked up at him with adoration.

Oalfus sputtered, coughing up his smoke as he looked down at her. She was brutally honest at times. He adored this about her, but it never made it any less shocking to hear.

"You are the only one to think so, *mien Liebchien.*"

"Most folk don't have the eye for true beauty" she shrugged, looping her camera faithfully around her neck as she tugged his jacket a little tighter around her. "Why are you smoking?" she finally asked.

"An old habit. I only do it when I am in the city, it seems. I surprised myself when I asked Viktor for some of his cigarettes just before the wedding. Tatianna finally got under my skin, I suppose."

Deirdre could have taken an entire roll worth of photographs that night, and all of them would have been of her beautiful Krampus. She trailed her fingers along the edge of his jacket, speaking in a small voice.

"I tried to stop her. I am sorry."

Oalfus stopped, shaking his head and turning to face his little demoness. He lowered onto one knee and pulled her in close to his chest.

"You are not to blame. I dealt with Tatianna and her big mouth. You are perfect, and I am sorry if you feel any discomfort because of this. I promise you, I will take care of you and our child. You will never be alone in this."

Deirdre slid her arms around his neck, sliding her fingers up into his hair and kissing him fiercely. Oalfus groaned, wrapping her tightly in his arms as he lifted her up off the ground. He consumed her, wrapped her in every inch of him. She adored how he encompassed every part of her in just his embrace.

"Let's go up to our room now. We have played our part," Oalfus whispered, kissing down Deirdre's neck and along her shoulder.

"Won't that upset Ricky?" Deirdre gasped, fisting Oalfus' hair and biting back her moans as his tongue trailed over her throat.

"He will get over it."

Whisking her off into the house, Oalfus rushed the stairs in twos and shouldered open their guest room door. Deirdre giggled wildly when Oalfus threw her onto the bed, yanking his tie off and pulling his shirt off. He flashed a wide grin at her, nodding towards her.

"Get that dress off, sweetling," Oalfus growled, his eye glowing faintly as he looked over her laying sprawled on the bed.

"Help me unzip it?" she asked innocently, rolling onto her front and kicking off her heels.

Oalfus growled, crawling onto the edge of the bed and straddling her hips. Deirdre squealed under his weight, looking back at him with a wide smile.

"With pleasure, *mein Liebchen.*"

Oalfus felt his cock strain against his pants as he slowly pulled the zipper down, licking his lips as he watched the silk fall away from her body. Deirdre had such a tantalizing shape, a delicious set of wide hips and precious little rolls of chub down her back. He groaned, running his hands under the material to hook around her midsection and pull her free of the dress. He grasped her stomach, pushing his nose against her throat as he moaned, feeling her bare body under his touch. His hips pushing against her plush ass, grinding slowly and moaning against her ear as he eased her down to the bed. Deirdre lifted her backside up against him. Feeling his heavy length pressing against her sent a flair of courage through her body. She loved how he reacted so freely to her; he seemed entranced by her and it filled her with desire, knowing he wanted her as badly as she wanted him.

She wiggled under him, rolling onto her back so she could run her hands down his chest. Oalfus let out a rattled growl as she dug her fingers into his clipped fur, his eyes closing and head falling forward.

"*Liebchen*, it is hardly fair what you do to me," he groaned, rocking his hips forward so he could grind his bulge against her lower stomach.

"Well, how about I take care of that for you?" she whispered, running her hands lower and gripping his length through his pants. A dark stain was already forming where his head was pressed firmly against the front of his hip. Oalfus growled as she ran her hand along his length, rubbing firmly over the outline of the spines along the belly of his cock. He sucked in a sharp breath, fisting the bedsheets beside her and panting from her touch.

"Be merciful. I will be spent if you keep that up," he panted, peering up at her with his blazing red eye.

She giggled, leaning forward and pressing her lips against his as she worked to free him of his pants. She held her hand at the ready, waiting to receive his length in her grip once he was free. Tracing her fingers over the gold ring still snug on his base, her mouth peppered kisses down his neck and chest, until she found her target. She took the gold ring hanging from his nipple between her teeth and gave it a tug, which immediately had Oalfus snarling and pinning her to the bed. Deirdre giggled, his big tail lashing behind him and thumping against the floor and bed.

"You play a dangerous game, sweetling," Oalfus snarled, grinding the head of his cock against her stomach.

"I like dangerous games," Deirdre said a little more boldly, her eyes darkening and her bright emerald eyes shifting to dazzling ruby red. Her braids were now tumbling out and hairpins scattered on the bed below her as thick green vines sprouted from her head and began crawling up along Oalfus' arms where he held her. He watched in utter fascination before letting out a loud gasp and looking down where several had coiled around his cock.

"This is new," he purred, trailing his fingers along one of the vines. He arched a brow at her as they continued to coil around him and seemed to tug him in closer. His cock was notched against her eager entrance, her hips lifting to meet him with an eagerness he was glad to see.

"They like you," Deirdre said shyly, her eyes hidden behind hooded lids.

Oalfus smirked, pushing the head of his length inside. Her head fell back as the first spine popped inside her folds. Grinning wickedly, Oalfus pushed harder and bucked once into her. She yelped and arched her back as he forced himself inside.

"Oalfus!"

"That's my girl, so eager to take me inside. No wonder my seed took so quickly. You are desperate for me inside you, aren't you, sweetling?"

"Yes! Oalfus, please!" Deirdre whimpered, her vines curling around his back and hips now.

"So needy," Oalfus growled, hooking his arms under her and lifting her against his chest. He spun around and fell back onto the bed, holding her hips as he bucked up into her hard. She was straddling his hips now, bracing herself against his chest.

"Work those gorgeous hips, sweetling," Oalfus purred, running his hands over her supple thighs.

Deirdre whimpered, leaning forward to lift her hips. Oalfus sucked in a breath as she began to work his length. He struggled to keep still, eager to watch her worship his cock. The desire to ravage her was boiling just under the surface. He refused to keep his hands off her, massaging her little breasts and tugging on her nipples. He trailed his hands further, gripping her throat and squeezing. Her body arched, her eyes fluttering closed as she struggled to take a breath under his grip.

"That's it, that's my good girl," he breathed, groping at her hips and urging her along.

Deirdre sucked in a greedy breath as he released her throat, falling forward against his chest and bouncing her hips as quickly as she could. Oalfus grit his teeth; the way she clung to him and worked his length, he was near ready to finish. It was agonizing, but eventually, he pulled her off him, grunting and flipping her onto her stomach as he looked down at her.

Deirdre peeked at him over her shoulder and raised her hips, her tail wagging as she let her hand slip down between her thighs and spread herself open for him.

"Please...I need you inside me," she whimpered.

He came undone. Caging her under him and pinning her against the mattress, he forced himself to the hilt inside her. One single thrust had the head of his cock bashing against her deepest inner walls. She screamed his name, her hands fisting the sheets. She braced against the headboard as he began his final relentless barrage on her.

He bit down on the back of her neck, snarling loudly as he felt his peak coming quickly. He shuddered on his final thrust, groaning in such a raw and guttural way that it nearly sounded painful to Deirdre. His head fell forward against the headboard as he let his jets of cum paint her insides. His claws dug into her hips and he bit the skin under her fur.

Glorious as it was to stay like this, he knew she needed her release as well. He forced himself to reach down between her legs and find her sensitive little pearl. She yelped when he circled it at first, shocked at the sudden sensation, then melted against the bed. He was still buried inside her, rocking his hips slowly to keep his seed planted firmly inside her, but his fingers were relentless.

"That's it, sweetling. Make those pretty little moans for me, I want to hear all of your desires."

She rocked into his fingers, her moaning turning frantic as he continued to work her clit with rigor. She was so close. His rocking turned into sharp bucks that matched each of her yelped moans. She shattered, screaming his name, and pleading for him to never stop. Begging for more of him, whimpering, and trembling until her cries finally died down and they turned to sobs.

She was crying, but it wasn't from pain or sorrow. It was from how *fucking* incredible it felt. Oalfus nuzzled her cheek, licking away her tears and soothing her. He couldn't feel an ounce of fear or pain radiating from her; he knew she was simply overwhelmed with the sensation, and, quite frankly, he was proud to have done it to her.

"Such a perfect girl you are," he purred, easing himself out of her slowly.

"Dont take it out, not yet," she gasped, clutching the pillow to her chest.

"You are already pregnant, *Liebchen,*" Oalfus teased, but he obeyed her. Rolling her gently onto her side, he cradled around her.

"I know...I just want to stay close to you," she whispered.

Oalfus smiled to himself, wrapping her tightly in his arms and pressing his nose into her neck. "I don't deserve your love," he murmured, kissing her once more.

"Yes, you do, and so much more," she mumbled, her words slurring as sleep was already taking its hold. Oalfus allowed his eyes to droop, sighing with content as he held his precious little demoness in his arms.

Chapter Twenty One

Oalfus groaned happily in his sleep, arching his back. In his dreams, Deirdre was sitting astride his cock and working herself into a frenzy. Had it not been for the sudden cry of pleasure that snapped his eyes open, Oalfus would have swore it was the most glorious dream. However, it was his reality. Instead of Deirdre simply riding him with a vigor unlike anything she had ever shown him, the whole room was covered in her vines. Her arms were tangled into them above her head and, when Oalfus' wits returned, he realized his legs were bound down to the bed and his arms to the headboard.

Then the overpowering scent hit him: the charm of a female lust demon. Mixed with the deep smokey-spiced scent undeniably belonging to Rikovic, a honey-sweet ambrosia smell had practically filled the entire house. Oalfus groaned as he became even more aware of it, a wild heady sensation dulling his better judgment and flooding his mind with desire.

Deirdre was completely lost in it. Her head had fallen back and a cascade of curls and vines were bouncing with her vigorous riding of him. Female lust demons were a class all of their own. While male demons were capable of heavy charms, female lust demons had a particularly strong one. Males could coax desire from those they use their charm on, encouraging the desire in their target to bubble to the surface. Females, however, forced the desire they felt onto everyone around them via their charm. It was like a drug, addictive and all consuming.

Oalfus was an ancient one, Old Order, so he had more strength to fight off this assault of charm flooding into their room. The trouble was, he was buried inside his mate, causing his better judgment to be thrown out the window. He ground his teeth, unable to budge under Deirdre's remarkably strong vines.

In any other situation, this would be alarming. Certainly, for someone looking in on them, they might be terrified at the literal jungle growing in their room, but Oalfus felt his mind melting under such circumstances. It seemed there was much more to this little demoness than he originally had thought. As he finally tore his eyes from her to look down at what she was doing, he was shocked to see the absolute mess she had already created. He had finished inside her twice, at the very least, based on the state of them both, and that realization made it very clear this could become dangerous if Deirdre continued to be exposed to this much charm. There were two experienced lust demons in the house, both of whom Oalfus could smell their charm.

Viktor's scent was much less prevalent; he must be far away from this mess. It finally dawned on him where this was coming from: *Carmen.* The Elder said she had *absorbed* the half of Rikovic's soul she had been wearing due to its corruption. Rikovic was a lust demon. It only made sense she was, at least in some part, a lust demon. If Carmen was the one causing this...oh Hell have mercy, she was in a state of *frenzy.* It was likely her first frenzy, which could spell disaster if Deirdre remained here any longer. Oalfus struggled harder now, snarling as he managed to tear his arm free and reach up to Deirdre.

"Deirdre, Deirdre, can you hear me?" He shook her slightly, though it was becoming much more difficult to focus as she let out a cry of pleasure. Every little touch was setting her off. She came once more on his length.

"*For the love of–*" Oalfus growled, and managed to push her off him.

A little realization came to her. She let out a whimper and looked at his face as if noticing he was there for the first time.

"Oalfus?"

"Let me up, *Liebchen.* We need to get you away from here right away." Oalfus tried not to sound worried as he tore his other arm free with some force. Deirdre winced when his claws cut through some of her vines, yelping in pain. Oalfus' eyes widened as the realization hit him: the pain cleared more of the haze from her mind. Deirdre looked mortified, her hands covering her mouth as she looked around the room.

"I haven't lost control like this since I was a little girl..." she whispered, covering her face with her hands as her vines quickly retracted back to her body. "Oalfus I am so sorry. I–I don't know what–"

"Don't worry about this, it isn't your fault. I think this might be because of Carmen," Oalfus said as he finally got to his feet and pulled on his discarded dress pants from the night before. He would clean them both up later when it was safe to come back into the house.

"What's going on?" Deirdre asked, the glazed look coming back to her face as she swayed and fell against him. Her legs were spent, she was exhausted and likely going to be *very* sore later.

Oalfus saw one of her sundresses crumpled on the floor. It was easy enough for him to slip it onto her before he scooped her up and opened the door of their room. It was much worse in the hallway. Oalfus groaned as he pressed Deirdre's face against his chest and his own nose into her hair. It was most certainly coming from Rikovic and Carmen's room down the hall. The feral noises echoing in the hallway were all too telling. Oalfus rushed down the stairs, and, just as he was about to head for the door, one of the house staff called him.

"Master Oalfus, Master Viktor and Lady Tatianna are taking their breakfast in the back greenhouse to stay away from...the current state of the house."

It was Safiya. She had a cloth tied over her mouth and nose as she waved for them to follow her. She pulled out a small bottle from her apron pocket and poured the clear liquid onto a cloth as she handed it to Oalfus.

"For Miss Deirdre. This will help clear her head," Safiya explained as they made it out the back kitchen door to the pathway leading to the greenhouse.

Oalfus held it over Deirdre's muzzle until she nodded and was able to hold it herself. It was likely a mixture of salt and rainwater, purifiers that helped dispel the effects of charms. Oalfus was glad for the fresh air, taking a deep breath and sighing with relief as his mind began to clear. He ducked into the greenhouse and nodded his thanks to Safiya.

Inside, Tatianna was nursing a headache, from the looks of her, the unfortunate side effects of being a non-lust demon and being exposed to that much charm. Deirdre wouldn't be far off from that now, but simple things like modern medicine would also help greatly. Safiya came prepared, placing a white plastic bottle on the table before dismissing herself. Tatianna hardly noticed the pair; she quickly opened the cap and shook two little blue pills into her hand.

"Bless the mortal who invented Ibuprofen," she mumbled, tossing them back with a gulp of her coffee.

"You look like hell," Oalfus chuckled, setting Deirdre down at one of the chairs at the bistro set where Tatianna was taking her breakfast.

"I feel it, and I am sure poor Deirdre will shortly, based on how ragged you both look. I think I nearly killed Viktor last night," Tatianna groaned, rubbing her head. For once, she was not polished, not perfect or pristine; she looked like a middle-aged woman hung over from a wild night of sex and alcohol. Oalfus tried not to laugh. Instead, he picked up the ornate coffee pot on the side cart and topped up Tati's cup, patting the woman's shoulder. He then filled Deirdre's cup and his own.

"You'll survive. I am sure he was hardly disappointed with such a turn of events," Oalfus mused, easing himself gingerly onto the cast iron chair beside Deirdre.

"You two certainly ran off early last night," Tatianna said with an arched brow, though her smug look quickly melted off due to her discomfort.

"You know I never liked those big gatherings. Be glad I stayed as late as I did," Oalfus huffed.

Deirdre wretched when she lifted her cup to her lips, covering her mouth with a wide eyed look of utter embarrassment. Suddenly, she was on her feet, bolting for the door. She nearly knocked

Viktor onto his backside as she pushed past him and turned the corner. The unmistakable sound of her becoming sick made them all wince collectively. Viktor and Tatianna then turned and looked at Oalfus with an expression that made him feel two inches tall.

He sighed, his shoulders slumped and he looked down at the table.

"I suppose there is no hiding it..." he muttered.

"I knew it!" Tatianna shrieked, then winced and held her head.

"You deserve that," Oalfus growled, but she was right.

Viktor arched a brow at him, looking disappointed. *"You really got that girl pregnant?"*

"I didn't even think it was possible, I never would have—" he stopped himself before the lie came out. He put his head in his hands and sighed. *"I didn't plan to do this, and I certainly had no intention of overshadowing Rikovic's day with this news. The Elder told us the day before last. Neither of us had any idea."*

"How could you not think this would happen, Uncle? You are both demons." Viktor shook his head; he almost felt as though he was lecturing his own son.

"I never imagined my seed would still take...I have never—" he growled in a low tone, his ears splaying back in embarrassment. *"I have never been with another demon. She is new order, I didn't think such things would be...compatible."*

"Well, clearly, there is more in this world than we know. Take, for instance, my new daughter-in-law," Viktor chuckled, rolling his eyes.

"A half-lust demon now I suppose, or maybe all? I can't even step foot into my own house without shifting," Viktor mused, stretching his lower back and letting out a grunt of discomfort.

"I take it we all woke up to unexpected activity," Oalfus muttered, trying to hide his smirk.

"Rather lovely, no?" Viktor teased, sitting beside Tatianna and running his clawed fingers through her hair. As weary as she was, she couldn't help but smile and lean against his side.

"Yes, though I can't say being covered in vines was expected. That girl has more power than she lets on," Oalfus half said to himself. Deirdre appeared in the doorway of the greenhouse, wiping her mouth and grimacing.

"Come here, poor girl," Oalfus cooed, holding his arms out to her. She whimpered, crawling into his lap and hiding against him.

"Take these," Tatianna offered her two of the pills she had taken while Viktor poured her a glass of water.

"Rise your mouth first. Just spit it into the plants, it won't hurt them," Viktor chuckled.

"We have had enough garden parties in here in the past that the plants are likely wondering where all the alcohol and vomit have gone over the last century."

"Viktor, don't be vile," Tatianna grumbled.

"Oh please, like you haven't been a part of that," Oalfus teased.

Deirdre smiled, despite the terrible taste in her mouth. It was nice to see him settled into this playful banter. He seemed calmer somehow. The anxiety he had felt on their arrival only a week ago felt like a distant memory. Even holding her hair back while she rinsed her mouth, he made jokes with Viktor.

Tatianna kept her eyes on Deirdre in a strange way, which Deirdre chalked up to her knowing what was going on. The men didn't seem phased by the overabundance of charm, scarfing back their breakfast with vigor. Tatianna and Deirdre, meanwhile, struggled to keep toast down. Oalfus explained that the effects of the charm would likely have her off her feet all day, and that going into the house was absolutely off limits, but Deirdre was desperate to clean herself off.

"I think we still have the old wooden tubs in the storage room. Perhaps I can have Safiya get some water boiling. Oalfus, would you mind helping pull them out?" Viktor offered.

As the pair made for the house Viktor whispered to him. *"I knew keeping them was a good idea. Who knew it would be my son fucking his wife that would give me an excuse to have a bath with my wife in the greenhouse again."*

"You've done this before?" Oalfus mused, arching a brow.

"Christmas of 1918. Got Tatianna drunk enough she would half-look at me. It was right after Rikovic went AWOL"

"She blamed you for that, did she?" Oalfus muttered as they went around the back of the house where there were a set of large doors that led to the cellar.

Viktor hauled the doors open and immediately, the scent of Carmen's ambrosial charm made them both growl. Viktor's straight horns doubled in length and curled around his ear, a tall prong splitting off near the front curve. His canines elongated well past his chin and his eyes shone bright red. He looked scruffier, his fur along his jaw shaggier, and there was a wildness to him that reminded Oalfus painfully of his brother.

"You look just like your father." Oalfus hadn't meant to let the thought out, and he quickly turned his gaze to the ground as they descended the steps.

"You mean I look like you?" Viktor chuckled, glancing over at his uncle. His smile slipped when he saw the pain in Oalfus' eyes. Viktor was not overly sentimental with the men in his family; he struggled to soften around them. However, in his attempts to re-

pair the tattered relationship with his son, he had found the task a little easier.

As they sifted through the crammed storage area searching for the old fashioned wooden tubs, Viktor finally found his courage.

"You know this will always be your home as well, Uncle."

"What are you going on about?" Oalfus failed at forcing a dry laugh, his back turned as he pushed another stack of boxes aside.

*"You don't have to stay in Germany anymore. You could come back. I don't know what your plans are but...you could stay with us. It would be nice, having my only living family close again. Tatianna is already talking about going off to visit her brothers in St. Petersburg. She even wants to go to visit the one in Paris. I envy her, in a way. I know I have Rikovic, but...he is not **mine**. He is our son, but you..."*

Viktor stopped moving boxes for a moment. He ran his thumb over the lid of the box he was holding as he struggled to find his words.

*"You are **my** family, my only close family left. I would very much enjoy having you nearby again. You know, it's foolish: I raised Rikovic to believe demons were above mortals. I raised him to think we did not need such trifling things as emotional bonds with family. Perhaps I only taught him such things because—"*

"You watched everyone in our family die or flee to the far corners of the world," Oalfus finished for him, the pain in his voice evident. His ears were tipped back and his shoulders drawn up tightly. He swallowed and audibly struggled to get his words out. Viktor nearly dropped the box in his hands when he heard Oalfus stifle a sob, his hand shooting up to cover his mouth.

"I hid all those years...I hid away because I could not bear the thought of watching...watching that sweet little boy my brother brought into this world die like he did. Then Rikovic was born and that fear only worsened.

He was so tiny, so small and fragile. I always thought you were so very small. Somehow, the bulk in our ancient blood didn't pass onto you and it made me so afraid of what might come. My brother and your mother were wiped out in a single night, your sister..." Oalfus croaked out his words.

"*Hardly four months old when they burned the house down,*" Viktor finished solemnly

"*I never should have turned my back on you two. I will live the rest of my life regretting my actions.*"

"*Then why not come back, settle down here? The property is big enough, we could have a second house built beyond the gardens for you and–*"

"*Viktor, you truly honor me with such an offer, but I already promised Deirdre I would go traveling with her*" Oalfus said quietly, looking over his shoulder at his nephew.

"*Where?*"

"*Everywhere, it would seem. She was traveling all over Europe when she stumbled onto my cottage. Now that I have put a child inside her, she has less time than ever to continue her journey. Her kind are also bound to their homeland. When her parents pass, she is duty bound to return to Ireland and take up their position.*"

"*Will you go with her when the time comes?*" Viktor almost feared the answer.

"*If that is what she wishes, yes. I will follow her until the ends of the earth.*" Oalfus spoke with unwavering confidence. He turned to face his nephew and gave him a gentle smile, placing his hands on the younger demon's shoulders. "*And a gate will always remain open for you, no matter what comes. I will never hide from my family again, I promise.*"

A deliriously giddy voice called from the cellar doors. The speech was slurred and cackling like a hyena between words.

"*What the hell are you two doing down there?!*" Ricky called, leaning sloppily against the doorway.

"*Oh great...*" Viktor groaned, finally spotting the wooden tubs under a covered sheet. He and Oalfus pulled two of them out, both of them exchanging weary glances as they approached Ricky, who was sitting in the grass with his wings splayed out behind him. He rolled his head to the side, a stupid grin on his face as he arched a brow at them. He looked drunk, but it was likely just his ridiculous indulgence in lust with Carmen.

"*What are you doing with those?*" Ricky snickered. His hair had long since fallen out of his pony tail and his tattered jeans were pulled on, but not yet buttoned or zipped.

"*You two made the house inaccessible, so we are improvising,*" Viktor sneered, kicking the cellar doors shut.

"*Were you crying, Uncle?*" Ricky looked a little more sober now, his eyes wide.

"*Shut up. Make yourself useful and go ask Safiya to heat some water,*" Oalfus grumbled.

Chapter Twenty Two

The greenhouse felt like a tropical rainforest with the two tubs filled with hot water. Condensation trickled down the high glass walls and steam fogged the domed roof. The flowers were not yet in bloom for the season, but the heavy floral oils in the water made the whole place feel much more exotic.

Oalfus shuddered as he lowered himself into the hot bath, water sloshing over the sides of the tub. He let out a deeply contented sigh. It was already a hugely oversized tub, but in order for Deirdre to fit in with him, he had to keep his knees bent or stretch his legs over the sides.

Deirdre seemed relieved to finally be getting clean. She melted against Oalfus as he insisted on cleaning her off. She had gone through so much with him in such little time, it was truly the least he could do. The greenhouse was an enormous place. Pathways and massive tropical plants that were several centuries old created much privacy for the two couples.

Viktor was curled up with Tatianna on his chest, his fingers trailing patterns on her back as she half-dozed laying against him. It had been a very long time since the two had been this intimate.

They had been having sex, of course, but this was a new level of closeness.

An ease had washed over Tatianna last night during the reception. Viktor had caught his wife having a private moment outside the tent, weeping alone. She had practically thrown herself into his arms and sobbed how it was all finally happening. How their family was coming back together, and that it had been all she had ever wanted. Viktor had confessed that it had been his desire, too, and now his wife was leaning against him and cuddling against him with ease.

That morning had been glorious, though he knew the charm had taken its toll on Tatianna. She was still a fierce wrath demon, tough as nails and vicious when she wanted to, but there was no denying that she was fragile in some ways. She had pushed herself hard as a dancer in her youth, and, even for a demon, there was irreversible damage from those long years of pushing her physical limits.

That morning, Tatianna had woken him up with oral, which had turned into her riding him, and then him getting much too rough with her. He had pinned her by her horn, taking her from behind until she whimpered in pain between his thrusts. It was only when he had finally torn himself away from her that he realized how much the charm was affecting him. She had not once complained or scolded him; they had just hastily dressed and rushed out to the greenhouse.

Now, she was curled up like his delicate little ballerina in his arms, and guilt was flooding in. Viktor leaned down and kissed the top of her snout, hooking a finger under her chin and tilting her head up.

"I am sorry, Prima," he whispered.

"Prima? Goodness Viktor, you haven't called me that since we were courting. Why are you apologizing?" Tatianna chuckled, her brows pulled together in confusion.

"I was much too rough with you this morning. I lost control and I had no right to treat you that way," Viktor said softly, cupping her cheek and kissing her forehead.

"You didn't mean to, I knew it wasn't your–"

"It was entirely my fault, and I promised you I would never harm you again. I am sorry, Tati, my sweet girl. I never want to cause you upset ever again. Forgive me, Prima?"

"How can I stay mad when you make such a sweet face? You look like Rikovic when he was a little boy getting into trouble," Tatianna giggled, stroking his cheek thoughtfully.

"I love you, Prima."

"I love you, too. Goodness. you are very sentimental today. Did something happen? You and Oalfus were gone for a while..."

Viktor rested his chin carefully on his wife's head, rubbing down her arm slowly. Glancing over, he picked up the metal case he had lent Oalfus for the wedding, pulling out the zippo and one of the remaining cigarettes. He lit it, taking a slow drag before tilting his head back to exhale. He held the cigarette out for his wife, resting his head on the edge of the tub as he sank lower into the water with her.

"I asked Oalfus to stay with us, but he said he had plans to travel with Deirdre before their child comes. I wish he wouldn't."

"Shouldn't you be glad he's finally venturing out? I think that girl is a blessing."

"I am, but don't you think it's dangerous for them to travel? Oalfus knows nothing of the world, and Deirdre will begin to show her pregnancy. It will make her a target."

"Oh, don't act as if we have any real grasp of this new world. We hardly know how to operate a television or wireless phone. I hardly think we have the right to be worried. This will be good, you'll see. Don't fret so much. You'll get wrinkles," she winked up at him.

"I fear you and I are much too late to be worrying about wrinkles, Prima," Viktor chuckled, nuzzling her cheek. She scoffed in disgust, crossing her arms and smoking indignantly. *"I think each one brings untold beauty. You are perfect just as you are,"* he muttered, kissing her neck and cheek.

Tatianna smiled despite herself, holding the cigarette out for him. He leaned in, his eyes locked on hers as he took a drag and exhaled it out his nostrils.

"You are quite the charmer, Viktor Petrokov," Tatianna giggled, kissing his forehead.

"And I belong to you, Prima. Mind, body and soul."

Tatianna threw her head back with laughter, hugging him closer to her and nuzzling his cheek. *"I don't know what sentimental old goat possessed your body, but I must admit, I love it very much."*

Oalfus mused hearing Tatianna's laughter. His nose was buried in Deirdre's hair as he lathered sweet smelling soap into her fur with great consideration. She was sore. Every inch of her throbbed with ache from their antics all morning, and Oalfus was determined to massage every bit of her.

"Sounds like they are having a good time," Deirdre whispered, giggling shyly.

"I think Viktor is in a rather tender mood. He and I had a surprising conversation down in the cellar."

"Is everything alright?" Deirdre asked, her genuine concern warming Oalfus' heart.

He dug his claws in and lathered deep into her back, nuzzling her head as he worked over her rump and thighs. "Yes, he wanted me to stay here instead of returning to Germany."

"O-oh...he must really miss you..." she swallowed hard.

Oalfus could hear the worry in her voice. He smiled and cupped water in his hands to rinse out her fur, rubbing a little deeper as he worked up her back.

"And I told him I had already promised to travel with you."

She perked up immediately, looking up at him with a glittering smile.

Oalfus chuckled, shifting her so she was sitting between his knees as he began working on her hair. "Though, could we perhaps consider an extended visit when you become too pregnant to travel comfortably?" he purred, lathering more of that sweet scented soap into her hair with considerate hands.

"My parents would be devastated if I gave birth away from home, I just know it. Fae are always born in their historical family plots."

"I am sure that can be arranged, perhaps part here and the final leg there? It would please Viktor greatly. I fear I might be becoming soft...I wouldn't want to disappoint him. He seems rather upset I turned down his offer," Oalfus admitted, toying with her curls longer than he needed to.

"I am sure he just misses you. We can make it work. You know I don't have roots anywhere just yet, I just know I would never hear the end of it from Mammy."

"I would never disrespect their traditions. Speaking of them, should we send a letter? I don't fully know what would be appropriate for our situation...what to even call *us*," Oalfus muttered, feeling his face growing warm. He was out of his depth; he wasn't even sure what to refer to her as.

"Do you think we could call them? Mammy had a phone put into the lighthouse on the moor. I'm likely due to call anyways. She's probably worried now, I haven't called since Berlin."

"I am sure Viktor won't mind. Let's call them before supper. Safiya has all the windows opened and, *allegedly* ,Rikovic and Carmen have pulled themselves off each other."

"Goodness, who knew sex could be so troublesome," Deirdre giggled.

Ricky and Carmen were lounging together on the couch when everyone finally came back into the house. It was late into the afternoon now, and while the suffocating scent of their mixed charms had greatly dissipated, it still clung to everything. Carmen looked different, her features a little more angular, and there was a sharpness to her gaze that wasn't there before. Her nails were a little longer and pointed and peeking out of her chocolate coloured hair were two petit horns. She looked deadly.

Ricky couldn't stop running his hands over her face, tracing his fingers along the curve of those horns and hugging her closer to him.

"I never knew I could feel this way," Ricky whispered, kissing Carmen's cheeks and forehead again and again.

"I never knew I could be so addicted to someone," Carmen whispered back, crawling on top of him suddenly. She dug her nails into his shoulders as she straddled his hips.

"Ah, Carmen, no! My father will murder me. They had to air out the whole house. You need to relax, *Milaya,*" Ricky laughed, pushing her to sit beside him on the couch.

"But–"

"*No buts.* I finally can walk into my own house without shifting," Viktor said behind them, crossing his arms and arching his brow.

"Sorry Viktor," Carmen said abashedly. "Ricky said I'm in a frenzy right now? I don't know much of what's goin' on." She shrunk down, her ears drooping.

"Where are Oalfus and Deirdre?" Ricky asked, leaning back against the couch.

"Making a phone call. Goodness, Carmen. You really did end up like us...horns and all." Viktor was leaning to get a closer look, his claw tapping her horn as he inspected her.

"The horns come and go. Once she learns how to control herself a bit, they won't always be there," Ricky mused, brushing the backs of his fingers along her arm.

"It is difficult. Rikovic was a mess for several months when his true nature started coming out. Luckily for you, you have a lust demon for a husband. He will certainly be able to keep up with you. However, should we have another ring made for *you*, Rikovic?" Viktor asked, arching a brow.

"I haven't felt drained. Are you sure that's necessary?" Ricky scoffed.

"Is it possible I could hurt him?!" Carmen asked, her face painted with worry. The charm felt sucked from the room, her horns retracting and fear taking hold of her.

"I am not sure, but it would be best to be careful. I can call my contact once Oalfus and Deirdre get off the phone," Viktor said, giving her a reassuring smile.

"Is everything alright?" Oalfus poked his head into the room. He involuntarily ran his tongue over his lips as the gorgeous scent of fear made his mouth water.

"Perfectly fine, Uncle. Gracious me, Carmen, you were that worried? Oalfus feeds on fear, you know," Viktor laughed, shooing his uncle back towards the office. *"Go on, your chat with Deirdre's parents is far more important."*

Oalfus sat beside Deirdre once more, placing a hand on her knee. She had been idly chatting with her parents, who were on speaker phone so they both could hear and talk with their daughter. She wanted to ease into the topic, so until she introduced Oalfus, he was to stay silent.

"Berlin was gorgeous, Mammy. Even better than you described. I have lots of photos to mail home. After Berlin, I went into the mountains," she said sweetly, her excitement genuine as she recalled her hiking and exploring, the quaint villages, and how each one warned her about Krampus. Her parents laughed; it seemed they were familiar with the old legends. Oalfus smirked to himself, leaning over and kissing the top of her head.

"...And then this freak snow storm blew in. I should have known better, but you know how I get with my camera. I was too busy taking photos to notice the snow, and then I was completely in the thick of it. I got really lucky though. I found a cabin with someone home. I ended up staying with him for a while."

"Another little romance on the road?" her mother chuckled. Oalfus could almost hear the eye roll on the other end.

"Actually, Mammy...he's here with me now. His name is Oalfus..." Deirdre said shyly, wringing her hands nervously.

"I thought you said you were in Moscow?!" her mother blurted.

"I am. I went with him to a family event. We really got on Mammy. Da I know you'd love him. He is older, really smart, and very kind. He takes such kind care of me, Mammy. I really...I think he might be—"

"Oh Deirdre, that is wonderful news," her father's voice came through, sounding emotional.

"I always hoped I would meet my other half like you and Mammy did, traveling and exploring the world. He wants to come on my travels with me. I know it's all so sudden and you must have a million questions—"

"It's exactly what we anticipated for you, sweet girl," her mother cooed. She sniffled and sighed.

"You said he was there with you? Can we speak with him?" her father asked.

"Of course. Oalfus, did you want to say hello?" Deirdre looked up at him with glossy eyes.

"It is a pleasure to finally put voices to your names, even though Deirdre has only referred to you as Mammy and Da with me," Oalfus rumbled out with a chuckle.

"Oh my, he sounds so handsome!" Deirdre's mother squealed, giggling the same way Deirdre did.

"She is still our little girl, I am afraid. Oalfus was it? My name is Cillian and my wife is Orla. Our little one never seems to fancy fellas. Never really tells us about any she has met. Glad to see she has finally decided on one. You are from Germany, then?"

"Da!" Deirdre shrieked, covering her face.

Oalfus rumbled out a laugh, wrapping an arm around her shoulders and smiling down at her. "I am rather fond of her myself, I do hope she keeps me. I was born in Moscow, but left for...personal reasons. I've lived in Germany for a very long time, but I think I might become a traveler, if it means I get to keep your daughter."

"Oh my, he certainly has eyes for you, sweet girl!" her mother giggled.

"So what exactly were you off to Moscow for? Deirdre said a family event?" Cillian asked, a fatherly edge came to his voice.

Oalfus smiled, appreciating the concern more than being offended. "I asked Deirdre if she would be my plus one to my great-nephew's wedding. He and his wife are living in the United States, but Rikovic knows how his parents treasure our traditions, so they had it here. It seems your daughter stumbled into my life at just the right time. It had been a long time since I last saw my nephews, and I was a little nervous to attend on my own. She has truly made this whole experience wonderful." Oalfus was entirely enraptured in Deirdre as he spoke, cradling her face in his hand and holding her hand in the other.

"*Great*-nephew?" her parents said in chorus. Oalfus went wide-eyed, swallowing hard and grimacing. Perhaps he had spoken a little too freely.

"Er– yes...Rikovic and Viktor are both my nephews, father and son. They are my closest family, so it was–"

"How old are you, Oalfus?" Cillian asked rather pointedly.

"Da! That is incredibly rude! Who gives a care how old he is? Weren't you just sayin' a moment ago how glad you were I had found someone?" Deirdre growled.

"Don't speak so coarsely to your father, Deirdre," her mother clipped.

Oalfus groaned. He had certainly made a mess of things already. Deirdre was going back and forth with her parents, her mother attempting to soothe and her father pressing harder.

Oalfus sucked in a breath, placed a hand on Deirdre's lap and squeezed. "If I may..." he said.

Silence fell from all parties.

"Cillian, you have every right to be concerned. I was concerned myself when these feelings began forming between Deirdre and I. There is a reason I lived in seclusion for so very long. I remember the days of mortal raids on demon homes. I watched too many riots break out in Moscow between mortals and demons simply because of what they were. I lost my entire family, my mother and father first. Then my brother and his wife...my darling little niece..."

Oalfus bit back the emotion; now was not the time for it. He sucked in a sharp breath and continued.

"I feared what might happen to someone who *looks* like I do in this ever-changing world. I am very old. I have lived a long time in hiding due to being Old Order. I certainly did not seek out your daughter. She and I found each other through fate, and it was fate alone that allowed us this opportunity. She has opened my eyes to the importance of family, and, frankly, had it not been for her, I doubt I would have had the courage to reconnect with my nephews. With my age comes old habits, and I have every intention of meeting with you face-to-face and asking your permission to court your daughter, though it might be redundant now, I suppose."

Deirdre held Oalfus' hand in her lap, her eyes brimming with tears as she looked up at him. He glanced over at her, a stiff smile pulling the corners of his mouth as his brows drew tightly together.

"This is certainly a shock to us," Cillian finally said. Oalfus could hear the reluctance in his voice.

"He has been very forthcoming, dear. Perhaps this is a good thing?" Orla said, though, from the sounds of it, she was speaking directly to Deirdre's father and not them.

There was a whispered conversation on the other end of the phone. Neither Deirdre nor Oalfus could make out what was being said. Deirdre crawled up onto Oalfus' lap, her head resting on his shoulder and she looped her arms around him.

"No matter what they say, I will always stay by your side," Deirdre whispered, pressing her face against his neck.

"Don't be foolish, your family–"

"We want you to come home, Deirdre," Orla said suddenly.

"Mammy! I'm in the middle of my trip!" Deirdre gasped, her ears splayed back.

"And you know how your father gets. I want you to come home for a few days, at the very least. We need to discuss this face-to-face. Do you still have your grandfather's hagstone?"

"But, Mammy–"

"Deirdre, honey. There are no 'buts' for this. If you are serious about this, then your father and I insist." Her mother asserted.

"Is a hagstone like a sigil?" Oalfus asked.

"In a way. Hagstones reveal Fae gates. All moor hounds live on fae gates, so once you find compatible veins of magic, the hagstone takes you back to the land it was carved from." Orla explained.

"Where in Moscow would there be a vein?" Oalfus asked, though Deirdre looked furious with him.

"I left the hagstone at your cabin," she hissed at him.

"Then we are going and getting it, Deirdre. I will not risk *us*," Oalfus growled back.

"Fine. Mammy, you win," Deirdre relented, her ears pinned back. "I will see you in two days." She snatched up the phone and hit 'end'.

Oalfus sighed. He knew she was upset, but he also wanted to gain the favor of her parents. They still had yet to tell them Deirdre was pregnant...

Chapter Twenty Three

It had been exceedingly hard to say goodbye, much harder than Oalfus had anticipated. Thanks to the help of Blednica and Cert, Viktor and Ricky were able to go on the first leg of their journey with them. Even with Oalfus' sigil closed, the two Chaos Demons were able to open a portal back to where they had discovered Oalfus.

In a whirl of nausea, Deirdre found herself standing in front of Oalfus' cabin once again. A flurry of emotions came with it, her fingers trailing over the doorway while Oalfus hesitantly showed his nephews into his home. A single room, nothing grand like where they had just been, simply rustic and natural. Viktor looked unimpressed, but Ricky kept smiling as he looked over everything.

"It is exactly as I remember it. You haven't changed a bit," Ricky teased, picking up one of the skulls sitting on Oalfus' window sill.

Something in Deirdre felt protective of the space. She didn't like how casually Ricky was picking up things and placing them back haphazardly. She and Oalfus made a move to straighten the objects Ricky had disturbed, their hands brushing and both of them exchanging a smile.

"Uncle, this is beyond a hovel," Viktor remarked, crossing his arms and leaning on the counter.

"Now I remember why I stayed away," Oalfus muttered under his breath.

Deirdre giggled. "I love your home, no matter how much others might call it a hovel," she said, giving Viktor a stern look.

Deirdre turned to find her backpack, delighted to have her own clothes back. As much as she appreciated the prettier clothing Tatianna had insisted she kept, it felt more comfortable pulling on a pair of leggings again. Viktor and Ricky exchanged surprised glances as Deirdre seemingly didn't have a care in the world changing in front of them. Oalfus snorted, glowering at the pair.

"What?" she asked, pulling on a purple jumper and a pair of army green cargo shorts over gray leggings. "Oh, grow up, you both have wives. I have stayed in plenty of hostels where you have no option but to change in front of others. I had underclothes on. I can't be *that* interesting to gawk at," she said dismissively, though her face burned with embarrassment as she slipped on her mustard yellow leg warmers and found her matching scrunchie. Pulling her mass of curls into a loose ponytail, Deirdre finally felt like herself once more.

Oalfus beamed at her. She looked just as she had when they had first met, though he did enjoy how sweet and innocent she looked in those sundresses.

"Tatianna would have a fit if she saw you," Viktor teased. "I'm going out to carve the sigil in one of the stones around the base of the structure. That way, you can't get rid of it so easily," Viktor said in an accusatory tone. He ducked out the door to join the two chaos demons, who were already preparing a spot for it.

"Carmen and I want you to have this," Ricky said, rubbing his arm awkwardly as he held out a small gift box to his uncle. "It was very last minute. I doubt it is something you would go for, but she and I didn't exactly get much warning you were leaving," he grumbled.

Oalfus shifted nervously, pulling the lid off and blinking as he looked down at a gold chain with a medallion that looked like a compass. Lifting the chain from the box, Oalfus felt an engraving on the back. Flipping it over, his eyes went wide. Etched into the gold was the new sigil Ricky and Carmen had created during their wedding.

"Give me a week before you use it, though. We are going home next week, and then I can open the gate for you. Now you don't have any excuse not to come see us in America," he said in a gentle tone.

Deirdre was eager to see as she stood on tip toes and her tail wagged wildly. "Oh, that's a brilliant idea! I have never been to America before," she gushed. "Oh wait! This gives me an idea!" Deirdre darted out of the cabin, leaving Ricky and his uncle alone.

They stared at each other for a long moment, before Ricky rubbed his neck and shrugged. *"Need help putting it on? You have stupidly long claws for such a little clasp."*

Oalfus smiled at his nephew's attempt at tenderness. He nodded and sat on one of the stools at his table so Ricky could reach. It fit well, though he imagined it would get buried in his fur by the time it grew back. Oalfus trailed his fingers over the medallion, it was roughly the size of a large coin.

"Why did you choose a compass?"

"Carmen thought it was appropriate. Compasses lead you home. That's what she said anyway..." Ricky shrugged, moving away from him and leaning on the counter.

"I like your Carmen, she is a smart girl. Her charm smells fantastic. I am sure you are very pleased." Oalfus thought a little flattery might lighten this odd tension.

"I am. She is everything I could have dreamed of. Deirdre seems like a good match for you, too. I hope you don't expect me to start calling her Auntie. That girl isn't even half my age," Ricky snorted.

"Don't remind me..."

"Oh Uncle, come on. Don't look like that, I didn't–" Ricky swore under his breath. *"It doesn't matter. If we looked at age that closely, the very same could be said about Carmen and I. She is only 29 years old, and I was pushing 515, last time I checked. Don't let mortal standards dissuade you from someone who is clearly meant for you,"* he said, stamping his hoof.

Oalfus smiled despite how annoyed Rikovic looked. He held his hands up and nodded. *"You are right, Nephew. I won't let it take away from this. When did you get so wise?"* Oalfus mused, moving to stand beside Rikovic. He hesitated, but finally wrapped an arm around his shoulders and spoke while looking away from him.

"I won't abandon our family this time. I promise I will visit soon, once I get things sorted. Deirdre and I need to come up with a plan. We have a narrow window to get travel in, and she wants that more than anything. I wish I had more time with you, but I will be back soon."

Ricky leaned against Oalfus. He felt like a teenager again. His big sturdy wall of an uncle promising to see him soon. He always worried, when he was younger, if Oalfus would really come back. This time felt different; he actually believed his uncle.

As much as the remaining Petrokov family was prickly and stand-offish, awkward with affection, and stumbling over moments like this, a new bond was forming. Oalfus had not recoiled in fear when he saw Ricky's corruption. He had been worried, above all else, when he found out Carmen was mortal. And now, he was emotional in leaving this time, having to say goodbye.

Part of Ricky had softened because of Carmen. She had wiggled into a crack in his armor, reminded him of the warmth and comfort that comes with love, and now, it was nagging at him with his uncle.

"I hope perhaps you will be a great-great-uncle someday soon. Hell, if you and Deirdre can have one, why can't I?" Ricky mused, tapping a considerate claw on his teeth. *"I never thought I would want children...especially after how things happened with Dad."*

"Don't be so hard on your father. He had a shit role model for what a father should be. I loved my brother, but he makes me look like a teddy bear." Oalfus rolled his eyes.

*"Who are you trying to fool? You **are** an overgrown teddy bear. You might have these mortals fooled, but we all know you wouldn't hurt a fly,"* Ricky snickered.

"I used to be ferocious, I'll have you know. You little shithead," Oalfus chuckled, ruffling Ricky's hair.

"You keep telling yourself that, old man. Wait a second," Ricky smirked wide to himself, looking up at Oalfus. *"If you have a child with Deirdre, does that mean I have a great-cousin?"*

"Stop reminding me of how damn old I am, you brat. Come on," Oalfus smirked, giving Ricky a shove to join the others outside.

Deirdre and Viktor were wandering around the surrounding trees. Deirdre was holding an odd triangular stone with a hole in the center to her eye and pointing. She passed it to Viktor and guided his eye to whatever they were looking at. Deirdre caught sight of Oalfus and beamed at him.

"You have no idea how much magic you've sewn into this land just by being here!" she said with awe in her eyes, her tail wagging wildly behind her.

"What are you going on about, *Liebchen?*" Oalfus chuckled as he and Ricky walked towards the pair.

"You are an embodiment of ancient magic. Being Old Order basically makes you a magnet for the magic that we all possess. You can almost see a map of your regular routines through the hagstone. The path you follow to cut wood, a path to the stream, different faint trails towards the villages. It is amazing!" Deirdre giggled. She had two stones in her hands as she turned back to Viktor, who was staring through the hagstone, open-mouthed.

"She is right, Uncle. It looks like yellow glowing trails. It's the most peculiar thing I have ever seen."

"What do you have, *Liebchen?*" Oalfus asked, pointing to the stones in her hand.

Deirdre smiled, holding up a stone the size of her palm that had Viktor and Tatianna's sigil carved into it. "I thought it would be a good idea to take with us, since we have one for Ricky," she explained sheepishly.

"You gave your uncle your sigil before me?!" Viktor complained, but Ricky just rolled his eyes and told him to be patient.

"And the other?" Oalfus asked, arching a brow at the plain stone in her hand.

"I was going to see if I could make a hagstone for here," she mumbled, shrugging a little.

"I thought these stones were only made for a Fae's homeland?" Oalfus asked, raising a brow. Deirdre shifted nervously, glancing up at Viktor and Ricky, still watching the pair. Her tail tucked and she looked down at the ground.

"I guess it's stupid," she suddenly blurted, dropping the stone and hurrying past him towards the cabin.

"Wait, Deirdre–!"

She shut the door before he could finish.

"Are you seriously such an oaf you couldn't see what was so obvious?" Viktor groaned, covering his face in his hands.

"Come on, Uncle..." Ricky scoffed, shaking his head.

"What?! It was how she explained it to me!" Oalfus snapped.

"This is painful. Come on Rikovic. We should head back. I can't watch this old fool blunder anymore," Viktor groaned, moving to the main sigil he carved into the base of the cottage.

"You will figure it out eventually, Uncle. I believe in you," Ricky mused, giving his hopeless uncle a pat on the shoulder before following his father. They both turned and called back to Oalfus, who was standing there very disgruntled and frustrated. He would never understand women. He was cursed to be a blundering idiot with these things.

"We will see you soon, right?" Viktor called.

"Of course you will, you both know that," he grumbled, moving towards the gate as it opened.

"Tell Deirdre we say goodbye. Good luck with her parents. You'll need it, old man," Ricky teased. The pair stepped into the swirling red circle and were gone in the blink of an eye.

Oalfus sighed heavily. He now had to sort out what to do with Deirdre. There was no way they were leaving while she was so upset. Carefully opening the door to the cottage, the big demon peered in to find her sitting at the table fiddling with her hagstone.

"Deirdre..."

"It was a dumb idea..." she whispered.

"It was not a dumb idea. I just thought you could only make one if it was your homeland," Oalfus said gently, kneeling beside her.

"This does feel like my home..." she whispered, tears blurring her eyes.

Oalfus felt his whole heart melt. He pulled her into his arms and kissed her forehead, her cheeks, then her nose and lips. He cradled her head against his chest and whispered to her.

"Then make as many as you wish. It will always be your home as long as you desire it to be."

"I'm sorry I didn't say goodbye to them," she whimpered again.

"They will see you again soon, and I know your parents are waiting for us. You don't want to show up in such a state, do you? I fear your father might hate me if he sees you so upset."

She nodded, sniffing and turning so she could wrap her arms around his neck. Her legs wrapped around his midsection next, and he rumbled contently as she squeezed onto him. She was so small in his arms, so *perfect*. He allowed his eyes to close, nestling in close to her and enjoying being in his home once more with his darling girl. He buried his face against her neck, groaning because he knew they wouldn't be able to stay like this for very long.

Chapter Twenty Four

Oalfus was greatly intrigued by the way the hagstone acted as a portal in place of a sigil; it was a nearly identical type of magic, in his eyes. Instead of swirling red, it was shimmering yellows and blues, and at the center, the portal almost appeared like a window.

A rippling view of a wide-open, rolling green cliff appeared, little purple flowers dotting the grass and, just beyond, was the boiling gray-blue ocean. Oalfus had never been to such a place. He knew of oceans and the famous emerald green hills of Ireland, but this would be his first experience there.

Deirdre held his hand tightly, taking a deep breath before stepping forward into the portal. Oalfus followed behind, ducking through as he shifted Deirdre's backpack off his shoulder to make sure he could fit through.

The first thing he felt was humidity, thick and cold all at once. His lungs felt heavy with his first inhale. His fur was almost immediately damp, and a steady drizzle was coming down. It was hard to say if it was actual rain, or just the crashing waves against the cliff they were standing on, but Oalfus was already sufficiently soaked.

Deirdre's curls were wild before, but within mere minutes of them standing there, her hair had doubled in volume. Oalfus tried not to laugh, her sour expression hard to ignore.

The scenery was almost as gorgeous as Deirdre. They stood in a meadow atop the cliff. Dotted with flowers of every colour, the tall wild grass brushed against his legs as he slowly turned to admire where they were. It suited Deirdre, being from this place. Lush and wild as she was, bright and brimming with life, even in the gloom of overcast rain.

"This place is amazing," Oalfus finally said, looking down at Deirdre.

She was hugging herself, giving a shrug as she muttered, "It would be if I hadn't been forced back so soon."

"Come now, *Liebchen*. Your parents are being diligent. I respect them for it. I promise we will start off exactly as you were planning once they are placated." Oalfus knelt down in front of her, rubbing her shoulders and smiling warmly. "Are we going to mention the...current development?" Oalfus asked, doing his best to be considerate.

"No! Oh good Lord, no. My Mammy might faint and Da will lose his head. They can find out later."

"Alright. Deirdre, if it should come about that they–"

"Don't even finish that thought. I know they will love you as much as I do." The words tumbled out of her mouth faster than she could hold them back.

They stared at each other in wide-eyed shock for what felt like ages before Deirdre clumsily tried to correct what she said. Oalfus laughed it away, urging her to lead the way back to her home.

The lighthouse where she had grown up was clear to see from here, but still Oalfus did anything to change the topic. The walk was tense and silent, though it did give them both enough time to clear their minds of their mixed up emotions.

Deirdre paused as she reached for the door, looking up at Oalfus. "Are you sure you want to go through with this?" she whispered.

"More sure than anything I have done in a long time. I have no doubts in my mind. You are my priority now," Oalfus assured her. He placed his hand on the small of her back as he nodded for her to carry on.

Deirdre took hold of the doorknob, and, pushing the big red door open, she poked her head into the house.

"Mammy? Da?" she called out.

There was a clamor inside, the sound of cutlery hitting porcelain and a squeak of wooden chairs across the old wooden floors. A red terrier, exactly the same build as Deirdre, rushed out of the kitchen into the narrow front hallway. Her hair was a darker shade of red, cut into a bob so wide from her natural curls that it almost looked like a half-circle framed her face. She was dressed in a crochet shawl made from granny squares of all different colours, a bright yellow jumper, and gray wool pants.

"Oh, my darling girl is home!" Orla wailed rushing towards the door with outstretched arms. The door swung open wide, and Orla yelped, frozen when she saw Oalfus looming a few feet behind Deirdre.

"Oh my stars..." Orla said, creeping forward slowly. Her wide brown eyes were just like Deirdre's. Oalfus did his best to smile at the woman; truly Deirdre took after her mother. The trouble was, those wide eyes were not kind like her daughters, they were hesitant. There was something in that look, something hard and stand off-ish, Oalfus couldn't place.

"Well, he is a big fella isn't he? He's taller than your father!" Orla laughed nervously, pulling her daughter into a fierce hug. "Oh my little shutterbug is home. I trust you have more pictures for us?"

Then another figure appeared. A massive wolf hound poked his head around the corner still holding a cup of tea. He had striking green eyes, a trait his daughter had clearly inherited from him. His wiry salt-and-pepper coat stuck in every which way, a shaggy crop of black hair atop his head, and a pair of heavy brows that gave the man the appearance of a constant scowl. He wore an old blue cardigan with brown patched elbows, a button up white shirt and a pair of loose brown slacks. His eyes went wide when he saw Oalfus, slowly stepping out of the kitchen and clearing his throat.

"Good day," he said, apprehensively.

"A pleasure to meet you both," Oalfus said, respectfully bowing his head and remaining at a safe distance. He was not aware if there were different customs with this order of demons, but Oalfus was hardly one to invite himself inside to anyone's home.

Cillian came to the door, tugging his bushy mustache and beard as he looked up at Oalfus. "Haven't seen an Old Order in many years now..." he remarked, mostly to himself.

The hound looked as if he was studying an old text book rather than another demon. He sipped his tea and stepped out so he could get a closer look. Oalfus felt a little perturbed by this, especially when Cillian started circling him and poking at him.

"I thought you lot had more fur normally, more animal-like. Huh, look at them claws. My stars... look at the size of that tail, Orla. He is gonna knock everything over with that thing."

"Oh, like you don't already, Cillian Shae!" Orla teased, snuggling her daughter closer in a hug only a mother could give. Deirdre didn't see the icy look her mother shot Oalfus as he cradled her girl more protectively than affectionately.

"Da, you're being awfully rude," Deirdre warned, giving Oalfus an apologetic look.

"Hm, I suppose. Never really got to look at an Old Order so close before, though. He doesn't look like the ones I've come across."

Oalfus snorted, crossing his arms and arching a brow. "Apologies for disappointing you," he huffed, though now he wished he hadn't. He internally kicked himself; he was trying to make a good impression, not piss off the father.

Cillian narrowed his eyes at him for a moment before throwing his head back in laughter, slapping Oalfus on the arm. "At least he has a personality! Alright you two, come in and Mum here will get you a nice cuppa. Don't you knock over my lamps with that tail, Mr. Oalfus. I will be right cross with you."

Cillian shuffled back inside and disappeared into the kitchen.

"Come on love, we were just having tea. You want some beans on toast with fresh tomatoes? Da went to the market this morning and got fresh bread."

"Oh, is it from Mrs. Gurdy's?" Deirdre asked, her tail wagging.

"Who else would we get bread from, sweetheart?" her mother laughed, hurrying off to the kitchen. Deirdre scurried inside after them, tugging off her mustard-knit cap and hanging it on a hook with her jacket.

"Are you coming, Oalfus?" she suddenly asked, realizing he was still standing there dumbfounded.

"That's it? No more glaring or questions? I just go in like that?"

"Well, Da will hammer you with questions over tea, of course, but he isn't scowlin' anymore!" she said, pulling him in by his arm.

Oalfus almost immediately banged his horns against the top of the door as he came into the cramped lighthouse. He hated being so big at times. Grumbling loudly, he attempted to stand upright and promptly banged the front of his horns on the ceiling.

Fantastic...I have to hunch.

Tea went as well as it could, though it was horribly cramped for the four of them. Oalfus opted to just half-sit, half-lean on the counter for fear of breaking their precarious-looking vintage kitchen chairs.

Everything in this house was mismatched. Not a plate or bowl was the same, every pot and pan was a mix up, the cutlery was all different and the *knick knacks*...the walls, every non-utility surface, and tucked anywhere they could fit were little baubles from various travels. Photos stacked in boxes, plastered on the walls, in albums, photos going back to when the lighthouse was first built by Deirdre's great-grandfather...this house was filled to the brim with memories. Oalfus had never seen such a way of living.

It seemed Orla was a knitter, crocheter, macrimer. If it involved yarn, she was making it. Every surface had a doily, every plant in a woven hanger. Oalfus thought it was rather charming, though he didn't appreciate the cold looks she sent his way every now and then. Cillian asked the usual round of questions one might expect: what were his intentions with Deirdre? Who was his family? Had he had any children out of wedlock? How big was his family? Why has he never married before now?

Things began getting more personal, cutting a little too deep as the conversation turned into more like an interview. Oalfus did his best to give half-answers, in order to preserve his own sanity and not get into such dark topics. He would much prefer not reliving his darkest days in front of perfect strangers, but it seemed nothing was off-limits to this man.

Orla had taken Deirdre and gone off to the other room to spread out her photographs and discuss her trip. Really, she wanted to give her husband a better chance at questioning this giant beast in her kitchen. Oalfus would have given his left arm to escape Cillian's sharp gaze and irritating questions. The hound leaned across the table, arching a brow as he spoke in a low voice.

"You say you lived alone in the mountains all those years, avoiding the world. Why? What were you so afraid of? Surely a beastie such as yourself can take care of any dangers with ease?"

Oalfus grit his teeth. This interrogation was becoming tiresome. He struggled to think of something civilized to say, anger beginning to seep into his bones. Oalfus' ears perked when a little shriek came from the living room where Deirdre and her mother were looking at pictures.

Oh no...

"Mammy, give that back!" Deirdre barked, but Orla appeared in the kitchen holding up several photos from when he had killed the deer.

"Do you mean to tell me Krampus is standing in my kitchen right now?!" Orla blurted.

Oalfus' stomach dropped. He stood in stunned silence and willed his tongue to work, but it refused.

Deirdre tried to snatch the photos back, growling as vines began to spring out of her hair. "Mammy I am warning you! I am not a little girl anymore, give me *back* those damned photos!"

Orla had a strange expression on her face; it didn't look like fear, and Oalfus smelt no fear on her, either. She looked bewildered and *offended*, but at least it wasn't *fear*.

"Krampus? Like the spirit who steals away naughty babes at Christmastime?" Cillian said, standing and taking the photos from Orla. His eyes bugged out of his head as he looked through them, then back at Oalfus.

"I don't take children. That is just a wild tale about a very odd turn of events!" Oalfus blurted, and promptly wished he hadn't.

"Turn of events?" Orla gasped.

"Mammy! For the love of the Ancients, if you don't stop acting like this, I swear we are leaving! Da, you have been unbelievably nasty, too! I am ashamed of you both!" Deirdre practically screamed, storming over and standing defensively in front of Oalfus. "How dare you give him such a hard time! Can you imagine the impression you have made?! You both should be ashamed! Oalfus' first time in Ireland and his hosts are being wretched to him! Yes, alright, he is Krampus, but the rumors of him stealing children are just that! Rumors! Those stories are hundreds of years old and you *know* how mortals exaggerate their stories! Oalfus has never killed anyone, not on purpose that I know of–"

"He could be *lying* to you, Deirdre!" her mother barked back.

Oalfus stamped his hoof and snarled, his eye burning crimson as he crossed his arms to hold back any more of his anger. "*Genug Unsinn! Das ist lächerlich!*" Oalfus snarled, his eyes closing as he pinched the bridge of his nose. "I have had enough family squabbling to fill my belly for a lifetime! Deirdre, your father is simply doing what any father would, albeit *very* personal. Yes, Orla. I am Krampus. No, I have never eaten a child or even taken one. I have no interest in such barbaric acts, but I do scare the daylights out of mortals so I might get a half-decent meal once or twice a year. I am an Old Order. Among my kind, we feed off emotions and, unfortunately for me, I ended up preferring the taste of fear. My nephews are both lust demons, and believe me, it would have made my life much easier to be like they are but, alas.

"I have no intention of staying where I am unwelcome, and I shall not cause any more fighting among family members. *Ich bin alt und müde. Dafür habe ich keine Geduld.*"

Deirdre watched helplessly as Oalfus stormed out of the cramped kitchen, the front door opening and slamming shut behind him. Her vines spiraled out of control, spreading across the counters and floor as she stood there biting back her screams of anger. Orla's eyes went dark, her inner demon being pulled out from the sudden strength of her daughter's shift.

"Deirdre—"

"No! No more Mammy! You two have never acted so beastly in all my days! You have been warm and welcoming to everyone you came across, and then today, you threw away everything I ever believed you to be! Why?! Because he is older than us? Because he isn't Fae like us?! You don't understand how much he means to me! He is *mine!* I chose *him* and now you have driven him away and I feel like I have to choose between my own parents and the man I love!"

Deirdre's voice was hoarse as she stood there yelling, her hands fisting her hair and vines as they began to spread wildly through the room. Containers of sugar, tea bags, a tea pot and dishes were sent crashing to the floor as her vines lashed out in a display of the rage boiling her insides.

"Deirdre Shea, you calm down!" her father barked, but it did no good. Her vines shot out and knocked him back into his chair, wrapping around the hand still holding the photos she had taken of Oalfus.

"Fine! If you make me choose, know I choose him over you! I will always choose him!" she shrieked, her vines snapping back to her as she forced herself past them and out the front door.

Oalfus had heard the whole thing, The windows were open, and Deirdre had been bellowing her words. She ran blindly, tears streaming down her face until Oalfus managed to catch up and pull her into his arms.

"Shh, shh *beruhige dich, meine Liebe,*" Oalfus soothed, cradling her in his arms. Her vines wrapped around him, uncomfortably tight, but he knew she needed this. The way her vines were wrapping him knocked him off balance, sending him down to his knees as he held onto her. Deirdre was crying and banging her fists against his chest.

"It isn't fair! They aren't my parents! They never ever treated people so coldly! How could they do this to you?!"

"*Beruhige dich, meine Liebe.* Calm down...I need you to take a breath," Oalfus whispered, pressing his nose against the top of her head. Her scattered photographs fluttered in the grass beside them as he looked up at the lighthouse. Orla and Cillian were likely watching from somewhere inside, the way the light was Oalfus could not tell, but he knew it wouldn't matter. He wiggled his arm free of her vines enough he could stroke her cheek, brushing her tears away from her eyes as he spoke carefully.

"They are only worried about you, *meine liebe*. Parents do strange things when they fear for their children. Worry is an odd emotion, it makes us fall to pieces. Just as you are right now, you would never shout at your parents if you were worried they might reject me. I am sure they are just worried if I am worthy of you"

"You said that again..." Deirdre sniffled.

"Said what?"

"*Miene liebe...* My love."

"Of course that's all you heard this whole time," Oalfus laughed, despite the situation at hand.

"Do you love me?" she asked in such a small voice, Oalfus nearly missed it over the wind.

"Would I go through all this trouble for someone I didn't love?" Oalfus murmured as he brushed hair from her eyes. "I know it's soon, but I won't deny it any longer," he breathed, pressing his lips against hers for a fleeting moment. "I hope you feel the same, though I am fairly certain you do based on what you shouted in the kitchen," he teased.

"You heard all that?" Deirdre said, her face heating with embarrassment.

"Yes, and while I do appreciate the sentiment, I would never allow you to abandon your family over me," Oalfus said firmly.

"I won't leave you!" she insisted, gripping onto his shirt.

"I am not saying you have to, *Liebe*. I am saying we need to get your parents comfortable with me."

Deirdre's anger rose again, her vines gripped him tighter and finally he could bear no more. He winced and ground his teeth together, his claws digging into her as he held her.

"*Liebe,* I need you to be a good girl for me. Listen to me now, take a deep breath and calm yourself. We can do this together. I won't leave your side no matter how many questions your father asks me. Just *please* loosen your grip..."

Deirdre's eyes widened with shock, her vines suddenly releasing him and retracting quickly.

"I'm so sorry, I'm sorry I never meant– oh Oalfus I am–"

"Hush, no fretting. You are just much stronger than I gave you credit for," he said with a kind smile, rubbing her cheek as he pulled her close once more. "Now be a good girl like I asked, sweetling..."

Deirdre felt a warmth creep up her legs and wrap her so completely. Sweet oranges, cinnamon and clove flooded her nose. Normally she would have been angry at Oalfus for using his charm on her, but this felt so right. Pressing her face into his neck, she took a deep breath of his scent, his hand trailing up and down her back.

"Good girl, that's my good sweetling. Relax. I promise to reward you *thoroughly* if you get through the rest of the day calmly," Oalfus purred, nuzzling against her ear.

"Are you bribing me with sex?" Deirdre giggled, her words a little slurred from the effects of his charm.

"I might be. Though, if it isn't working, I can try something else," Oalfus mused.

"Oh it's working. I might not let you go back into that house and have you take me right now," Deirdre confessed, her fingers trailing along the back of his neck and up into his hair.

"Mmm...As tempting as that sounds, I can't reward you when you have yet to earn it. Don't worry, *Liebe*. I can't wait to see how well you take me tonight. But first, we need to patch things up with your parents."

Chapter Twenty Five

It was tense, awkward, and, frankly, irritating. Oalfus offered to help Deirdre clean up in the kitchen, but her mother beat him to it. As it turned out, Cillian and Orla had watched Oalfus calm Deirdre down and coax her back up to the house. Now, he was forced to sit in their living room, desperately avoiding knocking or bumping anything in the cluttered little space. The furniture was too small for him to sit comfortably. That was one blessing of his nephew's home: everything was grand and airy so there was room for him to move.

Cillian seemed just as uncomfortable, sitting and fidgeting with his cup of tea, while he avoided looking towards Oalfus. A very loud whispered conversation was happening between Deirdre and her mother in the kitchen. Oalfus was able to pick up snippets between the sweeping of broken glass and debris. He wished he could be anywhere else, but he hoped that if he was patient, things would settle and he might be able to slip away somewhere quiet with Deirdre.

A little smirk toyed his lips. Did Deirdre still have a childhood bedroom in this house? How entertaining would it be to snoop through that? He imagined pink everything, but that quickly faded when he remembered just how *not into* pink Deirdre was.

He mused about what might be hidden above where they sat. There was a narrow staircase leading somewhere higher in the lighthouse. Perhaps there was a guest room he might be forced to sleep in, separately from Deirdre. He didn't put it past Cillian to insist he sleep away from his daughter. Oh, if only the poor man knew. Oalfus snorted out loud at that thought, coughing to try and cover it as he glanced over at the very stoic-looking wolfhound.

"Something very funny, Mr. Oalfus?" Cillian said, not looking up from his tea cup.

"Er— I suppose I was letting the mind wander. Apologies, I meant no offense."

"There is no need to apologize...I believe I am the one owing you an apology, in fact."

Oalfus raised a brow, propping his head on his fist as he attempted to relax his posture. "You are a concerned father. I imagine I might react similarly, if I was in your situation. My brother had children, not I. While I struggle to comprehend the true nature of a father's protective nature, I am fiercely protective of my nephews. Poor Dierdre ended up taking the brunt of my protectiveness during our trip to Moscow a few times, though she was very quick to put me in my place. Her bark is something fierce."

"She barked at you?!" Cillian looked mortified, as if he was about to leap out of his skin. "We always taught her to never use it in anger!"

"I deserved it, believe me. I made quite the ass of myself on that trip, and she still seems to desire my company. I suppose I must be doing something right," Oalfus chuckled dryly.

Cillian looked a little confused, his head tilting the same way Deirdre's did when she was mixed up.

"A story for another time, perhaps. I think I hear the girls now."

Deirdre and her mother emerged from the kitchen, neither looking overly happy. A little smile pulled the corners of Deirdre's mouths up, however, when she came into the room. Oalfus warmed immediately when she came over to him, perching herself on his knee. Her mother made a very unimpressed noise in her throat, eyeing the pair of them with a pinched expression.

"Mammy, not a word! You promised!" Deirdre hissed.

"*Liebchen...*" Oalfus' tone was one of warning. He wanted her to stop squabbling with her parents, above all else. It didn't seem she was off to the best start.

"She is being unreasonable, Oalfus!" Deirdre complained.

"You are being stubborn. As much as I enjoy you being so close, perhaps not right now. Let's not antagonize your poor mother," Oalfus said, nudging her off his lap and towards the empty space on the couch.

"Well, at least *he* has some manners. I mean really! She certainly is *your* daughter," Orla hissed at Cillina.

"Mine?!"

"This might be more the influence of my family. I apologize," Oalfus offered. "Two lust demons as nephews. I can fully admit they are much more...outwardly affectionate with their wives than most regular folk tend to be. There isn't a moment outside meals I can recall Tatianna was not draped across Viktor's lap or Carmen not on Rikovic's. We are an eccentric family, I suppose."

This comment did not sit well with Orla. Her nose wrinkled with disgust and she folded her hands tightly over her lap. As soon as she had discovered Oalfus was indeed Krampus, politeness left her.

Cillian, on the other hand, seemed to find this amusing. His brows shot up and he chuckled at the thought.

"I think my Orla might die of embarrassment if she were around your family," he teased, but Orla was in no mood for jokes. She stood quickly, dismissing herself to go begin preparing for supper.

Deirdre looked over the back of the couch after her mother, her brows pulled together and frustration pulling her features.

"Da, why is she being so...so horrible?" Deirdre hissed, looking to her father for help.

"I think she might just need some time, dear. Though if I am honest...she is reminding me of her father right now." Cillian looked a little disappointed, his gaze dropping to where he was running his thumb over the rim of his teacup.

"How do you mean?" Oalfus asked, before realizing that it might be an invasive question, based on the tense expression on the wolfhound's face.

"Well...when I met Orla, her father didn't very much approve of me. Moor hounds usually encourage their children to go traveling in their youth since they become bound to their ancestral lands when the time comes. I don't think he planned for her to meet the son of a grimm or fall in love with one. Moor hounds and grimms have always had odd relationships. Moor hounds protect the land of our ancients, and grimms guard graveyards. You would think they would get along, but for whatever reason there has always been a strange tension. My mother was a Cu Sith, just like Deirdre and her Mammy, but I took after my father. When his time passes, I will take up the torch of protecting the graveyards in this region. I am not bound to this land as tightly as Orla is, though, and I think her father resented me for that. He never approved of our marriage, and he never approved of me." Cillian let out a great sigh, pressing his hand to his face. "And I have been treating you just as he treated me," he groaned.

"I take no offense to it. You are just being a concerned father," Oalfus insisted.

"Aye, but it doesn't make the bite sting any less," Cillian sighed, looking up at Oalfus properly for the first time since Deirdre lashed out. "I am sorry for being so inhospitable, Oalfus. I appreciate your patience with me."

"No need to apologize, honestly. I expected worse. My niece-in-law cracked me over the head with a fire iron while I was there. My family likely puts most to shame with their dysfunction," Oalfus chuckled.

"By the Ancients, sounds like a wild one," Cillian gasped, rubbing his own head sympathetically.

"Wrath demons tend to be. I always marveled at my nephew for taking her on. She is a beauty though," Oalfus mused.

"Did you get any photographs of his family, Deirdre?" Cillian asked, his ears perking.

"I did, but I need to develop the film," she sighed.

"Well, we could always run it down to the shop, they are still open for another two hours yet. I bet old Joseph would do a quick develop for us. He hasn't seen you in ages!"

"Olafus, do you want to come to town with us?" Deirdre perked, her tail wagging.

As badly as he wanted to indulge her, the idea of going into a town was exhausting. He glanced towards the kitchen. Perhaps a moment alone with Orla would be beneficial. He might be able to get her to warm up again. Tapping a claw on his chin, he shook his head.

"You go, spend some time with your father," Oalfus finally said.

"He is certainly brave. I would run if I had the chance to get away from your Mammy when she is in a mood," Cillian chuckled as he and his daughter went to pull on their jackets. "Orla, dear. Deirdre and I are going to run to the shops quick. Do you need anything for dinner?" Cillian called, flinching in fear of her tone.

"Get something for coffee after," she clipped in an icy tone.

Deirdre scurried to the kitchen quickly, giving her mother a stern glare as she whispered. "Be kind to Oalfus, he is staying behind. I swear, Mammy, if I hear you were rude to him..."

"Go away with you, talking to your mother that way," Orla snapped, shooing her out of the kitchen.

"Be nice Mammy!" Deirdre called as the door closed behind them.

Orla stood at the kitchen door, her arms crossed and eyes narrowed as she looked at the oversized demon sitting in her living room.

This bastard isn't staying.

Chapter Twenty Six

Cillian and Deirdre were delighted to watch as Joseph ran the film into the machine in the photo lab. The pair were standing there like children, tails wagging as they watched the old man working through the steps. It was a mystery how it all worked to both of them, but it was fun to watch nonetheless.

Eventually, Cillian remembered he had been tasked to go find something for after supper. Tugging Deirdre away from the window of the photo lab, they wandered out of the pharmacy and up the street towards the bakery.

"You seem to be very fond of him," Cillian finally said, bumping shoulders with his daughter. As much as he acted like an old man, Cillian and Orla were only four hundred years old. They had been young when they married and had Deirdre, so it was an odd feeling having such an old demon as a prospective son-in-law.

"I am, Da. I love him," Deirdre said quietly, helping her father decide between a mixed pastry box or a cake.

"I believe you, shutterbug. I know you're not overly happy with your mother and I, but I promise I won't be rude from here on out.

He seems a very kind man, patient as a saint for putting up with your ol' da'," he chuckled.

Deirdre threw her arms around him, squeezing him tightly. "Thank you, Da'," Deirdre said, her voice tight with emotion.

"Come now, you know I would do anything for you."

The pair finished buying their sweets, browsing the shops a little longer before they were able to collect the photos from the lab. The whole way home, Deirdre flicked through photos from the wedding, showing pictures of Carmen and Ricky dancing, of Tatianna and Viktor kissing either cheek of their son, of all the posh demons dancing like it was two hundred years ago.

Cillian's jaw was slack, looking at the grandeur of the Russian wedding. He gawked at the photos of the house she had taken, laughing and remarking how Oalfus had been right about how lovely Tatianna was.

"His nephew is Viktor, and then his great-nephew is Rikovic?"

"Yes, Viktor and Tatianna are Rikovic's parents. Carmen is Ricky's wife."

"Whoa," Cillian was looking at the photos of Oalfus, the orange glow of the lighter making his red eye look even more sinister.

"Oh wow, those turned out so good!" Deirdre squealed, flicking through the others.

"You really know how to capture him," Cillian said with a smile.

"Thanks Da. It's just easy with him, I dunno. I am sure he is tired of me saying to stop moving and sticking a camera in his face," Deirdre laughed, rubbing her arm.

"He looks pretty happy to be your subject in these. Look at that grin on his face."

Deirdre leaned in to look. It was faint from the shadows, but pulling at Oalfus' mouth was a wide grin. It made the photo much more playful than its original sinister appearance.

Deirdre couldn't stop staring at the photo. She couldn't wait to get home to show him. Her father warmed greatly seeing this side of the old demon. He might be big and intimidating, but he wasn't as fearsome as Cillian once thought. His heart melted seeing his daughter so happy. Walking side-by-side, the two climbed the hills towards the cliff.

"Oalfus! Just wait until you see these photos!" Deirdre called, tugging her knit cap off and hanging up her jacket next to her father's.

No answer.

"Oalfus?" Deirdre looked into the living room. He wasn't there. Deirdre turned to the kitchen where her mother was setting out three plates, instead of four. Deirdre's heart dropped. She slowly approached her mother, who was acting as if nothing had happened.

"Mammy, where is Oalfus?" Deirdre asked in a very level voice, her hands trembling.

"Orla..." Cillian appeared, looking around the house and then his brows drew together as he looked at his wife. She was still ignoring them as she carefully laid out the cutlery.

"Mammy, where is he?!" Deirdre demanded.

"Deirdre Shea, don't you raise your voice inside!" Orla snapped.

"Orla, what have you done?" Cillian asked, sorrow bubbling up in his voice for his daughter.

"I just...told him the truth. This is likely a little phase, just like all the boys who have come and gone in Deirdre's life. I didn't want him to get any grand ideas, it was likely going to fizzle out."

Deirdre couldn't speak. Her stomach was boiling with rage as she stood with tears welling in her eyes. This woman wasn't her mother. She couldn't even recognize this witch standing in front of her. Her heart shattering, she ran for her bag, tearing open the pockets looking for the sigil stone Viktor had carved for them. Sobs broke out of her as her frantic searching turned to tearing the whole bag apart. She wailed uncontrollably with the realization that it was gone, her body curling in on itself as she sank to the floor.

"Orla, you are no better than your father was. How on earth could you have said that to him? You and I faced this sort of thing, and you promised me you would never act like he did!" Cillian bellowed, rage taking over his sorrow.

"Cillian, how could you compare me to him!? This is completely different!"

"How Orla? Because he is Old Order? Because he isn't Fae? Why?!"

"Because he is a monster!"

"The only monster I see is you right now, Orla. Look at your daughter and tell me you were right! Look at what you have done!"

Cillian grabbed her arm and dragged her into the hall where Deirdre was in utter shambles, sobbing and clinging to her packet of photos. Her words were so drowned out by sobs Cillian could scarcely understand her. He let go of Orla, dropping to his knees and hugging his little girl.

"H-h-he will n-never–" she sobbed, falling against her father.

"Shh, calm now my little one. We will fix this."

"How c-could you h-have done this!?" Deirdre shrieked, lunging at her own mother.

Cillian grabbed her around the middle, pulling Deirdre back and shaking his head.

"Come now, Deirdre. Let's go outside for a breath!"

Cillian shot his wife a disappointed look before hurrying his daughter outside, She collapsed into a heap, sobbing inconsolably once more. Cillian sat beside his daughter, patting her back, trying to soothe her.

"Come now, shutterbug. Breathe. We can get this sorted out."

"H-how will I ever find him now? He's gone back home! It almost took a year for me to get all the way to Germany!"

Cillian sighed, rubbing his face with his hands. He tried to think of how much money they had to spare right now. Maybe they could manage a flight? He was lost in thought, considering what he might be able to pull together, how he could help fix this mess. Deirdre shoved her hands in the pockets of her jumper, stiffening as she felt the flat smoothed stone Oalfus had given back to her just before they left.

"Da, how do you make a hagstone?" she blurted.

"Deirdre, I don't know how much that has to do with–" He looked to see his daughter holding a palm-sized dark stone, tears welling in her eyes once more as she looked down at it with a trembling lip.

"I said it was a stupid idea...b-but he insisted I try..."

"I have never tried to make one for somewhere other than our home. But magic is magic, I suppose."

The hope that lit up his daughter's eyes was enough to have Cillian leap into action, pulling her up onto her feet and leading her around the back of the lighthouse to his work shed.

"We can't completely cheat this process, but I can help speed this up. Goon down to the shore and find good, strong stones to grind with, preferably a flat one and a narrow one for the center hole. Fill this pail with water and be quick," he ordered, holding his hand out for the stone.

Deirdre held onto it tightly, her brows pinched with worry. "It's the only one I—"

"I won't start without you, I promise. I will be careful," he assured her.

"Okay Da...thank you."

Deirdre watched over her father's shoulder as he used the sea water to lubricate his drill bits as he slowly worked away at creating a hole in the center. He wasn't sure what kind of stone it was, so he worked with a delicate hand and incredible patience, even with his daughter hanging over him. He knew this meant everything to her, so he bit back his annoyed tone when he spoke to her.

"Deirdre, I love you, but please, stand back a bit."

"Sorry Da," she said meekly, backing away and pacing along the wall of the shed.

Bit by bit, Cillian bore his drill further into the stone he had clamped to a scrap piece of wood. He was glad for its shape; his daughter had chosen a very advantageous piece to work with. Finally wood shavings began spraying back from the bit. He smiled, his tail wagging as he pulled the small piece of stone out from the hole he had cut into it.

"Alright, Deirdre! The rest is up to you, shutterbug." He held up the cut stone, setting it in her palm. "Slowly, though. You will risk breaking if you rush this any further. Grind the hole in the center until it is smooth, just like the one your grandfather made. Then, work the shape of a triangle into the outer stone, just like the symbol for the elements. Make sure you use the sea water. The ocean connects everything in this world. It is vital you never let the stone dry while you work it."

Deirdre carefully placed the stone into the bucket of salt water and threw her arms around her father.

"Thank you Da. Thank you for believing in us," she whispered, emotions heavy in her voice.

"I always knew you would find someone. I just wish your mother was more understanding." He cleared his throat. "While you work that stone, I will work on your mother. We both have hard work ahead of us." He tried to laugh, but it came out bitter.

Deirdre nodded, taking his place at the workbench and laying the large flat stone she had found at the beach on the workbench. She had found several narrow pieces of stone with which to attempt smoothing out the inner circle, and her father had left a few sanding sponges for her, if push came to shove. Rolling up her sleeves, Deirdre set to work.

I promise I will be back home soon, Oalfus. I promise!

The solitude of her work brought back her rage and sorrow. While she ground the stone in circular motions, tears mixed with the sea water. Deirdre was running all the worst case scenarios in her mind, fearful Oalfus might reject her when she came back to him. She kept having to dispel those dark thoughts, leaving room for hope. She had to cling onto the hope that he would forgive her for what had happened.

The sun dipped below the horizon. Darkness fell and soon, Deirdre was working by lamplight. The drizzle from earlier in the day had turned into a downpour, but still, she kept working. Scooping sea water and grinding away, uncaring of the downpour, she would run down the steep slick path to the shore line and collect more water. She was soaked, but none of it mattered. She kept working. The once oval-shaped stone was finally starting to look like a triangle, the center hole less jagged and sharp from her father's drill. Deirdre sucked a breath, shakily holding the stone up to her eye and peeking through the center.

Nothing.

She stared at it in her hand, her hope dwindling. As if he could sense his daughter's discouragement, Cillian appeared with a covered plate of food.

"Let me have a look, shutterbug," he said, setting the plate down beside her.

He dipped the stone into the sea water, rubbing his fingers over the edge and on the inner circle. "Still plenty of rough spots. Don't give up, magic is a fickle thing. It wants to be comfortable. If you have too many rough edges the magic won't flow for you, take a break and eat something. Your mother says she is sorry, for whatever it's worth," Cillian added gently.

"She should come and say it to my face," Deirdre snapped. She frowned at her own tone, her ears tipping back and muttered, "Sorry, Da."

"You have every right to be angry. I told her she should come talk to you but..." He shrugged. "I'll keep working on her."

"Thank you, Da. I appreciate it."

"Anything for you, shutterbug. Take a little break, have something to eat," Cillian said, kissing the top of his daughter's head. "There's a big piece of cake for you in there, too," he said, winking at her

"You're the best, Da," she said with a sad smile, peeking inside the container of food.

Cillian didn't linger, so Deirdre returned to her work. She was determined to finish as soon as possible, but her father's words of caution kept her from making rushed movements or applying too much pressure. This stone was the only one she had from Germany. This was her only chance.

Chapter Twenty Seven

The sun was beginning to turn the sky brilliant shades of pink and gold, but Deirdre hardly noticed. Her hands were caked in salt and stone dust. They were cracked and bloody, but she refused to stop. It was nearly perfect now. Dipping it into the salty water once more, she smoothed over every inch of it with her pinky. It was the only finger not completely raw. It felt perfect, but would the magic think so?

The stone had smoothed out beautifully. It was a deep charcoal colour that reminded Deirdre of Oalfus' fur, and it was speckled with white and black dots. Tears welled in her eyes. Sniffling loudly, she pulled herself together and stood up.

Turning towards the light streaming into the work shed, she slowly lifted the smooth triangular shape to her eye. She had her eyes pinched shut out of fear. What if the stone didn't work? What if hagstones could only be made for her homeland? What if she had done something wrong? Fear swelled inside her like a storm cloud, but the image of Oalfus flickered in her mind and she swallowed her damned fear.

Slowly, she peeked one eye open. Her eyes were blurry with sleep deprivation and nearly a whole night and day's work, but a brilliant gold shimmer flooded her vision. She blinked several times. Rubbed her eyes on the back of her hands, she looked once more.

Brilliant rivers of shimmering magic spiderwebbed all over the meadow outside. Deirdre shrieked with triumph. Running out of the shed and around the lighthouse, she ran smack into her father, who had come running when he heard his daughter.

"Have you done it?!" he asked, a bright smile pulling his features.

Standing a few feet behind the pair still sprawled in the grass, was Deirdre's mother in her granny-square shawl and night dress. Deirdre's smile vanished. She simply nodded and handed the stone to her father to see for himself. Cillian peered through the stone and gasped, his eyes wide and a toothy smile softening his features.

"By the ancients! You made one damned powerful hagstone, shutterbug! I haven't seen such bright magic veins in ages!"

"It's because of all the love she put into it..." Orla said sadly. She was hugging herself and looking at her feet.

"Oh, now you want to talk about love?" Deirdre spat at her mother.

"Deirdre," her father warned, giving her arm a squeeze and placing the stone in her hand. "Your mother and I stayed up all night and day talking. We haven't slept much more than an hour. Listen to what your mother has to say."

"I don't want to listen!" Deirdre snapped.

"I know you are hurt, and I deserve your anger. I was just afraid I was going to lose my little girl to a monster," Orla said sadly, her ears drooping and tears welling in her eyes.

"Oalfus isn't a monster! I can't believe–"

"I know he isn't, Deirdre. I know I made a mistake!" Orla cried, covering her face in her hands. "I wish I could undo what I have done. I have no right to stand in the way of your happiness. I just...I wasn't ready to let go yet..." Orla sobbed.

"You let me travel Europe on my own," Deirdre scoffed.

"That isn't the same, shutterbug. You know it's a tradition for your kind," Cillian said gently.

"It isn't like I'm dying! I just found the man I want to be with."

"And that means you won't be coming back to take over the moor," Cillian said knowingly.

"You don't know–"

"Of course we know, because it makes no sense for you to. Your mother and I have decided to call upon cousins when the time comes. If Olafus was one of our kind, he might understand this binding life better. He isn't, and it isn't fair to impose our ways onto him."

"He knows my role, Da! He knew and said he would–"

"But it wouldn't make you happy either," Orla said sadly. "I was glad to take up my fathers mantle. I enjoyed my time away from the moor, but I was glad to come back to it. Deirdre, you never would have been happy being bound to this old place," Orla sighed, placing a loving hand on the lighthouse.

"But–"

"Don't try to deny it, darling. We know. Look at what you made. That hagstone is a symbol of your true home," Cillian said with a soft smile.

Deirdre looked down at the stone she had slaved over, her fingers wrapping around the sturdy object and holding it to her chest.

"It is...if he'll take me back," Deirdre whispered.

The pain in her voice brought her mother to her knees beside her. "I wish I could fix this. I would give anything to fix this disaster I have caused," Orla wept, wrapping her arms around her daughter.

Deirdre wanted to be angry, she wanted her stomach to boil with rage and for her mind to fill with venom, but instead, her heart only felt empty and sad.

"I know you were only worried. I forgive you, Mammy."

Her mother squeezed her tighter, pressing her cheek against her as she sobbed. "I love you, Deirdre. I am so sorry."

"I know..."

Orla's vines slowly curled from her hair, coiling and hanging at her sides. Deirdre's eyes went wide when her mother used her claw to cut through one of her vines. It instantly withered and became a thick, sturdy cord. Deirdre knew how painful it was to cut a vine. As her mother tied the ends together and looped it through the hagstone, Deirdre's heart ached for her mother.

"Now you will always have a little piece of me with you," Orla said, teary eyed.

"Mammy...thank you." Deirdre hugged her mother, squeezing her close.

"Just promise you will visit."

"I will. Oalfus would be furious with me if I don't."

"He is a good man. I am sorry I didn't see it at first," Orla whimpered.

Deirdre helped her parents to their feet, the three walking back inside as she began her mental checklist of everything she would need. When they stepped inside, her backpack was already packed and waiting, along with a small suitcase.

"Mammy and I packed what we thought you would need, but you can always come home if we missed anything," Cillian said gently.

"Oh!" Deirdre whimpered and took a hand from each of her parents. She was exhausted and emotional, and they were doing everything right in this moment. She only wished they had done this when she had arrived with Oalfus.

"I suspect you want to go alone, but I promised your Mammy I would go with you to make sure all was well first."

Deirdre nodded, grateful for her father to be at her side in case things went foul.

"I would give anything to come as well, but promise me you'll keep sending photos back to us. We love them, and you, so much," Orla whimpered, wiping away tears.

"I will, Mammy."

Deirdre stood with her hagstone in hand, still looped around her neck. Her grandfather's hagstone tucked safely in her pocket, and her father by her side with his own hanging around his neck, the pair stood, ready to depart. Orla lingered at the door, watching with a worried expression as Deirdre lifted the stone and peered through it while walking towards a thick shimmering vein of magic. Once she was in the center of it, she held the stone out and imagined Oalfus' cabin. The round rustic structure, the cutting log with his axe leaning against it, the fire pit in front, the moss-covered, wooden-shingled roof, and the sturdy log door. A rippling portal opened in front of her, swirls of blue and gold framed the humble cottage hidden in the German mountains.

"Ready, shutterbug?" Cillian asked.

"I was born ready," Deirdre said with a teary smile. "I love you, Mammy," she called, looking over her shoulder.

"I love you too, Deirdre, with all my heart! Please never forget how much I love you!" Orla called, waving frantically as tears poured down her face.

"I will come to visit soon! I promise I won't be gone forever," Deirdre said with a smile.

Holding her father's hand, Deirdre stepped through the shimmering portal.

Chapter Twenty Eight

Viktor jolted up from the table he had fallen asleep at, maps spread out under him and different flight itineraries scribbled on a dozen odd pages of note paper. He grumbled, pulling off the page stuck to his face. Oalfus had shown up at the house yesterday in a state. It took hours of begging him to speak and several bottles of brandy before the stubborn old bastard finally spilled his guts about what had happened.

Afterwards, the two had spent hours looking at maps, calling different connections Viktor had across Europe and trying to track down where Deirdre's parents might live. Oalfus, of course, had not even bothered to find out this critical detail to help them narrow their search. The old fool had stormed off in his anger at Orla and had not even considered the consequences of his temper.

Viktor, of course, could not deny his uncle's desperate pleas for help, so the pair were now trying to iron out what airport might be the smartest choice and when Oalfus could get on the next flight to Ireland. Viktor's head throbbed from a lack of sleep and hours squinting at maps. The reception at Oalfus' cabin was garbage; he had to climb up on the roof to get a half-decent connection, and even then, it resulted in an irritating amount of disconnected calls. Viktor had decided he hated modern technology.

Grumbling, he rubbed his aching neck, and then the sound that had woken him called out again.

"Oalfus?"

Viktor stood up so quickly the stool he was sitting on fell back behind him. He clambered for the door and threw it open. There, standing out in front of the cabin, stood Deirdre and some scruffy-looking dog. Viktor rubbed his eyes, and his brows shot up.

"Deirdre?" he called, squinting at her through the early morning fog.

"Viktor?" she called back, coming closer. Viktor couldn't believe his eyes; she really was standing right in front of him.

"What the fuck are you doing here?!" he exclaimed, hurrying down the steps to greet her. He wasn't sure if he should be angry or delighted to see her, but automatically he pulled her into a brief hug. "Who are you?" Viktor blurted, looking over at the wolfhound standing a few feet away.

"Er– I am Cillian, Deirdre's father. I assume you're either Viktor or Rikovic?"

"Viktor, yes. Rikovic is my son," he said, holding out his hand to him.

Cillian set Deirdre's suitcase down, taking Viktor's outstretched hand.

"Where is he?" Deirdre asked, the desperation clear in her voice.

Viktor rubbed his neck, shrugging and giving a big sigh. "I fell asleep trying to find a flight for him, but he must have gone off on his own. I am sure he will be back soon."

"A flight?" Deirdre asked, her voice tight with worry.

"He was trying to figure out how to get back to Ireland to find you," Viktor said with a sympathetic smile.

"To find me?"

"Yes, Deirdre. You mean a great deal to my uncle. He was in shambles when he arrived at our home. He was angry at first, raging so much that we could hardly understand him. Once the anger wore off and he got into the alcohol, he fell to pieces when he told me what happened. Your mother is certainly a colourful character," Viktor said with a sarcastic edge to his voice.

"Er— I would like to extend an apology on my wife's behalf. As her husband, I am here to take responsibility for her actions. She and I had quite the conversation and she sends her deepest apologies," Cillian said in a very formal manner. Deirdre was surprised to see her father acting so seriously.

"I am sure Oalfus will appreciate that in time. I know he will be glad to see you," Viktor said, turning to Deirdre. "How on earth did you get here though?"

Deirdre lifted the hagstone, holding it out to Viktor. His eyes widened, taking the stone before noticing how battered Deirdre's hands were.

"What did you do? Oalfus will be furious when he sees this," Viktor hissed, taking hold of Deirdre's wrist to inspect the extensive damage to her fingers and palms.

"I was making that hagstone. I couldn't sit around waiting!" Deirdre huffed, pulling her hand back.

"You made this in such little time?" Viktor said, looking at the perfectly smooth triangular stone in his hand. He lifted it to his eye and flinched when the brilliant glittering paths exploded into view. "Hell's sake! This one is brighter than the other!" he yelped, rubbing his eyes as he handed it back to her.

"Mammy said it is because of how much love I poured into making it."

"You certainly did. I don't think I have ever seen you work so hard on anything," Cillian said, smiling proudly.

"I am sure Oalfus will appreciate it once he recovers from the state of your hands. You know what a fuss pot he is," Viktor said, rolling his eyes.

Deirdre's eyes were glued to the forest, her gaze falling to the chopping stump. His axe was gone. Viktor watched her for a moment, her nervous tail wag and shifting from foot to foot made her emotions clear. He glanced up at Cillian, who was watching his daughter as well.

"Go," Viktor said kindly.

"What?" She looked up at him with wide eyes.

"Go find him," Viktor urged, shooing her towards the trees.

She needed no more encouragement. She tore off her backpack and dropped it in a heap, darting into the trees. Cillian sighed, collecting her bag off the ground and turning back to Viktor.

"She is normally more polite," he tried to say with a genuine smile.

"Politeness is for those who can afford it. Right now, she can't. Come, my uncle keeps a great stash of proper German Schnapps." Viktor picked up Deirdre's suitcase, grinning wide at Cillian, who gave a shrug and followed him inside the cabin.

"Oalfus! Oalfus!!" Deirdre yelled until her voice broke, darting through the trees until her legs and lungs demanded she stop to breathe. She leaned on a tree, doubled over and panting hard. As her breathing slowed, the faint but undeniable thudding of an axe into wood caught her ear. It wasn't a normal rhythmic sound, it was erratic and violent. Deirdre could hear muffled yells, a deep gravelly cry, filled with heavy emotion.

Oalfus.

Deirdre once more began running, now with a beacon calling out to her. Her legs and lungs burned but she carried on. The louder the rage-filled sound became, the harder she pushed until she tripped and fell hard against a tree.

Panting as she braced herself, she finally caught sight of him through the trees. He was lashing out violently, swinging so hard she wondered if it was the tree or the axe handle making the eerie cracking noises. His eye was blazing red, his fangs hanging low below his chin and his horns had curled viciously at the end. His fur stood on end, like a mohawk running down his neck and back. His tail was lashing violently and his claws were easily three or four inches long.

Oalfus swung back and smashed the axe so hard into the tree, the handle finally relented and splintered as it broke off at the axe head. He bellowed with rage, lashing at the tree with his claws and snarling like a wild animal.

Eyes wide, a strange tingling sensation ran up Deirdre's back as the scent of burnt cinnamon and fire filled her nose. That tingling sensation turned to knots in her stomach, the scent of fire growing heavier in her nose until she swore she could almost feel the heat of it. This was Oalfus' charm, the charm he used to pull fear out of those he 'hunted' on Krampusnacht. Deirdre didn't like this smell; it burned her nose and made her eyes water.

Her feet refused to move as she stood there, paralyzed with fear, watching the man she loved down a tree with his bare hands. Oalfus threw his shoulder against the tree, a deep groaning and splintering sound echoing all round them as the tree finally gave in to his abuse and began tipping. Deirdre's blood ran cold, her heart hammering in her ears as she watched helplessly.

His head shot up from where he was hunched over the violently splintered tree stump. He lifted his nose to the air, sniffing a few times before his head snapped in her direction. Oalfus couldn't see who was standing among the trees, as the sun was directly behind them and only left shadows in his view. He didn't care anymore; the sorrow and self-loathing in his heart was consuming him. He dropped to all fours and bellowed out a roar before charging directly towards whoever it was. A vicious grin spread over his face when they turned and ran.

Run all you want, little mouse, I will catch you. You are in my forest now.

He leapt up onto a low-hanging tree branch, launching himself from branch to branch in pursuit of the shadow below him. His senses dulled by rage, he couldn't even detect the familiar scent of fresh rainfall wafting off his prey. They were below him now. He snarled out his laughter before hurling himself down to the forest floor directly in their path. He was on all fours.

He heard them skid to a stop and begin backing away. Dark laughter rumbled out of his chest. Perhaps this time he would finally kill his prey. Why not? He hadn't fed properly in centuries, and their fear tasted sinfully delicious. Creeping forward, Oalfus finally raised his eyes enough to see mustard yellow leg warmers, gray leggings, a bright purple jumper.

He froze. His eyes widened and the glow slowly faded from his one seeing eye as he met the gaze of two terrified emerald eyes. He slowly rose to his feet, stumbling back from her as she stood there, trembling and panting.

"Deirdre?" he whispered, hoping this was some sick joke his mind was playing on him. She only nodded, her hands clutching a funny necklace she wore. Oalfus backed away further from her, his ears tipping back and a low whine slipping out of his parted lips.

"I am a monster..." he muttered. He turned away from her, ready to run, when two arms wrapped around him in a fierce hug.

"Please don't run away!" she sobbed, her face pressing into his back. "I tried to get here sooner. I tried so hard to get here–" her voice broke as she clung to him. "Please don't go!"

Oalfus fell to pieces, tears flowing freely as he spun around and hauled her up into his arms. He held her so tightly he feared he might break her ribs, but he couldn't let go. His hand cradled the back of her head as he broke into tears and kissed her between his own sobs. They both fell in a heap, Oalfus on his knees as he held her limp body against his.

"I am so sorry, Deirdre," he wept, holding onto her for dear life. "I never should have left you. Please forgive me," he said with a hoarse sob, his grip on her tightening.

Her body ached under his grip, but she refused to ask him to loosen it. She clung onto him, her fists in his hair as he hugged his head against her chest.

"I am so sorry!" she cried.

How could only one day apart cause such pain? It felt like a lifetime, the unknown of what each other was feeling like an eternity of worries. It had only been a day apart, but the ache was the pain of a lifetime for them both. Their bond only solidified in that moment, clinging to each other for comfort.

Oalfus was a mess of guilt for leaving her, for giving into her mothers cutting words, for hunting her. He felt unworthy of her, but at the same time, he could not express how grateful he was to have her back. Deirdre ran her hands over his face, smoothing back his disheveled fur and hair. She kissed his forehead and cheeks, his nose and lips, even the front of his horns. Her fingers ached but she didn't care, she gripped onto his shaggy fur and pressed her cheek against his forehead.

"I was so scared I had lost you," she whimpered, a little hiccuped sob bubbling up.

"I never should have left. I regretted it the moment I realized I had no way of finding you again. I was such a fool!" Oalfus groaned, his hand wrapping around hers, still cradling his cheek. He could feel the state of her hands, the coarseness of the fur from non-stop stone work. He pulled her hand away and his eyes widened in shock.

"Deirdre–!"

"Viktor said you would be upset, but I'm fine. I couldn't stop working until I could get back to you." Deirdre pulled the hagstone off her neck and held it in front of him.

"You...you made this? It worked?" He was baffled.

"How do you think we got back so quickly?" she said with a shy smile.

Oalfus held the stone in his hands, smoothing over it with his thumb. It felt like velvet, it was incredible how perfect it was. Lifting it to his seeing eye, Oalfus' jaw fell open as he saw the dazzling veins of gold snaking through the trees, ghosts of all the paths he had taken through these forests.

"It's beautiful," he muttered in adoration of her work.

"Now we will always have a way back home," she whispered, trailing her fingers over the edge of the stone in his hand.

"Deirdre, I told you I didn't want to come between you and your family. This is just a dwelling to me. When the time comes, we will return to your homeland as is expected. No matter where we are, as long as you and I are together, we are home," he said, brushing his thumb over her cheek.

She appreciated the sentiment of his words, but exhaustion was starting to set in. There would be time later to explain everything that happened. Her body slumped against him, her arms wrapped around his neck loosely, and her face pressed against him as she mumbled, "Can we go home now?"

"Of course we can," he said, cradling her against him as he rose to his feet.

She was exhausted, he could see it plainly, and as endearing as it was to carry her asleep in his arms, it sent off alarm bells. Oalfus walked cautiously, careful of every step as she slipped deeper into sleep against him.

He pushed the cabin door open quietly, nearly leaping out of his skin when he saw Viktor and Cillian sitting there.

"Hell have mercy, I forgot you were here," Oalfus groaned.

"Is she alright?" Cillian gasped, seeing his daughter limp in Oalfus' arms.

"Yes, just exhausted. Has she slept at all since I left?" Oalfus asked, easing Deirdre down on his bed carefully. Immediately Deirdre buried her face into the furs and sighed happily.

"She was up working through the night and most of the day. I doubt she even ate anything, even though I brought her supper last night. She wouldn't be deterred from her work, she was so distraught..." Cillian trailed off, looking over at his daughter with a tight expression.

"Foolish girl," Oalfus sighed, brushing her hair away from her face.

"She loves you deeply, and I am here to apologize on behalf of my wife," Cillian said in a grim tone.

Oalfus shook his head. "I don't hold any ill will. It was my own damn fault for storming off the way I did."

"Oalfus, I appreciate the kindness but I must insist. I am her husband and I need to take responsibility for her behavior. She told me what she said and I was appalled. I want you to know that you will always be welcome in our home. I promise you, my wife is sincerely sorry for her conduct. She was foolish and I am very embarrassed for how we both behaved."

Oalfus smiled to himself; it didn't surprise him when other creatures were cold towards him. Orla had certainly cut deep with her remarks, but he promised himself he wouldn't allow it to dwell in his mind. Deirdre was not a reflection of her mother, and vice versa. Deirdre had never been cruel or unkind to him. Quite the opposite, she was sweet from the moment they laid eyes on each other. Oalfus longed to just lie with her, curl himself around her and shut out the world.

Cillian softened seeing the tenderness Oalfus had for his daughter. The apprehension he had felt towards the old demon all but vanished in that moment. He knew he would take care of her, he would keep her safe, and, most of all, he would love her fiercely.

"I suppose I should be on my way," Cillian said, smiling kindly as he looked at Oalfus.

"Are you certain?" Oalfus asked, a look of suspicion flickered across his features.

"She has her hagstone for the moor. She can come home to visit whenever she likes," Cillian assured, pulling his own from his pocket.

"I will make sure she comes home soon, I–" Oalfus caught sight of the suitcase peeking out from behind Deirdre's backpack. "What is that?"

Cillian followed his gaze, chuckling and shaking his head. "Oalfus, you are a little slow on the uptake, eh?"

"No kidding," Viktor sneered from where he perched on the counter.

"Deirdre won't be coming home. Not permanently, anyway. This is her home now. The moor was never meant to be her fate."

"But I thought she had to take over her mother's role," Oalfus said quizzically, running a nervous hand through his hair.

"We have many cousins we can call upon if need be, but Orla and I are still young! I suspect we will be there a long while. Deirdre is much too wild to be trapped on the moor. It would snuff her out like weeds in a garden. She needs the wide open world. Orla and I see that now," Cillian said with a sad smile.

"You really mean...she can stay?" Oalfus whispered.

"It is hardly up to me, now is it?" Cillian laughed. "That girl would turn the world upside down to get her way. This is her path. *This* is her fate."

There was that word again...fate.

Oalfus stood and held out a hand to Cillian, which the wolfhound took and shook firmly. "I promise to take care of her," Oalfus said solemnly.

"I know you will, and when you both are ready, Orla and I would love to have you at our home."

"We won't be strangers," Oalfus assured.

"Da?" Deirdre's groggy voice called. She was sitting up and rubbing her eyes.

"I am off, shutterbug," Cillian said, going to her side and kneeling on the bed. "You are home now"

Deirdre hugged him fiercely, a peaceful smile on her face. "Thank you, Da," she whispered.

"I would do anything for you, my girl," Cillian soothed, running a hand over her hair.

Deirdre and Oalfus stood together as they watched Cillian leave. Deirdre tearfully waved a final goodbye when he disappeared through the portal. She promised herself she would bring another stone and make a hagstone to the cottage for her father the next time they visited.

Then it was Viktor's turn to leave. He hugged them both, which surprised Oalfus.

"Try not to show up in such chaos next time? You gave us all a fright," Viktor teased as he cut his palm and allowed the blood to drip over the carved sigil. A swirling red portal slowly bloomed open.

"I don't plan on it," Oalfus chuckled dryly.

Viktor turned to Deirdre, grasping her shoulders and grinning at her.

"You take good care of my uncle, or I might have to come check on you two unannounced," he warned, though it was a friendly tone he took.

"I will," Deirdre beamed.

They stood together, watching Viktor disappear through the portal. The red swirl shrank and disappeared. Deirdre leaned against Oalfus, hugging his arm and looking up at him.

"What now?" she asked.

"Whatever you wish," he purred back, cradling her face in his big sturdy hand.

She was finally home.

Chapter Twenty Nine

It turned out what both of them needed was several days of absolutely nothing. Deirdre and Oalfus ended up sleeping for nearly an entire day and night, sprawled across the bed, curled in each other's arms. The pair were spent, overexhausted, and worn out from everything they had gone through. How had it only been a month since they met? It felt like a lifetime. A lifetime worth of drama and emotions, a lifetime worth of love blooming between the two of them.

Oalfus was glad to be back in his sanctuary. As much as he said this cabin was simply a dwelling, he was delighted it could be their home. The pair lounged in his makeshift bed for several days, simply enjoying each other's company. They read one of Oalfus' books, each taking turns to read a chapter out loud to the other. They made countless pots of tea, and simply got lost in each other's presence.

Finally, they were both becoming stir crazy, so they ventured out into the woods. Deidre was delighted with how normal it felt. Oalfus even offered to carry her in his basket, which she giggled at. It felt so comfortable, so simple now that their feelings were known and, better yet, reciprocated. This magnetic draw between them was like the stuff of fairy tales, absolutely effortless and blissful.

Oalfus began teaching Deirdre the different barks and types of pine needles he used to make their tea, showing her how to discern poisonous berries from safe ones. The days melted into each other. Every day, they would hike out a little further, and every day, Deirdre filled more and more rolls of film with pictures of Oalfus and their home. They spoke of where they would travel to next, and Deirdre often found herself longing to pack up her bag and start a new leg to her adventure.

Finally, an excuse came one morning as Deirdre dug through her bag to find she had completely run out of film. She sat back on her haunches and looked at her bag with a frustrated expression.

"What's the matter, *mein liebe?*" Oalfus asked, glancing up at her from where he was making their morning coffee.

"I am out of film," she pouted, her shoulders slumping.

"Shit..." Oalfus huffed, looking down at the coffee in front of him and letting out a heavy sigh. "I suppose I should have seen this coming, I assume you want to go into one of the towns nearby?" he asked, rubbing the back of his neck as he considered what would be the best course of action.

"If it isn't a bother. I don't mind going alone, though, " she said hopefully.

"You're not going alone," Oalfus growled.

"Well, what should we do then?"

Oalfus dug through one of the wooden boxes tucked under his counter, grumbling and tossing things aside before he finally found an old map. He unfolded it, slumping back to sit as he scratched his brow and scanned it intently. Deirdre crawled over, sitting beside him and squinting at it. She gave up rather quickly, seeing it was all written in German. Finally Oalfus found what he was looking for, tapping his claw against the old paper.

"We are roughly here. These three villages are off limits. I would prefer not even going near them unless absolutely unavoidable..." he kept scanning over the map, scratching his chin until finally he tapped a claw on a town. "Wernigerode is big enough that there are likely demons there. It is a three day hike."

Deirdre whined, her ears tipping back. "Three days without my camera..."

"You will survive, *mien Liebe*" Oalfus chuckled, kissing the top of her head.

"I will stock up," she asserted.

Deirdre slumped down onto the ground beside Oalfus, her legs stretched out as she sat panting.

"Finally!" she groaned, looking down the hill towards the sprawling town down below them. "How are you doing?" she asked, looking up at Oalfus as he stood shifting his weight from foot to foot.

"I'm a little nervous," he admitted.

"I will be with you, I won't leave your side" she assured him, rubbing his arm.

"You better not," he growled, wrapping her in his arms and pressing his lips against her neck.

Deirdre giggled, rubbing the side of his head as they looked down to the town below. "It's our first adventure on our own," she beamed, pressing closer against him.

"Well, what are we waiting for?" he mused, trying to push confidence into his voice.

Deirdre took hold of his hand, looking up at him with a big smile. "One step at a time," she encouraged him brightly.

The town was bustling. Hardly everyone even looked at them as they wove their way through the streets. They spotted several demons among the market streets. Oalfus visibly relaxed after seeing other demons among the mortals.

Deirdre tried to ask for directions, but after two failed attempts, Oalfus could take it no longer. He sucked it up, found his courage, and poked his head into a small shop. The wide-eyed store clerk looked up at him with a slack jaw.

"H-how can I help you?" he asked.

"Could you point me in the direction of a shop where I can buy camera film? Perhaps somewhere to have photos developed as well?" Oalfus asked, glancing back at Deirdre, whose tail was wagging.

"Oh, uh, yes. Let me write down some directions"

The pair found themselves in a massive camera store, with a photo lab in the back that looked just like the one in the village near her parents house. Deirdre was delighted, though she couldn't read anything. Oalfus was stuck doing all the talking, asking clerks for help everywhere they went.

Deirdre was like a child in a candy store. Her face lit up at every turn as she admired the rows of new cameras on display. Oalfus felt a particular flair of embarrassment when he handed over the several rolls of film to be processed, knowing full well just how many photos of him were on them.

All that was left was waiting for the photos to be ready, which meant they needed to find lodging for the night. Oalfus groaned; he would have much preferred to camp in the woods, but Deirdre thought it would be better if they found something nearby. It was impossible for him to deny her. He knew he would have to get used to all of this hustle and bustle eventually, as his days of being Krampus in utter solitude were over. Perhaps, he thought, forever.

The realization was jarring. Would he never be able to enjoy another Krampusnacht again? Would Deirdre expect him to give up his little game?

Surely not he assured himself.

She seemed to enjoy the prospect, so perhaps he could involve her in his little game somehow. That idea pleased him greatly. Even if she could not be involved, the idea of being able to come home to her after Krampusnacht was equally pleasing.

They found a small hostel around the corner. It was one of the few with private rooms available, and Deirdre was delighted. She threw herself down onto the bed with a happy sigh, hugging onto one of the pillows and kicking her feet that hung off the end of the bed.

"It feels good to travel again," she sighed, rolling side to side with giddiness.

"You say that as you have been completely useless all day when it comes to the language," Oalfus snorted, arching a brow at her.

"Well, if someone wasn't so bloody picky about my German, I might have been able to work it out. I made it all the way to you without any problems, you know"

"Your German is atrocious," he muttered, shaking his head as he read over the several tourist pamphlets left in their cramped room.

"Well, you could always teach me, you grumpy gus" Deirdre retorted, her tone that of an insolent child.

Oalfus smirked at her, considering it a moment before he set the pamphlet down and crossed his arms. "I am a very strict teacher," he growled, his tone edging on dangerous as he loomed over her.

"Oh really?" Deirdre challenged.

"Oh yes. I will make sure to drill every word into your pretty little head. I won't tolerate any mistakes," Oalfus rumbled, caging Deirdre under him against the bed.

"I think I like the sounds of your lessons," she gasped, her eyes burning into his.

"I am sure you will. I am very thorough," he purred, leaning down and nibbling along her neck.

She instantly melted against the bed; Oalfus loved how sensitive she was in the crook of her neck and shoulder. His long tongue trailed along her throat and up her jaw before their lips crashed together.

Truth be told, they had not been overly sexual with each other since leaving Rikovic's wedding. Intimate, most certainly, but they had not actually gotten much farther than heavy petting and kissing. There was a fire blazing just beneath the surface, both of them could feel it, a magnetic pull bringing them together.

This time, there was a *need* to go further. Something about this first step into the unknown together had sparked a new flame in both of them. For Deirdre, it was the burning desire of adventure, breaking out of routine and exploring everything new. For Oalfus, it was simply taking the first of many new steps, as he had been a creature of habit for centuries. Deirdre was forcing him, for the first time in his life, to accept the unknown possibilities that lie outside his comfort zone. He never believed it would be possible, but here he was, eager and hungry for it.

"Oalfus, please," she whispered to him, her back arching up to meet his touch as he pushed her knees apart with his.

Oalfus growled, grinning wide as his hand ran down her sides with one hand and the other snatched up her wrists to pin them above her head.

"Beg, *mein liebe*. I want to hear you plead for me inside you."

Deirdre whimpered, her legs hooking around his waist and lifting herself up so her crotch was pressing against his. "*Please,* Oalfus, please, I need your cock inside me. I want to feel you split me in half. I want you to paint my insides and make me scream your name so this whole fucking city hears me."

Oalfus' fur stood on end. The ravenous look in her eyes and scent of her need was beyond anything he could have imagined. His claws dug into her hip as he cupped her ass, kneading her supple rump.

"I might break you if you keep begging so sweetly, *Liebe,*" he growled against her ear, pushing himself harder against her burning core. He could feel the heat of her desire through their clothing, and it was intoxicating.

"Give it to me, stop teasing!" she whimpered.

Oalfus grinned, leaning back from her and then completely backing away from the bed. He crossed his arms, his smirk only widening as he looked down at his very disgruntled little demoness.

"Take off your clothes, slowly," he ordered. His eyes burned into her very soul as he looked over her body with such hunger it made Deirdre shiver.

"You want me to strip for you?" she asked shyly, tugging off her leg warmers and windbreaker first.

Oalfus arched a brow, shrugging. "I suppose, but then you will be helping me out of mine?" he rumbled.

This had Deirdre up and on her feet. She was eager to get him out of those well-fitted dark denim jeans and skin tight black turtle-neck. He looked sinfully good in everything he wore. As much as he grumbled and complained about clothing, he was naturally gorgeous in everything. Oalfus had the features one sought out in models, high cheekbones and a strong jawline. His eyebrows were tamed back from his styling session in Moscow and it only gave his angular expressions further sharpness. His blind eye was mesmerizing. Somehow, the silvery tone of it wasn't sickly or milky like most blinded eyes; it was just as bright and expressive as his seeing eye.

Deirdre had become jealous of all the stares he got as they walked down the crowded German streets, but in this moment alone in a tiny hostel room, she was peeling off her layers of hiking clothing like it was priceless lingerie and she was the only woman in the world. Oalfus *looked* at her like she was the only woman in the world, and it made her chest swell with pride.

It was hard for the old demon to keep his hands off her. Stepping closer and trailing fingers over her arms and hips as she wiggled out of her shorts, she tugged her jumper and waffle undershirt off. Nothing about the way Deirdre dressed was sexual or extravagant, and it didn't need to be. Oalfus dreaded the idea of her wearing anything overtly sexy; he would be a floundering slack-jawed ne-anderthal if she did.

He loved how Deirdre's simplicity only accentuated all the things that drove him to feral desire. The way her stomach had a paunch just above the little red curls that crowned her folds, how her hips were wide, and that her thighs pressed together. The way she had the thickest mass of copper curls someone as big as himself could hide in them when they slept together. Her emerald eyes were practically boiling his very soul as she stared deep into his eyes while she wiggled out of her skin tight leggings to finally reveal her bare body. Oalfus almost whined from how tightly his pants were crushing his length, his clipped fur fluffed out on end when Deirdre's hands slid under the hem of his shirt and began sliding up his stomach.

"Deirdre...you are being cruel," he whispered, fisting her hair and crashing his lips against hers.

It was a wild kiss, not slow or tender, but heated and dangerous. His teeth tore her lip, and hers did his in return, but neither cared. She began pushing his shirt higher up his chest, her claws raking along his lower back as he finally pulled away long enough to struggle the fitted garment up and over his horns. He felt his breath hitch when two delicate hands slipped under the waist of his pants and began unbuttoning and tugging at the zipper. As much as Oalfus detested the irritation of clothing, he had not anticipated the sensuality of a woman taking it off him. He rumbled out a low growl, tossing his shirt aside and taking a firm grip on her hair.

"Down on your knees, sweetling," he growled, a grin spreading over his features.

Deirdre was more than happy to oblige; she rather liked bringing him pleasure. The idea of making this hulking man completely come undone with just her mouth brought a rush of confidence to her. Sinking slowly to her knees, she jerked his pants off his hips as she settled down in front of him. Oalfus' grip was hardly aggressive on her hair; he slipped his fingers over the top of her head and cradled her head considerately in his large clawed fingers. Deirdre eyed his length with a wicked grin, bringing the tip to her mouth before opening wide enough so that half his length slipped into her eager mouth. It tasted as incredible as she remembered, one of the many perks of having a demon as a lover. His slick pre-cum left a sweet flavor in the back of her throat as she greedily began rubbing her tongue over and around the three spines along the belly of his length.

Oalfus groaned loudly, whining low as he bucked into her maw. His mind was in a fog of pleasure, bracing against the wall for dear life. He was ready to crumble, the way her hand eagerly worked the lower half of his shaft while her mouth worked the tip. She suckled the spines along the underside of his cock, trailed kisses along his shaft, and ran her tongue over every inch. The more Oalfus squirmed, the bolder Deirdre got, first massaging the length only, then working her hand down to cup and rub over his sack. A strangled choke came out of him as she fondled and had her way with him. Oalfus fell back against the wall ready to crumble right then and there.

"You'll kill me at this rate," Oalfus half-joked, his knees threatening to give out.

"I like you this way," Deirdre mumbled around his length in her mouth.

"You are a wicked little minx," Oalfus groaned, finally pulling her off his length by her hair.

"No fair!" she complained, her hands still working his length.

"Enough, you witch," he hissed, pulling her up off her knees and tossing her onto the bed. "Clearly, someone enjoys teasing, so why not give some in return?" he growled, a wicked smirk spreading over his face as his one seeing eye shone brilliant crimson.

Deirdre tried to wriggle free, but Oalfus truly had her on size and weight. He pinned her arms above her head in one hand, her knees forced apart as he pinned her leg under his, his claws trialing down her side.

"M-mmn...Oalfus don't be cruel," she whimpered, her previous bravado melting away as the older demon took charge.

"Oh, what? My little *Liebchien* doesn't want to be teased?"

She gasped as his hand trailed over her stomach before dipping between her legs. He slipped two fingers over her slick folds, then, without warning, thrust both of them inside her to the knuckle. Deirdre let out a cry before Oalfus silenced her with his mouth, his tongue slipping into her mouth. Deirdre's back arched off the bed, her whole body trembling as Oalfus curled his fingers and found the tender little spot deep inside her quivering core. It felt like she was melting into the bed, her whole body shaking against his grip. Oalfus groaned into their kiss, his length grinding against her thigh. He finally pulled his mouth from hers, his tongue running over her maw.

"You're gripping onto my fingers so tightly, sweetling," Oalfus murmured, kissing down her throat.

"*Please*, Oalfus," Deirdre breathed, her thighs twitching as her depths tightened around his fingers.

"Tell me exactly what you need, sweetling. Tell me what you burn for," he groaned, his teeth grazing along her throat and shoulder. Deep in his mind, that wretched voice that had been nagging at the back of his mind began growling.

Claim her, claim your fate.

He willed the voices away, but his lower jaw trembled as he slowly opened his mouth. His teeth grazed along the crook of her neck and over her shoulder. How easily he could sink his teeth in and mark her as his own.

Claim what is yours.

Oalfus squeezed his eyes closed, taking a shaky breath as he edged his mouth away from her. He snapped his jaws shut, only allowing himself to drink in her scent. Deirdre felt his hesitation. His fingers had slowed inside her, his grip faltered on her wrists, and, all too suddenly, she realized he was trembling. She pulled her hands free of his grip, her fingers trailing over his cheeks and cupping his face as she slowly lifted his head to meet her gaze.

"Oalfus, what's wrong?" she whispered, her eyes searching his face desperately for answers.

His eyes opened slowly. They were blazing with desire, even his clouded blind eye boring into her very soul. He gripped the back of her neck; it was a possessive and dominating hold on her, his body caging her down. He growled out his words and she could hear his struggle to maintain control.

"Every part of me is fighting to claim you...to possess you...it is torture. Even now, I want nothing more than to replace my fingers with my cock and sink my teeth into your shoulder. I have planted my seed in you and yet, I want *more* of you..."

Deirdre swallowed, the realization coming to her. He wanted to mark her. She had heard about this in passing. The act was seen as very old-fashioned, which made sense, seeing as Oalfus was Old Order. The look on his face, however, told her it was beyond just an act of marking claim. This was *instinctual*, it was embedded in his very nature, and he was fighting it to spare her the discomfort. She wrapped her arms around his neck, pulling him in to kiss her as her leg hooked around his sturdy form, her hips slowly rocking into his fingers and little moans slipping out of her.

"I need you, Oalfus. Please stop tormenting me. I want you inside me. I feel so empty without you," she whispered against his lips, kissing him between her words.

He could hardly deny her. Pulling his fingers from her at an agonizingly slow pace, he watched her mouth form a little O shape as he trailed along her slick folds. Shifting over her, he grazed the tip of his length against her burning entrance. She whimpered, giving him such gorgeous doe eyes he could scarcely hold back. She gasped as he pushed his tip in. The spines popped into her melting depths one by one, and she shuddered and fell back against the mattress. He crumbled seeing her ecstasy. His hips thrust forward and he buried himself fully. Deirdre cried out in bliss, her legs wrapping around his hips and her arms tight around his neck. She shuddered and cried out under him as he continued his onslaught of thrusts. Her pleasure climbing, her courage took hold, and breathlessly she whispered to him through a flurry of moans.

"Claim me, Oalfus, I am yours!"

A brilliant crimson glow filled his seeing eye. His body felt as if it was a spring stretched to its limit. With those simple words, he was released, and that inner beast roared in triumph at her order. Buried inside her to his hilt, his arm cradling her against him and hand fisting her hair, Oalfus clamped his jaw down on Deirdre. He hesitated only a moment, but it was enough for her to place her own hand on the back of his head and give him the slightest nudge of encouragement. His teeth sank in, his mind went blank, and then his beast took over.

He snarled viciously, clamping his jaws on her while his pace suddenly doubled. Deirdre had no time to even perceive the jolt of pain before a vicious wave of pleasure absolutely wracked her body. She cried out, pleading with him to continue, begging to be allowed to cum, shattering entirely under his oppressive force. He didn't release her, even after her orgasm came and went. His teeth just sank deeper and his thrusting seemed to carry on without signs of stopping. His hands were everywhere, from her hips and stomach, to her breasts and teasing her perked nipples. He started teasing her clit, which sent another frenzied wave of ecstasy through her.

Finally he pulled his mouth away from her shoulder to admire the mark he had left on her. It was a grizzly affair to most, but Deirdre seemed utterly lost in the excessive charm pouring out of Oalfus. His sweet, citrusy spiced scent flooded every corner of her senses. Her mind was such a fuzzy haze of pleasure and bliss, she hardly registered him flipping her onto her stomach, and repositioning himself before slamming into her.

Oalfus was nearing his limit. Between her blood smeared over his muzzle and teeth, her heady scent was making him struggle to hold back much longer.

"I'm going to lose my mind!" Deirdre slurred her words, her tail wagging against his stomach as he edged closer to his limit.

"I fear we both might," Oalfus groaned, reaching under her and finding his prize, her trembling pearl.

Deirdre practically screamed as he began tormenting it, circling it with firm fingers. She shattered, the flood of her desire spilling down onto the sheets was too much for him, and he was finished. Flood after flood of their combined climax spilled from Deirdre, her body shaking from the waves of pleasure, Oalfus in no better a state. He snorted and huffed out several choked breaths, gasping and shuddering as he went rigid over her.

The pair collapsed in a tangled heap together on the little hostel bed, both spent and exhausted. The ache of her mark settled in, but

Oalfus knew immediately. His tongue ran over it, like a dog licking his wounds, and he refused to leave it be.

Eventually, Deirdre had to insist he leave it alone, but the low whine he made had her immediately relenting and melting at how sweet he was. She figured this was part of it, his more primal instincts demanding he nurse the mark he left. She knew by morning it would be a puffy pink scar, and in a few weeks' time, a less swollen silvery mark on her shoulder. The bleeding stopped quickly, Oalfus seemingly satisfied and he finally left it alone.

He was not speaking, only giving grunt or huffing noises in response. Deirdre assumed it was because he was so tired, but then he lifted her off the bed and squeezed into the tiny bathroom in their room. There was only a standing shower, so Oalfus opted to wipe her down by hand using the sink and a cloth. He still didn't speak, only nuzzling her occasionally and tending to her oh so tenderly.

Had Deirdre not been so damned exhausted, she might have been concerned, but the warm cloth was like magic and had her slipping between consciousness and sleep. She didn't recall exactly how she had gotten back to bed, most likely Oalfus carrying her, but just before her mind finally slipped into blissful sleep, the vivid image of little star shaped white blossoms filled her mind. She promised herself she would ask Oalfus about them tomorrow, but right now, laying on his chest, she needed to sleep.

Chapter Thirty

Oalfus groaned, opening one eye and immediately, both shot open. The room was covered in vines again, only this time it was covered in tiny white blooms. The normally light buttery scent of Edelweiss was overpowering the whole room. Oalfus sat up and pushed the vines off him. They were just a sprawl, growing denser towards the tiny bathroom in their room.

Oalfus heard the faint buzzing of Deirdre's toothbrush. He waited a minute, hoping she would come out, but she didn't. Stepping carefully though the sprawl of vines and flowers, Oalfus arched a brow when he saw Deirdre. She was staring in horror at the mirror, her mouth slack and the toothbrush hardly hanging on in her mouth.

"I don't think that's a very effective brushing method" Oalfus teased, but Deirdre didn't respond. He reached out and waved a hand in front of her face, which managed to draw her attention.

"Oalfus?"

"Yes?" He tilted his head looking at her.

"What are these flowers called?"

He snorted, arching another brow at her. "You are growing them and you don't know? They are Edelweiss flowers. Normally they only grow in the mountains"

"I didn't do this. I woke up and they were everywhere! I...I saw them last night as I was dozing off, right after you marked me..." Deirdre's fingers gingerly ran over the wide bite mark that covered most of her shoulder.

Oalfus grinned, moving behind her and wrapping his arms around her, being mindful of her mass of vines. "Breath, *Liebchien.* Deep and slow...can you do that for me?"

He looked at her through the mirror, showing her the kind of breath he wanted her to take. She nodded, spitting out her tooth-paste and taking in a shaky breath. Each one came easier, her eyes closed slowly as she leaned back against his rising and falling chest. It guided her breathing and soothed her right to her very bones. When her eyes fluttered open, her vines were gone. All that remained were little white flower petals scattered over the floor.

"Do you feel better?" he mumbled.

"Much...thank you." Deirdre turned and buried her face against his chest, nuzzling in and missing his shaggy fur desperately.

"Let's go get your pictures, then perhaps chart our next course," Oalfus whispered.

"You mean it?!" Deirdre jerked her head back to look at him. A warm smile spread over his face as he nodded, cradling her face in his hands.

"Anywhere you wish. I can't keep hiding from the world forever."

"How do you feel about Vienna?" Deirdre asked, her tail wagging wildly behind her.

"Whatever pleases you, *mein Liebchen.*"

And please her he did. It seemed every stop on their journey brought more and more photographs than Deirdre had ever taken. Almost all her photographs that she mailed back to her parents consisted of Oalfus in some capacity. Standing in front of monuments, shopping in markets, hiking through trails. The funniest were of him being very disgruntled in crowded forms of transportation.

Deirdre could read him like a book by the time they left Poland. Oalfus wore three smiles at any given time. The first was the one he saved exclusively for Deirdre, warm and all-encompassing like a warm blanket. The second was a pleasant grin for the general public, though it could morph into a forced expression when he was being stopped by the countless mortal tourists who begged for photos due to his 'resemblance to Krampus'. Little did they know they were taking photos of the actual monster of legend, but Deirdre only giggled to herself when he would *always* reluctantly agree. Part of her was certain he adored the attention.

The final smile was the one Deirdre always seemed to capture and squeal over. It was his 'Get me the hell out of here' smile. The one he would flash at her when he was crushed into a bus seat or struggling to shimmy through narrow markets with his backpack over head. They had found one big enough for him when they stopped in Berlin briefly to catch a train to Austria. It seemed Oalfus carried what was most important, clothing, food, and most of their camping gear when hostels or hotels were not available. Deirdre's pack consisted of film, photos, more film, and a few odds and ends she would collect as souvenirs to mail her parents. Oalfus realized her parents' knick knack problem was only worsened by their daughter.

Travelling had terrified the old demon. He dreaded it in the beginning, fearful of the reactions he would get. He had always known the major cities in Europe had demon populations, but he had avoided them out of fear. Little did he know, among Europeans, demons were as common as pigeons. No one gave much thought or care to them, and Oalfus was grateful at just how ignored he was. He would get stares, the occasional photos, struggling to fit in tighter spaces, but, for the most part, he was just another fly on the wall.

Seeing the passion in Deirdre's face as they moved further and further north to the Scandinavian regions was a gift in itself. It was a shame their travels would soon have to end. As Oalfus had feared, Deirdre was beginning to balloon in size. Her pregnancy was coming on fast, and it seemed that every city they stopped in, she was needing more and more maternity wear.

It all came to a head when they couldn't find a hotel. Deirdre broke down in tears in an alleyway. They were in a tiny village in Sweden, the hostels were full, and the only inn was at capacity. Deirdre sobbed against Oalfus' chest as they stood in the dark passage between the buildings.

"*Liebchen...*" Oalfus soothed, smoothing her hair back and tilting her chin up.

"I-I am s-sorry...I p-promise I w-will b-be okay," Deirdre sobbed, rubbing her tears away and whimpering.

"Deirdre..." His tone meant she was about to be told the truth. It was time to go home, it was time to accept that traveling in this state was beyond foolish. It was time to hang up the backpack.

"I d-dont want i-it to be o-over," Deirdre sobbed anew, hiding against him as her tail tucked between her legs.

"I don't want it to end either, sweetling, but we have been traveling together for some months now and you are not getting any smaller. We must consider your safety and that of...our little one."

It was the first time Oalfus had ever truly acknowledged their child. Deirdre herself had been avoiding the subject. In a way, they both were afraid to face this new truth. While it felt as if they had spent a lifetime together, it had not yet been a year.

Deirdre sniffed, wiping her face and letting her forehead fall against his chest.

"Where should we go?" she muttered.

"Frankly, I think back to Russia or Ireland. You need to see a doctor. This whole time, we have been very foolish and have not had you looked over once. The cabin is too far from anyone who could treat you, should things go wrong."

Deirdre nodded, rubbing her eyes and looking up at the old demon. She had fear in her eyes and Oalfus could feel that same fear in his own. They had avoided this too long, pretended things were fine and there was nothing to worry about. Now, the looming reality had them both startled. Oalfus cupped Deirdre's face in his hands, rubbing her cheeks to dry them.

"I promise, I will stay with you for every moment, you will never have to be alone in this," he assured her.

"Thank you...I...I am a little scared," she whispered.

"I am too, but we are here for each other," Oalfus promised.

"Okay...okay." She wrapped her arms around him and pressed in as close as she could.

Oalfus reached into her bag, pulling out the hangstone and the carved sigil before offering for her to choose.

"Wherever we go, it is your choice," he assured her, stroking her cheek.

"I don't want us crammed into my Mammy and Da's attic, I might kill someone," she joked, brushing her hair from her face. She was getting overwhelmed, he could tell by the look on her face.

"Then we will see them after the – after *our* child is born," he asserted, pushing a smile. It was a strained smile.

Deirdre hated that smile suddenly. Her brows furrowed as she searched his face. "You hate this, don't you?" she blurted, she hadn't meant to let the words out, but they spilled past her lips anyway.

"Deirdre..." Oalfus looked hurt, kneeling in front of her he pulled her close to him so they were nearly nose to nose and eye level. "I am simply anxious, just as anyone in our situation must be. This came on by surprise. Summer is nearly over and you look as if you are nearly ready to give birth. Neither of us have any idea what to expect, when you are due, *what* might come of our coming together. I have never cared about anyone as deeply as I care for you. I am just worried this might...that *I* might have ruined what is growing between us by burdening you with–"

"You never burdened me. I chose to sleep with you. It is equally my fault," she snipped at him.

Oalfus winced at her words. Was their child some problem they had created? He looked away from her, his ears tipping back as he swallowed hard. He struggled to find the courage to speak. He had been wanting to say these words for weeks, and yet, they felt as if they might choke him.

Looking down at her swollen stomach, Oalfus placed both hands on either side and pressed his forehead to it. Deirdre froze, her hands drawn up to her chest as she looked down at him, perplexed and rather uncomfortable.

"Deirdre...this child is not anything to lay *blame* on...they will be ours, a little *someone* we made together. I knew you were going to be special to me from the moment I laid eyes on you, I never knew just how damned special you would become. You are *mine,* just as I am yours...I love you, Deirdre." The words left his throat in a tight whisper.

After painful moments of her silence, he glanced upwards. Deirdre had her hands covering her mouth and tears welling in her eyes. Oalfus swallowed audibly, one of his hands moving from her stomach to her cheek.

"Please say something, *Liebchen*"

"I love you, too," she croaked, sobbing once more and throwing herself into his arms.

Oalfus nearly fell onto his arse from how fiercely she hugged him, laughing and lifting her into the air. He pressed his nose against her neck and drank in her scent, kissing her throat and jaw. She wrapped her arms around his neck, holding on tightly to him.

Moving further away from the main road, Oalfus managed to get a portal open. Both gave one last backward glance to the village they had *properly* confessed their love in. Oalfus made a mental note to remember this place and bring their child back here.

"Our child will most certainly be well-traveled. I suspect we will be back here before we know it," Oalfus mused.

Deirdre nodded, hugging him closer to her as the pair stepped through the portal back to Moscow. Back to where everything had really begun.

Chapter Thirty One

It was almost as if Viktor was expecting Oalfus and Deirdre to show up, though he had not expected Deirdre to be bursting at the seams. Tatianna swooped in, a private doctor called immediately.

Between Safiya and Tatianna, Deirdre was practically smothered in fussing. She was not allowed to do *anything* herself. She couldn't even go to the washroom without someone coming along with her.

The doctor was a demon herself, specialized in demonic pregnancy and seemingly confident that Deirdre was healthy but low on some of her vitamins. She was put on a rigid diet that was ruthlessly enforced by Tatianna.

Oalfus felt as though he hardly ever got to see Deirdre anymore. Between the constant doctor calls and Tatianna hovering like an irritating fly, Oalfus was stuck sulking in the sitting room most days. Viktor tried to distract his uncle with walks and ventures into town. Oalfus was almost as bad as a woman when they went shopping, as he was drawn to baby clothes and toys no matter where they went. Viktor indulged everything his uncle showed interest in, desperately trying to lift Oalfus' downtrodden spirits.

Viktor was melancholic in regards to the prospect of a baby being in his house. The last time there had been one present, it had been catastrophic. He pushed himself to smile at every opportunity. Oalfus needed the positivity, and Viktor was determined to keep things light. He knew his wife was becoming overbearing with Deirdre due to their painful history. Viktor could see it, plain as day, that she was compensating. Tatianna would collapse into their bed when she finally came to rest at night, and the strange sadness that both of them were pushing down hung in the air like a fog. Neither of them dared to voice their feelings; they had agreed that what was done, as done. As much as they agreed on this, the melancholy remained.

Oalfus may have been fretting over what was to come, but he was not a fool. He felt the strange emotions hanging over Viktor, the constant forced smiles no matter when he looked at him. As distracted and overwhelmed as Oalfus was, he also knew he was causing obvious strain.

Viktor had taken the old demon out into town once more. They were in a heavily demon populated area and Oalfus was a little more relaxed than usual. They strolled idly down the busy streets of Moscow, the world buzzing around them like a bee hive. Glancing over at his nephew, Oalfus cleared his throat awkwardly before speaking.

"I hope Deirdre and I being here has not been a...point of tension," he said carefully.

"Dont be foolish, Uncle," Viktor sighed, pushing his smile.

"There you go again, with that fake smile. Enough of the smiling, Viktor. I know this is hard on you and Tati, I am not an idiot," Oalfus grumbled, narrowing his eyes at his nephew.

"I– shit...I suppose it has been a difficult reminder, but I **wanted** you to come to us when you had need. I am glad you two are here, truly I am. I suppose...I am still feeling a little sentimental," Viktor shrugged, trying to keep the emotion out of his voice.

"You two won't talk about it, will you?" Oalfus asked.

"We agreed to leave it in the past," Viktor grunted.

"Leaving things in the past does not mean ignoring the emotions that arise when you are reminded of it. Believe me, I am very experienced with what ignoring the hard parts of life can do," Oalfus said with a humorless smirk.

"I do not want to fight with her," Viktor sighed, his ears tipping back.

"You don't need to. I can tell it is sorrow and not anger that plagues you both. I don't think you two ignoring this will make it go away. Perhaps attempt to start it in a sympathetic way, tell her you see her strain just as you feel yours," Oalfus sighed, giving Viktor's shoulder a squeeze.

"For someone who is such a hermit, you certainly have become wise," Viktor mused, a genuine smirk tugging his mouth.

"Age is a part of it. These last few months with Deirdre have certainly opened my eyes to much. Imagine how insufferable I will be once our child is born," Oalfus teased.

"Hell have mercy," Viktor snorted, but his face softened as he looked up at his uncle. "Thank you, Uncle."

"For what?" he snorted "Showing up on your doorstep unannounced and throwing a wrench in your life?"

"Perhaps we all needed this wrench," Viktor shrugged.

Viktor was glad to see his wife come into their room earlier than usual that night. She looked frazzled. She immediately moved behind her changing screen, groaning about how tired she was and passively making chitchat. Viktor was lost in his thoughts, trying to find the right words to start this touchy conversation.

"Viktor, are you listening?" Tatianna huffed, wiping away her makeup and tucking a cigarette in the corner of her mouth.

"Not really," he admitted glumly.

"What on earth is wrong?" she asked, a little stunned at his downtrodden face.

"Come here, Prima," he said gently.

Tatianna was disarmed. There he was, using that pet name again. She set down her cloth, walking over to him slowly and settling on the edge of the bed next to him.

"Has something happened?" she whispered.

"Of course something happened, Prima. We haven't spoken of it since it happened..."

"Viktor, we had an agreement," she said firmly, her voice edging into anger.

"I still stand by it, but it doesn't change the hurt I see in your eyes every night. The same hurt I feel. We never healed, we ignored this wound, and now it seems to have festered." He sighed, resting his face in his hands.

"I thought I was being careful," she whimpered, looking away from him.

*"We are both being **too** careful. We refuse to speak on what happened, and now it's staring us in the face. I know—"* he took a slow breath,

looking up at her. Viktor reached out and pulled Tatianna close to him, resting his chin on the top of her head. *"We both acted out of anger, for each other and what had come of our family. Loss is still loss, Prima. We...we lost our little girl,"* Viktor croaked, his ears splaying back.

"And you blame me," Tatianna spat bitterly.

"I caused your anger by forcing a child on you. It is just as much my fault as it is yours. I might as well have had my hand on her throat in that crib, too..." Viktor couldn't bring himself to speak above a whisper, shame tearing his heart to pieces.

"You've never said that before." Tatianna was shocked at her husband's words.

"I have never had the courage until now," Viktor admitted. *"I'm so sorry I've allowed you to carry the guilt all these years alone. I should have found my courage sooner. It kills me to see you force such a brave face alone, Prima. You are allowed to mourn her loss, you were not yourself. Neither of us were."*

"I have no right to cry for the babe I killed to spite you, yet this hole in my heart feels as though it will swallow me whole," Tatianna sobbed, covering her face with both hands.

Viktor wrapped her tightly in his embrace, pressing his forehead to hers. He wished more than ever to turn back the clock, to undo what had happened between them. He had not only forced a child on her, he had forced her to keep the child in their room. He had forced her to tend to it, not pass it off onto a maid. It had driven her mad with anger. She had been drinking herself into stupors to dull out the constant wailing of their baby girl. They had not even named the child, and four days after she had been born, she was laid to rest in their gardens. It was just as much, if not entirely, his fault that his wife fell apart, and he refused to allow her to shoulder the blame alone any longer.

"I would give anything in this world to undo what I did to you, Tatianna. I wish more than anything to right the wrong I caused. I don't deserve your forgiveness, yet, somehow, you found it in yourself."

"You are my husband. I will always love you," she whispered, pressing closer to him.

"If it causes you upset, Oalfus will understand—"

"No! I...I want to hear the little cries and coos of a babe in our home once more. I want to see their little baby brought into this world, just as I hope, one day, we might see Rikovic's child brought into the world." She whispered her confession against his neck, his hand stroking the back of her head.

"Perhaps we will be blessed with many grandchildren and...cousins?" Viktor half-laughed, nuzzling against his wife.

"Or perhaps...another child?"

"Tatianna," Viktor warned, his face hardening.

"Not now! Someday?" She sounded hopeful, which stirred something in Viktor's heart. He wanted to say yes, he truly did, but he knew better than to push this issue.

"Let's wait and see how you handle having another crying child in the house before we make such a big choice, Prima," Viktor finally said.

Tatianna hugged him fiercely, nuzzling against his chest the way she did when they were young. It made him melt; she was still the sweet young dancer fresh from Paris, even all these years later. Her golden doe eyes found him and soon, they were falling back against the bed in a heated kiss. Things were still going to be difficult, but the wound that had marred their marriage looked as if it was on the road to recovery.

Chapter Thirty Two

"Oalfus Petrokov, I will gut you for doing this to me!" Deirdre screamed at the top of her lungs as another wave of agony swallowed her body.

Six hours into labour, Deirdre was seeing red. Her vines had long overtaken the room and covered nearly every inch of the walls, floor, and ceiling. Oalfus had originally been in the room with her, but when the third hour came and went, he quickly became unwelcome.

He looked like a lost puppy, ears tipped back and helplessly pacing as he watched the door where Deirdre was bringing their child into the world. The sounds were wretched, her screams made him even more nervous, and he desperately wanted to be with her. He wished she would have let him hold her through his whole thing, but that had been a non-starter.

An agitated, nerves-fueled whine bubbled up from his chest. It wasn't exactly the sound one expects of a whine. Not high pitched or frantic like that of a dog; no, this was more of a low, distressed, growling loud, a few octaves higher than Oalfus' usual tone. He fisted his hair, gripping the bases of his horns as he marched up and down the halls. It was taking too long. This had to be much too long for one demoness to be in labor. She was so young, her true life only just beginning, what if this child was the end of her? Could he love it? What if the child did not survive?

Oalfus' mind raced and panic seeped into every inch of his body. His seeing eye burned crimson, anger filled him, and soon, he was glaring holes into the door. He would break it down to be with his girl if he had to. He had to be with her. He could not live with himself if she died labouring their child into the world without him. Just as he was about to bust the door open, a familiar hand took hold of him. Oalfus blinked at the old leather jacket-clad arm crossing the door in front of him.

"If I have learned anything in all these years, it is to steer clear of pregnant women. Especially when they are screaming bloody murder a the man who impregnated them."

Rikovic. Oalfus swallowed hard, stunned to see his great-nephew here. He blinked owlishly at him, then glanced up to see Carmen. She had changed. Two petite horns still crowned her head, and her eyes were an odd, almost metallic shade of green now.

"W-what are you two doing...?" Oalfus realized how foolish his question must have sounded.

Carmen threw her arms around him in a hug and beamed up at him. "Do you seriously think we would miss the birth of our newest addition?" she drawled, her southern accent still was novel to the old demon.

"I-I suppose not. How did you find out?" he asked, patting Carmen stiffly on the shoulder.

"Viktor came and got us. He said you could use some company," Carmen beamed, her sweetness still ever-present.

"How long has it been?" Rikovic asked, nodding towards the door.

"Six miserable hours..." Oalfus sighed, looking at the door anxiously.

"Come on, old man. Let's go downstairs and let the poor girl work it out."

Oalfus snorted at his nephew's nonchalant and grotesque way of referring to the birth of his child, but he didn't refuse. He followed, sulking and looking back at the door hopeful that it might open and he would be called back.

"You look like a scorned pup," Carmen cooed empathetically. She was guiding Oalfus down the steps and smiling sweetly. "You just let her be, it does her no good you fussin' and frettin' outside her door. How have you two been gettin' along? Have you traveled much?"

Oalfus sighed, pushing a smile to his face as he looked down at Carmen.

"You are truly a blessing. I am glad you both are here. Yes, and Deirdre has all the photographs to show our travels. They are in the living room if you'd like."

"Sounds lovely! I'll run and put a pot of tea on!" Carmen beamed.

Rikovic threw his head back at the strained expression on Oalfus' face in so many of these photos. Wiping tears from his eyes, he marvelled at all the discomfort his uncle went through to appease his woman.

"Look here, you look like a sardine crammed into that bus!" Rikovic howled with laughter.

"Oh, be fair to the poor man! It ain't common for folk to be so big!" Carmen exclaimed, grinning empathetically between giggles at the photos.

"I suppose the world is not made for creatures like me anymore, but I am glad to be seeing it now," Oalfus said, smiling as he flicked through the more scenic photos.

The old demon was grateful for the distraction. His nephew and niece-in-law were wonderful at keeping him occupied. Viktor and Tatianna were out of the house, though Tatianna kept calling every hour or so to check in. Oalfus had encouraged the pair to be away while the midwife did her work. It would be no use for the three of them to be chewing their claws and waiting. Truthfully, he preferred to be away from the melancholic couple. He loved them both dearly for all they had done, but this child business was making them sulk more than Oalfus could stomach. Oalfus assumed Viktor and Tatianna had spoken on the subject, as things had improved slightly, but it was still dreadful for him to watch.

"What country have you enjoyed the most so far?" Carmen asked, pulling him back to their current conversation.

"I suppose Poland was great, though I was eager for Norway. We shall plan a return once Deirdre and the baby are ready for such things."

"You want to travel *with* your baby?" Rikovic gaped, his eyes wide.

"Yes, and close your mouth, you idiot. You look like a fish," Oalfus grumbled around his tea cup.

"Deirdre seems the type to run all over the world with a baby strapped to her back and a camera in her hand," Carmen giggled.

"She already has a rubberized case for her camera and a body wrap for the baby. She even got me one," Oalfus mused, tapping a claw on his temple.

"You?!" Rikovic snorted.

"Yes, me. You think I won't want to carry my own child?" Oalfus snorted.

"Well, I suppose, but to swaddle them to your chest?" Rikovic sneered.

"Why the hell not?" Carmen barked.

"I knew I liked you," Oalfus grinned at Carmen.

"It is a woman's role to do– ow!"

Carmen had cuffed Rikovic so hard he fell out of his chair. *Good girl*, Oalfus thought.

"Woman's role my fuckin' ass. When our baby is born, you bet your ass you're carrying them around if I need help," Carmen fumed.

"I suggest you listen. From the smell of her, you already know one is on the way," Oalfus sneered at his nephew, who was picking himself up off the floor.

"You can tell?" Carmen gasped.

"You're a demoness now, your charm scent has changed. I never noticed with Deirdre because...well, I suppose I was in denial of the possibility. Her scent was different, once I accepted it and looked for the signs. She smelled of the forest and fresh rainfall, but now, there is a subtle spice behind her scent. It's similar to my scent. You were very *floral* when I smelled you last; now there is the smokiness of Rikovic lingering behind it. I take it this is a new development?"

"I only took the test last week. I was late, but I didn't think much of it until now. We...we certainly have been *active* lately, now that things have changed. Can't be more than a month or so," Carmen confessed, her voice edging with embarrassment.

"It does my heart good to hear our family is finally growing," Oalfus sighed with contentment.

Tatianna and Viktor arrived not much later. Tatianna looked frazzled and admitted she could hardly pay attention to their outing while she worried about Deirdre. Though she was insistent that it had taken nearly nine hours for her to deliver Rikovic, she still seemed antsy. The group had moved to sitting in the front room, all of them waiting in silence. Deirdre's screaming had ended, but no news had come down the stairs. Tension was getting to the better of everyone, but Oalfus could take no more. He stood and grumbled something in German before storming up the stairs, taking them in threes. Viktor stopped Tatianna from going after him; he figured it was best Oalfus go alone.

When Oalfus reached the door, it swung open before him. The midwife let out a little yelp, jumping back as Oalfus stood frozen. Deirdre was laying in bed, her vines gone, and though she looked absolutely ragged and exhausted, she was holding a bundle in her arms.

"Would you like to come see them?" the midwife asked.

Oalfus only nodded, gingerly walking into the room. He hesitated at the foot of the bed, craning his neck to catch a glimpse. The child was unnaturally silent.

"Oh, Oalfus...he is perfect," Deirdre panted. Her copper curls were plastered to her face still, her fur wet with sweat. She never took her eyes off their child, her fingers stroking his cheek and brushing back the little tuft of black hair on his head.

"D-did you say *he?*" Oalfus croaked.

"Yes! Come see your son, silly man," Deirdre laughed, finally looking up at him as her head fell back onto the pillow. Oalfus carefully lowered himself onto the edge of the bed, his hand trembling as it rested on Deirdre.

"Are you alright?" he breathed, his eyes shifting from the bundle to her face.

"Knackered as all hell, but alive," she chuckled, reaching one hand out to him. "Come closer, come see him," she whispered.

Oalfus obeyed, moving to sit beside her. Wrapped snugly in a red blanket was his *son.* On all accounts, he looked like a goat, as his nephews did when they were born. Deep chocolate fur, a tuft of black curls on his head, and two little brown horns poking through his hair. Oalfus felt tears burn his eyes. He reached out and brushed his knuckle against his son's cheek.

"He is like Rikovic and Viktor," Oalfus smiled, though he was a little disappointed at how mortal the child looked. Deirdre could see it in his eyes, and she only smiled wider as she pulled the blanket away from their babe for a moment. Out fell a long thin tail with a little tuft of black fur on the end. Oalfus gasped, his eyes going wide as his trembling fingers stroked it. Immediately, it curled around his finger, and tears blurred the old demon's vision.

"Hell have mercy...he is perfect," Oalfus groaned, wrapping an arm around Deirdre and pressing his forehead to hers. He swallowed his emotions, willing his tears to stop, when Deirdre let out a little gasp. He looked down and his jaw fell slack.

Three leaf green eyes were staring up at them. Two, placed as they should, and one vertically between the babe's brows. Deirdre looked confused, her brows knitting together before she gasped and let out an excited giggle.

"By the Ancients! He is a Pooka!"

"A *what?*" Oalfus asked.

"Pookas are a type of goblin. They usually resemble horses or goats. Mischief makers, not exactly good or bad, but never truly there to cause harm. They are earthen protectors, safeguarders of nature and the old world. Usually, you can tell a Pooka by a misplaced feature. Oversized horns, two tongues, or a third eye. Oh Oalfus, he is one of the Fae!" Deirdre sobbed, kissing the little one on the crown of his head over and over.

"Whatever he is, he is ours," Oalfus murmured, smiling at his delighted little demoness.

"He is perfect...oh, he is so wonderful!" Deirdre sobbed once more, nuzzling the half-dozing babe. "What should we name him?" she asked, her smile only growing.

"Moritz came to mind. There are old German stories about two naughty boys who pulled pranks. It might be setting us up for disaster, but I thought it might suit him."

"Moritz...I like that very much," Deirdre sighed, leaning against Oalfus as she kissed their babe once more. "Moritz Petrokov...it is perfect" Deirdre finally said, looking up at Oalfus with eyes brimming with tears.

"You wish him to have my name?" Oalfus asked.

"Of course I do, he is your son."

"You are too good to me, Deirdre," Oalfus sighed, smiling as he ran a gentle hand over their son's head. "Welcome to the world, Moritz," he purred, squeezing Deirdre even closer to his side.

"Are you two done yet, can we come see?"

Oalfus looked up to see Rikovic, Carmen, Viktor, and Tatianna all peeking into the room eagerly. Oalfus laughed, nodding and waving them in.

"Yes, yes. Come meet your cousin," Oalfus beamed.

"Oh look at him!" Carmen squealed, beaming down at the baby.

"Looks just like his father," Tatianna cooed.

"Wait...does he have *three eyes?!*" Rikovic gasped.

"Quiet boy, who cares? He is damned cute," Viktor rumbled, smiling at the little one.

As Oalfus had feared, their child became the center of everyone's world, and incredibly spoiled. Deirdre was well and truly bed-ridden; her birth had been more complicated than she had originally let on, and so everyone was not only fussing over Moritz, but Deirdre as well. Oalfus had not intended for his more primal tendencies to come forward; he had been fighting them for months, but with Moritz finally here, things had become complicated. He was territorial, incredibly protective, and irrational. It was difficult for anyone to come into the room once the shock of the birth had worn off. No matter if it was a midwife coming to check on mother and child or his own kin, Oalfus could not stop snarling from the corner of the room where he would get shooed into until their guests left.

Only Viktor seemed to empathize with him. He felt similar things when Rikovic had been born, but not nearly to such a degree. He worried his uncle would not be reasonable at some points, but as the days turned into weeks, the constant rattling growl shifted into apprehensive humming. Deirdre had been eager to go to her parents, but she was still in much too delicate of a state. What she needed was to go see a doctor, one who could perform the minor surgery she needed, but the trouble was convincing Oalfus to let her go. He had no objections to her going, but the part where he would have to wait behind for her was where he struggled. He needed to be with her, he knew she was weak and it was tearing him up inside that he could do nothing for her.

"We will be with you, Uncle. Nothing will happen, but if we don't go, Deirdre will be bed-bound for much longer than necessary. Let the poor girl go to the doctor," Viktor complained loudly over supper. Oalfus had hardly settled Deirdre down into her chair with Moritz when Viktor had started this argument yet again.

"Viktor, I don't want to talk about this again," he warned, narrowing his eyes at his nephew.

"Well, I will, until you see reason!" Tatianna clipped, her horns already growing longer. "Or must I smack you over the head with the fire iron once more?" she hissed.

"No violence, please!" Deirdre complained, shaking her head at this whole argument.

"Deirdre deserves to be taken care of," Viktor snapped.

"I *am* taking care of her!" Oalfus growled.

"You are keeping her prisoner and stopping her from getting the very simple treatment she needs," Tatianna bellowed.

"Enough! All of you! For the love of the Ancients, I will lose my mind!" Deirdre wailed.

All eyes fell on her, Oalfus looked hurt as his ears splayed back.

"Oalfus, I will go with or without you tomorrow. I am tired of pushing this appointment back, I need to go to the doctor," Deirdre insisted.

"But—"

"No, Oalfus! I need you to just *do as I say.* I need you to take care of Moritz while I go to the doctor, and if I can't trust you with that, what on earth can I trust you with?" she snapped, her tone cut like a knife.

Oalfus fell back into his chair defeated, his head hung and shoulder slumped.

"You're right...I am sorry, *Liebchene*. I have been unreasonable, I just..." he sighed, avoiding her gaze. "I won't be able to do this with you, I won't be able to help if something goes wrong...What if–"

"Oalfus, nothing will go wrong. It isn't a big surgery, I will be home by supper time. I need you to take care of our boy, there are just some things we *can't* do together," Deirdre sighed,

Oalfus looked deflated, his ears splayed back and tail limp at his side. She felt only a *little* sorry for her stubborn old demon. He was being a fuss pot because he cared, but still, she was eager to see the doctor.

Chapter Thirty Three

Deirdre's procedure at the doctors went off without a hitch, and, after a week more of rest, she was up on her feet again. The pair decided to stay in Russia while Oalfus moved back and forth between their home and the manor. He was determined to make their home more appropriate for their child, who was growing remarkably quickly. Demon children always did, usually walking and talking before they were a year old.

It wasn't long before little Moritz was wobbling along behind Oalfus like his shadow. He would cling onto his father's tail to keep him steady as he followed the hulking demon around. The child was fascinated by his father, all three owlish eyes always wide and glued to him. Rikovic had given Moritz his childhood gold band, a Petrokov tradition where all the boys wore a gold band on their wrist to show their status and which family they belonged to. Oalfus had cheekily admitted once he had grown out of his own gold band, he now wore snugly around the base of his cock, which made Deirdre practically scream with embarrassment. The gold bangle hardly stayed on the little one's wrist, as it was intended to be worn until the boy reached adulthood, so most of the time, it was pushed up around his little bicep. It shocked Deirdre how quickly her son was progressing. He was growing bigger every day, it seemed, and nothing she had gotten him to wear fit longer than a week before they had all but given up on dressing him.

"Don't fret, darling," Tatianna assured her. "When Rikovic was small, he grew like a weed in his first year, but they slow down after that. He raced around the house in nothing but cloth diapers and blankets wrapped around his shoulders. Capes were fashionable at the time, so he wanted to look like his father," Tatianna had giggled one night during after supper coffee.

Then there was the first visit to Deirdre's parents, where Oalfus had nearly lost his head. After several hours of shrieking and fussing, Cillian had been the first to warm up, cuddling the little Pooka and chuckling about how sweet he was. Orla had taken more convincing, still muttering bitterly about her daughter being trapped by an older demon. Oalfus had learned to let it go in one ear and out the other, as he certainly did not need a repeat of their last visit. By the time the pair had left, Orla was sobbing for her grandbaby and Cillian was rolling his eyes at his moody wife.

The time had come when Deirdre and Oalfus were finally ready to head home, back to their quiet cabin hidden in the Black Mountains, and Oalfus could not have been more thrilled. Months of secret changes he had managed to keep Deirdre completely unaware of were finally ready to be revealed.

Oalfus and Deirdre had decided to have a small wedding just before returning to Germany. It was truly an intimate affair, with only the pair of them, and Viktor acting as the sole witness. Tatianna had been furious; she had to simply sit and watch inside the small temple they had gone into for the ceremony, but she did her best to keep it to herself. She had always hoped Oalfus would want a grand wedding, though she knew that was a fleeting dream. Even Deirdre refused to have guests; her mother would not be allowed to attend, so no one but those legally required would be there. Tatianna did manage to capture several photographs of the quiet event, and Deirdre mailed them to her parents. Moritz had managed to steal the show; Tatianna had insisted on getting him a fitted suit, and he was darling in it in his father's arms.

Cradled in her husband's arms, with little Moritz in hers, Deirdre leaned against Oalfus' shoulder as the pair stood in front of the swirling gold portal. She waved one final goodbye to Viktor and Tatianna before looking up at her husband.

"Lets go home," she sighed.

"Happily," Oalfus rumbled, nuzzling her cheek as they stepped through the shimmering doorway to their home.

The cabin had looked much the same from the outside, but there were visible additions. The first being an actual addition onto the side of the house, and the others being *pipes* going into the side of the house.

"Oalfus what have you done?" Deirdre gasped.

"I had a well put in. I actually had to bring some poor sap all the way out here, though Viktor did help me find a demon who could do it. I built an extension on the side of the house for a proper bathing space. It's simple and we will still have to boil the water, but–"

"Oh Oalfus...you're incredible," Deirdre sobbed, wrapping one arm around his neck.

"Mama!" Moritz giggled, clapping his little clawed hands as he reached out and grabbed hold of Deirdre. She jolted, laughing as she wiped the tears from her face.

"I still can't believe he is already saying that!"

"Just wait until he starts talking properly," Oalfus mused, carrying his little family up the front steps.

Inside, the cabin was familiar and unchanged. The only things Deirdre noticed were things moved out of little hands reach. A full-sized proper bookshelf had lower shelves that were filled with children's books and toys. A crib sat beside Oalfus' big nest of furs. The addition was open so Deirdre could see it had a large wooden tub that Oalfus had clearly gotten from Viktor. It also allowed for more floor space, and a wooden toy chest with Moritz name painted on the front sat in the open.

What made Deirdre's eyes mist were the dozens of framed photographs all over the walls, including the very first portraits she had taken of Oalfus. Nothing in the world could have prepared her for such an incredible gesture, and as Oalfus set her down on her feet, she leaned against him as a sob broke out.

"Is it not to your liking?" he fretted.

"It is perfect, you big fool!" Deirdre laughed between her sobs, setting Moritz down to explore freely.

He crawled over the bed, wobbled all over the round room, and reached for everything. He was keen to touch and feel anything his little claws could find. Oalfus soon realized he would need to make more toys to keep his son's attention away from his skulls and dried flowers. He opened the toy chest, pulled out a little wooden train, and eased onto the floor with Moritz, oblivious to Deirdre admiring the cabin, just as she had the first time she had set foot inside.

"Mama!" Moritz called, rolling the train over so it bumped against her foot.

"Are you happy, *Liebchene?*" Oalfus asked, smiling up at his wife.

"There are not enough words to express it," she sighed, settling onto the floor with them both. "I love you," she whispered to him.

"I love you too, *Liebchen,*" Oalfus purred, glancing down at his son who was grinning widely at them both.

"Love!" he squawked back, rolling his train and crawling after it.

Oalfus felt his chest tighten, looking over at the woman who had turned his entire life upside down. His fate had come running through that door during a spring snow storm just one year ago, and now, the pair of them had the rest of their lives to figure out what comes next. He lifted Deirdre up into his lap, propping his chin on the top of her head.

"Love, indeed" he rumbled, basking in the all-encompassing warmth of this precious moment in time.

Epilogue

Two Years Later

"Uncle!" Rikovic called, beaming at Oalfus as he stepped through the portal. It was *hot* where his nephew lived, stiflingly hot. He groaned, pulling off the turtleneck he had been wearing before Moritz barreled through the portal and nearly knocked him over.

"Damnit boy!" Oalfus grumbled, but his frown melted when Deirdre rushed through after her son.

"Moritz, you little terror!" Deirdre laughed, bumping into her husband. "Oof!"

"You certainly have your hands full," Rikovic chuckled, watching Moritz catch sight of Gibel and Bezel sitting in the shade.

"Kitty! Puppy! I wanna play!" he cried, rushing towards them.

Bezel leapt up into the air, hovering just out of reach of the little demon, and soon, his eyes were set on Gibel. He frowned when the big hound melted into the shadows. Stamping his little hoof, he ran over and hid against his father's leg.

"Why won't they play?" Moritz complained.

"Familiars are not play things, but I am sure your cousin would like to play," Oalfus said, reminding his son of the reason for their visit. It was his little cousin's second birthday.

"Boone! Boone!" Moritz suddenly tore off towards the farm house, giggling wildly and nearly knocking over the little demon who was wobbly pushing the front door open.

"Cousin Moritz!" Boone giggled, the little caramel-coloured goat leapt for joy at the sight of his cousin, throwing his arms around him. The two held hands and quickly scurried off towards the grassy lawn where toys were strewn about.

"He is getting so big!" Deirdre giggled, waving hello to Boone who glanced their way.

"I knew I heard that little devil!" Carmen laughed, stepping out of the farmhouse.

"Carmen!" Deirdre beamed, hurrying over to greet her.

Oalfus and Rikovic smirked at each other, turning their attention towards their children. Shielding his eyes from the blazing sun, Oalfus glanced over at his nephew.

"Did you ever imagine it would end up this way?"

Rikovic snorted loudly, sticking his hands into the tattered pockets of his jeans and shaking his head. *"Not in a million fucking years."*

Boone's head shot up, pointing at Rikovic and squealing. "Papa said a bad word!"

"Damnit Ricky!" Carmen glared his way.

"Mama!" Boone gasped.

"Oh shi– Sorry honey bun!" Carmen called.

Oalfus and Rikovic snickered together, walking towards the two little ones.

"Would you go back and change anything?" Rikovic asked his uncle.

"Knowing what I know now? Not a chance in hell," Oalfus answered.

The pair smiled at each other. The same warmth Oalfus had felt when he first brought Deirdre and Moritz home, came flooding his heart once more. His sentimental moment was quickly stifled when two little hands came crashing down on his thigh, nearly doubling him over from the force.

"UNCLE OALFUS IS IT!" Boone cried.

"Yeah! Papa's it!" Moritz giggled, and the pair tore off towards the field where the goats were grazing.

"Damn your boy is strong," Oalfus grunted, glaring over at his nephew. He reached over to him, but Rikovic dodged out of the way. *"What the fuck, boy?"* Oalfus snapped.

"Are you deaf now, old man? You're it," Rikovic snorted, smirking like a child at him.

"You're a dead man," Oalfus warned before he bolted after his nephew.

No, he certainly wouldn't dream of changing even one moment of his life. Nothing could compare to this true and utter bliss.

Hello, and Goodbye!

I hope you enjoyed *Edelweiss*...

It has been a wonderful journey, writing these books for all of you. If you have been keeping up with me on social media, this might not come as a surprise to you at all, but if you haven't, it's time I explain...

Edelweiss is my final book under the pen name, KF Goblin. It has been such an amazing experience to write these books for all of you, but I have a new chapter to start! This isn't a final goodbye, more so a pivot into something new.

If you want to keep up with me, make sure you're following along on social media (@bookishgobliin on Instagram, Threads, and TikTok) so you can see where I will be going next.

I hope you all adored this book, and you'll follow along for more romance under my new name, *KF Thérèse*.

There are plenty more stories coming, just a little different, and I hope you'll enjoy them just as much!

Manufactured by Amazon.ca
Bolton, ON